# Deepwoods
## Book One of the Deepwoods Saga

## Honor Raconteur

 Raconteur House

verheimr

exlior sea

chopper sea

cogan's blue

orin

robarge

wymgaard

teherani

sllegton
talumae
talumae mountains
kapsey
seaboard
wingate
charnel pass
lino's point
blackspon
oatmian
winslde
turton
coravine
gibbons
nail channel
stoll
goldschmist
converse
whizlane
darping
goodliffe
ace channel
shatma mountains
mdgaara
saleren
quag
the grey bridges
sykes
teschner
kachina
brevik
robin's wake
elas
hemans
cymer
wako
kallmann
thamne
resic
lyce
malin

Published by Raconteur House
Manchester, TN

DEEPWOODS

A Raconteur House book/ published by arrangement with the author

PRINTING HISTORY
Raconteur House mass-market edition/September 2014

Copyright © 2014 by Honor Raconteur
Cover Illustration by Katie Griffin
Portraits by Christa Triumph

**ISBN: 978-1502392527**

www.raconteurhouse.com

To Darby Ann –
a faithful friend and companion for many years.
You will be sorely missed.

The only way to make a man trustworthy is to trust him.
-- Henry L. Stimson

# Siobhan Maley

# Chapter One

Siobhan leaned back in her chair, propped her boots up on the table, and sighed with ultimate contentment. Truly, today couldn't be going better. She sat within her guildhall, enjoying the peace while it lasted. Sylvie had pulled one of her trading schemes that borderlined magic and found a small bag of chocolate. Siobhan had promptly confiscated it and volunteered herself as a taste-tester. Just to make sure it wasn't poisoned, of course. For the sake of the guild.

A sizeable bowl of warmed chocolate sat at her elbow, another bowl of fresh strawberries next to it, and she dipped the fruit liberally before popping it into her mouth. No signs of poison yet, but it might take three or four strawberries before the poison took effect. These things took time after all. Easing back even further into her padded rocking chair, she snagged another strawberry and coated it nice and thick with chocolate.

"Siobhan!" Sylvie called from the front of the Hall.

Siobhan paused with the strawberry halfway to her mouth and cautiously looked toward the door. The sunshine outside was strong enough to make the room look dim, casting Sylvie and a strange man in shadow, so she couldn't make out much. It didn't look like any sort of trouble to her, though. "Yes, Sylvie?"

"Someone wishes to speak to you!"

Well that certainly left the door of possibilities wide open. "One or two?"

"Four!"

Four? Eyebrows quirked, she called back, "Bring him to me."

As Sylvie escorted the stranger inside, Siobhan popped the strawberry into her mouth and chewed, watching the man carefully. He didn't pay much attention to her at first, his eyes roving over the Hall instead. He took in everything from the high vaulted ceilings with their wooden rafters to the stone tiled floor, square oak tables, chairs, and the rounded bar in the far corner. She'd bought the two-story building ten years ago cheap from a failing guild and it was twice the size they actually needed. She kept thinking they'd grow to fit it, but it never seemed to happen.

His perusal of the Hall gave her time to study him without being caught staring. He didn't look like much. Of average height and build, he was far from physically imposing, and nothing about his features really stood out. Slightly shaggy blond hair, oval glasses that masked his eyes, clean-shaven fair skin, and an air of harmlessness. The only thing distinguished about him was his clothes. That thick wool sweater, dark suede jacket, and black trousers all said *money* from the way they fit him so well. His polished half-boots alone probably cost as much as her monthly salary. Now, what was a rich boy like him doing in a small guild like hers? Escort service? Men of his wealth normally went to the larger guilds. Actually, men like him didn't make their own travel arrangements at all but had one of their servants do it for them.

His eyes finally turned toward her and took her in from head to toe in a quick scan. He didn't look surprised by her dark auburn hair, green eyes, or fair skin—all of which were somewhat unusual in this corner of the world. It made her think that he'd done some asking around before coming here. She took her boots off the table as he stopped in front of her and stood to give him a proper greeting, hand outstretched.

"Siobhan Maley, Guildmaster of Deepwoods."

"Markl Hammon," he responded in a surprisingly pleasant tenor, grasping her forearm in a firm warrior's clasp. "Light and peace upon you, Guildmaster Maley."

"Likewise." Just plain Markl Hammon? No mention of guild or family connections? He couldn't possibly be related to Nuel Hammon, founding Guildmaster of Silver Moon, could he? The way he politely responded to her with Winziane greetings made her think so. No wonder Sylvie had said four. "Sit, please. Might I offer a strawberry?"

"Ahhh…" he paused and glanced at both bowls. "It looks very inviting, thank you. I saw you dip one into the chocolate. I've never seen that done before." His statement tilted up in tone, making it into a question.

"A habit of my own making," she admitted cheerfully. "It's quite divine that way. Try it," she encouraged, and not just out of generosity. Much could be learned by offering people food, but it also went against her culture to talk business without offering *something* edible.

A little gingerly, he picked up one of the smaller strawberries and dipped it into the chocolate before taking a tentative bite. Then his eyes went wide behind those thick glasses and his mouth turned up into a smile. "Mmm! It's good like this."

"Have another," she offered. "Wait, Sylvie, not *you*."

Too late. Sylvie already had the berry firmly in her mouth, dark eyes sparkling with laughter. "Escorting charges," the other woman defended herself, licking traces of chocolate from her lips.

Siobhan rolled her eyes and shook her head in resigned amusement. She couldn't help but notice that as

Sylvie left, Hammon's eyes strayed to watch her go for a moment. But she didn't blame him. The man would have to be dead and six feet under to not be attracted to their resident trader. Sylvie had been blessed with gorgeous dark hair, a voluptuous body, and an exotic-looking face—all of which she used ruthlessly to her advantage. No one got better deals than she when it came to trading.

"So, what brings you to Deepwoods?" Siobhan brought his attention gently back to her without embarrassing him.

"Ah, hmm." Hammon swallowed the mouthful he had and gave her a game smile. "Well, let me explain. I'm a scholar by profession, you see."

Actually, she didn't. Scholars were not a profession as no one paid them for their information. In fact, to call it a profession was the greatest oxymoron in the known world. But she had heard of families that were so wealthy that their children took on that title and studied whatever suited their fancies. Waste of time, education, and money in her opinion. Still and all, she didn't make a habit of judging paying clients, so she made an encouraging sound and let him continue.

"I want to study specifically the cultures of this world and the interactions each nation has with each other," he expanded, warming up to his subject. "I think if we all understood how the other cultures worked, we could have better relationships with them, especially where trade is concerned."

Oh? Well, what a surprise. At least he wanted to study something sensible instead of how air was formed or some such nonsense. "How do we come in?"

"I've come to you for two reasons." He held up two fingers in illustration. "One is that I'm informed that out of all the guilds, yours tends to travel the most because of your specialties in pathfinding and escorting."

Thereby meaning...what exactly? "So you want us to escort you all over the four continents?"

"Well, yes and no. I actually hoped to just stay with your guild for a time and whenever you take a job, I travel with you. It's less cumbersome for you that way."

Her eyebrows rose in surprise. He wanted to *live* with the guild? "What's the second reason?"

"Of the guilds in this city, yours is the most ethnically diverse. I understand you have people from five different nationalities here." He waited for her confirming nod before continuing. "I didn't hear wrong, then. Good. So you see, you actually have the perfect place for me to observe right in this Hall. Your people, despite their different cultures, get along peacefully and work well together. I can learn a great deal by watching them interact and asking questions."

'Get along peacefully' was it? That might be stretching things a tad. "So you wish to live with us."

"An unorthodox idea, I know," he admitted with a wry shrug, expression bashful yet somewhat charming. "I would of course be willing to pay you for the expense of having me."

Ohhh? So this study of his had funding to it? Siobhan sat back in her chair and regarded him frankly, the wheels in her mind spinning. She saw something in his eyes that made her pause before giving him an immediate answer. She'd seen it before—and it made all the difference to her. Logical reasons aside, she had a feeling why he had really come.

She could charge him some exorbitant price for the privilege of staying here, but she had a gut feeling it wouldn't work. Her people didn't esteem wealth. They would be polite to a paying guest but not welcoming. It would add tension in the guild, and she avoided tension like the plague.

She had half a mind to let him stay just because she rather liked what she saw. But she wouldn't be a guildmaster if she couldn't somehow turn this to her advantage. Right now she didn't need money so much as another set of useful hands. "Are you willing to work to stay here?"

He blinked at her several times, head cocked. "Work?

Well, certainly, if you prefer that. But, ah, what would you want me to do?"

"What skills do you have?" she countered. "We're a small guild. We can use a helping hand in almost every department."

It took a second for Hammon to answer her. "Well, I've experience in booking, trading, and research. I speak three dialects—"

"Which ones?" she interrupted.

"Blasden, Ellertish and Kaberrin," he responded promptly.

Oh? No one in the guild knew two of those dialects. It opened up trade possibilities if he chose to stay. "Good. Anything else?"

"I'm completely literate," he said dryly. Of course, as a scholar, he would have to be literate.

"Good skills," she commended. "I'd ask for your help in translating, when necessary, but we need someone to take over the books more than anything. I'm doing that right now and I frankly loathe it."

He smiled at her words but it didn't do more than flash across his face. His eyes studied her intensely before he asked slowly, "You'd prefer that I work over paying you. Why?"

"If you want the respect of my guild, you earn your bread. You don't pay for it."

His expression relaxed into a soft smile and he nodded once. "I understand."

"Hammon, I must ask a few questions first. Your family?"

"I'm from the southern end of Robarge. My family knows what I intend to do, and while they're not quite sure what to think of it, they have no problem with it either."

She frowned slightly at his wording. 'From the southern end?' Wouldn't it be easier to just name the city he was from? And why not say his family name? Siobhan smelled evasion. "I see. Do you mind if I ask how old you are?"

"Not at all. I just turned twenty-five."

"Oh, you'd be one of the younger members in the guild, then." In fact, Denney was the only one younger. "Are you registered with any other guild in Robarge?"

"Well, yes," he admitted reluctantly. "But I'm on an extended leave of absence with them and they understand it might well be years before I come back."

"Do I need to notify them?" she asked. In truth, she should, as it was a guildmaster's duty and courtesy to other guilds to do so.

"No, it's fine, I'll handle it."

Again, she smelled evasion. "Well enough, then. As long as you promise to not start trouble, I have no problem taking you on."

He gave her a half-bow, face brightening into a relieved smile. "Thank you. Then I'll take up those books, shall I?"

"Good enough." She'd get to the bottom of just who he was later, when he didn't have his guard up. Digging right now for answers would make him too uncomfortable and she'd prefer not to do that. "Now, I don't know how much you've been told, but here's the basics. Deepwoods only has nine members, including yours truly. Ten now with you. As you said, we usually do escorts and the like, but we don't pass up trade opportunities either. Sylvie's the best in that. If you want to do a trade or bargain, I'd run it past her first. Our rooms are all upstairs, and the one at the very top and to your right is empty. Take that one. Most of your meals can be had here, if you wish, but you're not bound to eat with us. We sometimes go out to eat as well. Clothes, weapons, and the like are your own expenses. Travel expenses are handled by the guild's coffers. Don't do anything to kill, maim, or bankrupt us and we'll get along fine."

"If you don't mind a question?" he waited for her encouraging motion of the hand before asking, "The numbers you and Sylvie exchanged. What do those mean?"

"Ah, that. It's something of a code that Sylvie and I have developed over the years. It cues me up to trouble. 'One' means that someone in the guild has seriously hurt someone else."

Hammon's eyes were in danger of crossing. "How often does that happen?"

"More than I care for," she grumbled. "But one of my enforcer's a Resken and another is a Teheranian, so I suppose fighting is inevitable. Anyway, 'two' means that something has happened that caused damage somewhere, damage that will cost me a pretty penny in restitution fees. 'Three' is a trade or business opportunity coming my direction. 'Four' is the unquantified. It's not trouble, but Sylvie's not sure if it's good news either."

For some reason, this made Hammon chuckle. "I suppose I fit the definition of 'unquantified.' Well, thank you for the explanation, Guildmaster Maley. If it's alright with you, I'll go collect my bags and then return here."

"Go, go," she encouraged with a wave of the hand. "But Hammon? A word of advice."

He paused partway out of his chair. "Yes?"

"The easiest way into the hearts of this guild is to bring them something tasty."

He gave her a thankful nod. "I'll find something suitable. How much should I bring?"

"As much as you can," she answered seriously. "I have several bottomless pits that masquerade as humans."

With a mock-bow, he promised, "I'll do my best. Then, if you'll excuse me, I should be back by this evening."

"Alright. Send word if you need help." She meant the words literally. No matter how unorthodox this situation might be, he was still a new member of her guild, and all the guild looked out for each other.

He seemed to understand her sincerity as his smile grew genuine before he gave her another quick bow and left as unassumingly as he'd come.

Before Hammon had completely left the Hall, Wolf

came and sat across the table from her, snagging a strawberry and dipping it in the chocolate. The wooden chair and table creaked slightly under his weight as he leaned over the surface.

"Oy!" she protested. "I haven't sufficiently tested that for poison!"

Knowing very well she was joking, he replied calmly, "You're not dead yet. I'll take my chances. Who was that?"

Pulling both bowls closer to her in a defensive manner, she said, "Our newest guild member."

Wolf gave Hammon's back a quick glance as he licked the chocolate off his thumb. "Don't look like much of a fighter."

"Scholar," she corrected with a wry twist of the lips.

Her giant enforcer had the blankest expression she'd ever seen as he repeated, "Scholar."

"He's going to work in the guild—" might as well get that out in the open now "—but his main purpose in staying with us is to study the different cultures and figure out how to improve trade relations between them."

"Hoooo." He looked thoughtful, white-blond brows screwed upward slightly as he processed this.

"Be warned, he'll probably ask you the most questions." For rather obvious reasons. As far as Siobhan could tell, Wolf was the only Resken in this entire city, and his looks sometimes invited trouble. No one could mistake him for anything else, not with that giant, powerful frame, ice-blond hair and deep blue eyes. Despite his propensity to find trouble, she thanked the stars he chose to remain with her. Wolf had become the dearest friend and brother in arms she had, and if he ever did choose to leave, it would be like losing an arm.

"No doubt." Wolf didn't seem the mind the impending interrogation. "Why did you agree?"

"He said he'd do the books."

Wolf chuckled as he reached for another strawberry. "*Now* it makes sense. What do we know about him?"

"Not enough," she admitted, swatting at his reaching

hand and missing. "But he had a good look in his eyes and he was respectful and willing to work, so I don't think he'll cause trouble."

Wolf glanced up at her face for a moment as he reached for the last plump strawberry. "I'll keep an eye on him anyway."

She knew he would, no matter what she said. Wolf didn't trust anyone the first six months they were in the guild. His caution had saved her hide more times than she cared to remember, so she didn't argue with him. He'd come around eventually. "Will you stay out of my strawberries?!"

Laughing, he stuck his finger in the chocolate bowl before going on his merry way.

Hammon came back well before dinner, arms weighed down by various bags. Siobhan saw his approach from the second story window, where she had been freshening up a room for him. Seeing that he was struggling to hang on to everything, she called down the stairs, "Someone go help Hammon!"

Even as she spoke, she hurried out the door and downstairs, intent on helping him herself if no one else had heard her. But as she hit the ground floor, she saw that Conli had beaten her there. Denney hovered nearby, eyes doing a toe-to-head sweep of Hammon before catching Siobhan's eye and mouthing, *That's him?*

Siobhan nodded confirmation as she strode around the table to the door.

"—take at least some of this from you," Conli offered, already lifting a wicker basket out of Hammon's hands. "How did you manage to get it all here without dropping something?"

"Who says I didn't?" Hammon returned with a wry smile.

"Uh-oh." Siobhan bit back a smile as she took in the bags. "Which one? Anything break?"

"No, likely not, as it was the bag with all my clothes and books."

"Good, good." She looked at Conli. "Did you introduce yourself?"

"Barely." Conli turned to Hammon and offered a hand, now that Hammon had one free. "Conli Rorona, the physician of the guild."

Hammon blinked at the word 'physician'—it was a rare occupation, as most chose to be bonesetters or apothecarists—but accepted the hand readily. "Light and peace upon you, Rorona. I'm Markl Hammon, Scholar."

"Welcome," Conli responded with a slight smile. "We're glad for anyone that will take the books away from Siobhan."

Siobhan gave him a dirty look, which he returned with a mischievous grin. "The love I feel from you is underwhelming, Conli, thank you. Hammon, I have a room set up for you at the top of the stairs. Throw everything in there."

"And after you do so, come see me," Conli directed. "It's procedure in the guild that I examine every new member that comes in."

Hammon pointed a finger at his own chest, head canted in question. "I'm not ill."

"No, you look perfectly healthy," Conli agreed pleasantly. "But this way, I know if you have anything that I need to be aware of, medically speaking. Like allergies to foods, or medicines that don't work well on you. It's best to know these things in advance."

"Ahh, I see. Then, I'll come see you in a moment."

"Denney," Siobhan directed, "play tour guide for him."

Hammon turned, just noticing the young woman standing quietly behind Conli.

Conli gestured toward Denney, then Hammon in an inviting manner. "Hammon, this is Denney Icean. She's our resident animal expert. Denney, Markl Hammon, our new master of finances."

"And language expert," Siobhan added. "He speaks two languages no one else does."

"And I certainly will learn more, when I can," Hammon agreed. He regarded the girl with obvious interest, perhaps because of her milky brown skin that didn't belong to any particular culture. He surely wondered where she was from, but aside from a brief, "Light and peace upon you, Icean," he didn't say anything to her.

Siobhan didn't miss the way his eyes darted from Conli to Denney and back again. True, the two looked similar enough that they could be kin. They had joined Deepwoods together six years ago and to this day Siobhan was not quite sure why. Siobhan had always suspected that the girl was Conli's daughter (with a twenty year age gap between the forty year old Conli and the twenty year old Denney, it was certainly possible), but had never felt it right to pry and satisfy her curiosity. She didn't know their precise relationship, just that Denney never strayed far from Conli's side.

Denney offered him a smile. "Come with me, and I'll show you where everything is."

"You're very kind, thank you."

She watched them go off toward the stairs, Conli following after with the basket still in his hands.

Strange, from the back, it looked like Conli and Hammon were kin. They both had the same tall build, fair hair, fair skin and that intellectual air about them. Though Conli was from Island Pass and Hammon from Robarge.

With them more or less sorted, she went and tried to put the books in some sort of semi-order for Hammon to take over. Right now, they likely wouldn't make an ounce of sense to him. They barely made sense to her. As she sat at the main table and struggled to make things add up, time more or less passed by without her notice.

"You really keep such detailed notes on each person?" Hammon asked, his voice mixing in with the sound of footsteps against the wooden stairs.

"Oh, I have to. I don't dare trust my memory," Conli responded with a half-laugh.

"For good reason," Denney muttered.

Siobhan turned and smiled up at the group as they came down, pleased by the way that Hammon respected Conli's skills. Physicians and pharmacists were not well received, although Conli's skills with herbs and surgery made most doctors look like quacks. He'd proven over the past six years of being in the guild that he knew his trade, and knew it well. His medical expertise had opened doors for her several times.

She opened her mouth, intending to call Hammon over, when a clatter from behind distracted her. Wolf came inside with a slightly guilty look on his face and his right arm clasped to his chest. Tran was right behind him, an evil smile of sadistic pleasure stretching from ear to ear.

Reading the signs well enough, Siobhan just groaned. "Wolf, you broke it *again*?"

"Broke what?" Beirly appeared from the back room like magic, his leather apron on and a hammer in his hand. He took in the sight of Wolf's hand and said on a growl, "You broke the hand *again*?"

"It was an accident!" Wolf protested.

Beirly crossed his arms over his chest, bushy eyebrow raised in challenge. "Oh, do tell."

"He was trying to hit me and missed, so he hit the wall instead," Tran explained, grin widening.

Despite being a good deal shorter, Beirly managed to reach up and snag the back of Wolf's neck, hauling him down to his own level. "That's not an accident, you fool! How in the world do you manage to constantly break *an iron hand?!*"

Siobhan, used to such a scene, simply rolled her eyes before standing and pushing away from the table. "Alright you three, hold on a moment while I introduce you to our latest member. Beirly, you can ream Wolf later. Everyone, this is Markl Hammon."

Hammon gave them a cautious half-bow.

"This is Tran Amar," Siobhan introduced.

"Hammon-maee," Tran greeted with a slight head
bow, his three long braids swinging forward with the
motion. Hammon blinked, slightly startled as he was
forced to look up to meet the man's dark eyes. Siobhan
had reacted the same way upon first meeting Tran.
Between his corded musculature, imposing height, and the
array of scars that mottled his pitch black skin, he looked
like a thug, really. No one would suspect that a highly
intelligent mind lay beneath that rough exterior.

"Beirly Kierkegaard."

"Hammon the scholar, how do!" Beirly greeted in
that slightly rough, deep voice he had, bushy red beard
quivering with energy. He clasped arms with the man, and
judging from the slight wince on Hammon's face, a mite
too strongly.

"Light and peace upon you," Hammon returned. He
lost some of his caution under the enthusiastic greeting.

Without waiting for questions, Beirly volunteered,
"I hail from Widstoe originally, but I've lived here in
Goldschmidt for nearly a decade and was one of the
founding members for Deepwoods. Siobhan, Grae and
I are childhood friends, you could say. As far as I know,
there's no dwarvish blood in me." He said this with a
half-chuckle as people usually assumed he had a dwarf
ancestor somewhere in the family tree. With his short but
stout build, he certainly looked the part. "I'm the fixer in
the guild."

"Fixer?" Hammon parroted.

"Blacksmithing, carpentry, leatherworking—if it
requires tools, I'm your man. I keep everything in repair
around here, and when we're traveling I'm responsible for
fixing anything that breaks." Pointing at Wolf's iron hand,
he said proudly, "That's a bit of my handiwork right there.
I fixed it up for him when he first joined us."

"It's good for fighting and working," Wolf added with a

slight smile. "But not for loving."

"I've never seen anything like it," Hammon admitted, torn between staring at the hand or at Beirly.

"Wolf will let you get a good look later, won't you, Wolf?" The question was clearly rhetorical as Beirly didn't pause before continuing, "He likes to show it off."

"Not as much as you do," Wolf retorted with a snort.

"And finally, Erik Wolfinsky," Siobhan finished. "We all call him Wolf, though."

"You're welcome to as well," Wolf offered him although his tone was neutral. "Forgive me if I don't shake hands."

"Quite understandable," Hammon assured him with his eyes locked on the broken iron hand.

Beirly blew out an irritated breath. "Alright," he directed Wolf, "come on back, I'll fix it before dinner."

"Hurry," Siobhan advised. "I'm assured it'll be on the table soon. Hammon, if you'll follow me, I'll try to explain my insane book-keeping method to you so you can take over."

"Oh, yes, certainly," he agreed.

As the boys tromped back into Beirly's shop, she led Hammon to the table and ran him through the books. He was more or less able to grasp what she wanted done the first time through, which Siobhan appreciated. So he truly did have the mind to be a scholar, eh? Seeing his intelligence at work pleased her.

They wrapped it up when their cook started setting dinner on the table. People filtered in from every direction—barring Sylvie, who had stepped out for an errand—and she waited until they were all gathered before snagging Hammon by the elbow, preventing him from sitting down. "I'll introduce you to the last two. This is Fei Man Lei, one of our enforcers."

Hammon perked up slightly meeting him, not unexpectedly. Hailing from the mountains of Saoleord, Fei fit the description of his people to the letter: slick black hair, pale skin, slanted eyes, small stature and the fighting prowess of a tiger. The Saoleorans didn't normally descend from the mountains, so finding one living here was a rare opportunity for the scholar. "Light and peace upon you, Man Lei."

Fei rose from his chair long enough to clasp hands with the man but didn't do more than say, "Hammon-jia."

Siobhan sighed at his antisocial tendencies and moved on. "And Grae Masson, our Pathmaker."

Grae leaned over the table long enough to briefly clasp arms with Hammon before quickly retreating back to his seat. She could tell Hammon wanted to speak with him and silently wished the scholar luck. She'd known Grae since they were teenagers and the man had always been shy and slow to warm up to people. Even as he sat there, he ducked his head to hide behind his bangs, not comfortable with a stranger's attention.

"Well, Hammon, that's everyone." Siobhan encouraged him to take a seat by nudging him in the middle of his back. "I'm told dinner's coming soon, so let's sit."

"Oh! Wait." Hammon turned back toward the stairs and grabbed his wicker basket, which he set with a slight clatter on the table. "I wish exaltations and blessings upon this house, family, and its companions. I brought a gift with me, as thanks for welcoming me into the guild. I wasn't sure of everyone's tastes, so bought a little of everything. There's sweet rolls in here," as he spoke he took things out and spread them over the table, "four bottles of apple brandy, and some white goat's cheese for the flatbread."

Siobhan silently applauded his choices. Neither Denney nor Tran cared much for meat, preferring fruits and bread instead, so his choices meant that everyone could enjoy the food equally. Lucky guess on his part? Or did he know enough about the cultures in this guild to know that might be the case? She caught his eye and gave him a nod of approval, which made him wink back at her.

As her guildmates good-naturedly passed the treats about, their cook, Sara, brought out several plates of spicy curry and rice, which everyone greeted with happy faces. Thick, spicy scents filled the air and set her mouth to watering. They ate with gusto for several minutes, the conversation overlapping and sometimes loud, as usual. Hammon didn't say much as he ate, just watched with slightly wide eyes. Wasn't used to this sort of scene, eh? Hopefully he'd get used to it quickly. Siobhan's guild could not be described as *quiet*.

Half of the food had been consumed when Wolf leaned closer and asked in a low rumble, "Where did Sylvie get off to?"

"I'm not sure," Siobhan admitted, turning in her seat to look thoughtfully at the front door. "She said she had a quick errand to run, but I expected her back by now."

"Sunset's come and gone," Wolf said, forehead furrowing in worry. "The streets are sure to be dark."

Looking around, Siobhan saw that Tran's plate was empty and she caught the man's eye. "Tran, done? Go look for Sylvie, then."

"Vahh." As he pushed back from the table, the front door clicked open.

Siobhan turned around again, this time relieved to see the brunette striding through the door. "Sylvie!"

"Sorry," she said, pausing long enough to close and lock the door behind her.

"Sylvie, we've talked about this." Wolf did not look pleased as he pushed back from the table to look her dead in the eye. "You're not to go out alone this late."

Sylvie held up both hands in a placating gesture. "I know, I know. I didn't expect to be gone so long. But don't worry, I had an escort back."

At the other end of the table, Hammon whispered, "Problem?"

Beirly answered in an equally low tone, "None of the girls are allowed out late without an escort. We've run into problems when they do. I guess it's just part and parcel of being beautiful, eh, Denney?"

"Like we ask to be harassed," Denney grumbled.

"Anyway, if we do need to go out, one of the men is expected to go with us. Just to avoid trouble."

"Ah."

Siobhan gratefully let them handle the explanation as she waited for Sylvie to cross to her. "So?"

"I was stopped by a messenger from Blackstone," she responded simply and held out a folded sheet of paper that had been sealed with black wax, the crest of the main guild of the city impressed into it. "Seems urgent."

Siobhan broke the seal with a quick twist of her fingers before unfolding the paper. Deepwoods had strong ties to Blackstone, the master guild of Goldschmidt, and often took on minor jobs for them. To be given a message like this wasn't unusual. To get it this late in the day, however, spoke of impending trouble. She scanned through the letter quickly and unease coiled into a cold lump in her stomach.

"Listen up," she called to the table, not taking her eyes from the letter. A hush instantly descended. "This came directly from Guildmaster Darrens. His daughter Lirah has gone missing."

"Missing?!" several people repeated in shock.

"She apparently was going to Sateren to negotiate something for her father but she never got there. He's verified that she went through Island Pass so she at least got to Wynngaard, but it's now three days past when she was meant to arrive and there's no sign of her." She raised her head and looked around the table, stating what everyone had already guessed. "He's asked us to go after her."

Hammon raised a finger. "Ah, can I ask why? As governor of this city, Blackstone can employ more than just this guild to go looking for her."

"Grae is the only Pathfinder in Goldschmidt," Siobhan explained succinctly. "We can get there faster than almost anyone else. Also, Darrens is aware that I have two people who are very familiar with Wynngaard."

"In other words, you're the perfect rescue team for this

situation," Hammon summed up with an understanding nod. "I see."

"I don't think we're the only ones he'll send," Sylvie put in, leaning over the table to snag a glass of apple brandy. "I think we're the ones he's sending *first*."

"Likely," Fei noted. "Siobhan-ajie? Leave at first light?"

"Yes. Pack and prepare tonight. Hammon, take only what you'll need for six days or so. Sylvie, Fei, I leave the food up to you. Beirly, how's our cart?"

"I just replaced the wheels but I'll double-check everything tonight," he promised.

She turned to Conli, a dozen what-if scenarios flashing through her mind as she tried to anticipate what they might need. "Conli, it's likely people are hurt."

"I'll bring everything we could possibly need," he promised. "Master Hammon? If I could enlist your help? Some of the equipment I want to bring is awkard to carry down those stairs."

Hammon blinked, surprised to be asked, but agreed readily. "Of course."

She didn't need to give exact orders to everyone, as they had been through similar situations before, so she simply rapped her knuckles on the table in an obvious signal. "Move, people."

# Chapter Two

They were up before dawn, everyone bringing down bags of supplies and equipment, loading it all into the cart pulled by their faithful reinmal. This far north of Robarge, a reinmal was not only an odd choice for pulling a cart but a rare sight entirely. Horses and mesans were the norm here. The breed was used more in Wolf's area of the world as they were made for the winter cold. Siobhan thought of them as an odd cross between a deer and a camel—they had the narrow legs, facial structure and coat of the deer but the robust size and color of the camel. If not for the fact their backs were more flat instead of humped, most people would probably mistake a reinmal for a camel.

Denney, hooked the reinmal to the cart while everyone loaded bags and boxes into it. Grae, always the one that worried about how much weight went into the cart, sat in the driver's seat and oversaw the packing. Siobhan packed for her and Sylvie both as she had sent the other woman to Blackstone to get more information about the party they were pursuing. She wanted an itinerary and a list of who was missing at the very least before they went hunting.

By the time she made it out of the building, the sun had just started to flirt with the rooftops and the air had gone from severely cold to just cold. She hugged the jacket's collar up around her ears a little more, feeling the bite at the exposed skin of her face. What a terrible time of the year to have to go searching for *anyone*. Winter was quickly approaching here, and in Wynngaard, it'd likely already arrived. Unless they wanted to search for people in three feet of snow, they'd best find the missing travelers quickly.

Hammon appeared at her side, cheeks rosy from the cold. "Guildmaster Maley. Anything I can help with?"

She'd passed him several times on the stairs as he helped carry things down. He seemed intent on being supportive, which was not a habit she wanted to dissuade. "Not a thing. I think we're more or less ready to go."

Grae must have heard her as he lifted his head and complained, "There's too much weight on the cart!"

"You *always* say that," Siobhan returned with a roll of the eyes.

"That's because it's *always* true," he grumbled. "You're not the one that has to carry the cart!"

"It'll lighten up in a day once we eat some of the food," she soothed, as she always did.

He gave her a long, searching look. "You're really not going to let me take anything off, are you?"

She met his eyes squarely. "Grae, I don't know what we're walking into. I don't know what equipment we might or might not need. I'd rather take shorter hops and be an hour or two delayed in the journey than to abandon something here that we might desperately need once we find them."

Seeing her point, he raised both hands in surrender and bent back to the cart, securing everything with a rope net.

Hammon lowered his voice as he asked, "Is pathfinding that hard? He seems legitimately worried about the weight."

"Hard isn't the word," she corrected. "Complicated is a better way to put it. But he's not going to be able to do any pathfinding until we're well clear of Goldschmidt. Why don't you ask him how it works as we travel through the city?"

He blinked at her. "Would he mind?"

She snorted. "No. But I warn you, the last time someone asked him that question, he spent three weeks explaining the answer. And that was the *short* version."

Far from being dissuaded, Hammon's brown eyes shone with anticipation. "Excellent. I'll ask. I've always wanted to know the specifics of how pathfinding works, but I rarely encounter a Pathfinder willing to explain it all."

Truly a scholar, this man. Siobhan couldn't be more pleased with his attitude. It killed multiple birds with one stone: it would help forge a friendship between Pathfinder and scholar, keep the scholar happily occupied as they traveled, and more importantly, keep *Grae* occupied. Her childhood friend had a bad habit of worrying about unnecessary things unless he had a mental task to chew on.

She stepped back into the thick of things, calling out a checklist of items and equipment to people, getting verbal assurances as she did. She'd done this so many times over the years that she only had half her mind on the task, and she let her eyes rove over the group, verifying for herself they were all ready. Wolf and Tran already had their leather armor on, winter coats and weapons strapped in place. Tran kept toying with the twin short swords strapped behind his waist, sliding them an inch out of the sheath and back in again in a bored fidget as he waited for them to move out. The man had the patience of a fruit fly most of the time. Wolf stood behind everyone else, standing there like an immovable stone statue, eyes making the same visual check she was.

Conli already sat on top of the wagon next to Beirly,

stifling a yawn behind his hand. He'd never been the best morning person. He had so many layers of shirts and coats on that he looked as round as a ball. Siobhan had a mischievous urge to push him off the cart and see if she could roll him down the street. Unfortunately, they didn't have the time for any playful wrestling, so she squashed the impulse. Fei, who hated mornings on general principle, had squirreled himself away in a cranny of the cart and had already fallen asleep. She couldn't see anything more than the tip of his ponytail trailing out from the edge of his collar. For his sake, she hoped he hadn't forgotten anything as she wasn't about to wake him up to ask.

Denney already had their dogs Pyper and Pete out. Pyper's pure black coat and Pete's mix of black and silver shone in the cold and they moved with an extra bounce in their step. But then, these dogs were bred for cold weather—their long, thick coats, padded feet and flopped ears had all been designed to protect them from the cold. Both dogs made the rounds and checked in with everyone, pushing their noses into welcoming hands in a greeting before moving on. At some point, they must have met Hammon as they didn't do anything but give him an extra curious nudge and a wag of the tail. Hammon, proving to be a man that knew how to charm people, knelt and gave both colliers an extra scratch behind the ears and a word of praise. Denney beamed at him. Siobhan had bought the colliers for the guild three years ago—dogs were excellent guards and traveling companions in their profession—but the whole guild knew that they were Denney's babies. Hammon had just won the girl over.

Seeing that they were ready, she retreated back to the Hall long enough to lock the doors and pocket the key before waving Beirly forward. "Go."

With a click of the tongue and a soft slap of the reins, the cart rumbled into motion. It went slow enough that they all kept up at a walking pace without trouble. The dogs, in fact, sprinted a short distance ahead, automatically scouting their road, before running back to the cart again. They'd steady out as they traveled, but would likely do this dozens of times before they left the city.

At this hour of the morning the city still lay half-asleep. Goldschmidt had become one of the major cities of Robarge over the past two decades, but even it didn't stay up all hours of the day. The brick and mortar buildings they passed all had their wooden shutters closed against the chill, the doors locked, and not a shred of light could be seen from the inside. A few businesses had opened their doors by the time they left the guild quarter and entered the main thoroughfare—mostly bakers and the like. Siobhan could tell by the sweet smell of bread baking that floated through the air. But they'd all munched on something as they'd packed this morning, and no one felt particularly tempted to stop for another breakfast.

As they walked, she heard Hammon join Grae on the back of the wagon, settling in with a slight squeak as the springs took his weight. "Masson, I wonder if I can ask a few questions?"

"Grae is fine," the Pathfinder corrected in his usual soft tone. "And by all means. We like to talk as we travel."

"Excellent. I thank you for the offer of informality. I wonder if you can explain pathfinding to me? I know very little about it."

Siobhan cast a glance back over her shoulder. She walked to the side of the wagon, so couldn't see Hammon's face, but she could see Grae's. He had noticeably perked up at Hammon's frank interest. Instead of sitting folded in on himself, he'd stretched his lean frame out, blue eyes alert and focused instead of hiding behind his dark brown bangs. *Here we go*, she thought to herself with a wry smile.

"Yes, certainly." Grae answered with noticeable animation. "I'm not sure how familiar you are, so I'll start with the basics. Pathfinding is actually an erroneous term in some respects. It's more like Path*making*. People who possess the ability to form paths can, with the right know-how, build a path that will take you over land. The ability gives you a way to travel significant distances within a few short strides, as you know, but there's many different aspects in making a path."

"Such as?"

"Well, there's certain factors that I must calculate before I can determine just how far we can travel. The condition of the land, for instance. The more natural power that resides in the land, the farther we can go on the path. Deserts are impossible to cross by pathfinding because of this. So, for that matter, are cities."

Over the sound of the wheels on the cobblestone came the *scritch scritch* of a pen on paper. Siobhan glanced back again, looking for the source, and nearly stumbled over her own feet when she found it. Hammon was actually taking *notes*? Grae was smiling from ear to ear, enthusiastic that someone took him seriously enough to record what he said.

She caught Beirly's eye, cocking her head to indicate the two happily talking on the back of the cart. The other man bit his lip to keep from laughing before mouthing carefully, 'There will be no livin' with Grae after this.'

Siobhan nodded in wry agreement.

"So assume that you have land under you that has inherent power," Hammon prompted, still scribbling away in the leather-bound book in his hands. "What other factors are there?"

"I need strong sunlight, as the power of the sun affects pathfinding as well. I also need water from a pure source, which I drop at certain intervals to open the path. But the hardest part is gathering enough stones to create the stepping stones. You see, it's not just finding a path in the soil—I have to create large stepping stones that tap into the land's power. Most places already have several paths available because people cross them so often, although only another Pathfinder can activate them. But if we're in an underpopulated area, I have to gather enough stones to make the stepping stones myself. Sometimes, too, the paths that *are* there aren't large enough to carry a party this size."

"Right picky he is about the stones, too," Beirly added over his shoulder. "We all pitch in and help him, but it's still sometimes a full day's work to make him happy."

"Would you rather be suddenly dropped in the middle of a swamp?" Grae shot back with false mildness. "Or the ocean? If a path isn't made correctly, that's what happens."

"Was I complaining?" Beirly retorted without looking back. "Just commentin' is all."

Grae grunted a "Ha!" under his breath. "*Anyway*, the more weight and people that I have to make a path for, the more complicated the pattern is for the stepping stones."

"Ahhh," Hammon said in understanding. "Is that why you were so concerned earlier about how much weight is in the cart?"

"I'm glad *someone* understands," Grae said sourly. "We always hover right between the balance of ten to twenty chuls of weight. With this amount of people, we should be fine at ten chuls. But then Siobhan insists on bringing the cart along, which adds two chuls all by itself, never mind factoring in Kit—"

"Kit?" Hammon interrupted in confusion.

"The reinmal," Beirly answered, still not looking away from the road ahead of him. "His name is Kit."

"Ah. Sorry, Grae, do continue."

"Well, Kit is about a chul and a half because of his size. So we pass over ten chuls and therefore have to use the snowflake pattern, which is much more complex than the rose pattern, and it takes more energy for me to use—"

Siobhan tuned him out at that point as she had heard this complaint before. Multiple times. In fact, she could probably give the lecture word for word from here on out. Instead she shortened her stride and fell into step with Wolf, who was guarding the rear. "Sylvie was supposed to meet up with us by now."

Wolf gave a grunt, eyes narrowed against the morning sun as he looked ahead. "I don't see her. Want me to go ahead and see if she's found trouble?"

"Well, now, that depends." Siobhan glanced at him from the corner of her eye. "How long has it been since you picked a fight with anyone from Blackstone? And how likely is it that they're holding a grudge over it?"

"It's been at least a week," Wolf defended himself mildly, putting a wounded hand over his heart. The gesture might have gone over better if it wasn't his steel hand. He'd broken many a man's bones because of that hand. "And I didn't start it."

She raised her eyes to the heavens and asked, not for the first time, why it was that she had two fight-loving idiots as enforcers. Siobhan honestly couldn't decide most days who was worse, Wolf or Tran. "Alright, you're out," she informed him before lengthening her stride and catching up with Tran who scouted a little ahead of the group. Wolf, obviously not minding, chuckled in a low rumble behind her.

Tran turned his head to answer her question before she could even give voice to it. "It's been a solid month, and no, I paid for his medical bills. No grudge there."

Except perhaps wounded pride. But it was good enough to Siobhan's mind. She wouldn't have to wake up a grumpy Fei to go fetch Sylvie. "Then go ahead. She might just be delayed weaseling more information out of someone, but the last time she went to Blackstone they tried to recruit her, and I don't want her delayed uselessly."

Tran gave a nod and sloppy salute with two fingers before he stretched out his legs and started running at a ground-eating lope. Siobhan watched him go in admiration, as she always did. Watching him run was like seeing poetry in motion. But all Teheranians moved like that. Out of all the cultures of the four continents, only they did not believe in riding animals but in using their own feet to get them wherever they wanted to go. The only exception to that seemed to be boats. (Probably because no one wanted to swim in the leech infested waters of Teherani.)

As they walked down the main road, the morning traffic started to pick up so that they weren't the only ones on the street. Siobhan hugged the side of the cart more to avoid the traffic going the other direction, keeping one hand on the wooden side as she tried to plan ahead. Once they reached the outskirts of town, they'd be able to use one of the paths that Grae already had built there. It would let them cross the hundred spans to the next city of Converse in one jump. Then they would hit their first delay, as crossing the man-made bridge that connected to Island Pass would be impossible with pathfinding. They'd have to travel as everyone else did, which would take a solid two days to do. But at that point, they would reach Quigg, the first city that led into Wynngaard.

And from that point on, she had no idea what they would do.

Darrens could confirm that his daughter made it to Island Pass. But after the island, there was another bridge that connected to Wynngaard's shores. Many travelers had not made it across that bridge because of the high tides. Lirah and her companions might be dead already, swept over into the ocean and forever lost. But if they could confirm that she had reached Quigg, then it opened up whole new sets of possibilities. She *should* have traveled due north from Quigg to Sateren, but Siobhan couldn't be sure of that until she reached Quigg and asked around.

Over the low side of the cart, Siobhan caught Denney's eye and asked, "What do you think happened? Traveling to Sateren from here is a bit risky to the unwary, but it's not *that* dangerous a trip."

"Especially for her," Denney agreed. "Like as not, she had quite the escort with her, being Darrens' daughter and all. There's no the bandits in that area I know of, and I can't imagine slavers willing to take on Blackstone enough to try to sell the girl."

It would be suicide if they did. Darrens had not reached the seat of power he had without being ruthless against his enemies. "So, what does that leave us? Sickness?"

"Possible," Denney said, although the way she frowned suggested she didn't think it likely. "I can't imagine the terrain is responsible for any delays. It's mostly farmlands, small villages, and a few foothills in that area. Honestly, I can only think of one real possibility." Denney looked distinctly uneasy as she said slowly, "That she actually did make it to Sateren."

Siobhan felt a cold chill go down her spine that had nothing to do with the outside temperature as she understood what Denney meant. "She went to negotiate with Iron Dragain Guild. You think they'd double-cross Blackstone?"

"They'd best have a very good reason for doing so," Denney responded grimly. "Let's hope I'm wrong. It's just a dark theory that occurred to me last night."

"I hope it's just you being paranoid and suspicious."

"Me too." Denney turned her eyes northward in the direction of Sateren as she repeated softly, "Me too."

Sylvie and Tran waited for them at the eastern gate, not looking at all worried or hassled, although Sylvie kept rubbing her arms against the cold. As soon as they came abreast of them, Tran took up his usual position at the front of the group and Sylvie fell into step with Siobhan.

"So?" Siobhan prompted.

"I have a copy of their itinerary but it's not anything unexpected. They were planning to travel straight to Sateren, no stops, and stay there for two weeks before coming back. She had an escort of fifteen people, three of them very experienced with Wynngaard, and the rest known for their fighting abilities. I recognized some of the names because Tran and Wolf have both tussled with them before. Siobhan, this isn't looking good. With an escort like hers, and the way that she was supplied for the trip, she shouldn't have run into any trouble she couldn't handle."

Siobhan rubbed at her head, feeling a brooding headache coming along. "I was afraid you'd say that."

"One more thing. Darrens came and talked to me personally and handed me quite the bag of gold to finance this trip." Sylvie tapped the leather bag strapped to her waist meaningfully. "He said to make sure to send reports daily to keep him updated."

"Don't blame him," Beirly grunted from atop the cart.

"He also said," Sylvie added, "that we're not the only ones he's sending out. Apparently he has friends near Sateren that he's also sent word to and they're searching for her even now. So this might turn out to be a wasted trip."

"Let's hope it is," Wolf said quietly.

"Regardless, we act like we're their only hope," Siobhan said firmly. "Darrens trusts us to save his daughter and we'll do exactly that. Unless someone else beats us to it." She looked through the iron and stone east gate, looking past it and to the open stone highway that led west. Only a few carts and pedestrians traveled out of the city at this hour of the morning and absolutely no one traveled toward Goldschmidt. They had plenty of room to use Grae's pathways without any danger of being jostled.

She studied the ground with a keen and discerning eye. She didn't have an ounce of talent where pathfinding was concerned, but after working with Grae for ten solid years, she knew how to judge the ground and sky and predict whether they could use the paths or not. "Grae? I'm seeing a lot of frost."

"It won't hinder us," he assured her, interrupted mid-sentence from his conversation with Hammon. "We're going to need another hour or so of daylight anyway before the sun is strong enough, and the frost will melt by then."

He could very well be right. It would take them an hour to reach his pathways too. But she'd timed their departure with that in mind. Satisfied, she waved them back to their conversation before turning to Sylvie. "Did Darrens say whether or not he could confirm that they made it through Quigg?"

"He said he'd sent word asking but hadn't gotten a response yet."

Quigg was an insane hub of traffic coming and going. Never mind people, large circuses could be lost in there without trouble. Even her plan of going into the city and asking for information was flawed and depended more on luck than anything.

She let out a low breath and wished, not for the first time, that the guilds that controlled all of the cities had better working relationships with each other. Or were at least on better speaking terms. Ever since the fall of the great four nations that had once ruled over these continents seven hundred years ago, the world had changed drastically. Now, each city had a guild that ruled over it like it was a miniature country. The economy, politics, and livelihood of a city survived on the trade and governing ability of the major guilds. Small guilds like hers always owed allegiance to a large guild because of that. On a day-to-day basis, the governing of independent guilds worked—more or less. It was just in times like these, when emergencies popped up, that she saw how flawed the system had become. The areas between cities might as well be a no man's land as far as the guilds were concerned. If you got lost traveling between one city and the next, well, you'd best hope you had strong allies that would come looking for you.

No one else would.

# Chapter Three

"Alright, everyone into the cart!" Siobhan commanded.

They'd reached the pathway exactly on schedule. To the novice eye, it didn't look like anything more than some elaborate stonework set into the earth, forming a straight line of stepping stones. In all actuality, there were two lines, one of which sat a hundred marks farther to the right, both of them well away from the main highway. It sat near a running brook—which had a thin layer of ice on it still—and so provided an excellent source for Grae's necessary water element. He preferred the far path above the one they stood poised to walk on for that reason. Well, that and the fact that this path was built to carry a smaller load. The other path was made to handle large groups, like caravans. (Hence his habitual arguments with her about weight.)

Grae left the paths in place without worry because so few Pathmakers existed in the world. Anyone without a Pathmaker's ability couldn't use them, after all. But leaving a bunch of stones buried in the earth didn't mean that they would stay obediently in place, so Grae hopped out of the cart and carefully checked to make sure that nothing had moved.

The day had not noticeably warmed up as they traveled, even though no clouds obscured the sun. Grae muttered under his breath things like "sun's not strong this morning" and "wish we could wait another hour" but he didn't pause in dipping his leather flask into the brook and fetching water, so Siobhan assumed that in spite of his mutterings, he still felt it safe enough to continue.

Used to the routine, everyone that hadn't already been riding in the cart climbed on top. This proved to be a little challenging as one small cart couldn't really hold eight full-grown adults, much less two giants. The dogs, also used to the routine, jumped up at Denney's urging and found a human to cuddle in with.

Sylvie, playing on the moment, batted her long eyelashes at Hammon and purred, "Mind if I do?"

"Eh?" Behind his glasses, his eyes went wide. "I-uh, pardon, what do you mean?"

"There's not enough room to sit separately on the cart," Denney explained, already sitting on Conli's lap. "So to avoid trouble, the women usually borrow someone's knee until we're through the path."

"Ahhh." Hammon reverted back to his usual good-natured expression and waved Sylvie forward. "In that case, my knee is your knee, Waverly."

Sylvie giggled in true amusement as she slid into place, putting both arms around his shoulders. "You truly aren't the lecherous sort, are you, Hammon?"

Hammon gave a one-shouldered shrug as he answered, "I have a mother and three sisters who made sure of that."

"Bless them for it," Sylvie responded, only half-joking.

Siobhan stayed on the ground and watched to make sure that everyone had found a good spot and wouldn't be knocked off if someone shifted unexpectedly. She did *not* want to repeat that mistake. It'd taken four days to find

Denney in that gods-forsaken marshland.

As she oversaw them, Hammon asked why they were on top of the cart to begin with, and Sylvie explained that it was easier for Grae to transport them all at once this way. Not to mention avoiding anyone accidentally putting a foot in the wrong place. Kit had been trained to put his feet only on the stepping stones, and the cart would follow where the reinmal went.

Grae came around to stand at the front of the cart, flask at the ready, and called back to Siobhan, "We can go!"

Good. Siobhan put one hand on the cold wooden side of the cart and looked around in slight perplexity. Well, everyone else had settled, but where was *she* supposed to go?

Wolf, seeing her confusion, extended a hand and offered dryly, "Need a lap, Siobhan?"

"If you're offering, I'll take it." She gripped the hand he extended and swung nimbly up and onto his lap. It felt rather like sitting on a carved wooden chair. Wolf didn't have a spare inch of fat on him anywhere.

He put both arms around her waist to secure her better and complained, "You're too light, Siobhan. You need to eat more."

"Wolf," she said patiently, for what felt like the thousandth time, "*Anyone* would be small compared to you."

"She has a point," Conli piped up. "And Wolf, I disagree with you. Medically speaking, she's in the peak of health."

How had they gotten on the subject of her weight, anyway? Hoping to cut the topic short, she called forward, "Alright, Grae!"

The cart inched forward, wheels bumping and clacking a little as it crossed the multitude of small pebbles forming the stepping stones. She had no pathfinding sense and never had, but even she could feel it when Grae worked his ability. The air became softer, more distorted, and it felt

43

heavy and humid. The area to either side looked strange as two different landscapes mixed and overlapped with each other, their colors mingling into odd blurs. To the naked eye, it seemed as if they moved at a snail's pace but, in fact, they were crossing spans upon each step. She preferred staring at the stepping stones the most, as they glowed under Grae's power, sparkling blue-white and reflecting the light in a dazzling display.

She glanced at Hammon and found him staring with wide-eyed wonder, mouth slightly agape. "Have you never traveled by path, Hammon?"

"Once before," he admitted without looking at her. "But I was a small child then. My memory is a little hazy."

"Ahhh." That explained his reaction. It reminded her that she still didn't really know who he was. He had mentioned a family earlier, so he wasn't an orphan. He kept presenting a growing puzzle to her, though, the more she discovered. Most people who were wealthy enough to be scholars traveled by path often. Why had he only done it once? And despite his very sensible, logical reasons in joining her guild, she couldn't help but feel that he could have found an easier way to do his studies, especially if he was funded as he claimed to be.

Rain and drought, but she really wished they'd had a day or two more in Goldschmidt so she could have done some discreet inquiries about Hammon before traveling with him.

"Then basic rules." Sylvie ticked off points on her fingers. "First, don't fall off the cart. If you land on anything other than a stepping stone, you'll leave the path completely and we have no way of knowing where you ended up. Ask Denney sometime about that."

Denney stuck her tongue out and looked away with a *humph*, refusing to be baited.

Hammon took in this interaction with arched eyebrows. "I take it something happened."

"It's a long trip," Sylvie assured him with sadistic cheer. "I'll tell you the story sometime. Anyway, rule two:

only Grae can end the path so don't climb down until he says so. Rule three: if you do fall off, no moving. We can find you a lot easier if you're not wandering around in circles. Isn't that right, Denney?"

"You're forgetting something, Sylvie," the woman told her with a dark glower.

"Oh?" Sylvie looked innocent. Or tried to, although her lips kept quivering as if she suppressed a smile.

"Yes." Denney growled out, "I know where you sleep at night and you're a deep sleeper. I'd be concerned if I were you."

"Why should I?" Sylvie snuggled in closer to Hammon, making the man blush a little. "Hammon will protect me."

"Ah..." Proving he could play along with their teasing, he gave Sylvie an apologetic smile, "I'm actually a very deep sleeper as well. My house was struck by lightning once and I slept right through it."

Sylvie pursed her lips as she studied his expression. "I'd best find a different protector."

"I certainly would," he responded with a distinct twinkle in his eyes.

"We're almost through!" Grae called back to them.

Siobhan let out a subtle breath of relief. She couldn't really tell Wolf this, but that steel hand of his rested right against her ribs and pinched a little. Normally, when he touched someone else, he took great care with that hand so as to not accidentally cause any injuries. After all, he couldn't feel anything through it except distant pressure. He'd broken more things accidentally than she could recall. But she didn't dare say anything to him about it— the last time she had, he'd been so regretful of leaving a mark on her he hadn't touched her for nearly two months. She could put up with a bruise on her ribs rather than reliving that awkwardness.

The stepping stones faded, returning to their normal color of brown and grey. The distorted and humid pressure of the air also dissipated and Siobhan knew they were through before Grae could get out the words, "We're here! You can get down!"

Wolf gave her a hand down—with his natural left hand—which she used gratefully to clamber off the cart. A slight breeze washed over her, causing an errant shiver to dance over her skin, and she grimaced. Sitting on Wolf might have given her a bruise, but at least he'd kept her warm. "No one fell off, right?" she teased as her boots touched the ground.

"Ha ha ha," Denney shot back sarcastically.

Wolf put a hand on the side of the cart, levering himself up. "I think we'd know—"

Tran, an evil smirk on his face, reached out a hand and grasped Wolf's ankle before yanking hard. Wolf had just enough time to gasp, eyes wide in panic, before he face-planted into the grass, sprawled out like an abandoned ragdoll.

Dead silence.

When Wolf didn't do more than twitch, Siobhan dared to ask, "So, ah, how you doing down there?"

Without lifting his face, Wolf growled, "Me? I'm dandy. I'm so happy I'm eating grass."

Tran threw back his head and roared.

With an outrageous twinkle in his eye, Hammon turned to Conli and asked mock-seriously, "Doesn't grass have several medicinal properties?"

"Actually, it does," Conli agreed in the same tone. "It's quite good for the digestive system."

Beirly twisted about in his seat to add, "Animals eat grass, so makes sense to me."

"That confirms a few things," Tran said to no one in particular.

Wolf finally rolled over to his side and lifted himself up, giving Tran a glare hot enough to melt steel. Siobhan had no doubt that later—when they were out of her sight and hearing—there would be revenge.

Well, as long as they didn't kill each other. Shaking her head, Siobhan looked around. They'd reached the end of the path without mishap, bless Grae's skills, and had come to the outskirts of Converse. Siobhan had been in, through, and around this city often enough to know it at a glance. Converse sat at the very northern tip of Robarge, placed at the opening of the Grey Bridges that connected to Island Pass and through the island to Wynngaard. To label it a 'trading city' would be a severe understatement. Despite that, it had never become particularly large. Goldschmidt took up three times the amount of land Converse did and saw far more livelihood. Most people passed through Converse and did a little business as they went, but few chose to stay.

But then, the high tides of the Mother Ocean could likely be blamed for that.

People who wanted to stay on the cart did—Fei actually went back to sleep—but most chose to dismount and continue walking alongside. Siobhan studied the city as they angled their way across the wild grassland and toward the stone highway. Quite a bit of traffic went up and down the road, either leaving Converse for another destination further east or heading toward the west with plans to pass through. The western gate leading into the city stood wide open and traffic flowed through unchecked. From here, only the tallest structures remained visible beyond the high stone walls. Bells tolled out over the city, telling the time, and she could faintly detect the smells of food baking, all of it saying no trouble lay ahead. She never quite knew with this city whether they'd be walking into a dangerous situation or not.

After all, everyone had to go through Converse to reach Robarge. Good and bad alike.

"Seems peaceful," Wolf said quietly from behind her.

"Let's hope it holds true," she responded just as quietly. Now, next important thing to consider: how much time did they really have? It took a solid eight hours to cross the first section of the Grey Bridges and reach Island Pass. Siobhan always tried to give them an hour's leeway just in case something went wrong—like a wheel unexpectedly breaking—so they didn't face the dangers of being left out on the bridge when the tide rolled back in. Centuries ago, when the bridges were first constructed, they were meant to be passable at all times of the day and night. But over time, the seas had risen, cutting the travel time down significantly. If you wanted to pass safely and not face being swept away by the ocean, you crossed at low tide. By the time high tide came in, the bridges would be awash under several feet of seawater.

Now, let's see...the bells had tolled out the ninth hour just now. By the time they reached the bridge itself, it would likely be closer to ten. Thereby leaving them eight hours until nightfall. Ouch. On the one hand, they'd had new moons just two days ago, so the tides wouldn't be as high as during full moons. If they walked quickly and didn't have any difficulties in crossing, they'd make it to Island Pass. But just barely.

On the other hand, every day that passed without them actively searching on Wynngaard made their rescue that much harder. Did she dare delay for a full day in Converse and wait to travel over the bridge in the morning?

Siobhan stared sightlessly ahead and weighed the pros and cons. "Grae!"

Her Pathfinder came around the cart and stopped long enough for her to catch up to him before falling into step. His eyes scanned her face, reading her like an open scroll, and guessed, "You're not sure if we have enough time to cross today."

"How high is the tide likely to be?"

"Not as dangerous as the last time we crossed," he assured her. "It'll take a full hour after sunset before the bridge is truly covered in water. I think we have enough time and even a little leeway if we need it."

He knew tides and seasons better than she. His pathfinding ability depended on such knowledge. Humming thoughtfully, she mulled that over before raising her voice slightly to ask Beirly, "Bei, how sure are you that the cart's in good shape?"

"Might could break unexpectedly," he returned,

48

twisting in his seat as he answered. "Can't predict the future. But it's as solid as my head and won't break of its own accord. Kit's fine as a fiddle, too."

If anyone became unable to walk, for whatever reason, she could just throw them onto the cart. Making a snap decision, she said to the group, "We'll cross today then."

Hammon raised his hand to get her attention. "If I may...? Guildmaster Maley, I have an old family friend in the city that runs a stable. We could likely rent horses from him and make it across much faster. His business partner is on the other end in Quigg and will take the horses from us at that point."

Thereby avoiding having extra weight for Grae to transport. Siobhan perked up at the idea. Horses would make crossing the bridges much faster and lower the risk considerably. "We'll do it. How much will he charge?"

"Depends on who asks," Hammon responded dryly. "Miss Waverly, if you'll do the honors, he'll surely drop it down to half his usual price."

Sylvie gave him a casual two-finger salute. "Consider it done. Although it's not like price is really an issue. Not with that fat purse Darrens gave us."

Too true. Though Siobhan didn't intend to squander it little by little with unnecessary expenses either. They had no idea where this trip would take them, after all.

It took a remarkably short amount of time to visit Hammon's friend, rent their mounts, and get through Converse. In fact, they arrived at the beginning of the bridge before the bell could toll out the tenth hour. Siobhan couldn't remember a time they'd made it through a city *that* quickly.

They exited the western gate while leading the horses, nodding respectfully to the gate guards as they passed. Siobhan led them off to a small waiting area off the side of the road and gestured for everyone to gather around. She mounted her horse so that they could all easily see her.

"Alright, everyone hear me? Good. Usual rules of crossing the bridges apply—we go at a quick walk, nothing faster than that. I don't intend to waste our stamina if we don't need to. If any of the horses pull up lame or something, tell me immediately."

Grae raised a hand and pointed toward the bridges. "You did see the storm front moving in on us?"

"I did," she grimaced, shooting the sky a look over her shoulder. "Getting rained on won't kill us, so I don't want to hurry across the bridge unless we absolutely need to." For one thing, making several horses run on stone could become deafening after a while. But they'd all learned the hard way that a steady pace would get them across faster than trying to run the distance, losing their strength, and stumbling to a near halt.

Shaking off the worry, she finished, "Everyone mount up!"

They all climbed aboard their horses—all except Beirly and Fei, that was. Fei chose (for some inexplicable reason) to not ride but stay in the cart, and of course Beirly was driving. Siobhan watched long enough to make sure they were all ready to go before she kneed the placid mare around and led them off in a steady walk onto the bridge.

Nothing could be quite as cold as the sea with winter approaching. Siobhan rode ahead of everyone else with Tran, leading the way across, and as they moved it felt like the wind cut right through her heavy jacket and cloak. She shivered hard, once, and urged everyone to go a little faster. The sooner they could reach the island, the better.

Not many chose to travel at this time of the year and the scant traffic on the bridge emphasized the season well. Aside from them, only one caravan and a family group with a professional escort traveled toward Wynngaard. Since they all traveled at different speeds, a gap developed between them, and soon it felt as if they were on the bridge alone. Almost no one came from the other direction either. It brought up a question that Siobhan hadn't thought to ask before. Why had Darrens sent his daughter at *this* time of the year to negotiate some kind of trade deal? Couldn't it have waited until spring?

Grae came up from behind to ride at her right side. He usually looked a little brooding, but now he looked outright worried. "Siobhan, do those look like rain clouds to you?"

She looked north, where he pointed, and narrowed her eyes slightly. The clouds did look ominous, although they didn't pitch and roll like a thunderstorm would. In fact... "No, they look like snow clouds."

His shoulders slumped. "I was afraid you'd say that."

Poor Grae. He only hated a few things in the world, but snow made the top of his list. Right now, she rather agreed with him. The bridge they were on had been made so that eight carts side by side could cross with plenty of space in between. She'd been in buildings less solid and the way the grey granite stones had been overlain made it nearly impregnable to anything nature could throw at it. But despite its width and strength, no one in their right mind would choose to be on a bridge during the middle of a storm. They had no shelter available here—nothing but tall railings on the sides of the bridge. If the sea did get stirred up because of the storm, they could easily be washed over the sides before they even knew what was happening.

Siobhan looked out over the railing and toward the sea. The water looked green-grey and choppy, the waves coming up into white peaks. It even smelled like a storm, air heavy and moist. Hardly a good sign. "Maybe it'll blow past us," she offered with weak optimism.

"*This* is why I hate bridges," Grae grumbled, glaring at the sky. "There's no natural power in structures like these. Even if something happens, I can't open a path and carry us out of safety."

"I know," she soothed. "But all we can do now is pick up the pace and hope we make it to the island before that hits us."

Grae's eyes cut to her in an exasperated look. "Siobhan...doesn't anything ever rattle you?"

"If I was easily rattled, you and Beirly wouldn't have

unanimously decided I had to be the guildmaster," she pointed out dryly.

From behind, Hammon asked in a carrying voice, "Is that how you became the master?"

She twisted around with a slight creak of leather to answer. "That's how. I actually had no ambition to be guildmaster. But for some reason, everybody likes for me to be one."

"It's because she's tolerant of the boys' antics," Denney explained to Hammon, not untruthfully. "As long as they don't kill anyone or bankrupt the guild, she won't throw them out."

"I do have a *few* more limits than that," Siobhan protested.

"No you don't," at least five people said in unison.

Hammon bit his bottom lip in an obvious attempt to keep from laughing. "That lax, eh?"

Siobhan opened her mouth to object and paused when she couldn't automatically think of a good argument.

Conli, ever helpful, started ticking things off on his fingers. "Wolf caused a riot in the Blackstone's main hall and you only fined him for the damages."

"That was an accident!" Wolf protested. He didn't sound at all defensive with that wide smile on his face.

"Tran nearly killed three men only a month after he joined the guild," Conli continued, not fazed by the interruption.

"They were hassling the pretty girl that serves at the Three Crowns," Tran explained to Hammon, completely unworried about this open airing of past sins.

"The pretty girl he had a crush on," Sylvie explained further and smirked when Tran shot her a warning look.

Conli ignored that byplay too. "Fei got drunk from that apple cake and went around the town scrawling bad poetry on all of the walls with red paint."

From the back of the cart came a soft warning, "Conli-ren, another word on that and you will not sleep peacefully tonight."

The doctor gave the cart an uneasy look. "Well, ah... you get my drift, Hammon."

"I do," Hammon agreed, although he looked torn between being flabbergasted or amused. "I just have one question, Man Lei? If you don't mind."

Fei lifted up just enough for his eyes to appear over the cart's edge. His black hair looked a bit mussed from his nap and stuck out slightly on the right side. "You want to know how I got drunk from apple cake."

Hammon shrugged and gave him an expectant look.

He ducked back into the wagon, voice ordering, "Conli-ren, you explain."

With another wary glance at the cart, the doctor complied hesitantly. "He's allergic to sugar. Odd, I know, but that's the only explanation I have for how he reacts to it. He acts drunk after he's consumed any real quantity of it. Natural sugars, such as those coming from fruits, seem to be fine. It's the processed cane sugars that his body can't seem to handle."

"So don't offer him any food with sugar in it," Siobhan half-pleaded. "He's a truly unmanageable drunk."

"I will be careful," Hammon promised her. "But I now see their point. I've never heard of a guildmaster as tolerant as you."

"It's why they won't let me quit," she complained, half-serious.

"We never will, either," Beirly promised her.

Resigned, she turned back around and faced forward. "Let's just get to the island, alright?"

# Erik
# Wolfinsky
# "Wolf"

© 2011 Christa T Rumph

# Chapter Four

Alas, the snowstorm overhead did not care about the puny humans traveling along the bridge, or their travel plans, or the fervent prayers about them making it to shelter before the storm unleashed. Before their party had even made it halfway across, the sky opened up in a steady stream of snowflakes. The wind howled over the sea, sending the snow flying about in whirls and eddies, cutting through all layers of clothing and making everyone shiver.

Siobhan grimly told herself to keep the horses to the quick walk they'd been doing for the past two hours. Any faster of a pace than this, they'd be spent by the time they reached the island. That said, she really wanted to at least go at a trot.

Fei, Denney and Conli rearranged the cart to clear out a hole near the front of it so they could huddle together and share body heat. It must have been working, as those three were the only ones who had the energy to talk. Everyone else grimly hung onto their reins and kept moving forward.

With the storm clouds blocking the sun, the only difference between day and sunset was a slight darkening. Siobhan lost all track of time because of it. But they had to have made good time, as the water had only come up to the bridge's base level by the time Island Pass's gates came within view.

Island Pass had existed before the bridges had been built. It had probably been nothing more than some line shacks then, but now the city sprawled out over almost every square inch of the island and proceeded to grow up on top of itself. Under the heavy layer of snow, it looked like a fairytale ice castle more than anything. What little she could see of it, anyway. The storm and the encroaching darkness obscured most of her vision.

Everyone perked up when the main gate came into sight. Siobhan anxiously peered ahead, trying to see through the falling snow. The gates stood massively tall, with thick granite walls and stairs that led up on either side so that a person could climb to the very top. A ramp led up from the bridge so that the bottom of the gate never had seawater touch it unless a wicked storm passed through. But what she really wanted to see were the lights. Someone had designated a coded system for travelers to know how much time they had to get to the gates before the tide rose to a dangerous level. Three lanterns on either side of the gate burning meant they had all the time in the world. Two lanterns meant they had about two hours. One lantern: one hour. If no light could be seen in the gates, you'd better run like your life depended on it.

Right now, she saw two lanterns...no, wait. One of the lanterns bobbed and moved as if—wind and stars! Someone up there had just snuffed the lantern. Only one remained burning now.

Siobhan eyed the distance between them and the main gate. She'd traveled this way often enough that she knew the distance well. They should be able to make it with a little time to spare, but... "Pick up the pace!" she called over the storm, the air freezing in her mouth.

As tired as everyone had to be at that point, they moved up to a trot and started covering ground more quickly. The rattling of the wheels and the clacking of hooves against stone became louder, almost loud enough to penetrate the wind howling in her ears. Really, with the storm's roaring, it was amazing anyone had heard her. Or maybe they had seen the light go out for themselves and guessed what she must have said.

They stopped at the gate with a slight huff of mixed relief and exhaustion. The granite pillars on either side almost had enough width to them to make the wall of a house, and the roof loomed high overhead, blocking most of the storm. It still felt unreasonably cold, and the guards had a hidden brazier on either side of the gate so that they wouldn't freeze. She felt sorry for them, but not sorry enough to stay out here and keep them company. Siobhan reached into her shirt pocket and took out the leather encased seal with her guild's mark on it and flipped it open to show the two guards on duty.

"Deepwoods Guild. Party of ten."

They'd been through here so many times that the guards nodded in recognition, one of them jotted down their arrival in a large book that leaned in a wall alcove, and the guild was waved through.

Despite it being such a late hour, the streets were lively. People of every possible age, gender and profession seemed to be out and about, scurrying from one building to another, bundled up against the snow. But through the glass windows came a great deal of light, and the faint tones of raised voices and laughter.

The main road they traveled on went straight through the island and served as the main causeway. Because of that, the governor of the island had deemed it illegal to encroach on the road with any building projects and make it narrow. They had an easy time going up into the city, heading for the inn they habitually stayed at. The trouble came when they had to turn onto a side road. People had been fighting with limited space for so long that they'd gotten creative in their building habits. Now, little add-ons jutted out from the sandstone walls here and there, while brick overpasses and second-story levels arched over the street. Anyone that had a problem with enclosed spaces would have found it unbearable to travel down this street.

Siobhan blessed the crazy building habits at this moment simply because it blocked a large majority of the snow and wind. Despite being surrounded by stone on all sides, she felt almost warm in comparison to being on that thrice-cursed bridge.

The cart had to squeeze through in a few places, but they made it to Sunrise Tavern without a problem. The inn's windows in the front had light blazing out of them, and through them she could see quite the crowd huddled around the two large fireplaces on either end of the main room. Hopefully they still had a few rooms available. Siobhan forced her half-frozen hand off the reins and slowly creaked out of the saddle, dropping heavily and hissing as pins and needles shot through her legs at the impact. She hadn't frozen to the point of frostbite, but it had been a little too close for comfort. With any luck the storm would blow over tonight and it would be clear tomorrow. She didn't think anyone would be able to travel through a storm like this again. Herself included.

"Siobhan?" Wolf came over and hunkered down slightly to see her face. "Your lips are turning blue."

She turned a glare on him. *He* looked fine, and the unfairness of it rankled. That Northern blood of his made him almost immune to weather like this. "Wolf, don't you ever get cold?" she demanded, almost whining.

He grinned at her in a quick flash of slightly crooked teeth. "Not like you do. Let me see to the rooms, alright?"

"Make absolutely sure they come with hot baths," she insisted.

Patting her shoulder lightly in reassurance, he opened the door with a slight creak of hinges and pushed through, bellowing as he went, "Master Gramms! We need rooms!"

Gramms, looking as burly, surly, and round as ever, turned from where he stood near the bar and bellowed back in a rough voice, "You best be willing to make do with three of 'em! It's all I've got left!"

"They come with baths and dinner?"

"They do."

Wolf turned slightly and cocked an eyebrow at her. She nodded confirmation. They'd make do. They'd done so before. If Hammon hadn't gotten comfortable with their party yet, he would need to do so quickly, as he would be bunking down with at least two of them.

"Stop hovering in the door, then, and letting in all that cold air!" Gramms commanded, bushy eyebrows pulled together.

Beirly stayed in the driver's seat long enough for everyone to scamper off and gather their bags before he went through the narrow pass with the cart to the inn's stable yard in the back. Two young boys, Gramms' sons, came out and took their horses and led them the same way, letting the cold and weary party enter the inn. The close confines of the tables, already loaded with customers, made it hard for them to cross the room without bumping into anyone. A few gave them curious glances but did nothing more than that.

Everyone had plates of food in front of them and the sight and scent of it filled her head in a sweet, intoxicating way. The aroma set her stomach to rumbling petulantly, reminding her she'd only had cold fare for lunch several hours ago. But the thought of food came in a distant second to the idea of soaking in a large tub of scintillatingly hot water.

By the time Siobhan made it across to Gramms, her skin tingled painfully. Gramms had three keys in his hands, but he watched her instead of handing them over, dark eyes looking her over carefully. "Hot baths before dinner, I think."

She managed to move her frozen muscles into a semblance of a smile. "That obvious?"

"With you, at least." He gave the keys over and pointed up the stairs. "Back three rooms on the left. Women's and men's baths have hot water in 'em, and towels and soap, so come down when you're ready."

Never before had she felt like kissing the innkeeper as much as she did now. "Bless you."

"I'll have Maddie bring up pallets and such," he promised, shooing her on her way.

She trudged up the stairs, her pack bumping along on her back, sorting out the keys in her hands as she went. They were simple black cast-iron keys with a ring on them and a small leather square with a number embossed. It didn't take any brains to put the right key to the right room, and when she did, she left the key in the doorknob to let the boys sort themselves out. She would take the far back room, the one that sat over the kitchen. She had absolutely no intention of being cold tonight.

Siobhan entered the room and took a glance around. Two narrow beds, one on either wall, with enough space for a pallet on the floor between them, a fireplace that sat cold but with logs ready to be lit, and a single washstand holding up the corner. Large enough for the women, certainly, but she didn't know how Tran or Wolf could begin to fit on those beds. They normally had the larger rooms when they stayed here. She'd never seen Gramms so full before. The storm's doing, perhaps?

Choosing the bed closest to the door, she set her pack down and started rummaging through it for a set of clothes that would be comfortable enough to sleep in but decent enough to wear downstairs. Sylvie came in after her, setting her pack on the opposite bed and doing the same search. Siobhan could hear the men's low voices next door as they talked amongst themselves.

Denney came up a few minutes later and without ceremony dropped her pack onto Siobhan's bed. "Phew! Got that sorted."

"The dogs?" Siobhan asked. In her preoccupation to get warm, she'd temporarily forgotten about them.

60

"Gramms had some of the scraps brought in from the kitchen and made them a place near the fire. Said they'd be fine there while we had our bath and he'd keep an eye on 'em." Denney smiled as she spoke, digging out a loose sweater and matching pants. "I do love the man."

Actually, Gramms' easy-going nature about having dogs stay in his inn was one of the reasons why they always chose the place. His surly attitude aside, the man knew how to be a good host.

"Good enough. Bath," Siobhan said firmly. Clothes tucked under her arm, she headed back downstairs.

The baths had sensibly been put in the same hallway as the kitchen so that hot water could be easily carried over. Siobhan's stomach started rumbling all over again as she passed the wealth of delightful smells coming from that room. She ordered it firmly to be quiet as she kept right on going into the women's bathing room.

She took in the sight of the six wooden barrels and their steaming water with a smile of delight. Little benches sat next to each barrel, holding clean towels neatly folded and bars of soap. She went directly to the nearest one, setting her clothes under the towel, and quickly stripped of her shirt, vest, coat, riding skirt and boots. Someone paused long enough to draw the curtain in front of the door closed (thereby preventing any accidental shows for whoever might be in the hallway). Sylvie and Denney went to the barrels near her, and they didn't pass a word among themselves until they'd settled into the hot water with a long sigh of pleasure.

Knees folded up slightly, Siobhan laid her head against the side of the tub and let the water erase every trace of cold from her skin. Ahhhh. Paradise. Her hair still felt frozen against her head, so she unbraided it and let the long length of it flow into the tub. Mmmm, better.

Companionable silence descended for a long moment as they soaked and enjoyed. But silence could never last long with Sylvie in the room and eventually the woman broke it. "So...what do you two think of Master Markl

Hammon?"

"I've never seen such an easy-going, amiable man," Denney answered promptly, lifting her head so that she could look at everyone properly. "He's been very helpful ever since he joined."

"And he's honestly interested in everything," Siobhan added thoughtfully. "And I do mean everything. He told me he came to us because he wants to study the different cultures of this world, find a way to make trading easier. But his curiosity certainly isn't limited to that."

"Truly." Denney shook her head, sending her honey-colored hair swirling on the water's surface. "You should have seen Grae's face when he actually took *notes* on pathfinding. I don't think I've ever seen our gloomy man openly beam like that before."

A thought occurred and Siobhan asked Sylvie, "Did you happen to ask around? Find out if he really is related to the Silver Moon Hammons?"

"Oh, he is," Sylvie answered with an odd smile on her face. "But at the same time, he's not."

Siobhan set herself to be patient as she weaseled the full tale out of the woman. Sylvie didn't enjoy anything more than a good secret to share. "Do expound upon this matter, Mistress Storyteller."

Sylvie giggled slightly and sat forward, dark eyes shining with enjoyment. "I asked Charlin, you know, Darrens' head assistant, and he told me the full story. Apparently, over two decades ago Hammon Senior had a bit of a drunken affair with his first wife's sister—"

Siobhan's eyes widened to the point they were in danger of falling out of her head. "You're joking!"

"No, I'm not," Sylvie assured her. "It caused quite the scandal at the time. At any rate, it caused one Master Markl Hammon to be born into the world. At first, no one was quite sure what to do with him. The sister certainly didn't want him, as he endangered any future marriage prospects she had. So Hammon Senior took him in as a son, which enraged his wife and made her leave altogether. But, as it turns out, the split became a blessing. Hammon Senior met and married a woman with a much better character about a year later, and she gave him a whole passel of children and raised Markl as if he were her own son."

"The mother and the sisters he mentioned earlier," Denney said thoughtfully. "True, he did sound genuinely fond of them."

"With good reason, it sounds like," Siobhan added just as thoughtfully. So a mother that rejected him, a step-mother that wouldn't claim him, but a third mother that married in and loved him unconditionally. Talk about a rocky start in life. But he seemed to have come through it just fine.

"So while he is the firstborn son," Sylvie continued, "he's not a legitimate heir and so technically shouldn't inherit anything. Rumor has it that his father actually gave him the choice of whether he wanted to inherit the guild or not and Markl chose not to. But he's obviously still got a lot of family support."

"And funding for his chosen path," Siobhan mused, sinking a little further into the tub. It also rather explained why he so readily joined their guild to pursue that path. Loved or not, he didn't choose to stay in the family business. He might very well be looking for a place of his own, somewhere that he felt he truly needed to be.

"He's a good man." Sylvie said this with uncharacteristic sobriety, expression soft. "His mother did well raising him. I was teasing him earlier, getting on his lap like that, but I was also testing him. I wanted to see what he would do. He kept his hands properly on my knees and didn't do a thing to make me uncomfortable. Do you know how many men I've met that would have taken advantage of that position somehow?"

Far too many. One of the tests that Siobhan put men through when applying to the guild was how they reacted to Sylvie. Most responded with lecherous intentions, to one degree or another. Tran, Fei and Conli hadn't, hence why she'd let them into the guild. She had no use of men that treated women disrespectfully.

"I knew he wouldn't."

Sylvie quirked an eyebrow at her, slightly surprised. "How?"

"When you brought him to me, he was more interested in looking around the Hall than at you," Siobhan explained with a slight smile. "Of course he noticed you, but a blind man would do that. He didn't do anything more than give you a look of appreciation. That's when I knew he was trustworthy."

Denney shook her head wryly. "I knew he had to be a good man because the dogs liked him. But you know, Siobhan, the other reason why we like you to be the guildmaster is because you have an uncanny knack for judging people."

Siobhan snorted. "No, I'm pretty sure it's because I let you lot get by with anything short of murder."

"And that," Sylvie agreed serenely. "Well now, what else shall we discuss while the men are out of earshot?"

True, opportunities like this were rare, especially while they were on the road. "Actually, I need to ask something else about Hammon. Do either of you know if he's skilled in fighting?" To not be a capable fighter in this world was strange, but so was the idea of being a 'scholar' so she felt like she had to ask.

"I would assume he is," Denney volunteered. "I saw him pack a sword spear this morning."

Oh good. Siobhan let that weight roll over her shoulders. She'd forgotten to ask that pertinent little detail before shipping out this morning. But it seemed an odd choice of weapon for him. A sword spear was part blade, part staff and would stand taller than the man himself. Tran had trained in it at one point and told her it took considerable skill to be able to wield it without leaving yourself open. And why would a Robargen's choice of sword be a Teheranian weapon?

Siobhan made a mental note to ask Hammon that

later, if the opportunity ever arose, and went to the next topic she wanted to discuss. "Is Fei sick? I've never seen him sleep this much."

"Bit of a hangover," Denney explained. "He came in to see Conli about it late last night. The sweet rolls apparently had enough sugar in them to make him a bit tipsy."

She'd barely detected the sugar at all. Siobhan rubbed at the bridge of her nose. "Really? He's *that* sensitive?"

"Conli says it's getting worse as he grows older." Denney made a face. "Poor man. He's going to have to be careful about what he eats."

Oh joy of wonders.

A soft knock came at the door and Beirly's voice floated through the wood. "I'm looking for three beautiful women that belong to the Deepwoods Guild. Have any of you lovely water nymphs seen them?"

All three women laughed. "We're here!" Siobhan assured him. "Is dinner ready?"

"And waiting," Beirly answered, tone rich with unvoiced laughter.

"Then we'll be out shortly."

# Chapter Five

Siobhan, a habitually early riser, came awake naturally as the sun started to rise over the horizon. The bed might have been on the narrow and small side, but she'd gotten a good night's rest regardless. She sat up and raised her arms over her head, stretching and getting the blood flowing again. From downstairs wafted the smell of baking bread, sizzling meat, and something spicy cooking. Mmm. That smelled like good motivation to get moving.

As she climbed out of bed, both dogs came alert and stared up at her, tails thumping softly against the wooden floor. They had started out on top of Denney's bed (and because of the narrow size of the bed, on top of Denny as well) but had at some point in the night moved to lie right in front of the door instead. Well, it had likely gotten too hot in here for them to stay on the bed. What with the heat rising up from the kitchen under them, and the fireplace in here blazing merrily along, it'd nearly gotten too hot for Siobhan at one point. Not that she had a mind to complain about that, not after the day she'd had yesterday.

She rose and dressed in something warm, pulling on her boots and trying not to fall all over Sylvie, who had chosen to sleep in between the beds. The dogs didn't help as they got up and kept circling her as she moved, nosing at her legs in a clear signal that they wanted to go out when she did.

"Alright, alright," she muttered softly. "Wait a minute, will you?"

Denney lifted her head a scant inch off the pillow and pried open one eye. "Uhhh?"

"I'll take care of 'em," she told the still mostly asleep woman.

Reassured, Denney's head dropped back down and she went right back into a deep sleep.

Opening the door, Siobhan let the dogs go out first before following after, shutting the door firmly behind her. She didn't get more than a step before Fei came out of the room two doors down. He took in the sight with nothing more than a good morning grunt.

"Morning," she greeted wryly. She, Fei and Wolf were the only three in the guild that even tried to wake up early. But while Fei might be moving, it didn't mean he had properly woken up yet, and she didn't try to really talk to him until he'd downed either food or tea.

They all clumped down the stairs and toward the front door. Siobhan stepped outside with the dogs, fully expecting Fei to stay indoors and simply keep an eye on things from the window. But he surprised her by coming out as well, stopping on the threshold. Her eyes turned up to the sky but it looked just as angry and grey as it had the day before and even on this narrow street, snowflakes fell with regular consistency. The storm had not yet passed. She blew out an irritable breath. Will ye or nill ye, they were stuck here for another day it seemed.

She kept only the most casual of eyes on the dogs—they knew better than to get out of her line of sight—and stood so she could look sideways at Fei. "Are you awake or not?"

"Tran-ren snores."

In other words, awake. Right. "So you ended up with Tran and...?"

"Hammon-jia."

Oh? So that's where Hammon ended up. "He strikes me as a good man."

"Yes, from what I've seen," Fei agreed. After a long pause, he added thoughtfully, "He's certainly intelligent. He was respectful in asking me questions last night, but also very curious. Why did you let him into the guild?"

"He agreed to do the books," she responded cheerfully.

Fei gave her quite the look, as if he knew she was only half-kidding. "Siobhan-ajie. Why did you let him in?"

He wanted a serious answer? She took a half step to face him more fully and answered honestly, "For the same reason I let you into the guild, and Conli, and Tran. Because you all had a look in your eyes as if you were trying to find a proper place to belong, a place that would be home for you unconditionally. He gave me multiple reasons for coming to Deepwoods, and I'm not sure if even he realizes why he's really here, but I think that if we give him time he'll find what he's searching for. Besides, he's one of the few men that I can trust around Sylvie."

Fei inclined his head in agreement.

"You've seen that sword spear he carries around?" She waited for Fei's nod to continue, "Find a way to subtly test his skills with that, will you? I need to know how strong he is. I'd rather not put him in more danger than he can handle."

Fei seemed to find this funny, as his eyes crinkled up. "You don't worry about that with Tran-ren or Wolf-ren."

"That's because they think danger is *fun*," she bemoaned. "If I tried to pull them out of trouble, they'd give me a look like a pair of dogs being denied a treat. You're the first sensible fighter I've ever seen."

He shrugged.

The dogs came back to her at that point and nosed at her hands. She patted them and gave them a good scratch behind the ears, and almost got knocked down by wagging tails of happiness. With a wave, she ushered them all back inside, shivering a little as she went. When they came through the door, she found Wolf already seated at one of the tables and three plates of steaming food set out. Oh good, he'd ordered for all of them.

As they took a seat, he whistled for the dogs, pointing them toward bowls of scraps and water that sat next to his chair. As they happily munched, the humans dug into their own food with happy smiles.

Only with her plate clean did Siobhan sit back and asked Wolf, "Is this cold typical of Wynngaard? The only time we've been through here is during high summer or late spring."

"And we came this way during those times for good reason," he informed her dryly. "It's only going to get colder."

She made a face. Not the answer she wanted.

"That said, this snowstorm is unusual for this time of the year. We should have another month or two before it gets this cold. I think it's just an unseasonal storm that's sweeping through." This would have sounded vastly reassuring if he hadn't added, "Or at least, I hope it is. Otherwise we're in for a cold winter up here."

"It didn't seem as cold to me this morning," Fei piped up, lingering at the table with a hot cup of tea warming his hands. "We are out of the wind here, though."

"Let's check with the tower guards, see if they noticed any other storms coming our direction," Wolf suggested. "From their lookouts, they've got quite the view."

Not a bad thought. Siobhan nodded in agreement. "We can't travel a full eight hours again in a snowstorm. Not without risking fingers and toes. But if there's another storm coming, I'd like to get ahead of it and be in Quigg when it hits. We're going to need to spend a few days there, likely, to find if Lirah Darrens even made it over the bridges. I want that confirmed before we travel any further north."

Wolf scooted back from the table in a rough scraping sound and stood. "I'll go ask the guards, then."

"Take hot tea or hot bread with you," she suggested. "Your questions will go over better."

He thought about that for a moment, shrugged agreement, and reversed directions to the kitchen instead.

"Do you always feed people?" Hammon asked from behind her.

Siobhan started in her chair, twisting about so she could see the scholar. He had moved so quietly that she hadn't the faintest notion he'd joined them downstairs. He looked a little mussed around the edges, but he was fully dressed and obviously ready to start the day.

"I do," she answered him after that startled heartbeat, waving him to join them at the table. "Well, among my people, we believe in feeding people for taking the time and trouble to help us, no matter how minor it might be. Offering food—especially to men and children—is an easy way to make friends, too."

Hammon seemed to find this amusing somehow. "So that's why you offered me strawberries and chocolate."

"That's why," she agreed. "How did you sleep, Hammon?"

"Surprisingly well."

Her brows quirked at this. "You must be a deep sleeper, then. Fei tells me that Tran snores."

His smile broadened so that it became mischievous. "I put wax in my ears."

Siobhan threw her head back and laughed aloud. "What, and you didn't share?"

Fei gave the blond an unamused look. "Next time, you will."

Hammon held up both hands in a gesture of surrender and placation. "Next time, I promise. I'm surprised to see we're the only ones awake."

"There are certain people that you do not wish to awaken if you can help it," Siobhan informed him, not at all joking. "If we leave them to their own devices, they'll

71

come down eventually. If not, we sic the dogs on them."

Fei pointed at the large clock sitting on the mantel. "Isn't it about time for that?"

"If we're stuck here for another day, no sense in upsetting people when I don't need to."

"Coward," Fei teased.

"I prefer to call it survival instincts," she corrected loftily.

"Ahhh…" Hammon glanced between the two of them, unsure if they were joking or not. "For my information and future safety, who isn't safe to wake up?"

"Conli-ren, Sylvie-jae, and Tran-ren," Fei said.

"But for entirely different reasons," Siobhan couldn't help but explain. "Tran's first instinct on waking is to maim or kill anyone leaning over him. He apparently had an interesting childhood. Conli doesn't wake up so much as *leap* into wakefulness. He comes awake as if there's an emergency and he has to be in motion right that second. We've bumped heads quite a few times because of it. But Sylvie doesn't want to wake up. She's quite stubborn about it, actually. She doesn't really do anything but kick at you and grumble. It's what she does afterwards, to get revenge, they make men tremble."

"As bad as a cat, that one," Fei grumbled. "Her methods are devious and underhanded."

Hammon caught the muttering and inclined his head toward the Saoleoran in question.

Siobhan carefully mouthed, 'Bad experience.'

His mouth formed a silent 'Ahhh' but didn't say anything more than that.

One of the kitchen girls came out bearing a steaming plate and a large tankard of tea, which was plopped down in front of Hammon with nothing more than a 'Good morning to you, sir.'

Hammon dug in and lingered over the first bite before saying with approval, "This is quite good."

"Gramms is a good host and has good cooks," Siobhan informed him after taking a long swallow of hot tea. "It's why we always stay here."

"Just that?"

"And he likes the dogs." Fei looked down at Pyper's upturned face, moving an arm so he could scratch behind one floppy ear. "And what do you want, hmm?"

"Your unfinished plate," Siobhan translated dryly. "Isn't that obvious?"

Fei played along with a straight face. "I thought she finally came to me for affection."

"The more you feed her, the more she'll love you. It's the rule of dogs," Hammon offered, eyes dancing.

Hoping to get a little more information about her newest guildmate, Siobhan asked casually, "That sounds like the voice of experience. Had a dog, did you?"

"A collier, growing up," he admitted just as easily, eating steadily. "He was more mischievous than these two. Is it Icean that trained them so well?"

"It is," Fei answered. Giving up, he lowered his plate to the ground and let Pyper lick it clean.

Wolf came back into the room with his usual heavy stride, making the floor vibrate at his passing. Siobhan looked up in surprise, protesting, "You can't possibly have gone to the watchtowers and back that fast!"

"Didn't," he agreed, bracing both hands on the table's surface and leaning over it slightly. "Gramms beat me to it. The guards report stormy skies in every direction, but there's a warm wind picking up from the south. Mayhap the storm will pass today, or so they say."

She let out a breath of relief. "Thanks to any god listening for that. Alright, then we need to get ready to leave tomorrow. We might as well spend today doing a little research and getting Hammond a ring."

Hammon quirked a brow at that. "A ring? What sort?"

In demonstration, she held up her right hand, which had a silver ring embossed with the basic arch of a bridge on it. "Bridge rings are what we call 'em. They're specifically for Island Pass. See, the rule they have for visitors here is that you're only allowed to use the hostels, inns, and stores as you pass through. It prevents mischief from happening in the more residential areas of the island. But if you wear this ring, you're a trusted man by the officials and allowed to wander in wherever you will and access records as you need them. If you plan to stay with us for any length of time, you'll need a ring. We come through here often and the rings help us with our clients."

"May I...?" he asked, with a gesture toward her ring.

"Oh, sure." She slid the ring off her middle finger and handed it over so he could more closely inspect it.

"It's not a very elaborate design," he observed as he turned it this way and that.

"There's different levels of rings," she explained, taking it back from him. "This is a more basic level, one that doesn't have a lot of power to it. It goes like such: silver, gold, then bejeweled. The bejeweled ones have either mother of pearl or crystal inlaid on top."

Hammon stared more intently at the ring before glancing up at the ceiling, a frown of concentration on his face. "A golden version with inlaid mother of pearl, you say?"

"Conli has one," she answered the unspoken question written all over his face. "He's from a prominent family on Island Pass."

From the blank stare he gave her, Hammon hadn't expected something like that. "He is?"

"He is." She splayed her hands in an open shrug. "Why he's in Deepwoods serving as our physician, I can't explain. He's never volunteered that information and I've never felt it right to pry."

"You're dying to pry, though," he said in a knowing tone.

"I hate unresolved riddles more than any other thing," she grumbled. "But if I do, I'll drive him and Denney away, and I'd rather not lose good people. So, I bite my tongue."

"Why him and Denney?"

"They come as a set, those two. Which is another riddle I want answered. The most Denney has ever told me about herself is that she's half-Teheranian, half-Wynngaardian—which I'm sure you've guessed, judging from her looks—but I know precious little of her background aside from that. Those two came in together six years ago looking for a guild and work, and I took them on because of Conli's medical skills. I haven't once regretted that decision, either. Although there are days when I *do* wonder what they're doing with us..." she trailed off, her own eyes straying up the stairs to where the two in question were still fast asleep. "With Conli's doctoring skills, he can work wherever he wishes to. I'm thankful to have him, mind, and certainly don't wish to see the back of him. I just don't understand what I did to gain him, either."

"Your stunning and dynamic personality?" Hammon offered artlessly, with an innocent blink of the eyes.

She threw her head back and laughed. "That I doubt! But I thank you for the flattery." Actually, while Denney was upstairs and still asleep, this would be a good time to warn Hammon of certain things. "Hammon, have you ever been to Wynngaard before?"

"I was three at the time," he answered with a wry shrug. "I don't remember much."

"Ahhh. Then you might not know this." She waved him closer and lowered her voice to a more confidential murmur. "I want you to be on your toes as we reach Wynngaard. There's a stigma attached to people like Denney, who obviously have mixed blood. They mistake her for a prostitute or some lower-class worker all the time. If she stumbles into a crowd of Teheranians, it's especially bad, which might happen in Quigg. There's quite a large neighborhood of them in the city."

Hammon raised a hand in a staying motion. "Wait, why?"

"As it was explained to me, there's one thing that Wynngaardian and Teheranian culture have in common: they don't tolerate half-bloods. Those poor souls that are born to mixed parents are in for a rough life afterward.

I think that's why Denney chooses to stay in Robarge, as we don't have that prejudice." That was pure guesswork on her part, though, as Denney had never said a word one way or the other. "Regardless, when we're in Wynngaard, keep an eye on her and step in if you need to."

He gave her a solemn nod and promised, "I will."

"Good man."

"Ahhh...speaking of her...." Hammon's eyes started twinkling in a devilish fashion. "I was promised a story that I never got to hear. Something about her falling off the cart while on the path and getting lost for several days?"

Siobhan's expression melted into an evil smile. "Oh, that? True, I do need to tell you that. To serve as an example and prevent you from repeating her mistake, of course."

"Of course," he agreed with a straight face.

"It happened about, oh, two years back." Siobhan relaxed in her chair, crossing her hands over her stomach, and prepared to tell the tale. "We were taking a small caravan from Cymer to Kaillmark, then escorting them back again. On the way back, Denney got concerned about one of the dogs not being seated properly, and as she moved to adjust the dog, *she* lost her balance and fell straight off the side of the cart. Tran and Beirly both saw her going over and called a halt right there, but when a person leaves a path, you can't see them. Grae marked the spot, but he couldn't just stop, as our clients had a ship to make in Dykes. So we went all the way through the path and took them to Cymer, then Dykes. That took about an hour, mind you. I split the guild up so that half made sure the caravan got loaded on the ship as they were supposed to, then I took Grae and Tran back with me to go get Denney."

Just remembering the whole situation made her shake her head.

"Grae had run some calculations and did a little wizardry, and he figured out more or less where she must have landed. We took a smaller path he already had built and he took us to the right area. Or what should have been the right area, if Denney had stayed put. But no, in her infinite wisdom, she'd decided to walk the remaining distance to Cymer and save us some trouble."

"Correct me if I'm wrong," Hammon's brows were furrowed in bemusement, "but isn't the distance between Kaillmark and Cymer about ninety spans?"

"Indeed it is," she assured him, like a proud teacher of a pupil. "Someone paid attention when they were being taught their geography. But Denney was under the impression that since she'd fallen from an active path, she had traveled most of the distance. But this gets better: you see, she has no sense of direction."

Hammon blinked. "At all?"

Wolf snorted. "The girl can, and has, gotten herself lost just going up the stairs."

"If not for the dogs, I wouldn't let her go out of the guildhall by herself for fear we'd never see her again," Siobhan added sourly. "Why she thought she could navigate all the way to Cymer, I haven't the foggiest notion. So, instead of going toward Cymer as she intended, she instead headed *west* and ended up in the marshland near Priyam's Waters. If not for Tran, we'd never have found her."

"Why Tran especially?"

"Oh, he's an amazing runner."

"Most Teheranians are," Fei added.

"Tran can run great distances and speeds without tiring. When I realized that Denney had gotten herself lost, I had him track her down and bring her back so we could travel by path to Cymer. Even with his help, what should have taken an hour or so took four days. We had to wander in every direction looking for her, as with Denney, you never know what direction she'll take."

Hammon coughed in a poor attempt to disguise a laugh. "She's never going to live it down, either."

"Never," Siobhan agreed with a genteel smile.

Conli chose that moment to come downstairs, stifling a yawn behind one hand. "Morning, everyone."

Everyone returned the greeting in their own way and Siobhan called back to the kitchen for another plate of food to be brought out.

As Conli sat, she caught his eye and said, "We'll be delayed here a day as the storm hasn't passed yet. Since that's so, I think we should speak to the guards and get more information about Lirah's party. Were they in good condition when they passed through? Any signs of trouble before she came or after she left? Any information right now will help."

"You think you'll need me," Conli held up his left hand and the bejeweled bridge ring he wore, "to find all that out?"

"I don't know," she admitted frankly. "But I *do* know that we'll need your help to get Hammon a ring while we're here. So why don't the three of us go get that done and ask questions while we're about it?"

"It's not a bad plan," he agreed readily. "Although I'm a little surprised, Hammon, that you don't already have one."

"I was very young when I left Robarge and traveled elsewhere," he explained. "After I turned ten, I never really went anywhere else until a few months ago, when I left home."

"Ahh, is that right? Then we'll get a ring for you and show you what you can use it for. We occasionally take side jobs separate from the guild, and when we do, the rings come in handy as we travel."

"You can take on side jobs in this guild?"

"I don't prohibit it, as long as it doesn't interfere with guild work," Siobhan explained absently. Her attention was on the second floor, as half of her guild had yet made no signs of wanting to wake up. "Errr..." She looked up at the stairs, debating on how to handle the slumbering dragons still in their beds. "Wolf?"

"I'm *not* waking any of them up," he said vehemently.

"And you can't make me."

Hammon paused mid-bite and looked at Wolf with mild alarm. "Are they truly that bad?"

Wolf nodded several times in vigorous confirmation.

Rolling her eyes, Siobhan said patiently, "I was about to say, sic the dogs on 'em."

"Oh. That I'll do." Relieved, Wolf whistled for both of them and headed up the stairs, the dogs climbing ahead of him with happy bounces. But then, for them, waking up sleeping people counted as 'fun.'

Ignoring the outraged yells coming from the second floor, Siobhan prudently decided to hunt down Gramms and settle their account. She'd worry about looking for information *after* the three grumps had breakfast.

# Chapter Six

The storm passed by noon, leaving traces of snow behind that collected along the sides of the streets and in shadowy corners. By that point, they'd gone through all the bothersome paperwork and procedures to get Hammon a ring of his own. Since she had Conli with her, they inquired about the Blackstone party, even going so far as to cross from the eastern gate over to the western gate, questioning the gatekeepers themselves and looking at the records.

They found nothing out of the ordinary.

According to the records and the guards' somewhat hazy memories, the party had come through and traveled on the bridges on a fair weather day. They hadn't looked distressed, preoccupied, or in any way worried about their journey. In fact, their attitudes and condition had been so completely normal that the guards couldn't remember them at first, and it was only the unusual size of the party that struck a mental chord with them. Usually people that traveled were much smaller in number or a great deal larger, such as merchants and caravans.

Having only been able to confirm what the initial report said didn't satisfy her, but at least Siobhan knew that whatever had happened hadn't happened here.

They couldn't leave for Quigg that day, as they wouldn't have enough time to get over the bridges before the tide rose, so they had several hours to kill. That in mind, she led the men back to the inn and had everyone grab their weapons, announcing to the guild that since they had the time, they might as well spar with each other and get a feel for how their new member fought.

Wolf and Tran were all for this idea, and they quickly led the way up to the inn's roof, which had a flat area open for guests to relax in. Gramms probably had some notion of turning this place into a garden, as he'd put flower pots and benches up here, but it was never used for relaxing. Not with her group, at least. In this overly crowded city, the rooftop had the only open space available for sparring that didn't risk striking a wall.

With everyone gathered, she caught Beirly's eye and motioned with her chin toward Hammon. Catching her drift, Beirly lifted a hand and waved Hammon down.

"Why don't you and I spar first?" he invited with a wide smile behind his bushy red beard. "I've never fought against a weapon like yours before and I'm curious."

"That's fine," Hammon agreed readily.

Siobhan leaned against the cold stone wall, safely on the sidelines, and watched with interest as Beirly and Hammon picked up their weapons and faced each other. She was very curious as to what Beirly would do, as he only had a long sword in his hand. In reality, the sword spear that Hammon used was one of the deadliest and most effective weapons in the known world. It combined two dangerous elements: it was essentially a short sword on the end of the spear. It gave its wielder incredible reach and range, effectively cutting the opponent's offensive power in half. Of course, being able to wield something six feet long without accidentally slicing your own foot off brought its own challenges, but from the way Hammon carried that thing, he'd been well trained in it.

The only way to really face a sword spear was with a shield, which Beirly didn't have. In truth, Wolf should be Hammon's opponent as he normally fought with shield and longsword. But pitting Wolf against the scholar seemed totally unfair. The man was a demon when it came to fighting. Only Tran and Fei seemed to be able to fight toe-to-toe with him. Beirly, being no slouch when it came to fighting, seemed a fairer opponent for this testing of skills.

Hammon settled into a wide stance, both hands on the wood in a steady grip, eyes on Beirly. Beirly had both hands on his sword hilt as well, the tip of the blade circling ever so slightly as he eyed Hammon. For several seconds, both men sized each other up, weighing options and tactics.

Without warning, Beirly lunged forward, sword striking Hammon's blade, attempting to knock it far to the side. Hammon didn't try to force it back, just slid the blade abruptly down, robbing Beirly's thrust of its force, before he reversed directions and snapped the blade back up. Beirly was forced to rapidly retreat or lose part of his beard.

"They do remember they're not trying to hurt each other, right...?" Siobhan muttered anxiously under her breath. Maybe she should have insisted that they leave the weapons sheathed before doing this.

"They're fine," Tran assured her in a low tone. "They've got good control right now, and it's obvious neither of them are fighting at full speed."

Well, true, they were obviously holding back. But she knew from experience that these things could get out of control very quickly and neither man was wearing any sort of protective armor.

Thwarted, Beirly circled back and tried again. Hammon wasn't giving him any opening this time, however, and moved the sword spear in a series of quick thrusts, the wood sliding in his forward hand, so that Beirly had to dodge every direction to avoid getting a foot of metal in his gut.

Beirly seemed to realize that if this kept going, he would dramatically lose the fight. In a short burst of speed, he closed the distance, sliding his sword against the staff, keeping Hammon from putting the blade into play. But Hammon didn't hesitate or panic, he simply raised the staff above his shoulders, forcing Beirly's sword up as well. Beirly had time to give a wordless protest before Hammon brought his knee up and rammed it into Beirly's chest, forcing him backward.

Losing his balance entirely, Beirly stumbled and collapsed onto his back, sword falling from his loosened grip. Hammon lost no time in putting the edge of the sword spear against the redhead's throat.

In good humor, Beirly spread his hands in surrender. "You won that bout, friend."

Hammon grinned at him. "You almost got me, though. A little faster, and I wouldn't have been able to stop you."

"Ha!" Beirly didn't believe that for one second.

Grin widening, Hammon retracted the weapon before leaning forward, offering Beirly a hand up. Beirly took it and came easily to his feet.

Siobhan watched this scene with open satisfaction. Yes, Hammon had the skills to defend himself and then some. She needn't worry about that in the future. She clapped her hands together. With that settled, they might as well go in—

"Me next!" Wolf said with unabashed excitement.

She stared at him in horror. "What? Why?"

"I haven't faced a sword spear user in quite some time," he responded as if the answer was obvious. "A man gets rusty if he's always sparring with the same opponents."

"Pull the other leg, man!" Beirly responded, amused. "You spar with the whole city!"

"They're still the same opponents," Wolf argued,

already drawing the shield from his back. "Besides, I want to see if he knows how to get past a shield."

"You can hold a shield and fight?" Hammon asked, tone not condescending, but honestly intrigued.

"Of course," Wolf assured him. Turning sideways, he demonstrated for the other man. "Beirly made it so that I can lock the hand in place. See? Once I have the fingers through the handle, I use the thumb here to latch the others in position. It won't release until I pull this lever here."

"Ingenious," Hammon breathed, leaning in closer for a better look. "Beirly, have you considered selling this design? Actually marketing it? I know you'd only be able to make limbs for people able to afford them, but I still think you'd make a pretty kor from it."

"Now that is a good business proposition." Beirly stroked his beard as he thought about it. "What do you think, Sylvie? You think you can help me sell it if I make it?"

"Beirly," the brunette drawled, "I can sell your beard to apes if I've a mind to. The reason I didn't suggest it before is it's hard to market something you have to custom make for people. I saw how much time you've invested in Wolf's arm, making it so that it fits him just right."

"There's a drawback, alright." Beirly frowned in thought, still tugging at his beard. "But in the beginning, it was all trial and error. I bet I can do it faster now, not fumble as much."

"Debate this over dinner," Wolf suggested, clearly not interested in business deals when there was new blood to spar with.

Hammon good-naturedly raised his weapon again, ready to take on the next opponent.

Siobhan leaned back against the wall with a sigh. Well, if it truly did start to get out of hand, she'd send Tran in to break it up.

✦ ✦ ✦

In an unusual turn of events, Siobhan was not the first down to breakfast the next morning. She came downstairs to find that Hammon, Grae, and Beirly had beaten her there, with half-consumed plates in front of them.

"—was actually for my sake that the guild was formed," Grae explained to an attentive Hammon. "You see, I studied under a master Pathmaker in Widstoe—that's our hometown—and became a master there myself. But once I had the ranking, I discovered that most of the people in the city still went to my master for work. He'd been doing it for over twenty years, so I guess people were just used to dealing with him. But that didn't leave a lot of customers for me, so I did a little research and discovered that Goldschmidt didn't have a Pathmaker but it *did* have the size and demand to support one."

"So you moved there?" Hammon guessed.

Ah, Hammon must have asked how the guild was first formed. Siobhan silently joined them at the table, serving up a plate of food for herself from the dishes in the middle, and started eating without even trying to interrupt.

"Well, I was set to do that, but I'm bad with people." Grae gave a self-depreciating smile. "I don't deal well with strangers, especially. But Siobhan, she's always been good with people. So I asked her to form a business with me— she'd handle the clients, I'd build the paths."

Hammon glanced at her.

"I thought it a good business plan," she said easily. "So I agreed."

"Right before we left, though, my master warned me that most Pathmakers don't do well unless they're part of a guild," Grae continued. "It's the protection of belonging to a guild more than anything else. Otherwise people try to pressure you into joining up with their guild, and you end up in a place where you'd rather not be. But it takes at least three people to form a guild, so..."

"So they asked me," Beirly piped up, stroking his beard in a reminiscent manner. "I'd built myself a carpentry business by that point, and had run it for two years, so I knew more about forming a guild than either of them. It didn't set right with me, either, sending them off alone to a city that they'd only heard of. I couldn't convince their parents to talk them out of the idea—they're both from large families and I think they were just as glad for one less child to feed—so I thought, I'd best go with them. Turns out to be the best decision I ever made."

"Somehow—mind you, I don't remember hearing this discussion at all—they talked about it behind my back and nominated me as guildmaster," Siobhan couldn't help but add dryly.

"We took a vote," Beirly defended himself mildly.

"The majority carried," Grae tacked on with a small grin.

"Ha ha ha." She glared at both of them, muttering under her breath.

"Although I almost rethought that decision after two months," Beirly admitted ruefully to Hammon. "See, we got a guildhall for cheap, and set up business easily enough. With Grae's skills, we had a good number of clients within the first month. We'd barely gotten our feet wet when she stumbled across a black market and saw Wolf. Siobhan's always been the sort to take pity on outcast souls, and after one look at him, she couldn't leave him there. So she bought him."

Hammon's eyes crossed. "You *bought* Wolf?"

"For fifty-eight kors," Beirly stated factually. Cocking his head, he asked rhetorically, "Has he ever paid that back?"

Siobhan snorted. "I couldn't begin to tell you. Considering how often I've had to dock his pay or fine him for damages, it's a miracle he has any money at all."

Beirly waved this away as unimportant. "We thought she was crazy at first. I mean, who buys a former dark guild mercenary with a missing hand? Especially one that's as big as a giant and strong enough to snap your neck like a chicken's? But he was so grateful for any show of kindness, I realized she was right to take him from there. That's when I thought, if he just had that hand of his back, he'd be a force to reckon with. We needed a good fighter in the guild with all the traveling we did. So he and I made a deal. I'd make him up a hand so he could fight if he promised to stay until we could find another enforcer to replace him with."

"Whoa, whoa, wait!" Siobhan threw up both hands to stop him. "I never heard about this! When did you two promise that?"

Those big brown eyes blinked at her. "You didn't know he promised me that?"

"No, I didn't know!" she responded in exasperation. "When did he?"

"Oh, not long after you brought him to the Hall." Beirly scratched at his beard and looked thoughtfully toward the ceiling. "Hmmm, a week or two after? Remember that one squinty-looking man who was trying to trick us into moving stolen goods to Stott? The one that Wolf squashed flat when he tried to flee? It was after that."

"That happened the first month he was with us," Siobhan said faintly. Several memories sorted and flipped themselves in her head, forming a completely different picture than they once had. "Wait, so when I asked him to stay on long enough to pay back what I'd spent on him, is *that* why he gave me such a funny smile?"

Beirly gave a one-shoulder shrug. "Don't know anything about that."

Hammon put his knife down, apparently too engrossed in the conversation and history of Deepwoods to care about a trivial thing like eating. "So what happened next?"

"Sylvie," Grae said, like a man explaining that a typhoon had hit.

Siobhan smothered a laugh, as it rather had been like that. "You see, the whole incident with the smuggler had taught us a clear lesson. We didn't know enough about trade, and I'm not a good trader anyway. None of us are. So I started looking around for another member, someone that would understand the business, and give me good guidance. It wasn't long after that we found Sylvie. She'd left Orin and come through Converse, looking for a guild that had a female guildmaster. I suppose she felt it would be safer that way, or something. Anyway, she heard that I was looking for a tradesman and came to me. We bonded over a bowl of chocolate strawberries."

"And the guild hasn't been the same since," Beirly inserted, eyes crinkling. "She wasn't too sure what to think of a male-dominated guild like ours at first—she's a bad history with men trying to take advantage of her—but we worked it out with her quick-like. The first day she was out late, and Wolf went looking for her, she came back with the widest smile on her face. She'd run into trouble and was in a fine pickle before Wolf showed up. It was the first time a man had defended her and not asked something in return, see. I knew then, she'd never leave of her own accord."

"It took us some time to figure out how to protect her properly," Siobhan admitted with a long sigh. "But she's worth every bit of trouble and then some. Although we haven't had as much trouble with that in Goldschmidt the past few years. People more or less know now that if you hassle her, you'll be dealing with every other person in Deepwoods, and there *will* be broken bones."

"It's given her space to breathe." Grae tapped the table to get Hammon's attention. "Be careful with her. Please."

"And Denney too," Beirly added.

"And…?" Siobhan encouraged them with a smile of anticipation.

Both Grae and Beirly looked back at her blankly.

"And what?" Beirly asked, looking for all the world as if he hadn't a clue what she wanted.

"And what am I?" she snapped back, irritated. "Chopped liver? Why aren't you worried about protecting me?"

"Shi, I feel sorry for anyone that tangles with you," Grae informed her bluntly.

"No kidding," Beirly muttered. "The last time a man hassled you, you'd taken him down before Wolf could do more than turn his head."

She glared at them murderously. Without turning her head, she growled, "I see that smile, Hammon. Wipe it off your face right now."

He gave a fake cough. "Wasn't smiling."

'Wise of you,' Grae mouthed.

Grumbling under her breath, she stabbed the knife into her food with more force than necessary.

"What are you two on about?" Wolf asked them. He'd apparently come down without her noticing. He came around the table to pat her gently on the head. "She's a beautiful woman, isn't she? Of course you should look out for her."

Her bad mood disappeared without a trace and she beamed up at him. Putting both arms around his waist, she laid her head against his stomach and crooned, "You wonderful man."

In an undertone, Beirly murmured, "He always spoils her like that."

"If either of you had any sense, you would too," Sylvie informed them as she sauntered around the table to the empty seat next to Hammon. "After all, she controls your paychecks."

Grae and Beirly gave each other nervous looks.

Siobhan started cackling like a mad crone.

Sylvie grabbed Hammon's spoon and without a by-your-leave snatched a bite from his plate. "Mmm, good."

Hammon regarded her with open surprise, not expecting his breakfast to be stolen.

"She does that," Beirly warned him belatedly. "If you sit next to Sylvie, expect to only eat about half your plate. She can't resist eating both her food *and* yours."

"Is that right?" Hammon glanced at her, expression

thoughtful and weighing. Then without another word, he reached out and piled another spoonful of everything onto the plate before nudging it a little closer to her.

Sylvie's mouth parted in surprise. When he simply looked back at her, expectantly, she softened into a sweet smile. With his generosity established, she didn't hesitate to steal another bite, although she did give him his spoon back first so he could at least try to eat.

Siobhan watched this play out with open satisfaction as Wolf took the chair next to hers. Well now. She'd known Hammon to be a kind soul from their first meeting, but this rather proved it to the whole guild. Sylvie had probably been half-testing him on that first bite—she routinely tested everyone she came into contact with—but now that Hammon had proven he wouldn't judge her for her bad habits, they would likely be much more at ease with one another.

They chatted over breakfast and ate but did not dawdle. With the storm past them, Siobhan didn't want to waste any time staying here. They knew everything that could be learned about Lirah's party and it was time to go.

Denney
Icean

Christa Triumph 2011

# Chapter Seven

Fortified with a hot breakfast, steaming tea, and a good night's rest, they took to the road once more. Leaving the isle took a matter of minutes, as it didn't have any real width to it, just length, and then they stepped onto the second half of the Grey Bridges. The whole party let out a sigh of relief when they felt the warm wind flow over them. The air still had a distinct chill to it, but it didn't even compare to the wind-cutting, bone-rattling cold of before.

They crossed the bridge without incident, sometimes nodding or saying friendly hellos with the people that passed them on the other side. With fairer weather, the traffic on the bridge picked up considerably as people tried to take advantage and get to their own destinations.

Siobhan kept an eye on Denney as they went. The girl had never been comfortable in Quigg, despite it being her hometown. Or maybe it was because of it. Wynngaard and Teherani both had interesting opinions about half-bloods, and Denney usually ran into trouble at some point when they passed through the city. The closer they got, the more openly she stuck herself to Conli. He put an arm around her shoulder, comforting, but also in a clearly protective mood.

She caught Wolf and Tran's eyes, inclining her head toward Denney. They nodded in grim understanding, accepting her silent order to keep an eye on her.

Still, the day passed pleasantly enough, and by late afternoon, they arrived in the thriving, bustling, and sometimes dangerous city of Quigg.

Quigg had never been designed or organized in any way as it was constructed. People had added on streets, neighborhoods and whole markets wherever they felt a need to have one. People who had been born and raised in the city still got lost in it, or so the rumors said. Anyone going to Wynngaard had one of two options: find a ship and sail there yourself or go through Quigg. Sometimes people had stopped there instead of continuing on, and the city reflected the very diverse cultures it housed. Every possible style of architecture, masonry, and signs could be seen as soon as the guild stepped through the main gates. Siobhan flinched from it a little, overwhelmed by the clash of scents, voices speaking loudly in different languages, and the press of bodies wearing every possible style of clothing.

She could tell it unnerved the men, too, being surrounded and jostled on all sides by pedestrians and other travelers. They immediately formed ranks around the cart, Wolf guarding the back, Fei the middle, and Tran coming ahead to ride alongside her. Raising her voice to be heard over the din, she said to him, "Is it my imagination, or is this place more crowded than it was last year?"

Tran grimaced agreement.

Sylvie stood up in the cart and called, "Siobhan! Should I go ahead and see if our regular inn has room for us?"

Instinctively, she felt it a bad idea. Shaking her head, she raised one hand and made a circular gesture, signaling

94

the group to stick close together. Siobhan just knew that if they separated in this crowd, for any reason, they'd have a terrible time finding each other again. She especially didn't want any one of them going off alone—no telling what trouble they'd find doing so.

They blazed a path through the crowd easier as a group, but even then their pace was slow. Siobhan couldn't clearly remember which street their preferred inn sat on, so Tran took the lead (bless the man's memory) and led them off the main thoroughfare, which took them away from that crushing crowd. Siobhan breathed a sigh of relief to leave that noisy, somewhat smelly, mass of people behind her.

Tran led them confidently up another two narrow streets and onto a wider, more appealing road that emptied into a pretty courtyard. There lay the North Bay Inn, its doors facing the courtyard, looking different than the last time she'd laid eyes on it. Strange, her memory said that the three-story building was brown with dark green trimming. But it now looked creamy white with blue trimming. Had someone painted the place? It didn't look different in any other way. She took a peek inside the large floor-to-ceiling windows on the front of the building as she rode toward the door. The inside seemed to be different too, as if the floors had been replaced with a lighter wood and the walls inside had been given a fresh coat of paint. Well now. Business must be good to afford a renovation like this.

"Sylvie," Siobhan called back.

"On it," the other woman assured her, already leaping lightly from the wagon. Straightening her hair, she walked confidently through the main door and out of sight. A few moments passed in silence before she came back out again, a smug smile on her face. "Five rooms left, most of them with larger beds, which includes breakfast, dinner, and baths. I got him to cut the price down by saying we only have the cart and two dogs."

Then they'd need to return the horses tonight. Well,

likely best to do that anyway. They'd served their purpose here and the group didn't need them anymore. "How much?"

"Twenty-seven kors."

"Oooh, not bad." Siobhan gave her an approving nod. She turned her eyes up to the sky and made some quick calculations. "I think we've got about two, perhaps three, hours of daylight left here. Everyone, throw your bags into your rooms. Hammon, if you and Fei will return the horses? Good, thank you. The rest of us will split off in pairs and see if we can't find confirmation that our missing party went through here. Who knows? We might get lucky and find something out today."

"It'll take some luck, Shi," Beirly warned her.

She grimaced a smile at him. "Don't I know it. Wolf and I will take the streets. Conli, Denney, Grae, take the inns. Beirly and Tran, take to the gate guards on both sides, see if they have any record of who came through. Move, people."

Siobhan had no idea what the world had been like when governments still ruled this land, but now every level of people existed from the most wealthy and powerful to the completely destitute. Every class of people had their own groups, their own places of gathering, even if they didn't officially belong to a guild. She had learned early on that if someone really wanted to know something, then finding the area of the city controlled by the street gangs was one of the best ways to go about it. Street rats thrived on information. More accurately, they survived by knowing the comings, goings, and dealings of every person in their city. The trick would be finding the right person with the right information and somehow bribing them into talking to her.

She had some experience in this, having done it

before, so she stopped by several food stalls and stocked up, asking about the 'dangerous' places in the city of the people in the marketplace. Once she had a good idea of its location, she and Wolf headed straight there with two heavily laden bags in hand. (Siobhan would actually do better if Wolf didn't go with her, as he would scare any child at first sight, but he categorically refused to let her go into the rougher sections of the city alone.)

The difference between this shadier area and the more affluent section they'd just left was like night and day. Siobhan felt a shiver go straight up her spine as she looked at her surroundings, not sure if she felt it because of cold or unease. The buildings here looked gutted, with no windows or doors aside from the odd tattered cloth pinned up. They looked lifeless, and it took no imagination to believe that spirits haunted this area. The streets were littered with odd refuse. No lamps lit the streets, of course, and the narrow alleyways didn't let in much natural light. It smelled cold, dank, and rotten. She swore she could hear the skittering of rats in the shadows, too.

Maybe Wolf had a good point about her not going in here alone.

She kept her hand carefully away from the long daggers at her waist and tried not to look unnerved. Somewhere...somewhere in here there had to be signs of life. She kept her eyes peeled for it, scrutinizing everything. Where did this group normally hang about? Oh? Up ahead a small fire burned in a brazier that had seen better days. No one was in sight, but they'd have bolted for the nearest cover upon seeing her and Wolf. The brazier gave her a good stopping point. Not to mention some much-needed light.

She stopped in front of it, kicked an upturned crate onto its side, and used it as a table of sorts to spread her bounty of food on. She made sure that the thick loaves of bread, cured meat, wheels of cheese, and the last haul of apples for the season could be plainly seen from every angle. Then she sat back on her heels and called out in a strong, loud voice, "My name is Siobhan Maley. I need information. Is there anyone that is willing to eat and speak with me?"

Taut moments passed. Finally, a tenor voice called out from the shadows, "'o's he?"

"Ah, this is Wolf," she introduced pleasantly, as if this was an everyday introduction. "He's my friend. He was kind enough to help me bring enough food for everyone."

Very, very slowly, a thin body stepped out of the shadows. The boy couldn't have been more than fourteen, and while he looked scrawny, he had a full set of clothes on, so he had to be fairly successful at some sort of livelihood. He came forward with a steady but slow pace, his eyes looking them over intently with the air of a cornered animal. Siobhan pegged him as the leader of the group as no one else dared to make even a peep.

She met his eyes levelly and stayed very still, letting him come in at his own pace. He stopped a good five feet away, not daring to get any closer. He kept darting looks at Wolf, expression blank but body language uneasy.

"Wolf," she muttered from the side of her mouth, "Will you stop looming and kneel? You're scaring the kid."

"I'm not doing anything!" he protested softly.

"You're breathing. That's enough."

With a put-upon sigh, he sank to one knee beside her, hands carefully in view.

"Come eat something," Siobhan invited with a charming smile, beckoning the boy closer. "Among my people, we eat when we talk business."

With Wolf's silent intimidation somewhat weakened, and under the charm of all that food laying out in the open, the boy ventured in closer although he clearly wasn't sure if that was a good idea or not.

"Ya...ya don't look like slavers."

Siobhan blinked. Is that what he was afraid of?

"No, we're an escorting guild. We're actually here to find some missing friends of ours." Seeing him eye the food hungrily, she broke off a piece of bread and popped it into her mouth, proving to him silently that she hadn't drugged it in any way. As soon as she did so, he grabbed the loaf and starting stuffing whole chunks into his mouth.

Someone, at some point in time, had tried to trick these kids. It made Siobhan boiling mad to think of it. What, their lives weren't difficult enough? They had to worry about being caught and sold as slaves, too? Without a word, she picked off a small piece of everything and ate it, proving it all safe. When she did so, more children started coming out of the buildings, although they didn't come to where she sat. She counted fifteen, but who knew how many there actually were.

When the whole loaf was consumed, the boy sat back and offered, "I'm Lenney. So what's yar business, guildie?"

Now she was getting somewhere. "Like I said, we're looking for missing friends. We don't know if they made it through this city or not. I can prove they came through Island Pass, but I want to know if they made it to Quigg. I also want to know if they left and where they were going."

His dark eyes narrowed thoughtfully. "How many we talkin' 'bout?"

"It was a group of sixteen from Blackstone Guild."

"How long back?"

"Hmmm...I'd say over a week. They're five days overdue in Sateren."

He shrugged his ignorance. "Don't know 'bout 'em."

"You can't keep track of every person that comes and goes in a city of this size," she agreed, not bothered by his response. "But I bet you can find out."

His lips parted in a grin, revealing crooked teeth. "Eh, I can. So what's the info worth to ya, guildie?"

She dug into her shirt pocket and held up two gold coins, which was a fortune to these children. Siobhan enjoyed watching his mouth drop open. "Two coins if you can give me the day they entered. Four coins if you can tell me when they left and which direction they were headed."

He recovered his composure and swallowed hard before saying through a dry mouth, "It'll take a good day or more to find out."

"I'm searching in other ways to find them," she warned him. "So you better find out quick. But when you do, I'm at the North Bay Inn. Ask for me and I'll come to you."

He nodded slowly, having a hard time taking his eyes off those coins until she put them away again.

"In the meantime," she stood back up, waving at the food, "think of this as a good faith payment and eat up."

"Ya drive a hard bargain," Lenney complained. From the way his eyes shone, he didn't mean it but hoped to weasel more out of her.

"I'm downright generous, and you know it," she retorted with a grin. "Come to me with good news quick, Lenny. And be ready to give me details, otherwise I won't believe you."

He looked offended that she thought he would lie, but they both knew he would if he thought he could get by with it. With a last wave, she turned and headed back the way she had come.

Twenty feet away from the children, they finally dove into the food like ravaging wolves. She didn't pause, but kept walking, finally turning a corner and passing completely out of sight.

Wolf leaned in and murmured, "You think you can trust the boy?"

"About as far as I can throw him. But four golds will take care of that entire group throughout the winter, so he's going to make sure to earn it, one way or another."

"Is that why you offered such a high price?" Wolf shook his head. "Siobhan, I never know with you if you're being shrewd or generous."

"What, I can't be both?"

He just shook his head, amused, and refused to rise to the bait.

They walked in companionable silence for several minutes as they passed out of the street rats' territory and back into the normal hustle-bustle of the city.

"So, say they made it through here and went on to

Sateren as they should have," Wolf said with a strange look on his face. "I assume that you want to use Grae's pathfinding to get there quickly."

Siobhan quirked an eyebrow at him. What did that expression mean? "Of course."

"You also remember that he doesn't have a pre-built path made to go to Sateren with?"

She opened her mouth to respond and froze, nothing but a croaking sound emerging. It actually had escaped her immediate notice that they had never gone to Sateren before and so of course Grae didn't have a path ready that went that direction. "Oh," she said weakly.

Wolf nodded, unsurprised. "I knew it. You hadn't thought that far ahead."

Siobhan's head dropped so that it hung in despair. "We're going to be digging around in cold ground for stones, aren't we?"

"We certainly are." He tried to smile but it came out as more of a grimace. "Digging in the cold ground with a fussing, nitpicking Grae hovering around issuing orders. Now isn't that something to look forward to."

"Shut it, I'm trying not to think about it." Actually, just imagining it gave her a headache.

"Maybe if we made it clear we're in a hurry?" Wolf trailed off and rubbed his chin. "Although that didn't do any good last time."

"Or maybe Hammon will distract him with more questions and he won't be as naggy this time," Siobhan offered hopefully.

"You realize that's wishful thinking."

"If you don't stop that, I'm making you sleep outside tonight."

He raised both hands in surrender and didn't say another word.

No, Wolf was right, no way would distracting Grae work. On the other hand.... "Since we're going to be here for a good day anyway waiting on informants to get back to us, maybe I can split up our manpower a little? Say, have three people go out to start putting a path together, while the rest of us search the city?"

"The question is, which two people do you hate enough to send out with Grae?"

"As the newest member, Hammon is automatically going," Siobhan decided on the spot. "He'd likely enjoy the experience anyway, with all his interest in pathfinding. Hmmm...but who else?"

"Denney?" Wolf suggested thoughtfully, stepping to the side to avoid a wagon before crossing the road with her. "All she does is get lost in this city anyway."

A very good point. Sending their directionally challenged animal tamer out with two other people would keep her safely out of potential trouble. "Denney will be our sacrifice, then." Looking at him from the corner of her eyes she added, "If that's alright with you?"

He gave a one-shoulder shrug. "Why wouldn't it be?"

"I'm just not sure if you trust the man yet or not."

"You've sent him out with only one other person before this."

"I sent him out with Fei. That's not the same thing as Denney and Grae. Answer me, Wolf. Has the man won your trust yet?"

Wolf chewed on that question for a long moment, stepping around to walk at her left side to shield her from the late evening traffic still on the road, before he finally said, "I don't think him a threat. Don't smile at me like that, Siobhan. I didn't think him a bad man from the start. You're too good a judge of character to let someone sleazy into the guild. But that doesn't mean I trust him to watch our backs, either. I don't know how this man fights or reacts to danger. Is his first reaction to protect or run? Does he have the awareness to recognize danger before it actually hits? I can't trust him until I know."

Siobhan's open palm ceded the point to him. She didn't know any of that either, and they wouldn't know until the first real danger hit them as a group and they could see how Hammon reacted. It was not the best way to find out, not by any stretch of the imagination, but it was the only sure-fire method of knowing. "But you trust him enough to go out stone hunting."

"Enough for that, especially with the dogs going along," Wolf agreed.

Good enough for the time being. Wolf's faith in her judgment aside, she knew very well that she was fallible. She trusted his instincts as much as she trusted her own and if he had some issue, then she wanted to hear it.

They returned to the inn only to find that everyone else had beaten them there. Not only that, but they had already claimed a back table in the main room and ordered dinner, no less. Siobhan called to them as she navigated around the tables, "At least tell me you ordered dinner for us too!"

"We didn't know when you'd be back," Beirly responded carelessly with a toss of his hand. "Order your own."

"A fine bunch *you* are," she grumbled, finding an empty seat and taking it. As Wolf took the empty seat next to hers, she caught Hammon's eye and asked, "Horses sorted?"

"Safely returned, no extra fees to pay," he assured her.

Excellent. She so hated hidden fees. "Perfect. Tell me some good news, people."

"If they ran into trouble, it doesn't look like it happened in this city," Conli reported to her. "We asked the guards here and no party of sixteen people or any mention of Blackstone appeared in their records."

Well, that was something, anyway. "Anything else?"

"Blackstone does have a trading branch here in the city," Sylvie piped up, idly stirring a bowl of hot stew. "I stumbled across them quite by accident, but they were rather helpful. They gave me a list of every inn that the guild has an affiliation with. I figure they would have used an inn they knew, so I'll start there."

Bless Sylvie's brains. If she was right—and she probably was—that would no doubt save them some time.

"How big is that list?"

Sylvie grimaced. "That's the bad news part. It's quite the list."

Well, Blackstone couldn't be considered a 'small' guild by anyone's standards. "Big enough to divide up? Alright, then let's split it between people. However, Wolf pointed out to me that we don't have a ready-made path leading up to Sateren. So while some of us are investigating, I want others stone hunting for Grae."

Every single person but two looked at her with outright dread. Grae looked happy—he hated talking to strangers on general principle—and Hammon didn't seem to mind either option. But then, the scholar stood to learn something new either way. "Hammon, as the newest member, you draw the short straw. Denney, you're joining them."

Denney let out a wordless protest.

"The dogs can go with you and serve as a lookout while you're working," Siobhan told her patiently, having already anticipated this reaction and planned a response to it. "You know they obey you better than anyone else. I can't spare another person to protect everyone while you're working. The dogs are a neat solution to the problem."

Denney slumped in resignation.

"Don't worry, it shouldn't be as many stones as last time," Grae attempted to reassure her. "It's only...er, how far is it to Sateren exactly?"

"One hundred and eighty-three spans," Hammon supplied.

"Oh? That far? I assumed it was closer because the itinerary said it would only take them three days to reach it from Quigg." Grae frowned as he calculated things at high speed. "Probably a little optimistic on someone's part. Well, regardless, the soil is quite rich around this area, so as long as we have good sunlight, hmmm...." He muttered to himself in complex mathematics that no one at the table could or tried to understand before he nodded, satisfied with his own conclusion. "Yes, we'd only need about ninety stepping stones altogether. So, it's just 3,150 stones we need to find," he assured Denney with an innocent smile.

Denney groaned and banged her head against the table.

# Chapter Eight

They spent all of the next day going from one inn to the next, trying to pinpoint where Lirah's party had stayed. By the time the afternoon sun threatened to sink past the horizon, Siobhan's feet were throbbing. In fact, her legs were threatening mutiny if she didn't sit down soon. She finally gave up and went back to the inn with Wolf, meeting other people in the main room who had already called it quits for the day. After an hour of sitting there, however, there was still no sign of Grae or the stone gatherers.

Concerned that Grae, in his preoccupation, would keep them out past dark, she told everyone to order dinner and left the inn, intent on fetching them herself. She'd barely gotten to the main road when she spied Hammon coming her direction and waved him down. "Why are you alone?"

"Denney and Grae are just behind me," Hammon assured her. He half-turned to look behind him. "I lost them in the crowd crossing the main intersection, though. You don't suppose Icean got lost, do you?"

She let out a wordless growl. Yes, with Denney, that was entirely possible.

Grae appeared from behind a group of chattering housewives and, spying them, weaved his way toward them. "Siobhan! I lost Denney in the crowd back there. Has she come this way?"

She dropped her head and shook it in absolute despair. "Of course she didn't go in the right direction."

"Uh-oh." Grae glanced behind him. "This isn't a good city for her to be lost in."

"Are the dogs with her?"

"No, she sent them back to the inn several minutes ago. They were whining about being hungry."

So, in other words, Denney was completely alone and without one reliable guide to get her back to the inn. Heaven preserve her.

"Grae, you go back to the inn. If we're not there in twenty minutes, send out a search party. Hammon, you come with me."

"Right." Grae shot a worried look at the darkening sky. "Find her quick."

"Will do," she confirmed. Brows knitted together in concern, she started off for the intersection.

At this hour of the day, everyone was going home from work, closing up shops, and making last minute stops to pick up dinner ingredients. The place was a madhouse with people going in every possible direction. Denney, with her directionally challenged senses, likely wouldn't know up from down after five minutes in this crowd. Siobhan's concern tripled, and she started calling out the girl's name as she went down one street and then another, hoping that by some miracle she'd find Denney before trouble did.

"Let go! I said let go! LET GO OF ME!"

Siobhan's head jerked around, alarm shooting through her. That was Denney's voice! In this crowd of people, it was hard to see her, but she was absolutely certain that had been Denney, somewhere to the right.

Grabbing Hammon's arm, she tugged him hard. "This way. Quickly!"

"What is it?" he asked in alarm, instantly following her.

"I think Denney's in trouble. I heard her yelling just now."

"Icean?" Hammon raised up on his toes, using his height to see over the crowd. "Yes, I see her. Straight ahead."

"What's happening?" Siobhan demanded as she used her hands and elbows to shove people out of her way.

"Two men have her by the arms and are dragging her toward that alley." Hammon raised his voice to a bellow. "LET GO OF HER! NOW!"

Siobhan felt her ears ring at the volume, but she felt grateful he had yelled, as she certainly didn't have the lung power to be heard over this din.

Instead of just following behind, Hammon stepped around her and blazed a trail straight ahead, still yelling for them to stop. Siobhan stuck close to his back, afraid to lose him in the crowd as people just melted back into position once he'd pushed his way through.

Finally they reached a semi-clear area. She took in the whole scene in a second. Denney was leaning backward with all her might, fighting the hold of two men that were trying to drag her forward. They had both hands on her wrists, using considerable strength to hold on to her. Both men were tall, muscular, and obviously Teheranian. Denney had tears streaming down her cheeks, sobs pouring out of her mouth. When she saw Siobhan, she lit up in relief and screamed, "SIOBHAN!"

Siobhan reacted instinctively. She closed in the final distance in a flash, and with all the strength that she could muster, struck both men hard in the sternum, driving the air from their lungs.

Gasping for breath, their hold on Denney loosened. Hammon lost no time in grabbing Denny around the shoulders and hauling her away from them completely, bringing her to his own chest in a fiercely protective move. Denney openly clung to him, shaking and crying.

Siobhan drew both swords and assumed a guard position in front of them, eyes snapping with anger. "What is going on here?" she gritted out between clenched teeth.

One of the men—she dubbed him as 'Drunkard' because he stank of cheap alcohol—pointed to Denney with an outraged shake of the hand. "That woman belongs to us!"

"That woman is Denney Icean, member of Deepwoods Guild," Siobhan riposted icily. "I am her guildmaster. You want to rethink that statement, you gleeking clodpole?"

"She belongs to us," the other man asserted with quiet authority. He looked angry as well, but composed instead of flaring like his companion. "She has since she was born."

"No!" Denney refuted strongly. "My uncle bought me from you! I owe no debt to you!"

Uncle? Bought? What by the wind and stars was going on here? Siobhan wanted to ask questions—she desperately wanted to ask questions—but this was not the time or place to get things sorted out. Whatever the history, she knew one fact to hold true: Denney had no business going with these men.

"Your uncle is not here," the man responded with that same eerie, irrefutable tone. "When you are out of sight of your owner, anyone can lay claim to you."

By Teheranian culture and law, that was unfortunately true. Siobhan tried to think hard and fast to get out of this without needing to fight them for the right to keep Denney.

"Her uncle also belongs to Deepwoods." Hammon's voice was like a quiet rumble of thunder, low but full of dangerous power. "What belongs to one guildmember belongs to the guildmaster. Her guildmaster is before you. You cannot claim ownership here."

"That is not true by the laws of this city."

Siobhan knew in that moment that whatever was said,

these men would not be convinced. They wanted Denney, and they didn't care if they had to resort to tricks or break a few laws to have her. Her grip tightened on her swords.

"I don't care if it's true by your laws or not. You have no claim over her and you can't have her. Go your own way."

"Or what?" Drunkard challenged, lip curling in a sneer.

Tran melted from the crowd and with deliberate movements took up a stance next to Siobhan. Grae must have sent out a search party as she'd requested. She stole a glance at him and felt fear shake her inner core at the dark expression she saw there. Never before had she seen Tran so openly *enraged*. It scared even her, and that anger wasn't directed at her.

"Take one step," Tran crooned darkly, voice promising death. "Come near me and mine, if you wish to put your lives in my hands."

They eyed him from head to toe and back again, and for the first time, looked nervous.

"Guildmaster, take her," Hammon encouraged.

Siobhan glanced over her shoulder and found that Hammon was already unsheathing the sword spear, ready to fight. Denney was reaching for her short sword, too, but her hand shook as she did so. She was in no condition to fight. Siobhan made a snap decision and sheathed her swords before turning back and taking Denney into the circle of her arm, giving the comfort that Denney so desperately needed.

Hammon stepped forward to take her place, standing shoulder-to-shoulder with Tran and not looking any more calm than the dark giant. In fact, his features looked hard with anger.

Drunkard, not able to take a hint, pointed angrily in Denney's direction. "That woman belongs to us! We owned her mother, and by birth rights, she belongs to us!"

"Why?" Hammon asked with soft menace. "Because she's an illegitimate child? That's it, isn't it? Because she's a half-blood, and a love child, you think you can do whatever you want with her?"

"By the laws of the land, we can!" Drunkard snapped, his hand finally reaching for the sword strapped to his side.

Hammon moved so fast that even Tran could barely keep up with his speed. The haft of the sword spear snapped out, hitting the man's wrist with a sickening crunch. Drunkard gasped in pain, the sword dropping from his numb fingers. Hammon wasted no time in following up that attack with another sharp strike to the man's head, striking him squarely in the temple.

Drunkard's eyes rolled up in the back of his head as he slowly sank to the ground, out cold.

The other man didn't stand much of a chance either. Tran didn't even bother to draw a weapon, just lashed out with a fist and hit the man squarely in the gut. When he folded over, choking, Tran grabbed him by the back of his head and rammed the man's face into his knee. It surely broke his nose, as blood spewed everywhere. With a disgusted snort, Tran tossed the man aside like a dirty rag.

Hammon spat on their bodies. "You are boils, malcontents, nothing more than rump-fed measles!"

"You know, Hammon, I believe that's the first unforgiving thing I've ever heard you say." Siobhan felt more than a little surprised at it, too. He was such a gentle, soft-spoken man most of the time. To hear such vehemence coming from him startled her.

"I'm angry." He didn't even try to apologize for his words. "Even I get angry, Siobhan."

"Oh, I never doubted that. But this is the first time I've actually *heard* you get angry at someone or something."

"Ahh." He shrugged slightly. "My father taught me that the tongue should have three gatekeepers: Is it true? Is it kind? Is it necessary? If it's not one of those three, it's best not to say it."

"Wise council," she agreed. Considering his father's reputation, she had to wonder just how well he heeded his own advice. Or perhaps this was one of those matters where a father wanted his son to follow what he *said* rather than what he did.

She shook the thought off. "For now, let's go back to the inn."

Tran knew where people were searching and they gathered up Wolf, Beirly and Fei as they retreated to the inn. Everyone took in Denney's shaken expression and closed in ranks around her, but tactfully didn't ask any questions.

They'd made it all of three feet inside the inn's main room when Conli spied them. He took in the iron grip that Denney had on Siobhan's arm, and the waxy complexion of her face, and came out of his chair so quickly it fell in his wake.

"Denney?!"

Denney reached out for him, arms latching around his waist, and for the first time, she breathed out in relief like a drowning man finally putting his feet on solid ground. Conli returned the embrace just as firmly, his eyes locking with Siobhan's, silently demanding an answer.

She didn't feel it right to say anything now, not with the room already half full of people and more coming in behind her. Instead, she turned her head and caught Sylvie's attention. "Get us a back room to talk. Private one. Now."

Sylvie took in the atmosphere around them with a glance and gave her a wave of the hand in acknowledgement before hunting down the innkeeper. In moments, she was back, silently encouraging everyone to follow her.

The whole guild trooped after her, most of them uneasy and wondering what was going on, all of them concerned with how uncharacteristic Denney was behaving. The dogs especially were sticking close, constantly nosing at her sides, although it took a few minutes before she was able to let go enough of Conli to pat them in reassurance.

The private room was nothing more than a rectangular table with chairs around it and a door that kept out the noise from the main room. With ten people inside, it quickly felt cramped, but Siobhan closed the door anyway and stood in front of it, guaranteeing that no one tried to casually enter.

Wolf looked from one face to another before asking in alarm, "What happened?"

"Now that's a question I can't fully answer." Siobhan kept her voice level, painfully even. "Denney. Conli. I haven't asked this question for six years as I felt I didn't have the right to pry or poke at old wounds. But that comes to an end tonight. What is your relationship with each other?"

Conli stared at Denney's bowed head, where it rested against his chest, for a long moment. Then he sighed in resignation before finally looking up. "She's my niece."

Everyone stirred, half-surprised at his answer. Even Siobhan hadn't expected that. She'd always assumed Conli as Denney's father. "Niece."

"You know I come from a family of apothecarists on Island Pass?" he asked. "Well, we often took goods and supplies to Quigg or Converse, distributing them there. My brother went to Quigg, I went to Converse, usually. But then one day he said he was tired of going that direction and asked to trade. I didn't think anything of the request and switched with him." Conli's face twisted into a bitter smile. "For ten years I didn't think anything of it or why he avoided Quigg entirely. Then one night, he and my father got too far into their cups, and started talking. I discovered my brother had tangled with a Teheranian woman in Quigg, leaving her with child. I was outraged that he had so casually abandoned her there. *Here*, of all places! By doing that, he'd consigned both of them to a life of either drudgery or prostitution. He knew that. He *knew* that." Conli's eyes closed in a pained manner. "I argued with him, my father, my mother, begging them to at least go get the child. They wouldn't."

"And then?" Hammon prompted quietly as Conli stalled.

"I left the family." Conli looked at him with sad eyes. "Our relationship wasn't good to begin with, as I liked to study surgery, which they thought was beneath our family. But knowing that I had a niece or nephew out there, abandoned to the world, when that child should have had all the benefits and protection of my guild...I couldn't live with that. I packed up and went to Quigg. It took me three months to find her."

"My mother had been sold to a brothel after having me," Denney picked up the story quietly, although she didn't release her hold on Conli. "I was ten, turning eleven, when Conli found me and bought my freedom. My mother felt she deserved to be there, so she wouldn't leave. No matter how we pleaded with her, she refused to go. So I left with him instead."

"We haven't heard from her since," Conli admitted with a heavy sigh. "I try to check up on her whenever we pass through the city, but it's so easy to lose people here. I haven't heard a word about her for the past decade. Anyway, after I had Denney, I knew we couldn't stay anywhere in Wynngaard. It was too dangerous for her. So we went east instead, into Robarge."

"We stayed in Converse for a while, but we didn't like it there so much," Denney admitted. "And then we went on that trip to Goldschmidt with a caravan, the one that Deepwoods was an escort for."

"And you were so welcoming to her, so kind, I couldn't help but think it was the right place to stay," Conli finished heavily. "The rest you know."

Yes, so she did.

"I'm sorry," Denney whispered. "I'm sorry. We should have told you before this."

"You should have," Tran agreed. Stepping forward, he stroked her head in a gentle sweep of the hand. She looked up at the gesture, startled by it, only to see him looking back at her with kind eyes. "If you had, Denney, we'd have known how to protect you better. You'd never have been threatened by those men."

"We understand why you didn't, though," Wolf added softly. His mouth curved in a sad way, empathy and dark memories chasing their way across his face. "At first, you were scared to say anything, right? Because you don't want to bring your past with you when offered a fresh start on life. And then, this new life is so warm, so bright, that you feel like you can't say anything. In time, the fear of losing everything you have gained clogs your throat, so that you can't bring yourself to say a word at all."

That rang with the voice of experience. Siobhan watched him as he spoke, seeing the sincerity in it, and realized that in this regard he and Denney were exactly alike. She'd never thought it necessary, but at this moment, she needed to treat Denney as the wounded soul she was. As they both were, as Conli had sacrificed much in order to save his niece. Stepping forward, she wrapped her arms around both of them, which likely squished Denney in the process. The girl didn't utter one word in protest, though.

"You...don't think less of me?" she asked in a threadbare whisper.

"Never." "No." "Of course not." Several voices protested at once.

Tears started streaming from her eyes as she raised a hand, hugging one of Siobhan's arms to her.

"What is this?" Beirly demanded, reaching out and wiping the tears away with a thumb. "No tears, girl. It unsettles a man, it does. Tran, did you properly squash whoever it was that hurt our Denney?"

"At the time, I thought I had." Tran cracked his knuckles into an open hand. "I'm thinking I might have left the job half-finished now."

"Well, you were in a rush," Beirly mock-consoled him. "Wanting to get her to a safe place first, and all. It's fine, we'll go settle it properly a bit later."

Denney started giggling, a watery half-choked sound. "You're not really going to destroy their business or something, are you?"

"Wolf's the expert on breaking buildings, not me," Tran protested.

"I'd best go with you, then," Wolf volunteered in a dark rumble.

Siobhan eyed the three and wondered just how serious they were, or if this was just an attempt at some light hearted jesting to put Denney at ease. Then she saw the way that Fei eyed Denney, and the hard set to his jaw, and realized that every man in the room was truly planning on dismantling that brothel later tonight.

Right then and there, she decided not to ask. In fact, she'd pretend she hadn't noticed that little exchange between her enforcers.

"Thank you." Denney's voice was soft, still a little muffled against Conli's chest, but it carried throughout the room. "Thank you, Siobhan, Tran, Hammon, for coming to my defense even though you knew nothing."

"We knew you didn't belong with them," Tran assured her. "And that's all we needed to know."

# Chapter Nine

Siobhan's street rat informants came through with the confirmation she needed in just one day. The missing party *had* gone through the city without mishap and were sighted leaving through the north side of the city, for all intents and purposes heading toward Sateren, as they were supposed to. While this was good news (Siobhan did not want to search for them in this crazy, confusing city), it also confirmed a dark suspicion she had been harboring in the back of her head. Whatever had gone wrong had happened either close to or inside of Sateren.

And if it had been severe enough to wipe out a party of sixteen people, her own party of ten didn't stand much of a chance.

Siobhan started mentally planning for the worst even as she hoped for the best.

Her team of stone gatherers did not manage to find 3,150 stones to satisfy the picky Grae—she hadn't expected them to—so the next morning, they all trooped out to help finish the task. This was just as well, as she had no intention of sending Denney out again unless the whole guild went with her. Today especially, the girl stuck close to them, as if afraid of a repeat of events. From the protective stance that Conli and Tran assumed, they were itching for a fight with those men.

She felt sorry for anyone that tried to tangle with Denney today. Well, almost.

Siobhan bundled up against the morning cold, rubbing her gloved hands together briskly as they went well outside the city limits and to the place where Grae had started building his path. She noted the location with interest—it was near a seaside beach, no doubt so he could draw directly from the ocean's power, but far enough away from it he didn't have to worry about a tide sweeping his hard work away. It was rather a picturesque place to put a path, actually. The grass grew thick and lush here, ending rather abruptly near the ocean and becoming grey rock instead of sand. The ocean looked blue from a distance, but the closer she came to it, the more it seemed green to her. Her nose wrinkled at the smell, which seemed very pungent and salty at first whiff.

Grae stood on the edge of the rocky beach and directed people to different spots like a general deploying his troops. She good-naturedly went where he pointed, hunkered down in the rocks, and started sifting through pebbles. What had he said the size was, again? The size of a kor? Something like that, anyway.

Wolf and Hammon were within arm's reach of her, and they all unanimously found a flat rock to put their finds on instead of trying to hold everything in their own hands. Siobhan had to watch her footing, as the rocks here were cold and smooth, and one careless step would send her sliding into a sharp, uncomfortable bed. She shivered now and again as a breeze came in over the ocean. "It is my imagination, or is that sea breeze making the air colder?"

She hadn't directed her words to anyone in particular, and it was Hammon that turned enough to answer over his shoulder, "It is. At least, it feels that way to me."

"Was it like this yesterday too?"

"Worse," he assured her with a dry smile. "I think the cold spell is passing."

"How many did Grae say he needed again?" Wolf asked.

"Another two thousand and something," Siobhan

answered, not remembering the full number either.

"2,673," Hammon informed them, eyebrow quirked.

She gave him an interested study. "You *do* have a good head for numbers, don't you?"

"I learned it at my father's knee."

And did well at it. Hmmm. Come to think of it, this was the perfect opportunity to dig a little into his past without being obvious about it. After all, the only way to pass the time was to talk. She opened her mouth to ask him a question, but Hammon apparently realized the same thing at the same moment, as he beat her to it.

"So, Wolfinsky, how did you come to join the guild?" Hammon asked with sincere interest.

"You're wondering how a Resken ended up so far south, aren't you?" Wolf replied with a wry twist of the lips.

"It's very rare to see your people outside of Reske for any length of time, much less choose to live elsewhere," Hammon pointed out.

"True enough. Alright." Wolf sat back on his heels, hands draped over both knees, so that he could look directly at Hammon as he answered. "Hammon, are you asking for my story?" The words were oddly formal, as if part of a tradition.

Hammon picked up on the nuance as well because he abruptly straightened, much more focused than he had been before. For that matter, everyone else also went still, drawn to this discussion between the two men. Even Siobhan turned her full attention to it, despite having heard this story once before and being a major part of some of it.

The scholar felt the weight of everyone's attention but he answered steadily, "I am."

"I am Erik Wolfinsky of Reske. It was there I was born and there I grew until I came into my fourteenth spring. At that time, I was captured by a band of slavers." Wolf's eyes darkened in memory. "I was not the only one taken. I was, however, the only child that was not recovered.

The slavers that took me paid dearly for their stupidity, as my village hunted them down, but two managed to get away with me in tow. To this day, I'm not sure how, as I was heavily drugged throughout the journey. I was sold to the mercenary guild in Wingate shortly after and there I stayed, fighting in every conflict that Wynngaard and Robarge had until I was nineteen. My life there was darkness. I lost my heart, my hope of returning to my home, and was in danger of losing my very soul before fate took an unexpected turn. It was in a bloody skirmish between two major guilds in Land's Point that I lost my hand." He held up his right iron hand in a silent illustration. "The mercenaries who owned me deemed me unfit to fight, useless, and so dragged me to the black market as soon as I was semi-healed. Because of my missing the hand, I was being auctioned for a very low price." At this, Wolf let out a bleak smile. "Fortunate, that. I'm not sure how things would have turned out otherwise. But Siobhan, Grae and Beirly saw me by chance at the auction and recognized my heritage. Out of pity, Siobhan bought me and took me back to the guild. I didn't know what to make of her, at first. Here was this beautiful woman, barely younger than I, who treated me with unreserved kindness and sympathy. My size alone scared her, I could see it sometimes in her eyes as she spoke to me, but never once did she shy away. She gave me the option of staying and working off the money she'd spent on me, or taking me home to Reske and letting the village reimburse her instead. I chose to stay."

Hammon blinked. "Why not go back?"

"Oh, I did," Wolf assured him, smile becoming more genuine. "Siobhan wouldn't hear of it otherwise. We stayed for a good month, too, visiting. But I owed the woman a debt I might not ever be able to repay. It wasn't just the money she spent on me—she rescued me from a hellish life without thinking twice about it. This, on top of being a brand new guildmaster! I stayed to protect her, to return whatever I could. Beirly made up the hand for me as soon as my arm fully healed, and it helped me regain the strength I'd lost." Wolf held it up and looked it over thoughtfully. "Actually, for combat, it's even better than the flesh and blood hand. After the first year of being in the guild, I came to realize that I wouldn't leave it by choice. I'd forged a strong bond with them, and I wasn't suited for a quiet village life anymore, not after experiencing life in a good guild. I was born in Reske, and it will always be a part of me, but my home is Deepwoods." With the same formality he had used at the beginning, Wolf ended with, "That is the story of Erik Wolfinsky."

Hammon didn't quite seem to know how to respond to this. Finally, he managed, "I thank you for the telling."

"Ooh, good response!" Wolf clapped him on the shoulder—with his left hand, fortunately—and grinned. "You're close to what should be said."

The scholar canted his head at this. "So there really is a proper thing to say? What is it, exactly?"

"It was a fine telling, and I thank you for it," Wolf responded as if quoting something.

"I shall make note of that," Hammon promised. "But formality aside, yours is an incredible tale, Wolf."

Those clear blue eyes softened. "Siobhan made it incredible. If she had not taken a chance on me, my story would be a tragedy."

Beirly came in close enough to knock into his shoulder with a gentle thump of the fist. "What are you on about, man? Without you, *our* stories would be tragedies." To Hammon, he explained, "Wolf's saved our skins more times than I care to recall. All those years as a mercenary sure have paid off, to my mind. I've never seen a man that can get the drop on him, although Tran's tried for it a time or two."

Tran grumbled and growled to himself. Everyone ignored him.

A grin split Wolf's face from ear to ear, but he tactfully didn't take advantage of the moment and rib Tran any. (Siobhan would have boxed his ears if he had.) To Beirly, he said, "Like you haven't done the same for me? For that matter, Siobhan's saved my skin a time or two, as I recall."

Siobhan snorted, well knowing what he referred to. "The first time, you had that terrible ear infection that wouldn't let you stand upright without swaying. And you still fought two men off in that condition!"

"Still saved me," he retorted, an outrageous twinkle in his eyes.

"And the *second* time," she directed this to Hammon, as he was following all of it closely, "his foot got tangled up in a thick rope that was dragging him quickly to the bottom of a lake. I dove in and cut him free. But the reason he was being dragged down to begin with was because he jerked me out of the way before *I* could get tangled up in it. So I don't think that properly counts."

"It counts," Wolf defended mildly.

Siobhan rolled her eyes. "As you can see, the only chance we ever get to return the favor is when the nigh-unthinkable happens and a string of bad luck hits Wolf so strong that he can't save himself. But that's happened a whole three times in the past ten years he's been with the guild."

"I don't mind this trip down memory lane," Grae cut in, still perched on the edge of the beach where he sorted through his gathered stones, "but can you people work while talking?"

With good-natured grumbling, they went back to the task at hand.

"Speaking of..." Wolf raised his voice and called to Grae, "Will this be done tonight?"

"I doubt it!" Grae responded, pausing just long enough to answer the question. "You might be through gathering, but it's going to take a bit longer to build the path."

"In that case," Wolf turned back to Hammon, "tonight we need to spar."

Hammon nodded ready agreement. "Of course. After all, the situation is becoming more dangerous the farther north we go."

Oh, so he'd caught on to that, had he? "Hammon, you're from a large guild, aren't you?"

"I am," he confirmed, although his tone sounded slightly wary.

Siobhan itched to ask him a slew of questions, but that reaction made her think he didn't trust them with his whole life history yet. So she bit back a good half of them and went with what she truly needed to know. "Then you'll know how this works better than I would. Is it possible for a sizable party of guild members from a foreign guild to enter a city without attracting attention?"

"No," he responded immediately, without even needing to think of the response. "There's too many other guilds that would notice that and report it to their guildmaster."

She'd assumed as much. "The information couldn't be lost on its way up the chain of command?"

At this, he did hesitate and think for a moment. "I highly doubt it. My guildmaster doesn't rely on just one person to report everything to him. He meets regularly with all of the different masters of the guilds and gets information directly from them. I understand that this system is common and how most large guilds operate."

"Mmmm." She let out a sigh. "In that case, we've really only got two options. Either they really didn't make it through Sateren's gates, or they did."

"And we're dealing with betrayal," Wolf summed up darkly.

"Which guild were they supposed to be meeting with?" Hammon asked. "You said the main guild of Sateren, so I assume it's Iron Dragain?" At her nod, he gave a thoughtful hum and sat back for a moment, focusing on speaking. "They're well-known to be good business partners. They have a reputation for being fair at trade and generous in their dealings. I can't imagine that they would betray another major guild like Blackstone. I can't even think of a good reason to do so."

"I can't either," Siobhan confessed. "It's just a dark

125

possibility that Denney voiced and I can't get it out of my head. I'm hoping I'm wrong. I'm hoping that we're not dealing with a large guild out for our blood." The trip to Sateren was hazardous enough without dealing with that threat. "But it begs the question, if it's not that, what happened?"

"A rival third party that knew about the trade agreement and wanted to destroy the possibility before it was formed?" Hammon suggested in an objective tone of voice.

She paused, her mouth half-open, as the words struck her. "Now why didn't I think of that?"

"It's just a possibility." Hammon splayed his palms up in a shrug. "I don't know of anyone that would go to those lengths to stop a trade agreement, either. I mean, if it's ever found out who it was that attacked them, then I don't imagine Darrens would let it rest until he wipes the guild out completely."

True, that.

"But they could very well get away with it if they hire a mercenary or assassin guild to do their dirty work for them," Wolf pointed out. "It's nigh impossible to track those requests back to their source without a lot of persuasion of a physical nature, if you catch my meaning."

And he would know. Siobhan blew out a breath. "In that case, if we show up looking for Lirah, wouldn't we become a target too? No one would want us to find out the truth, after all."

Both men gave her unhappy nods.

"Well, isn't that a chipper thought?" Siobhan rubbed at her forehead, feeling a headache brewing. "As soon as we've let for Sateren, we're sleeping in shifts."

"Probably for the best," Wolf agreed.

Not at all happy with her dark thoughts, she bent back to the stones and sifted through the ones on the ground with her gloved hands. She had no desire to keep going toward Sateren, not after this conversation, but she'd taken on the job, so they had no choice but to see it through. She might as well get this over with sooner rather than later.

# Markl Hammon

von Christa Triumph

# Chapter Ten

Grae finished the path by noon the next day, so they loaded everything back up in the cart and went to the newly placed stepping stones. Grae activated the path and took them through without mishap, and they arrived within sight of Sateren's walls.

Like most of the major cities of the world, Sateren looked like a veritable fortress from the outside. No one really worried about invasion from an army or the like, as it would take a united front from several major guilds to even pull an army together, but the walls *did* protect from other dangers. If nothing else, it served as a way to regulate the traffic coming and going through the gates and let the major guild in charge of security have a better handle on their visitors. Siobhan took a long second to really look at the place.

The walls stood three stories tall—a bit of overkill, there—made of dark grey stone that looked cold even from here. The gate in front of her stood wide open, the door made of thick wood that could be used for a ship's mast, it was so dense. What she could see inside of the city didn't look that different from any other major city she'd visited. Oh, the roofs had more of a slope at the edges, and the buildings tended to use shingles instead of thatch, but the people bustled about on business like in any other part of the world.

"What now?" Hammon asked her.

"Now we split up and ask questions," Siobhan answered promptly. She'd been thinking about this all last night and this morning, coming up with a plan. "I don't believe that our people ever made it to the city, but in case I'm wrong, I want two people to go to the gates and see if anyone there spotted them. The guards will have a record of a group that large. The rest of us are going to split up and backtrack a little." She indicated the docks not a stone's throw away, and then to the highway that led off in a south-westerly direction. "Odds are if they didn't make it to the city, then they retreated one of these directions. If they didn't, that means we've gone too far north, and we'll have to travel back southward on horses and look as we go."

Hammon pointed toward the western highway. "Why go there?"

It was Wolf that explained. "Wynngaard is not like most countries. The cities, sure, they act like any other guild-run city you might come across. But the people that live in the villages and towns, they're a separate matter altogether. They don't take kindly to guilds, they're not known for coming to the city unless it's a dire matter, and they tend to keep to themselves."

"It would make for a perfect hiding place," Siobhan added as she jumped lithely off the cart. The ground made a squishing noise under her boots, and she realized with a grimace she had just landed in mud.

"These lowland villages trade more with the cities than us mountain people do," the way Wolf said this suggested he didn't think much of that custom, "so odds are good that someone either coming to or from the city would find a troubled group and be more likely to help. If they did, they could hide easily and lick their wounds with no one the wiser. Thing is, they wouldn't be able to contact anyone outside the village either."

Yes, and for several reasons. If Lirah had done this, she wouldn't dare reveal her true identity because if the villagers discovered her ties with a guild, they'd kick her back out immediately. The distaste for guilds ran strong in this area of the country. In Lirah's shoes, Siobhan would take advantage of any kindness offered to her, lay low until her party was healed up again, and *then* try to make it back to Sateren. Or even outright retreat back southward to Quigg.

All of this assumed, of course, that Lirah had even made it this far north. They could be searching little pockets of villages near the main road all the way down to Quigg for the next month and might not find her.

And oh ye little gods, she hoped that wasn't the case!

Praying silently to any god that might be listening, she divided up her people into groups of three and sent them different directions. They had orders to reconvene here, at this exact spot, when they had the information they needed. Or if by some miracle one of her teams found a sign of the missing party, they were to signal via the horn. Most of the time when traveling, the guild stayed together, but on rare occasions, she found it necessary to split them up like this. When she did, she either had a meeting point and a designated time for people to return or she made sure they each had a horn with a predetermined signal. In this case, it was one blast for no sighting, two blasts for solid information, and three blasts for danger. On this flat plain of grassland, the sound of a horn should carry for spans without trouble.

She, Wolf and Beirly stayed with the cart and consulted a map on the good chance that they would soon have to search more inland.

Wolf sat next to her on the back of the cart, the map laid out over their respective laps, and bent over it slightly.

"Siobhan, can't you find a better map than this?" he complained for what had to be the thousandth time.

"Wolf, you say that *every time* we go into Wynngaard," she retorted in exasperation.

"That's because you haven't replaced the map yet!"

"Have you seen a more accurate one?" she challenged, giving him a stink eye. "Because I certainly haven't. If you feel like this is a sorry excuse of a map, make a better one! You can probably do it from memory, you know this country so well."

That adequately shut him up. With a grumble and snort, he pointed at a nearby village. "This is Vakkiod and it's much closer than the map indicates. Really, if Lirah Darrens made it within sight of Sateren before running into trouble, then this is the place I expect to find her in."

Assuming she and her party weren't in a shallow grave somewhere, that was. The thought hung in the air, unspoken between them. Siobhan cleared her throat to move past that heavy atmosphere. "Fine. Assuming that they didn't get this far north? What's the next best bet?"

"The next village is much farther south, a full day's travel from here. The Gainsborough, or the Gain's Furrow, depending on who you ask. They're not far from the highway, so again the odds of them helping out wounded travelers are fairly good. There's other possibilities the further south we go, but..."

She held up a hand to stop him. "Let's focus on just these two for now. You said Vakkiod is close. How close?"

"Three hours?" he scratched at his chin as he mulled over distance. "With the cart, at least."

"And if I sent Tran ahead?"

"An hour and half, maximum."

Well, that certainly made it clear to her what she should do. She often sent Tran ahead in circumstances like this because he was a fast runner that could go incredible distances. (Not truly unusual for a Teheranian.) But he sometimes would get bogged down because of the landscape or city crowds. Apparently, this wouldn't be the case here or Wolf would think it would take him longer.

From Sateren's gate came a short blast from the horn, followed almost as quickly from the port. She frowned at the reports, but in truth, it didn't surprise her that Lirah's party hadn't been sighted either place. Lifting her own horn from her back, she let out a long note, calling them back to her.

Tran's group came back first, as they had simply gone to the gate, and she motioned him closer. "Tran. Wolf thinks it's a good possibility for Lirah's party to be in Vakkiod, which is here." She pointed it out on the map, waiting for him to give her a nod before removing her finger. "He estimates it'll take you about an hour and a half to get there from here. Will you go ahead and check?"

"Vahh," he shrugged in agreement, although a smile lit his face. Tran loved a good run, and after days and days of either being on a cart or on a horse, he had to be itching to stretch out some. "Same signals?"

She thought about it. The same signals should work, but... "Do four blasts if they're actually there."

He tapped his heart twice in non-verbal understanding before turning on his heel and taking off at a fast clip.

Hammon watched him go, the only one that looked concerned, and asked, "Is it safe for him to go off alone like that?"

Siobhan snorted. "I pity the fool that tries to attack Tran. It would make his day." She sat back on the wagon a little more, getting comfortable as she waited for her port people to return. As they had a little further to go, she expected it to be another half-hour before they could make it back to the cart.

Once everyone did return, and because they didn't have anything better to do, they broke out the cooking gear and made lunch. Some might have wondered why they didn't just go into Sateren for lunch—after all, the city was little more than a stone's throw away—but she didn't want to breach the walls yet. Sending even a few people to the gates and asking after Lirah's party was enough to signal that there were people searching. She didn't want to alert the possible assailants more than she already had by actually going into the city.

Besides, out here she had no noise to camouflage Tran's horn when he chose to use it. The city's din would surely cover up the sound if she went inside.

Hammon broke the companionable silence with a soft clearing of the throat. "Man Lei, do you mind if I ask you a question?"

Fei looked up from scraping his plate clean. "Go ahead."

"I've noticed you add honorifics to people's names. What do they mean? I mean, what do they signify?"

Fei's brows rose slightly. "There's quite the list. It would perhaps be better if I told you the ones you will actually hear me say, as some of them are so old that no one uses them anymore."

"That's fine," Hammon assured him as he pulled his leather notebook out of his side pouch. "Are these ones that I will encounter during trade as well?"

"Some of them, yes." Fei seemed pleased at the respectful way Hammon asked and he set his plate aside to focus more fully on the conversation. "From most formal to least formal, it is in this order: zhi, jia, gui, ajie, ren, jae, xian."

"Wait, wait, repeat that please," Hammon requested as he scribbled frantically. "Zhi, jai—"

"Jia," Fei corrected, pronouncing it more carefully. "Gui, ajie, ren, jae, xian." He shifted up onto his knees briefly to check Hammon's writing, but not finding anything to correct, he gave a brief nod of approval before relaxing again. "Zhi is something you use when speaking to an older person of great importance. Someone such as the leader of a town, city, or guild for instance. Jia is for a person of higher status than you, such as a master tradesman or an older relative. Gui is for a stranger that has no special significance. Ajie is for an elder sister or relative."

Hammon looked up at that. "I've heard you call Guildmaster Maley that."

"Yes." Fei softened into a slight smile. "I have been in this guild for eight years. At first I referred to her as 'zhi' but she is now my sister more than my master."

Siobhan couldn't help but lean over and hug him. Fei chuckled indulgently and patted her on the head. "Yes, ajie, thank you."

"He's the sweetest thing," she told everyone and no one in particular.

Fei waved her off and went back to the explanation. "Ren is for a kind elder brother, or an older male friend."

"You call most of the men in this guild by 'ren?'" Hammon's tone made this a question.

"They are all older than I," Fei explained patiently. "I am twenty-six, and one of the youngest in the guild. Only Denney is younger than I, I believe."

"Not anymore." Hammon grinned at him. "I'm twenty-five."

Fei blinked in surprise. "I had thought you older."

"Hence why you called me 'jia?'" Hammon asked, not at all offended.

"Well, and that, yes." Fei scratched at his cheek, somewhat nonplussed. "In truth, I suppose I should be calling you Markl-xian."

"Xian meaning younger brother, or younger male friend, or something along those lines?"

"Exactly so," Fei agreed.

"Then do," Hammon encouraged him. "I realize I'm here provisionally, but it might be years before I finish my goals. I can be here a long time, and because of that, I don't want to be considered a temporary guest."

Siobhan felt in that moment as if he were not speaking to just Fei, but to everyone. They all had adopted the pattern of calling him by his last name, a formality that no one used with the rest of the guildmembers. Had she really been treating him as an outsider, in spite of what she instructed the rest to do? Shaking her head at herself,

Siobhan answered in Fei's stead. "We'll do that, Markl."

He flashed her a sunny smile that stretched from ear to ear. "Then can I do likewise? I realize it's rather awkward at this stage to ask permission."

"It is," Fei acknowledged ruefully, "but I for one am glad you asked. Formality should not exist among friends."

Some underlying tension that had hovered in Markl's shoulders eased upon hearing this. "Thank you. I'm glad."

Fei inclined his head in understanding. "The last honorific is 'jae' which is used for younger sisters or close female friends. I call Sylvie this, despite the fact she's my age."

"He called me 'ajie' only once," Sylvie explained with a dark pout.

"She threw something at me," Fei explained in a stage whisper. "I never dared to do it again."

Markl's mouth formed in a silent 'ahhh' of understanding, eyes crinkling up in a silent smile.

The culture lesson ended there temporarily as they focused on finishing lunch and getting ready to move. They'd eaten, cleaned everything, and packed it all back in without hearing a single sound. In fact, they were debating on rooting through the bags and finding their ever trusty deck of cards when faintly the sound of a horn carried through the air. Siobhan sat up abruptly, ears straining. "I counted five blasts."

"As did I." Out of the bunch, Grae had the sharpest ears. He turned so that he was half-standing in the cart. After a long moment, the horn sounded again. "Five blasts," he confirmed with a bemused look. "What's that supposed to mean?"

"Something unexpected happened?" Markl offered. "Something that the previous signals don't cover."

Siobhan grimaced. It looked like sending Tran ahead had not been the easy solution she hoped for, for whatever reason. "Beirly, hook Kit back up. Let's go to Vakkiod."

✦ ✦ ✦

Tran met them at the village entrance, as impassive as a stone statue carved out of black rock. Siobhan couldn't quite figure out why he looked that way.

Her eyes took in the village in a quick sweep. From what she knew of Wynngaard, this village seemed to be rather normal. Houses built haphazardly with no real clear-cut roads, corrals and stone fences branching off to encircle the village as a whole, most of which was filled with different types of sheep, pigs, and cows. The place looked sturdy with its brick and wood buildings, although where they had gotten enough wood to build this place was anyone's guess. She hadn't seen a stretch of woods for quite some time. But the place looked quiet, not at all rife with trouble or tension.

She hopped off the front seat of the cart as it moved and jogged ahead, meeting Tran half-way as he loped toward them. "What by the great stars does five blasts mean?" she demanded of him.

He gave her a quick, impish grin. "It means come to me, Shi-maee. And look, without even knowing what I meant, you came! It's like magic."

She growled and grumbled but couldn't refute his logic. Curse it. "Alright, what's the problem? They wouldn't talk to you?"

"Nearly got stabbed just coming near the entrance," Tran admitted, casting a dark look over his shoulder.

For a moment, Siobhan looked at him from a different perspective instead of as someone that knew him well. With him so tall, so covered in scars, with that dark skin of his and long braids, he probably screamed *danger* to someone from a backwater village like this. Of course no one from Wynngaard would automatically trust him enough to answer his questions.

Fool. Why hadn't she thought of that?

Siobhan raised a hand while giving a long sigh. "Sorry,

Tran. Didn't think this through. If the villagers here are really that cautious, then of course they're not going to speak readily to a Teheranian. Let's try this again." Turning, she looked over the people behind her. Really, when it came to approaching the villagers, she only had two options. Either Wolf, who looked so obviously native, or Denney, who was half-Wynngaardian herself. Well, no, probably not Denney. She was also half-Teheranian, so they might not know how to react to her either. "Wolf?"

"I'll try." Wolf strode forward and to the thick wooden gates ahead, careful to keep his hands away from any weapon.

Blowing out a breath, she rocked back on her heels and watched him go. Hopefully this worked better, although really, even though he was Wynngaardian, Wolf was intimidating in his own right, too. Perhaps Markl would be the better choice, with that quiet, unassuming air of his. Besides, he had the strangest talent for charming people into talking to him. He might succeed where no one else could.

"Are they normally this paranoid?" Tran muttered under his breath, dark eyes scanning the area keenly. "I know Wolf said that they were unusually cautious when it came to foreigners, but I couldn't even get a word out before they were coming at me with swords bared."

That bad? Oh dear. "His description didn't lead me to believe they were so wary. No, wary isn't even a strong enough word."

Wolf stopped at the gate, speaking to the group of men that had gathered there. He shook his head several times, hand raising in gestures, his right hand carefully kept behind his back the entire time. She couldn't hear from here what they were saying, and probably couldn't have understood anyway with her limited knowledge of the language. In a few minutes, he came back at a half-trot, a dark scowl furrowing his face.

"So?" she asked him.

"They were hit by a sneak attack a few weeks ago

and so are not very forthcoming with information," Wolf explained, irritated. "They wouldn't even tell me they were attacked, I had to figure that out from what they carefully weren't saying. They want to know who we are, and why we're asking, which makes me think that they're hiding *something*."

Siobhan rubbed at the bridge of her nose in a pained way. "We can't move on from here simply because they don't want to talk to us. One way or another, we need to confirm it. Alright, Plan C. Markl?"

Markl hopped lightly out of the cart and came to her side, head cocked in question.

"You go," she ordered.

"Me?" he objected. "My understanding of Wynngaardal is limited at best."

"They speak some Robargean," Tran offered. "It's how I was able to talk to them, or at least, understand the curses they were hurtling at me."

Robargean? Well, that had become a semi-universal trade language over the past few generations. She hadn't expected them to speak any of it here, though, so far away from the trade routes.

"Oh. In that case..." Markl trailed off, looking at her askance.

"You're the least assuming of us that doesn't look completely foreign," she explained to him. "Sending in Tran and Wolf might have given them the impression that we're mercenaries, but your mild manner and way of speaking will dispel the notion. You've got a better chance of getting answers."

"Ahhh," he intoned. "In that case, I'll do my best."

She waved him on and watched as he strode confidently forward, his weapon still in the cart. Brave thing, wasn't he, to go in unarmed against hostile natives. Markl got stopped at the gate, no surprise, but he lingered far longer there. Siobhan perked up, straining her eyes to see clearly. "Is it my imagination, or are they sheathing their weapons?"

"They are," Sylvie said in amazement. "One of them even smiled for a moment!"

Siobhan made a mental note right there. From then on, she would send Markl in first.

Markl gave the men a short bow and made a staying motion with one hand before he turned on his heels and came back to the group. The expression on his face made her think he had not only succeeded in getting an answer, as he looked strangely triumphant.

"You found them, didn't you?" she demanded as soon as she was within earshot without needing to yell.

"I did," Markl assured her. "They're all here."

"Your tone says there's a problem, though."

Markl let out a breath. "Miss Lirah apparently didn't tell the villagers here that they were guildmembers."

"It was us showing up that revealed who she was?"

Markl gave an unhappy nod. "They're threatening to throw her out."

Siobhan rubbed at her face. Her relief at finding the missing party faded quickly under this new problem. "How badly injured is everyone?"

"Bad, from their descriptions. I'm amazed she could move them at all, even to here." Markl looked disturbed by his own words.

Tran and Wolf didn't look happy to hear this either. They might get into regular scuffles with everyone in Goldschmidt, but they were also friends with a good majority of them. She knew for a fact that at least three friends of Tran's were in Lirah's party.

"Then they can't be moved, Shi-maee," Tran inserted. "Not yet."

Which meant that before anything else, Siobhan and Lirah had to work out some means of letting them stay here. Right. "Markl, did they tell you where they were? And they'll let us in? Good. Show me to Lirah first."

Conli seemed to realize something serious was going on, as he also jumped out of the wagon and quickly caught up to them. As Markl led the way past the first cluster

140

of houses, she explained in an undertone the situation, eyes darting about. At this time of the day, people should be busy getting the usual daily chores done. Should be. Siobhan saw people at every house staring suspiciously at them. My, my, word had indeed spread fast on who their injured guests were.

"Wolf, how bad is this?" she muttered from the side of her mouth.

"It will take some fast talking and a gesture of goodwill to smooth this over," he responded, mouth in a flat line.

Marvelous. She was afraid that would be the answer.

Markl took a right, weaved his way in and around several small yards and their stone fences, then stopped in front of a house clearly meant for storage. Stacks of bound bales, barrels and boxes stood on the porch, no doubt to give room to put people inside. Sitting on the steps was Lirah Darrens, although she stood as soon as Siobhan stepped into the yard.

"Siobhan!" she greeted with abject relief. "I've never been so glad to see a familiar face."

Siobhan stepped forward and gave the woman a long hug, as she looked like she needed one desperately. Then she stepped back a foot and scrutinized her for a moment. Lirah's usual perfect blonde hair had been tied off into a messy braid, dark circles prominent under her blue eyes, and she had aged at least five years since Siobhan had seen her three months ago. Her clothes looked wrinkled and slept-in, which they might well have been.

"Lirah. What happened?"

"We were attacked just within sight of Sateren's walls, by professional assassins or mercenaries, I can't tell you which. It all happened so fast, without any warning, that we were barely able to defend ourselves." Lirah's voice shook. "We were able to fight them off, somehow, and they eventually retreated. I think it's because they assumed we were mostly down. Some..." her voice choked and she had to take a deep breath before she could clear it, "...some of my men looked dead and for a moment I thought they

141

were. It's a miracle I didn't lose anyone."

More so than she could imagine. Although…something about this story felt wrong to Siobhan. She couldn't quite put her finger on what, though. Shaking it off to think about later, she encouraged her to continue. "And then?"

"I was floundering, not sure what to do aside from putting some emergency treatment on people's wounds, when a group from this village stumbled across us. They were on their way back home from Sateren, and when they saw the situation and heard my story, they agreed to shelter us while everyone healed. That was nearly two weeks ago, now, I think." She raised a hand to her forehead, slightly shaking. "I lost track of time at one point."

"It's actually closer to a week and a half," Wolf corrected her. "At least, from what we understand of your plans. You told no one you are from Blackstone Guild?"

"They don't like guilds here. I picked up on that quickly. And I wasn't sure why we were attacked, or by who, and I didn't want word getting out that everyone had survived. I thought it best to just lay low, wait for people to heal, and then travel back to Quigg before trying to send word home."

All in all, not a bad decision. Siobhan would have made the same in her shoes. "Tran tells me that you can't move yet, that people are badly wounded. I'll send Conli over, see how much he can help. But we need to deal with—"

"Lirah Darrens!" an aged, deep voice called out.

Siobhan turned around sharply. Standing at the gate was an old man that seemed to be in his late seventies or eighties, stooped over slightly with age, white hair long and tied up into a high ponytail, skin bronzed from the sun. He wore the long white robe of a village leader, so Siobhan pegged him as the local Ahbiren.

His eyes narrowed on Wolf, then switched to Siobhan with the same suspicions. "Who might you be?"

Siobhan took in a breath before she faced him

squarely. "Siobhan Maley, Guildmaster of Deepwoods. This is Erik Wolfinsky."

"Deepwoods?" he repeated without any recognition.

"We are a guild from Goldschmidt," she explained bluntly and without apology. "We have been looking for Lirah and her people for the past week."

His lip curled slightly in distaste at the word 'guild.' "Then take them away."

"We cannot at this time. They are too injured to move yet."

He slammed the staff in his hands on the ground—which was not for support, but a bo staff—and repeated, "They are to leave! They are not welcome here. They misled us, abused our hospitality, and brought a threat upon this village. I do not want them here!"

"Ahbiren, respectfully, this is not a matter of wanting to move or not wanting to. We *cannot* move them. We risk killing these men if we do so. Would you have innocent blood on your hands because you feel misused and taken advantage of?"

"I do not believe that they will die just moving them back to Sateren! You should be in a city—that is where the guilds belong. We of this village do not deal with the guilds. This woman has abused our trust by pretending to be a normal traveler and—"

Stubborn, arrogant, old— "Ahbiren," Siobhan said firmly, cutting him off mid-rant, "have compassion. Lirah is far, far from home in a land that she does not understand. She's in a culture that is confusing, with no allies or friends to rely upon. Worse, she was attacked by hired professionals with no warning, leaving her stranded here with wounded people to take care of and no way of knowing who attacked her or why. Why do you blame her for keeping her identity secret? Why do you judge her so harshly for trying to protect her companions? She had no choice but to keep her identity secret, not only for her own safety, but also for the fifteen lives that are depending upon her!"

143

The Ahbiren looked uncomfortable at her scolding and he flushed red, eyes not quite meeting hers. "What she did was a betrayal to us."

Siobhan resisted the urge to start beating sense into him. She took in a long breath and blew it out again. "I understand that your feelings are hurt and that you are not pleased with her choice. I can see your point as well as hers. In the interest of improving relations between the two of you, and letting her stay until her people are well again, is there anything we can do to make amends?"

At 'amends,' he looked up again with a light in his eyes that scared Siobhan. She knew, instinctively, that she would not like what he would say next. "You offer to take one of our troubles as your own?"

Trapped by her own words, she put on a game smile and said through gritted teeth, "That's right."

Like a fox that had found a way into the henhouse, he gave her a smug smile and pointed to a far off lean-to. "Then I ask that you deal with that."

She turned to look. In between a dozen buildings, down a weaving, narrow path, she could barely see the kneeling figure of a person, although she couldn't tell whether it was a man or a woman. "And what is that, exactly?"

"An assassin that came here to kill me several weeks ago."

She blinked. An assassin?! "You look remarkably well in spite of the attack."

"He never reached my home," the Ahbiren told her with satisfaction. "My people prevented that."

Riiiight. "And, ah, he looks uninjured as well?" After trying to kill their leader, she would have expected someone in the village to kill him.

The Ahbiren cleared his throat again but this time he looked more irritated than before. "He's quite skilled. It took all we had to subdue him."

Skilled enough to evade death even when in a Wynngaardian village? It made her wonder just how good this man was. As good as Wolf, Tran or Fei? Better? (Although she couldn't wrap her head around the idea of someone better.) "I see. And the reason he's still alive even though he's in chains is because...?"

"He comes from one of the dark guilds of Sateren." The Ahbiren probably didn't mean to sound nervous when he said this, but he looked like a scared rabbit. "We do not wish to invite their wrath by killing one of their own. But no one has come to claim him. We are not sure what to do. But *you* are of the guilds. You will know of the proper thing to do. Take care of this situation, free us of him, and all hard feelings will disappear."

She stared at him in dismay. Her? Deal with a dark guild assassin?! Great wind and stars, how was she supposed to know what to do with him? In desperation, she looked at Wolf, hoping he had an idea.

He cocked a brow back at her, expression saying, You got us into this. You can get us back out again.

Some help *he* was. Grumbling mentally, she plastered a smile on her face and assured the Ahbiren, "I'll take care of it personally."

The Ahbiren—crafty old fox that he was—smiled back at her and said sweetly, "You are a true friend, Guildmaster."

Siobhan was sure that she would like his smile better after she knocked a few teeth out of his head. Reigning in the impulse, she turned on her heel and headed for the assassin. She had no idea what she would do next, but getting more information seemed like a good first step.

# Chapter Eleven

Siobhan stared at the assassin from several feet away. Funny, he seemed so un-assassin-like at that moment she had a hard time imagining him as some murderous man lurking in the shadows. He sat hunched in on himself, pale and tired, beyond bored with life. In many respects, he looked every inch the Wynngaardian—the ice blond hair, naturally pale skin and blue eyes were very typical of this people. But unlike most of them, he didn't have the enormous build or height. Despite being slumped over like that, she could tell he wouldn't stand very tall and he had a wiry structure to him instead of a massive muscularity like Wolf. Malnutrition, perhaps? She'd seen children of this country fail to grow to their full potential simply because they didn't have enough to eat in their formative years.

He turned his eyes up to meet hers and a hint of something crossed his face. Curiosity, perhaps? She reacted to his stare without thinking, moving toward him. Wolf caught her arm before she made it a full step and dragged her to a halt.

"What are you doing?" he murmured to her in a low tone.

"I want to talk to him," she responded instantly.

"Why?" Wolf's eyes narrowed with suspicion. "Siobhan, there isn't a thing you need to know about that man. He came in here to do a dirty job and failed. He's now a problem to the village, a problem I can quickly solve by separating his head from his neck."

She took in a deep breath for patience. "Do we know that? Really? Wolf, think about this. He's been sitting here locked up for three weeks and not one soul has come here to either see if he finished the job or died in the attempt. *No one has come looking for him.*" Wolf opened his mouth to respond, paused, and closed it again as he took on her meaning. "You understand what that means, right? You should, even more than I. When a member of a dark guild fails, he isn't helped. He's gotten rid of."

Wolf looked away at that. She didn't press the point, as Wolf had experienced firsthand what happened to someone who was no longer useful to a dark guild. They were disposed of, one way or another. Wolf had been insanely lucky to have been sold when he was deemed "useless." Most were not dealt so kind of a fate.

"The only reason he's sitting there, alive, is that his guild assumed he was killed in his failed attempt."

Raising a hand, he scrubbed at his forehead roughly. "So? If you understand that, what's the point of talking to him?"

"Because he's a valuable resource. And I don't waste resources." Shaking off his restraining arm, she marched dead ahead again and paused two feet away from the assassin.

He watched her with cold blue eyes, not with any hostile intent, but with open wariness. She didn't see any signs of fear, though. In his situation, she would think he would feel some fear of what was to come. "I'm Siobhan Maley, Guildmaster of Deepwoods. You are?"

This civil greeting surprised him, a little, and he sat

up straighter, becoming more animated as he responded, "Most know me as Bloodless."

"Is that a description of your occupation or a warning?" Surely it couldn't be a name.

"Yes," he admitted with a slight shrug, mouth quirked in amusement. "What, ya haven't heard of me? I'm rather famous in certain circles."

"I'm from Robarge," she explained. "And I'm not associated with the darker guilds. Sorry, your name won't ring any bells with me."

"Ahh, Robarge." He nodded understanding. "Although that doesn't explain ya toweri'n Resken guard dog there."

"I adopted him several years ago," she answered half-truthfully, and smirked when Wolf choked behind her. Her bantering answer was calculated to see how the assassin would respond. So far, he seemed to have a rather dry sense of humor, which she hadn't at all expected.

"Siobhan..." Wolf growled out in warning.

Ignoring him, she went to the task at hand, all the while studying Bloodless carefully. "The people here don't know what to do with you. They want to be rid of you but aren't sure if killing you outright will be a wise idea. They're afraid that if they do so, your guild will come and exact revenge. But they're wrong, aren't they? No one will come to rescue you. No one cares if you're alive."

"That's right," he confirmed.

*There's nothing in his eyes.* A chill went up her spine as realization hit. His eyes were empty. Completely void of fear, caution, curiosity...all emotion. His mouth smiled, he reacted as if he were truly engaged in the conversation, but in truth his heart failed to feel anything at all. If he were older than twenty, she'd shave her head. Just what had been done to him that he couldn't feel anything even in the face of his own death?

Without taking her eyes from him, she asked Wolf, "What would you call sending a lone assassin into a Wynngaardian village with the assignment he had?"

"A suicide mission," Wolf answered bluntly. "You

send a squad of ten or more to do what he was sent to do. Less won't cut it. I bet he ticked someone off, or made the wrong man his enemy; that's why he was sent out here alone."

It fit with what she knew of the dark guilds. "So in truth, I can kill you right here and there's nothing that will happen to me."

"Will ya?" he leaned in a little closer and said in a confidential tone, "I prefer ta die at the hand of a beautiful woman like yerself."

"Oh? But I have a different idea in mind." Ah, *that* had gotten his attention. "How well do you know Sateren?"

"Born 'n raised there," he responded swiftly. "I know it better than the back of my hand."

"I want to send a message to Iron Dragain without raising any flags of where we are or that we even exist. Can you do that?"

He kept his voice carefully level as he responded, "Yes."

"I need a guide to bring us through the city and safely deliver us into Iron Dragain's main building. Can you do that?" she asked in the same tone he used.

"Ya'd have ta move very, very fast ta manage that, but yes, I know several routes ta take ya there." He lifted his bound hands and gave the chain a rattle. "What are ya offeri'n for my knowledge and help? Freedom from these?"

"I can do you one better." She sank down to her haunches so that she could be at eye level with him, eyes locked onto his. "If you promise to help us—*truly* help us, guide us, guard us, even when I don't know the right command to give you—then I'll do more than free you. I'll take you from here and right through Island Pass. When we reach there, you can go any direction you please and I will not stop you."

He didn't react, but that lifeless quality drained from his eyes. "Ya'd have ta act like I was a guildmember to do that. No one willi'n lets a member of a dark guild travel anywhere."

"I know. But it won't be an act. For the foreseeable future, at least until we're able to leave for Robarge, you'd *be* a member of Deepwoods. I won't be able to convince the villagers here to release you unless you agree to be in my custody."

Wolf let out a hiss and snarled a few choice words under his breath. She steadfastly ignored him.

"Yer guard dog doesn't like this idea," Bloodless informed her with sadistic cheer.

"He doesn't like a lot of things. It hasn't killed him yet."

"What if I betray ya?"

"We'll kill you." She said it matter-of-factly, but inside she knew it wouldn't come to that. She was his best ticket to getting out of here safely and into a different continent. His only chance of making a new life for himself without constantly having one eye over his shoulder would be to leave Wynngaard completely.

Bloodless glanced up at the hovering Resken, the unspoken question in the air, *What if you betray me?*

Siobhan answered it as if he'd spoken it aloud. "Don't worry about Wolf. He growls a lot, but as long as you don't provoke him, he won't do anything to you."

"Well, in that case...." He held out a hand to seal the deal. She took it without hesitation, gripping his forearm, surprised that it felt like she gripped an iron bar. He was deceptively stronger than he looked.

Bloodless shook his head in wry amusement. "Don't ya know better than ta come within arm's reach of an assassin?"

"You're not going to kill me," she responded with absolute certainty. "My death won't profit you anything."

He reclaimed his hand and asked Wolf, "Is she always this crazy?"

"No," Wolf growled in true agitation. "Sometimes she's worse."

Bloodless grinned. "My sympathies."

Siobhan ignored this by-play and rocked back up to her feet. "Alright, sit tight. I'll negotiate you out of those chains in a minute. But there's one last thing."

Bloodless cocked his head at her, silently questioning.

"I'm not calling you Bloodless," she informed him bluntly. "That's the name you give a hunting dog, not a human being. Don't you have a true name?"

"Not that I know of."

The answer told her more than he probably intended. Just how young had he been abandoned to the cold mercies of the world that he didn't even remember the name his parents had given him? If he'd had parents at all, that was. She didn't like the return of that lifeless quality in his eyes, either. Blowing out a breath, she flipped her hand palm up, letting that pass.

"Then is there a name you prefer to be called by? Or shall I choose one for you?"

He blinked at her, nonplussed and confused.

Wolf cleared his throat behind her. "Siobhan, the only person that can name another is their parent, or someone who acts as a mentor. It'd be very strange for you to name him."

Oh? Ooops. She hadn't known that little fact of Wynngaardian culture.

"Ya can," Bloodless said suddenly, eyes intent on her. For some reason, the expression on his face reminded her of a hungry animal, although why, she couldn't begin to understand. "Ya can name me."

She stared back at him for a long moment, trying to figure out why he said so. Was he afraid of upsetting their deal by denying her? That didn't seem to be it, though. She glanced up at Wolf, but he seemed just as puzzled by this.

Well, alright, he was willing and she truly couldn't bring herself to call him by a pet's name. She thought on it for a moment before offering, "Rune. It means 'secret.'" Heaven knew the man had a boat-    load of them.

"Rune," he repeated and smiled slightly as he said it, as if liking the taste of it. "Sure. I'll be ya secret, sweet

Guildmaster."

"Not quite how I meant it," she denied with a shake of the head. "But fine. Rune, sit tight. I'll have you out of those chains in a few minutes."

The Ahbiren did not at all like her proposal. In fact, he was with Wolf on this one—the only good assassin was a dead assassin. But after much discussion, promises, and such, he finally relented. Siobhan was well aware that she only got permission because Wolf cheerfully swore that if Rune acted up at all, he'd kill him without hesitation.

Siobhan decided not to care as long as she got Rune out of those chains and under her custody.

She went back to Rune with the key for the manacles in hand, knelt, and undid the chains, taking in his overall condition with a clinical eye. He looked—and smelled—terrible, as if he had been completely neglected except for the odd meals shoved his direction. Assassination attempt aside, how could anyone treat another human being like this? She understood anger, and retaliation, but outright cruelty was beyond her ken. She couldn't stomach him being left like this.

"Rune, listen to me carefully. The Ahbiren does not like the idea of you living one little bit and he's going to keep a close eye on you. So stay close to me and don't cause trouble, alright?"

"Yes, ma'am," he promised without a hint of sarcasm.

"Good. Now, first order of business, bath."

He blinked at her, as if he couldn't possibly have heard her right. "Bath?"

"Bath," she repeated firmly. "While you're washing, I'll rummage up some clothes for you to change into. These need to be in a waste-bin. Then we'll have Conli—he's our doctor—take a look at your wrists. Are you hungry? When did you last eat?"

For some reason, Rune watched her with a strange look on his face, as if he was having trouble following what she said. But he opened his mouth and managed, "Yesterday morni'n they fed me."

"Yesterday?" she parroted in exasperation. "You're a grown man, for pity's sake! Were they trying to slowly kill you through starvation? Never mind, I'll get a meal together while you're washing as well. Where's Beirly?" she stood and turned on her heel, looking about. "Ah, there he is. BEIRLY!"

Her friend looked up from the box he was moving and called back, "What?"

"Find some clothes that will fit him!" she ordered, pointing a finger down at Rune's head.

Beirly scratched at the back of his head, stared at Rune for a long second, and then asked, "Why?"

"Because he's ours for the time being."

Even from twenty feet away she could see Beirly's reaction to *that* piece of news. "Shi! Tell me you didn't just adopt an assassin!"

She grinned. "I've done stranger things!"

"Name one!" Beirly challenged, although he laughed as he retorted.

Well, actually, she couldn't think of anything that counted as 'stranger' right off the top of her head.

Rune chuckled in outright delight. "Ya can't think of anythi'n."

"I'm sure something will come to me. Later. In the wee hours of the morning." She shrugged, unconcerned. "Come along, Rune. We need to find a large tub of hot water."

# Chapter Twelve

Finding hot water took a good hour and a half, due to complications. They could not put an additional eleven people into the house/converted storeroom that Lirah's people were using, so another storeroom had to be cleared out before Deepwoods could get situated. With everyone pitching in, they managed to clear a sizeable area in short order, giving them a place to sleep right next to Lirah's building. As impromptu lodging went, it wasn't half-bad. Siobhan had certainly stayed in worse. This building had housed grain, mostly wheat, and so it smelled slightly musty. But the wooden floors, brick walls, and thatch roof overhead had a nice solidness to them that kept out the weather. Best yet, the doorway and ceilings had enough height for even Tran and Wolf to clear without danger of knocking their heads into something.

A lean-to had been added onto the building at some point, although it was not currently in use for anything. Siobhan declared it a bathing room and had a half-barrel rolled into it for washing. Someone had put in a small well and pump out in the back of the building, and through an open back window, they were able to cart in enough water for washing. She scrounged up a towel, a bar of soap, and a dirty assassin and shoved them all into the room without further ado.

Rune laughed as he went aside, amused by her insistence, but didn't complain as he closed the door behind him. She stood close-by for a second, waiting to hear the sound of splashing water. *Ah, there. Good.* Turning, she shooed everyone out of the building and onto the front porch so she could have this conversation outside of Rune's hearing. Well, hopefully outside of his hearing.

"Alright, Shi, what's the real story?" Beirly asked in a confidential tone.

She looked around at the circle of faces which, for the most part, stared back in confusion. "In short? The Ahbiren here agreed to let us stay if we took care of a problem for him."

"Ahhh." Fei pointed toward Rune's general direction. "Problem?"

"Assassin who failed to kill the Ahbiren," she explained with a grimace. "They weren't sure what to do with him once they caught him."

"That's a problem, certainly," Markl agreed. "And the reason why you brought him into the guild?"

"He knows Sateren." Siobhan had, in the course of setting all this up, finally seen the hole in Lirah's story. "Listen, I think we need him. I think we need him more than I first realized. Lirah said that they were attacked by professionals, either assassins or mercenaries, and that they retreated because they thought most of her people dead. But that doesn't make sense. Why were they attacked? Not robbery—Lirah still has most of her equipment. If it was a hit, then why leave with the job half finished?"

"If Iron Dragain was behind it, they wouldn't want witnesses left behind," Wolf continued her train of thought aloud, brows beetling. "And the guild that did the job wouldn't leave without making sure all were dead. Unless they were ordered to leave some alive. Sloppy work like that will lose you customers."

"Right?" she agreed. "It's like the attack was *designed* to make us think Iron Dragain had betrayed Blackstone. They waited until Lirah was close to Sateren, left her alive with all of her people, all so they can cast suspicion on Iron Dragain. But I don't think it was them. I think it's that third party that Markl thought up in Quigg."

"There's no reason for a third party to attack, though," Markl pointed out.

"That we know of," Sylvie corrected. "But we don't know every business dealing that Blackstone and Iron Dragain are involved in. There could be something else going on behind the scenes, something that would explain this."

"We don't know who to trust right now," Siobhan sighed, "but I'm inclined to trust Iron Dragain. I honestly think them innocent in all of this. That said, I want to send a message to them. They're the closest safe harbor we've got, if we can get to their main holdings. I don't want to risk that open road again, not until we understand what's going on."

"Which is why you want him." Tran inclined his head toward the building, indicating Rune. "You think he can get into Sateren without raising any attention."

"He said he was born and raised there. He knows the city better than any of us. Fei, I'm going to put together a message and I want you to deliver it with Rune."

Fei quirked a brow at her. "Because you don't trust him?"

She shook her head in wry amusement. "Would you? But also, I think Iron Dragain is more likely to trust any message I send if someone from Deepwoods delivers it."

Fei pondered that for a moment before stating, "I want to test his skills before we go."

"Fair enough."

The front door opened and a damp assassin poked his head out, a towel hanging around his neck. He looked remarkably better with all of the dirt and grime off of him. He also, strangely, looked younger. In fact, Siobhan realized after a startled blink that Rune couldn't be far past his teenage years. "Testi'n me aside, I don't think ya should contact Iron Dragain yet."

Siobhan had a flash of chagrin that he'd overheard their conversation. Shaking that off, she turned to face him squarely. "For future reference, how sharp is your hearing?"

"Quite sharp." He grinned at her, a surprisingly boyish expression. "I promised ta help ya even when ya didn't know the right question to ask. If ya want ta know who attacked yer friends, I can help ya find out."

Siobhan blinked at him in surprise. "You can?"

"Easy, easy," he assured her. "My old guild is the largest assassin's guild in Sateren. All requests went through them first. I don't know if they were the ones that actually did the work themselves, but they'd certainly know who commissioned it."

She rubbed at her chin thoughtfully. Granted, it would help a great deal if they knew who was behind the attack. She would at least know who to trust. "What do you need to pull this off?"

"I need ta arrange a meet between ya and one of the karls."

"Karl?" she repeated, having never heard the term before.

Rune gave her a strange look in return. "Ya don't know what a karl is? How do Robargean guilds rank the people, then?"

Markl chose to explain. "From lowest to highest, it's initiate, guildmember, sentinel, officer, advisor, guildmaster. But this is only true for the largest guilds, there's a different structure in small ones."

*Or little structure at all*, Siobhan reflected in wry humor. Herself aside, no one had a rank in Deepwoods.

"Hehhhh," Rune drawled out as he processed this. Then he shrugged. "Sounds like it's simpler here. We only have four ranks—praell, karls, jarls, and guildmaster. Praells are like the guildmembers, I guess, and the karls are like the officers. Jarls are the highest up, and they work directly for the guildmaster. For what we need ta know, any karl will do."

While all of this sounded very promising, it didn't really ease all of Siobhan's concerns. "Is it safe for you to meet with anyone from your old guild? I mean, all things considered." She jerked a thumb at the village in illustration.

His face became rigid with a fake smile. "Ya called it earlier, when ya said I was sent on a suicide mission. If by some miracle, I succeeded, they would have forgiven me and kept me in the guild. But I didn't, so I'm outcast from them. Since they were the ones cutting ties, they won't care what I do."

She glanced at Wolf, who knew the inner workings of a dark guild better than she, silently asking if that were truly the case. Wolf held a bleak expression and he nodded ever so slightly in confirmation.

Why? Questions swirled around in her head without answer and she turned her eyes back to Rune, unsure if she could give voice to any of them.

Rune took a step closer to her, closing the gap, which put Tran and Wolf distinctly on edge. Only then did she realize he was exactly her height, as their eyes were on the same level. "Ya want ta know," he said quietly, voice unusually gravelly. "If I knew it was suicide, why go? Yer big wolf here doesn't ask, cause he knows. Ya don't switch guilds in a city. No dark guild will trust ya if ya leave one ta go ta another, and the other guilds will just as soon throw ya in a cell as look at ya. I couldn't leave here—I didn't have the supplies ta travel. I'd be dead if I took ta the road. Odds were, I'd die tryi'n ta kill the old man, too, but at least the odds were better taki'n the job." That humorless smile darted over his face again. "So ya see, I had nothi'n to bargain with. Ya got rooked, Guildmaster."

She met that smile without flinching. "I bargained for an expert on Sateren. Did you lie to me about that?"

His brows compressed briefly in a small frown. "No."

"Then I'm satisfied." Judging from the way his mouth soundlessly moved, he had no idea what to think about that, much less how to respond. Taking pity on him, she clapped a hand to his shoulder. It felt like she grasped a warm wooden post. Was he nothing but bone and muscle? "We'll talk about how to contact someone from your old guild in a bit. First, introductions. This is Markl, Conli, Denney, Sylvie, Wolf, Tran, Beirly and Fei. The dogs are Pyper and Pete. Everyone, this is Rune. He'll be with us until we return through Island Pass."

There were some nods and greetings around the group, all of them said warily. Rune greeted them back cheerfully, enjoying their awkwardness.

Siobhan let out a sigh and hoped the mood would pass as everyone got used to him. "Rune, ground rules are these—treat everyone with respect, the women especially. If we ask you for an escort, do so. If something's broken, go to Beirly. If there's danger, Wolf, Tran or Fei needs to be told first. They're my enforcers. If it's trade-related, talk to Sylvie. If it's medical, talk to Conli. Got all that?"

Rune had that odd look on his face again, as if he couldn't understand what she was doing or why she was doing it. But he responded, "Yes, Guildmaster."

"If it doesn't fit any of the above, you're always welcome to talk to me," she assured him, hoping he would do so. She needed him to trust her, otherwise this dangerous situation would get a lot worse. "For now, Conli, take a look at him. I'll get some food while you do that."

"Sure thing." Conli replied. His eyes were already scanning Rune and he frowned as he noted the same problems Siobhan had spotted earlier. "This might take more than a few minutes. Rune, those manacles roughed up your skin quite a bit. It looks like more than bruising

160

to me." Silently urging the boy back inside, she could hear him asking questions as they went to where his impromptu medical center had been set up. "Are you hurt anywhere else? Hmmm? Oh, no, I probably won't need you to swallow anything."

Siobhan tuned it out and went to the next thing. "Sylvie, can you buy some food for us, enough to last us another two weeks or so? Lirah said it would take at least that long for people to be recovered enough to move."

Sylvie gave her a silent salute before moving off the porch.

Almost belatedly, she told Markl, "Help her. I'm sure it'll be too much for one to carry."

"Of course." He readily fell into Sylvie's wake.

That started, she went to the next thing. "Fei, talk to Lirah's group and get an exact accounting of what happened. Get me details—what they looked like, what weapons they used, which direction they retreated to, you know the drill. The more information I have, the better."

Fei nodded and silently went to do as bid.

Let's see...what else.... "Tran—"

"I'm not going anywhere," he refused in a low rumble.

"Ahhh..." Remembering that Rune's hearing was unusually good, she instead pointed in his general direction, head cocked in question. Tran nodded sourly. Wolf backed him up with a nod as well, arms crossed over his chest in a stubborn manner. Siobhan blew out a breath. So, neither Tran nor Wolf would let the boy out of their sight, eh? Well, for the time being, that was probably prudent.

"Fine," she sighed in resignation. "I'll find a plate of food for him and some better fitting clothes." The ones that Beirly had handed her hung on the boy so bad it was a wonder his pants stayed up. She also had to figure out where Rune's weapons had been put. Surely the villagers had kept them instead of just throwing them out. Whether or not she would hand them over immediately would be a matter to decide later.

Finding readily available food for an assassin in a, if not hostile, unwelcoming village proved to be quite the challenge. Siobhan ended up paying more money than she intended, but her grocery shoppers hadn't returned yet (probably because they faced the same challenges Siobhan had) and she was worried about Rune's condition. He put up a strong front, but there was no way to disguise the slightly grey color to his skin or the heavy way he moved, as if it took extreme effort on his part. She wanted decent food in him as soon as she could manage it.

When she returned, she found that Rune hadn't quite escaped Conli yet. Her resident physician was wrapping the younger man's wrists with a white bandage, issuing instructions to keep it clean as he did so. Rune had that inscrutable expression on his face again, as if he didn't know how to react to any of this. Maybe he didn't. Wolf had told her stories, from time to time, about what life in a dark guild was like. It had made her hair stand on end. Worse, she was fairly certain he only told her the milder tales. The darker ones he never spoke of.

She walked through the doorway and put the wicker basket in Rune's hands. "Eat all of it," she commanded.

Rune opened the basket and peered at the loaf of bread, wedge of cheese, smoked ham, and apple tart inside. He nearly started drooling. "No problem."

As Rune enthusiastically dug in, she settled cross-legged next to Conli and asked him, "How's his condition?"

"Malnourished, dehydrated, and exhausted," Conli replied promptly, his mouth in a flat, unhappy line. "I could whip these people for how they treated him."

Rune paused in devouring the ham and gave them an odd look. Around a mouthful, he managed, "I *did* try ta kill one of their own."

"They should have executed you for that or bargained with your guild to send you back for a hefty fee," Conli responded angrily, slamming the rest of the bandages back into his pack. "You don't starve and neglect people.

That's just cruelty."

Siobhan agreed with him one hundred percent. She didn't like how they'd handled Rune either. "His wrists and ankles?"

"Bruised and chafed, but not serious," Conli assured her. "That said, I don't think you should send him out today. Or tomorrow. He needs good food, a lot of liquid, and some uninterrupted rest for at least two days before you send him anywhere."

She understood the sense of his advice as he said it.

Rune, not understanding, protested as he ripped a chunk out of the loaf of bread. "I can go today."

Siobhan shook her head firmly. "No, Rune. You're not in the best of shape right now. I don't send weakened men into potentially dangerous situations. You might be able to go into Sateren and arrange a meeting with a karl without a hitch. Then again, you might be in for quite the fight. We don't know what will happen. I'm not sending you anywhere until Conli says you're strong enough."

He looked between the two of them with expressionless eyes, not saying a word. Siobhan was really beginning to hate that look. "Fine," he finally capitulated with a shrug. "Yer the guildmaster here."

Too true.

# Tran Amar

Christa Triumph 2014

# Chapter Thirteen

No one really complained about having a few days to rest in one place, not after the traveling they'd done. The problem Siobhan faced lay in that no one wanted to stay in close quarters with Rune. No one trusted him, and it was hard to relax in the presence of someone you didn't trust.

Siobhan wouldn't swear that she could trust Rune either, but she did believe that he would hold up his end of the bargain as he honestly couldn't afford to break the deal. She felt like saying, *Look, he won't bite. He's a nice assassin, see?* Alas, no one would likely listen.

She tried to ignore the uncomfortable atmosphere for the first day, giving people time to come to terms with him on their own, but by afternoon of the second day, the tension got to her. Giving up, she dug out the deck of cards and a brush pen from her pack.

People had more or less sorted themselves out in the narrow house. The bedrolls were rolled up during the day, as frankly there wasn't enough floor space to leave them out, with the packs laid against the walls. Wolf and

Tran seemed intent on polishing weapons, Conli eerily imitating them by polishing his medical tools. Markl had his notebook out, writing something down, but Sylvie looked beyond bored as she unbraided and re-braided her hair.

"Sylvie," Siobhan invited while waving the deck in the air. "Up for a game?"

The other woman perked up. "Sounds good. What are we playing?"

"Thirteen Cards," Siobhan responded. "Course, it's hard to play with only two people...Rune, care to join in?"

No one was fooled by this casual invitation. But Rune seemed glad for something to do aside from ignore everyone's not-stares. "Well, a game sounds fun, but I don't know this one."

"It's not hard," Siobhan assured him. She sat cross-legged near him, Sylvie joining her on the other side so that they formed a circle. "Are you familiar with card games?"

"Somewhat," he responded carefully.

"Then here's the rules. You have thirteen cards in your hands. Your goal is to get rid of them, and the first person with no cards left wins. You can lay down pairs, sequences, or multiples of cards, but whatever you lay down has to match what the first person lays down. Got that? Good. If you can't lay something down, or don't want to, say 'go.' We'll play rounds, eliminating people, until only one person is left."

He nodded understanding, watching as she quickly shuffled the deck of slim wooden cards before passing them out between the three. "What are we betti'n? This is a gambli'n game, it seems."

"Of a sort," Sylvie agreed. "But there's a long established rule in the guild that we don't bet money with each other. It leads to bad blood later. So instead, we have penalties." She smirked as she held up the brush pen. "The winner gets to scribble whatever she wants to on the loser's face."

Rune seemed intrigued by this, and if that quirk of the mouth were any indication, amused. "And, ah, how permanent is that ink?"

"Very," Siobhan assured him cheerfully.

"Warni'n taken." Rune took the cards from her and started sorting through them.

The first few minutes, people were busy sorting through cards and figuring out how to best play them. Then Siobhan nodded to the assassin. "We always start left of the dealer. So, you go."

"Pairs or sequences, right?"

"If you have three or four of a kind, you can lay that down too."

"Got it." He laid down a pair, starting the game.

Perhaps it was beginner's luck, but whatever the case, Rune proved to be a tough opponent. Siobhan barely squeaked by in getting rid of her cards before he did. Sylvie wasn't so lucky. With an outright smirk, Rune leaned forward with the brush and painted a sloppy star on her right cheek.

Making a face, she picked all the cards up and shuffled them. "I deal this time."

"Can you deal me in?" Markl requested.

Siobhan waved him forward, secretly relieved that he chose to do so. They all shifted their positions enough that he had room to sit with them. "Are you familiar with Thirteen Cards?" she asked him as he settled between Sylvie and Rune.

"I listened to the instructions, I think I know how it works," he assured her.

With the way the game was set up, no more than four could play. But as Sylvie dealt the cards, and Siobhan started them off by laying down a five-card sequence, she could feel Wolf and Tran paying very close attention.

With two beginners, Siobhan didn't play as ruthlessly as she normally did, which proved to be a mistake. After three rounds, both Markl and Rune proved that they had the strategies of the game down and she lost magnificently, getting a circle painted around her eye for her troubles. Sticking her tongue out at a grinning Markl, she played much more seriously after that.

Time passed quickly, the rounds becoming quicker and more hilarious as people got interesting things painted onto their skin. With no mirror, they had to ask what was painted, and Siobhan was sure that no one had told her the truth about what Sylvie did on her skin.

Beirly came in as the dinner bell in the village rang, took in their faces, and burst out laughing. "Playing Thirteen Cards, I see!"

"Beirly, they're ganging up on me," Sylvie complained with a mock-pout. Considering that she had a mustache painted on her face, the pout didn't have *quite* the effect she was aiming for. Beirly doubled over laughing, wheezing for breath.

Fei came in behind him, looking the situation over with a suspiciously straight face, as if he were laughing internally. "I see that Markl-xian is winning so far."

Considering Markl only had a black spot on his nose, an eye on his forehead, and a heart on his cheek, that was a fair judgment to make.

"It's a near thing," Markl admitted without an ounce of modesty. "Rune's wicked with cards. He's almost gotten me these last three rounds."

"And yet here I be with more scribbles on my face," Rune drawled, which made Sylvie and Siobhan laugh. Truly, he looked like a demented clown. Rune had black circles painted under his eyes, high on his cheekbones, over the tip of his nose, and a fat lip around his mouth.

"I'd suggest stopping now," Beirly managed in between guffaws. "If you start scrubbing, you might only have faint spots on your face tomorrow."

Siobhan imagined going to a meeting with a karl with traces of ink still all over her face and grimaced. Perhaps the game hadn't been the best of ideas. Although Sylvie and Markl, at least, were now much more comfortable with Rune, so it had paid off. "Right. And someone needs to start dinner. Who's on duty tonight?"

"Fei and Denney," Conli answered.

She blew out a secret breath of relief. That meant the food would be decent. Both of them were good cooks. "Where is Denney?"

"Coming," Fei assured her. "She and I went fishing earlier."

"Fishing?" Siobhan repeated blankly. "Fishing where?"

"We're not that far from Drahn Lake," he responded with a casual shrug. "An hour's walk will get you there."

"You went fishing in Drahn Lake?" Siobhan's eyes crossed just trying to imagine that. "The lake that never completely thaws, *that* lake?"

He grimaced. "It was unpleasantly chilly. But the fish were biting well."

In near-freezing temperatures? What kind of bait had they used?! Shaking her head, she dismissed it. She wouldn't turn down fresh fish for dinner, for sure. "Alright. While you cook, I'm scrubbing."

Fei snickered behind her as she marched resolutely for the inner bathing room. Rune, Sylvie and Markl had beaten her there and were already crowding around a pail of water, using the reflection to see enough to scrub with. The small towels and strong lye soap in their hands were doing a fair job of getting the worst of the ink off.

Resigned to the inevitable skin irritation this would likely cause, she grabbed a towel herself, soaped it up, and commenced scrubbing. As expected, the cloth felt rough as she tried to take off three layers of skin.

Since those three hogged the water-mirror, she was scrubbing blind. Her eyes roved over everyone as she had nothing to focus on. Rune had gotten off the black circles under his eyes, the one on his nose, and most of what was around his lips. The cheek facing her had a good swipe of black ink still left, though, as if he couldn't properly see the sides of his face. Maybe he couldn't.

"You missed a spot, Rune," she told him. Without asking permission, she grasped his chin with one hand to hold him still and used her own towel to start scrubbing at it. "Ah, there, it's coming off now."

He looked at her from the corner of his eye, his whole body completely and carefully still. For a moment, something flashed across his face, an expression there and gone so fast she couldn't begin to read it.

She pretended not to notice, instead shifting his chin to the other side so she could see his right cheek. "Ah, here too."

"You're so worried about his face, but what about your own?" Sylvie asked in rich amusement. She leaned across the water to attack Siobhan's face.

Siobhan tried to duck, protesting, "Let me take care of him first! You're likely to get soap in my eye at that angle."

"He's fine," Sylvie responded in exasperation. "It's all off his face."

"But there's this spot on his arm—" Siobhan started, only to cut herself off as she got a better look at the black ink etched into Rune's upper arm. Right below his shoulder was a long dagger, plain in design, with one drop of blood coming off the blade. It looked...eerie. She knew without asking what it was, but still the words came out of her mouth. "Your old guild's emblem?"

"Silent Order," he stated quietly. "Yes. It's an unsaid rule here that all members of a dark guild carry their emblem somewhere on their body."

Thereby trapping them into that life? Anger coursed through Siobhan in a red-hot wave. She choked it back. "I see."

"Conli might be able to take that off," Sylvie ventured slowly. She came around to get a better look at it. "How long have you had this, Rune? Ten years or so?"

Rune nodded cautiously. "About that."

"A cream likely won't work, then. But he's taken off scars and tattoos before. I've seen him do it." Sylvie glanced up at him. "If you want him to, that is."

"I have no reason ta keep it." Rune shrugged. "In fact, it'd be better if it were off."

Yes, if other people saw this in the future, when Rune was away from Wynngaard, they would likely make life difficult for him. It might even prevent him from building a new life somewhere. Decided, Siobhan turned on her heel. "I'll go ask."

Sylvie caught her arm and spun her back around. "He's a grown man, Siobhan, he can ask for himself. We need to get that ink off your face before you go to a meeting with a dark guild member looking like a demented ghost."

Siobhan stuck her tongue out in a childish gesture.

"And if you keep sticking that out at me, I'll wash that too," Sylvie threatened, waving the rag at her with an evil glint in her eye.

She promptly sucked her tongue back into her mouth.

Markl chuckled and even Rune smiled.

"If you four are done playing in the water, dinner is nearly done!" Denney called from the other room.

Sylvie wouldn't let go of her until all the ink had been taken off, along with about five layers of Siobhan's skin. Her face felt hot and probably looked as red as a tomato. By the time she made it back to the group, where they had congregated outside, the food was already being dished out. She accepted a loaded plate of fish stew from Fei, mouth watering. With rich anticipation, she put a spoonful in her mouth and sighed in bliss.

Denney passed around biscuits, a specialty of hers, and they gorged themselves with hearty thanks to the cooks. Siobhan kept an eye on everyone, making sure they had enough to eat, although Fei and Denney had cooked enough for everyone to have not only seconds, but thirds. The only one that didn't take advantage of this was Rune, who sat a little apart from the group.

Still not comfortable with them, eh? Sighing, she put her food down and went directly to him, grabbing his plate. He didn't protest, handing it over easily at the first tug. She filled it up to the brim, put two biscuits on the side, and gave it back. Catching his eye, she ordered firmly, "Eat all of it. And if you're still hungry, get another plate."

He took the plate in both hands, regarding her with an expression that might have been amusement. "What if I'm full?"

She snorted. "You're male. You're never full."

Every other man in the guild choked, laughing. "Wait, Siobhan," Conli said in disagreement, though his tone was distinctly amused, "I'm afraid that being around the men here have skewed your perceptions. There *are* men in the world who have limits on their appetites."

"Ha!" she scoffed, not believing that for a minute.

"Considering what we spend on food expenses every month, you can't blame her for not believing you," Denney pointed out.

"We saved seventy-five kors alone when we sent Wolf on that one-man escort mission this spring," Sylvie observed.

"I don't eat *that* much," Wolf protested.

"Yes, you do," at least four people disagreed in unison.

This started off a round of bickering on who ate more. Siobhan decided she didn't care to be in the middle of that debate and went back to her plate. As she moved, she saw Pyper approach Rune with a slow tread, her nose sniffing him curiously. Rune regarded her approach with the same caution, not at all sure how to respond to her.

Denney, bless her, went and sank down next to the dog, her tone neutral as she asked Rune, "You got experience with dogs?"

"Only hunting dogs, not like these," he nodded toward Pyper and Pete. "These are friendlier."

"Colliers," she supplied. "They're more watch dogs than anything. Smart ones, these are. Pyper's trying to figure out if you're a friend or not. You feed her something, she's likely to think you are one."

Rune listened to this advice carefully. "She like bread?"

"They both do."

He picked a biscuit off his plate and offered it to Pyper

on a flat palm. She sniffed it for a second, then tilted her head sideways so she could pick it up daintily. Typical of dogs, she then proceeded to swallow it whole, without seemingly chewing at all.

Being a dog, her affections were then sealed, and she nosed at Rune's hand in thanks before circling around once and settling down right at his feet, her head resting against his legs.

"Well." Denney beamed at him openly. "Glad she likes you."

Rune smiled back, seemingly out of sheer reflex. "That's good."

"It is. In many ways." With that cryptic statement, she rose back onto her feet in a smooth movement before going back to her plate. "Pete! You stay out of my stew, you rascal."

Siobhan watched all of this play out without a word, smiling in satisfaction. If the dogs approved of him, she knew that Denney would too.

That left the rest of the guild still to go.

# Chapter Fourteen

Since the first day Siobhan had become guildmaster, she had developed the habit of walking through the area and double checking everything before going to bed. Even in their own guildhall she did this. It set her mind at ease that all was well in her corner of the world and she could let the worries of the day go in favor of much needed rest. Here, especially, she felt a strong need to do a patrol around their little house.

The night air felt cool against her skin, unpleasantly so, and she rubbed her arms as she walked, scanning everything around her with sharp eyes. The village had mostly gone to bed, only a few hearth fires still sending plumes of smoke twirling into the night sky. In this open country, with little to no trees to bar her view, the sky overhead was a brilliant show of stars. She paused on the path in front of the house and turned her face upwards, drinking it all in. Rarely had she seen such a breathtaking display.

"Beautiful, isn't it?" Fei observed quietly from nearby.

Startled, she jerked around first to the left, then to her right, but she could see no sign of him. "Fei?"

"Up here."

Even with this vague direction, she almost didn't see him. He sat quite comfortably on the roof, as if the slanted angle didn't bother him any, dressed in an array of clothing that blended in perfectly with the night. She looked up at him in exasperation. "I realize your shin-tei training makes being sneaky second nature to you, but will you please try to breathe loudly? Clear your throat now and again? *Something* so that you don't constantly sneak up behind me and give me heart failure?"

He seemed to find this amusing, if that glint of white teeth was any indication. "I'm sitting in plain sight, Siobhan-ajie," he pointed out, tone laughing.

"Ha!"

"You were also the one to set me as first watch, were you not?" he continued, grin widening. "You should have known I was out here."

"And at the highest point possible, yes, alright, I'm the fool for nearly leaping out of my skin," she riposted sarcastically. "Obviously, with my amazing powers of deduction and clairvoyance, I should have known before asking exactly where you would choose to sit."

"Precisely."

Siobhan threw her hands into the air, giving up.

Without a trace of noise, he shifted to the edge of the roof and lightly leaped down, landing in a crouch. Siobhan eyed him curiously, not sure why he had decided to move from his perch. Fei came to stand very close to her, barely inches away, even bending his head slightly to put their heads on the same level. Only then did he speak, voice barely above a murmur. "You should put Wolf-ren and Rune-gui on the same watch tonight."

Fei had this remarkably bad habit of thinking things though at great length and then only sharing his conclusions aloud. Siobhan was certain he had several very good reasons for this suggestion, but dragging them all out of him would be akin to pulling teeth from a sick, wounded alligator. Bracing her feet, she met him eye to eye and responded in the same soft tone, "And why is that?"

"It would do them both good."

"Fei," she requested with forced patience, "start from the beginning, please."

"Rune-gui is like a lost child." Fei's brows furrowed slightly as he spoke, as if he struggled to put into words something that he only understood on an instinctive level. In the cool lighting of the stars and bright moons overhead, the words he spoke felt like a forbidden secret. "Your kindness baffles him. And yet, he gravitates to you, drawn to that kindness. Wolf-ren, watching this, is uneasy."

Yes, she had noted that unease herself. "Because by watching Rune, he's reminded of himself in the past."

Fei nodded agreement. "That is part of it. But he sees what I see...Rune does not let you out of his sight for long. Wolf-ren does not understand why and assumes the worst."

Something in Fei's tone said he didn't share the assessment. Siobhan cocked her head slightly. "What do you think?"

"I think even Rune-gui does not understand his actions right now. I think speaking to a man that has been in his place will help both of them."

Now there was a thought. Siobhan turned it over in her mind and found that she couldn't find any fault in Fei's logic.

"Scribbling on faces only works for some people, not all," Fei added, chuckling.

So he'd caught on to her ploy, eh? "I had to do *something*. The tension was killing me."

"It worked well on those two," he agreed, shrugging. "But the same tactic will not work on all of us."

Truly. But that did beg the question... "If you're volunteering all of this, it means you've come to trust him?"

"He does not wish us harm." Fei sounded absolutely certain of this. "He doesn't know what to think of us, or how to respond to the kindness shown him, but he has no ill intent. I also feel that given time, he will prove himself to be an invaluable friend, as Wolf-ren proved to be."

Until he said those words, Siobhan hadn't thought of Rune in that light. But with it now said, she instinctively felt that Fei would prove to be right. Wolf had not reacted like Rune in the beginning, not in some ways, but the way he'd frozen when kindness was shown to him, as if lost on how to respond to it, *that* was exactly the same. Siobhan freely admitted that her mothering impulses had been in overdrive with Wolf the first year he was in the guild. Rune's behavior made her react the same way.

Those mothering instincts were not certain about putting two survivors of a dark guild on watch, in the dead of night, without witnesses around. Especially when they didn't trust each other. But she didn't believe for one second that Wolf would harm the kid without very good reason. She also trusted Fei's assessment of the situation— so far, she had never seen him wrong, not on matters like this. So she blew out a breath, running a hand over her hair.

"Alright, I'll rearrange the schedule so they're both on watch after you."

Pleased, he nodded in satisfaction and headed back toward his perch.

More than ready to crawl into a warm bed, she headed inside. A blanket had been draped over the rafters, cutting the room in half, women sleeping on one side and men on the other. Siobhan stuck her head into the men's half, unsurprised to find that Wolf was lying on his side with one eye open, watching for her return. But Rune was also still awake, sitting up in his bed, idly flipping a dagger around his wrist. Hmm? Why would he bother to stay up...? Ah, never mind, it didn't matter. She paused long enough to catch Rune and Wolf's eyes. "Both of you stand the next watch."

For just a moment, they were strangely in sync as they gave her the same expression of surprise.

"Why...?" Wolf asked slowly.

With no compunction whatsoever, she shifted the blame to someone else's shoulders. "Fei suggested it. Night!"

Before they could start an argument, she let the curtain fall back into place and retreated to her bedroll near the door. Siobhan put the twin swords at her hip on the ground, resting above her pillow, then shimmied out of the boots, pants, and thick jacket she wore. Now in just thick leggings and a billowy shirt, she felt more comfortable. Siobhan slithered into her blankets with a small smile, more than ready for this day to end.

She awoke to the sounds of battle.

KLANG ching ching shiiing.

What in the—?! Siobhan rolled to her feet, both swords in hand, before she could get her eyes properly open. The blankets wanted to keep her left foot, and she had to shake it free even as she scurried for the door. Whatever was going on seemed to be happening in the front yard, as the noise came from there.

The morning hadn't really started yet, as the sun barely had its head above the horizon, and most of the world seemed intent on sleeping a little longer. (Siobhan rather agreed with this after taking the third watch.) But Fei and Rune seemed to be of the opinion that if there was light, then it was a good time to fight.

Siobhan stumbled to a stop on the porch and watched with an open mouth as the two men went at each other with ferocious intensity. Fei had his wadoki short sword in one hand, the metal scabbard in the other which he used like a shield, although he hadn't put on his utility belt.

Dare she take that as a sign that this wasn't meant to be a serious fight?

Rune had the iron gloves she'd retrieved from the Ahbiren on his hands, which covered everything from knuckles to elbow, but other than that she didn't see a weapon on him. Not that she believed for one second he was unarmed. He could make daggers appear and disappear at will.

Both of them flew back a pace, giving each other some breathing room, and then leapt forward again with a baring of teeth like wolves going at each other's throats. Fei's sword sliced through the air with a whistle of noise, Rune catching the edge of the blade on one of his knuckle guards before diverting it away, his free hand coming up in a sharp jab aimed at Fei's stomach. Somehow Fei blocked it with his scabbard, knocking the fist away, although he grunted at the effort.

They parried and sliced and punched at each other with such speed that Siobhan could barely track it all with her eyes.

Wolf ghosted up behind her and murmured, "Relax. It's just a test."

"*That's* a test?" she repeated in amazement, unnerved by the ferocity.

"It started out friendlier," he offered.

"Yes, that makes everything all better," she retorted acidly. When he chuckled, she shot him a look from the corner of her eye. "If I didn't know any different, I would say they're trying to take each other's heads off."

Unconcerned, Wolf shrugged.

She rolled her eyes to the heavens, praying for patience. Well, what had she expected? Wolf's idea of 'danger' and hers were as different as moon and sun. Her main question was, why hadn't Fei called a halt to this? She could tell after ten seconds that Rune had incredible fighting skill. They'd been at this for several minutes.

Clapping her hands loudly, she called, "Alright boys, quit!"

Fei paused with his sword in mid-swing, aiming for Rune's head. The other man had both hands up in a guard position, and he looked at her over one shoulder in an open pout.

"Awwww," Rune whined. "It was just getting fun!"

"Yes, that's why you're stopping," she informed him dryly. "I'd rather not have a body on my hands, thank you."

"We wouldn't have hurt each other, Siobhan-ajie," Fei assured her. *Much*, his tone added.

"Uh-huh." Siobhan stared him down. Why did she feel like a mother scolding two young boys for playing in the mud? "It's alright, the two of you can play more after breakfast."

Fei and Rune perked up.

Rune asked the obvious. "Meani'n it's time ta go into Sateren?"

"A-yup." Siobhan checked her mental schedule and realized with a groan that she was in charge of cooking breakfast. Curse all the luck. "Do I need to write a formal note to send along with you?"

"That'd be best," Rune admitted.

She'd do that after breakfast, then. "So your guards weren't damaged in any way?" she pointed her chin to indicate the metal guards strapped to Rune's arms.

"Oh, no," he said happily. Raising them up a little, he flipped his arms both ways, so she could see either side. "Just fine."

She still felt a bit bemused that the guards and a few random daggers were his only weapons. After seeing the multitude of weapons Fei carried around, or the long swords that most of the men in the guild favored, she would have thought that just two long hand guards would put Rune at a severe disadvantage. But after seeing him fight on par with Fei, she would have to put that idea to rest. Perhaps he had been called "Bloodless" because he chose to break bones over shedding blood? His hand-to-hand combat skills made her think so.

Shrugging, she let it go and went back inside to get dressed and start the day. After having the light scared right out of her, she didn't feel like snoozing for a few more minutes.

As she went about cooking breakfast and nudging people awake—cautiously, in Tran, Conli and Sylvie's cases—Siobhan kept a weather eye on Wolf and Rune. Despite standing on guard with each other for three hours last night, they didn't seem to be on better terms. Not that she had expected them to bond or anything, but it would be nice if they stopped eyeing each other like two yard dogs after the same bone.

Breakfast happened without mishap, and Siobhan sat down to write a very carefully worded note to any karl of Silent Order asking for a meeting. Markl actually stepped in and helped her write most of it. He was far better at crafting words than she.

She rolled the letter in on itself and stuffed it into a carrier tube, which she handed over to Fei. Both he and Rune stood just in front of the porch, fully ready to go. Fei took it from her and slipped it into an inside pocket in his jacket before he refastened it.

"I know it's a long way for a day trip," she told them both, feeling uneasy about sending two men into that huge city. "But try to make it back tonight. If I don't hear from you by noon tomorrow, I'm coming in after you."

"We'll be back tonight," Rune assured her. "This won't take long."

She certainly hoped not. "Be safe."

Fei gave her a nod and a casual salute before spinning on his heels and heading off at a ground-eating trot. Rune gave a cheery "Bye!" before following at Fei's heels, a noticeable bounce in his step.

"It's almost like two young boys going out on a fishing trip," she muttered to herself. Where was their sense of danger?

"While we wait, what to do?" Tran asked from the doorway.

"Let's talk to Lirah," Siobhan suggested. "I think we need to make some contingency plans in case I'm making some bad assumptions."

# Chapter Fifteen

Time could, under the wrong circumstances, creep by like an old man with a broken cane.

Siobhan went through the motions, doing everything that she should be doing, but she always had one eye on the sky, marking the sun's position. She spoke with Lirah at length about what they should do if it turned out Iron Dragain really had betrayed them. She helped Conli in changing out the bandages on Lirah's men, which was harder than she expected it to be. Siobhan was no novice when it came to wounds but these were horribly inflicted, and after seeing the damage with her own eyes, she felt it was a miracle direct from the gods that they hadn't lost anyone. Through blood loss, if nothing else.

But when evening came, she ran out of things to do. The injured were cared for, the plans were made, the evening meal cooked and cleaned up. To keep from openly fidgeting, Siobhan fell to Tran and Wolf's habit of sitting on the front porch, her legs dangling over the edge, slowly sharpening both of her swords.

"We're back!" Rune greeted, voice loud and cheerful in this still evening air.

Siobhan jumped so badly that she nearly sliced her thumb off on her own sword. "Rune! Great wind and stars, don't do that! You nearly gave me heart failure!"

The ex-assassin popped his head over the edge of the roof so that he could look down at her. She glared up at him. (And just when had he gotten up there anyway?!) "I thought ya wanted us to come back quickly?"

"Appear *normally*," she scolded. "That's all I'm asking."

"But that's boring, Siobhan-ajie," Fei protested, also sticking his head over the edge of the roof to look down at her.

Siobhan put the swords down so that she could turn and look at them squarely. Just who was corrupting who? "How did it go?"

"Well," Fei assured her. He flipped off the roof in a quick, heels-over-head movement, landing lithely on the ground. "Rune-gui found a karl to speak with almost before we were through the gates."

Rune hopped off the roof as well—minus the extra acrobatics—and explained to her, "That was a bit of good luck, that. Ya don't normally find a karl that quick."

"But he agreed to meet tomorrow, early in the afternoon," Fei continued. "For a fee, he'll tell you what you want to know."

For a fee, eh? Well, she hadn't expected anyone from a dark guild to do something from the goodness of their heart. "Fine. Then early in the morning, we leave for Sateren. Rune, you didn't have any trouble in the city?"

He shook his head. "Not a bit. One thing, though..." he openly hesitated.

"Yes?" she encouraged.

His hand covered the tattoo on his other arm. "This... needs ta be taken off. Ya could see people wonderi'n what I was doing with a good guild."

Fei nodded in grim agreement. "I thought a few people

186

would actually step in, ask what he was doing with me. Ajie, before we go into Iron Dragain, it has to be removed. It was clear to me today that he won't be accepted everywhere, not even if we say he's with us, as long as that mark is on his arm."

Yes, she had been wondering about that. Turning her head, she called into the house, "Conli!"

She heard someone stand up and the heavy tread against the floorboards, but waited until Conli actually appeared in the doorway before speaking. "Rune needs his tattoo removed. Can you do it?"

"Sylvie mentioned this to me," Conli responded, stopping on the edge of the porch to avoid getting his shoeless feet dirty. "I won't know until I look at it. Rune, come closer."

Rune obediently came forward three steps, turning so that Conli had a clear view of the tattoo.

Conli bent and peered at it for a moment. "You said it's been here about ten years?"

"Yes," Rune answered.

"Hmmm, looks that way. It's a simple enough design, not heavy on the ink, so I think a deep scrub will suffice."

Sometimes—most of the time, actually—Conli would say things that wouldn't make an ounce of sense to Siobhan. She sighed in exasperation and requested patiently, "Explain that."

"Tattoos stay on the skin because the ink goes through the first layer and down deep, toward the muscle." Conli lifted both hands and tried to illustrate in the air. "In most cases, like this one, it's a matter of lifting off all the layers of skin and simply scrubbing the ink out of the tissue. This is better than cutting the tattoo free, as it doesn't do as much damage or leave scarring in its wake."

Turning back to Rune, he added, "It also won't take as long to heal. I warn you, the scrubbing will leave you sore and aching for a good week at least. It's not a pain free experience, it's just relatively pain*less*."

Rune shrugged, the amount of pain not fazing him.

"It's fine. I just want ya ta take it off."

"We can do that tonight. It won't take more than an hour or so, I think." Pointing at the porch, Conli directed, "Sit here. I'll fetch what I need."

"Do you need more light?" Siobhan asked his retreating back.

In a slightly muffled voice, he responded, "Please!"

It didn't take more than a few minutes for the preparations to be complete. Siobhan fetched three lanterns, one of which hung from the porch's roof, the other two elevated by some chairs so that Conli had plenty of light to work by. Rune sat on a bench, Conli side-straddling the bench right next to him with an array of tools on another empty chair brought out for that purpose.

Siobhan, having been treated for a skin disease before with a method that sounded suspiciously similar to what Conli planned now, knew how this would feel. In sympathy, she sat on Rune's other side, one of her hands holding his.

Rune kept stealing glances at her, obviously unsure what she was doing.

"Conli will apply this salve to deaden the pain around your arm," she explained to him, knowing what would happen next because of past experience. "But it still feels odd. Uncomfortable, almost. It's tingly and feels like needles are poking underneath your skin. When that happens, it's best to squeeze someone's hand, take the pressure off."

"Geta," he said with a nod of understanding.

Markl, as if appearing by magic, came out of nowhere. "What was that?"

Siobhan turned to give him a wry look. "How is it that whenever someone uses a word not in the Robarge dialects, you can appear out of thin air?"

"It's a gift," he told her mock-seriously. His ever-present leather notebook came out of his side pouch, a small pencil tucked into its pages. "Rune, what did you say?"

"Geta," Rune repeated in bemusement. "Languages ya thing, Markl?"

"I like to study them," Markl explained, eyes lit up in an enthusiastic gleam. "They're fascinating. What does 'geta' mean, exactly?"

Rune paused and thought about it. "Got it, understand, know what ya mean?"

"So basically a way of giving affirmation," Markl noted as he scribbled this down. "Something like the Teheranian *vahh*, perhaps."

Seeing Rune's growing confusion, Siobhan had pity and explained, "Markl is actually a scholar, you see." Rune's look at her said that no, he didn't see anything of the sort. She had to bite back a smile, remembering her own reaction when Markl had introduced himself. "He's traveling around with us learning cultures, languages, and such. He wants to use that knowledge to improve trade relations between the four continents."

"Oh." Rune blinked, turning this over in his mind before he offered a ginger nod. "Not a bad thought, that one."

"I rather thought so." Markl gave them a brief, small smile. "Rune, this word strikes me as being pure Wynngaardal, almost of the old form of the language. Are there any other words like this one?"

Rune lifted one shoulder up into a shrug. "Hard ta think of one if ya ask me all of a sudden. Hmmm."

Fei, sitting somewhere up on the roof and out of Siobhan's line of sight, offered, "The man we met today said something to you."

"Eh? Ahhh." Rune nodded, remembering. "Sameign vi hofuo. De soemd lan risna."

...come again?

He grinned at seeing two blank expressions. "Don't ask me what it means exactly. Couldn't tell ya. But it's what ya say traditionally when ya make a meet with someone important from another guild. It means, roughly, that ya'll only meet with the head of the group and that if they'll pay, ya'll host the meeti'n."

Markl requested, "Say that one more time. Slowly."

Rune obliged, repeating it twice so that Markl was sure he was recording it right, before adding, "The 'soemd' bit is the most important. If ya don't hear that, hightail it out of there. Soemd means they will deal with ya fairly. But if they don't say that, ya should keep a close eye on the wallet."

Siobhan made a mental note of that for the future. Not that she intended to deal with the dark guilds in Wynngaard after this, but one never knew.

Conli interrupted the language lesson by pushing a finger into Rune's shoulder. "Do you feel that?"

"Ya not hurti'n me," Rune assured him.

The older man lifted his eyes to the heavens in a clear bid for patience. "Rune. I realize you're new, so I'm going to explain to you what I've had to explain to every *other* fight-loving idiot in this guild."

Siobhan, knowing what was coming, choked on a laugh.

"Pain is not your friend," Conli said in a tone that brooked no nonsense. "Pain is not a simple byproduct of a fight. Pain is the way your body tells you that something is wrong, something that needs to be fixed. I don't want you to ignore it when your body is in pain. I want you to come to me so that I can help address the issue, whatever that is." Showing that he had been paying attention earlier, Conli asked, "Geta?"

Rune's eyebrows shot up in surprise, but a grin took over his face. "Geta."

"Excellent." Conli shot a look at the hovering Wolf, who was ostensibly polishing his sword and not paying any attention to what everyone else was doing. "If you really do understand me, then you just proved yourself to be more intelligent than Wolf."

Quite a few people started laughing at that. Wolf put his sword down and turned to give the physician a dirty look.

"Ahhh, they picki'n at ya, wolf-dog?" Rune couldn't resist rubbing it in, smile wide in challenge.

"Don't start with me, kiō," Wolf growled at him. "You won't like the result."

Rune's challenging smile didn't falter but his hand suddenly tightened around Siobhan's. She tilted her torso a bit to see around his shoulders and saw that Conli had taken something that looked a great deal like a wire scrub brush and started in on the tattoo.

"Wait, kiō?" Markl interjected. Perhaps fortunately, as it headed off a fight.

"Child, or kid," Wolf translated.

"Although I'm not *that* much younger," Rune added, lip curling at the insult.

"Ten years, give or take." Wolf lifted a shoulder in a nonchalant shrug. "Close enough."

Rune blinked. He'd apparently thought Wolf younger.

What Siobhan wanted to know was, when had they developed nicknames for each other?

Rune's hand on hers tightened to a stranglehold and he let out a slow hiss between clenched teeth.

"Sorry, sorry," Conli apologized, not stopping in what he was doing. "I know it stings, but this will clear out the last of the ink *and* keep it from getting infected. Bear with it a minute more."

"Ahh, *that* stuff," Siobhan said in recognition. Even without Rune's reaction, the sharp smell was enough to tell her what he was using. It was a mixture of Conli's that, as far as she could tell, was almost pure alcohol. "The only time I've ever seen Tran yelp was when Conli poured some of that on an open wound."

"I can see why," Rune gritted out. "It stings a mite."

Siobhan searched for a topic to take his mind off things. "Rune, your hair is actually quite long, huh. Do you like to keep it past your shoulders like that?"

"Eh? Oh, no." He sounded distracted as he responded. "Actually, it's a bit of a pain that long. But I haven't had much time ta get it cut."

"Denney can do that for you after this?" Siobhan offered.

He gave her an amused smile, although it looked strained around the edges. "Ya not offeri'n to do it yerself?"

"You don't want me cutting hair," she assured him dryly. "Trust me."

"She gets it crooked every time," Conli tacked on. "You should have seen what she did to Wolf's hair the last time she tried."

"Took Denney two haircuts to really straighten it out again," Wolf remembered with a grimace.

Denney put her head around the doorframe to say, "I don't mind. How short you want it, Rune?"

"Bit shorter than Markl's, here."

"Oh, that's easy." She paused and really looked at him for a moment. "I saw a man in Quigg that had an interesting hair style...it was shorter on one side, a little longer toward the front. It looked sharp."

Rune asked in an undertone, "Do ya trust her ta play with a man's head?"

"She's never made a hash of it," Siobhan assured him.

Turning his head, he gave her a nod. "Do as ya like, then."

"Oh good." She ducked back inside, her words floating on the air. "Let me find some scissors."

"Well, Rune, you're going to look like a brand new man by tomorrow," Siobhan observed. "Conli, are you going to wrap the arm?"

"To keep it from being infected," Conli responded without looking up. "Alright, Rune, the worst is over. I've got some salve I'm putting on—you like that? Yes, it has a cooling effect. Feels quite good, but it also promotes healing. In three weeks, no one will tell by looking at your arm a tattoo was ever there. But for now, we're going to change that bandage once a day, keep things clean, with lots of this salve on it. Geta? Good man."

Rune finally let go of her hand with a sigh of relief.

She tousled his hair, playfully, before getting up. "He's all yours, Denney!"

"Oh good, a new victim!" Denney caroled back, appearing with a towel, scissors, and a comb.

Rune eyed the two women with growing alarm, although he smiled, as if knowing they were teasing. "Ah... is it too late ta take it back?"

"Yes," Denney informed him seriously.

"Just do a man a favor and leave me my ears?"

Denney cackled like a mad crone.

# Grae Masson

# Chapter Sixteen

While they had been waiting in Vakkiod, Grae had been busy. Siobhan didn't want to travel for hours at a time if they didn't need to, especially with wounded people. In fact, as soon as they were well enough to sit in a wagon, she wanted them out of this village and in a safer place. The question was, where was that mythical place of safety?

Anticipating the need to go into Iron Dragain, she'd directed Grae to build a path to Sateren. If she didn't get the confirmation she expected to, she'd have him build another path toward Quigg from there. Several people in the guild had had nothing but time on their hands, so they'd helped him search for stones. That said, he was building a snowflake pattern, as it was large enough to carry their whole group, and that took 35 stones per stepping stone. According to Grae's calculations, it took 1,400 stones to build a path. And that was only one direction! He'd build another, smaller path near Sateren that would lead back to the village at her request.

In this cold earth, digging up rocks had not been the most pleasant of jobs.

But Grae had finished it, and Siobhan took full advantage of that the next morning so that she didn't have to travel three hours just to reach Sateren. She rose leisurely, had a calm and unhurried breakfast, not in the least bit worried about getting an early start.

From the rafters above her head, Rune cleared his throat. "Ah, ya do remember the meeti'n is at noon?"

"I do," she responded calmly, tugging on her boots. "Worried we'll be late?"

"A mite."

"Don't be. Grae will take us."

"Ah, ya mean by path?"

"Yes."

There was a ruminative silence for a second. "If ya had a path made toward the city, why did Fei and me go the long way?"

"Grae didn't actually finish it until yesterday before dinner," she explained. "You were on your way back by then."

"Ehh."

Siobhan got to her feet and then bent long enough to scoop a cleaning rag off the side of the wash bucket. Without looking, she tossed the rag up toward the rafters. Rune handily caught it. "While you're up there," she informed him dryly, "you might as well put your time to use."

Rune chuckled. "Yes ma'am."

Judging it about time to leave, she went out onto the porch, calling people as she moved. "Wolf, Fei, Grae, you ready?"

"Waiting on you," Grae responded wryly, standing on the road leading out of the village. He did indeed look ready, as he had a flask of water hanging from one shoulder, a book tucked under his other arm. He planned to just sit and wait for them, eh? Well, not a bad thought. If something went wrong, and they needed to retreat in a hurry, she'd prefer to have him standing by.

Wolf and Fei just looked ready for a fight. Well, Wolf always looked ready for a fight, but even Fei seemed to expect trouble of some sort. They both had weapons bristling from every limb. In this northern city, Wolf and Rune would stand out the least, as they clearly hailed from here. Or near here. It would be Siobhan and Fei, with their unusual coloring, who would attract unwanted attention. Maybe she should reconsider having just her twin swords....

As she cleared the door, she felt the floorboards vibrate under Rune's landing. He followed her out without a word.

They all trooped out to the path. In deference to his need for fresh water, Grae had not built his path near the village's front entrance, but at the very back, near a spring that fed into Drahn Lake. Siobhan actually blessed that decision, as it prevented unwanted gawking by the villagers.

Grae took them through the path with only a brief warning to Rune of "Step only where I do" and to the outskirts of Sateren without mishap.

Siobhan stood staring at the front gates of the city with a vague sense of foreboding. Even though this whole thing was her idea, she didn't care for it one bit. "Grae," she murmured for his ears alone, "If we're not out in three hours, send a message to Blackstone and tell them everything."

He gave her an alarmed look. "You expect trouble?"

"Call it woman's intuition."

"Siobhan, your woman's intuition is scarily accurate."

She grimaced. "Don't I know it." Patting him on the shoulder in reassurance, she moved past. "Alright, Rune, lead me."

Her assassin did exactly that, taking the front position and guiding them into the city.

Sateren strongly reminded her of Goldschmidt in some ways. The men guarding the main gate asked her the same questions, and recorded their passing in a very similar fashion. The cramped stores and buildings just inside the gate were the same, all of them offering foods and services that a traveler might be in need of. The din of noise from people going every direction, the overripe smell of too many people living in too small a space, all of it was similar. If not for the tall, sloping roofs and the grey stone everywhere, she might have thought Grae had taken her to the wrong place.

This city had been built centuries ago, when there were still formal governments in the world. According to the briefing Rune had given them last night, parts of the city were so old that no one knew who had actually built them. He'd also assured her that there was so much trade and foreign business here that two more foreigners wouldn't warrant a second glance. Siobhan saw now that he had spoken simple truth. At least a third of the pedestrians on the street were from other continents, and her ears picked up every possible dialect as she passed different groups of people.

The main street connecting to the gate had wall-to-wall people, but Rune didn't stay on it for long. He quickly switched to a side street that had half the traffic, flashing her a smile over his shoulder as he walked. "Less crowded here."

"And I'm thankful for it," she responded with a breath of relief. "At least I can hear myself think now. Will this road take us the right direction?"

"Mostly."

"It's another street over," Fei volunteered from behind her. "We scouted it out yesterday to make sure it was a good place to meet. It's a small shop, like a miniature tavern, and sits on a corner. It gives us two ways out if we need them."

Good to know.

Siobhan kept her eyes peeled, but really, the way that the streets crisscrossed each other at random quickly baffled her. Why did she have the feeling that this place was even more confusing than Quigg?

Rune navigated it with ease, taking them to a quaint little shop that seemed to have been there since the city's founding. It had a fresh coat of paint on it, and someone kept it in good repair, but there was no disguising the age of the building. Siobhan liked the atmosphere of it, though.

They took a seat near the front table, which gave them good line of sight in all directions. Siobhan took a better look around, trying to see more of the place. Fei had described it fairly accurately—it looked exactly like a miniature tavern. It only had eight tables, and one long booth dominating a wall with every possible liquor known to man for sale. Not wanting anyone drunk while trying to meet with a dark guildsman, she ordered salted chips and apple brandy, one of the few non-alcoholic drinks to be had in Wynngaard. Taking their cue from her, everyone else did the same.

"Ya must be the guildmaster."

Siobhan's heart tried to leap into her throat. She had a hand on her sword, halfway out of her chair, on sheer instinct.

"Whoa there, didn't mean ta startle ya." A man with quite possibly the ugliest face she had ever seen came into view as he stepped more fully into the light. Half his right ear was missing, nose misshapen into a blob, with a lazy right eye. His clothes were in good condition, though. Or at least, she assumed they were. It was hard to tell under all the knives. He had a band of them around his waist, two on each arm, and four strapped to each leg. Even in this cool weather, he didn't wear more than a leather vest and simple pants tucked into high boots.

Siobhan put her sword back into its sheath before spreading her hand carefully away from the weapon. "Quite alright. I'm Siobhan Maley, Guildmaster of Deepwoods. You are?"

"Knives, Karl of Silent Order." He gave a brief inclination of the torso to her. "Pleasure. One of these I've met before…" he eyed Fei, then Wolf. "But who are ya?"

"He's Wolf, a guildmember of Deepwoods," Rune introduced.

"Oh, Bloodless. Almost didn't recognize you with short hair." The man smiled, or at least his mouth moved in the semblance of a smile, but there was no emotion reflected in his eyes.

It sent chills going up Siobhan's spine. Rune had looked at her like that, the first day they'd met. He'd slowly thawed toward her over the past few days and now she could see genuine emotion from him. This man… Knives. He didn't feel human at all.

Knives gave Wolf a cautious nod before he took a side-step, head slanting as he studied Rune's shoulder more carefully. The former assassin hadn't put on a shirt this morning either, content to wear his sleeveless vest. (Perhaps they were just that used to the cold?) Knives jerked a chin to indicate the bandage. "What, ya had the tattoo removed?"

Rune just stared back at him, not saying anything.

"Well, well." Knives stroked his chin idly. "I did say, if ya didn't kill the old man in the village, ya could leave the guild for all I cared. Didn't think ya'd do it, though."

Siobhan didn't like where this was going and stepped in, trying to head things off. "Karl, if you wouldn't mind? I have someone waiting on us, you see."

"Oh?" His black eyes were flint hard but he nodded amiably. "Sure, sure. Ya note said, ya want to know who it was that attacked a party coming toward the city? About a week ago?"

"That's right."

"Hmm, well, I looked into it a bit. There was two jobs then, and we took on both. One of them was a caravan comin' from Teherani."

She shook her head, indicating that wasn't the one.

His eyes narrowed slightly. "The other was comin' from Robarge. That one had an odd request to it, it did. We was to rough people up, bad, but not kill."

Siobhan clenched her hand into a fist so tight her nails bit into her skin. So, she'd been right in that regard. "Can you tell me who requested the job?"

"Well, now, it's bad business to talk about clients, ya know."

Rune stepped in closer, body tense as if ready to explode into action at the barest hint of danger. "Knives. Lives depend on her knowi'n."

The two men locked gazes for a long moment. The air became stifling, hard to breathe, under the tension.

"I wasn't really sure it was ya, back when I got the message." Knives cocked his head in a gesture of curiosity that seemed, for once, to be a genuine feeling. "It's more than odd to see ya here like this, and bein' protective of someone else. It looks like ya switched to another guild, Bloodless. Why?"

"She gave me a name," he answered with quiet simplicity.

"Did she now." Knives eyed Siobhan from head to toe and back again. "Well now. That's interestin'."

"A name, Knives," Rune pressed.

"Can't give ya one." Knives shrugged, uncaring. "Don't remember it. But it was a guild from Coravine, that I remember."

Coravine? She blinked. "Coravine, *Orin?*"

"That's the place."

"Ì fregn soemd. Ella jarn eiga hqfdi," Wolf rumbled in a low voice.

Siobhan's Wynngaardal was limited to, "Hello", "Thank you," and "How much is this?" Anything after that went quickly over her head. But even she could hear the unspoken warning in his tone.

Knives held up both hands in a placating gesture. "De soemd lan risna."

Oh? That phrase she recognized. Or at least the word soemd. So he was answering in all honor, eh? She looked first at Rune, then at Wolf, but both men seemed to believe the karl. Phew. "I thank you for the information," she responded politely. "Rune mentioned to me that you have a fee for this information?"

"Rune?" he repeated before his eyes darted to the young assassin. "Ah, ya new name? I see. The fee is twenty kors."

She couldn't quite conceal a wince. That was half the purse Blackstone had given them! But it was her fault for not asking a price and bargaining before spitting out questions. Mentally kicking herself, she pulled her purse out of an inner coat pocket and started counting it out. Halfway through, she paused as a thought struck her. "What if I gave you information in return? Information that might save your life."

Knives held his ground. "It'd have to be good, lady Guildmaster."

"It is. Do you know who you attacked on the highway?"

He weighed her question for a taut moment before slowly shaking his head. "A group of sixteen from Robarge was all we was told."

"It was an escort, actually, for Lirah Darrens." When he gave her a blank look, she elaborated. "The daughter of Blackstone's guildmaster."

The blood just drained from Knives' face. Attacking caravans or old village leaders, that he could do without a qualm. But attacking a large guild was a serious taboo. After all, a guild that influential and powerful could track down any dark guild and raze it to the ground without breaking a sweat. Worse, any good guild of the city would help them do so, because they didn't want a dark guild in their territory to begin with. "...Daughter?" he repeated faintly.

Siobhan gave him a sweet, sympathetic smile. "How about this as a fee? I won't say 'Silent Order attacked your daughter and subordinates' to Guildmaster Darrens. I'll just leave it as 'a dark guild of Sateren.' I'll also make sure to tell him it was a guild from Orin that hired you without telling you any specifics."

Knives gave a jerky nod. "Pl—ahem. Please do." With a

bow to her—an actual bow this time—he spun on his heel and disappeared, no doubt heading straight for his own guildmaster to report this conversation. At least, if he had any wits, that's where he *should* be heading.

Siobhan saw Rune give her a strange look and she quirked a brow at him. "Yes?"

"I get it now. Why they made ya the guildmaster." A smirk broke out over his face. "Ya can be scary when ya have a mind ta."

Wolf snorted. "Kiō, you have no idea. Alright, let's go. This information needs to get back to Lirah, and quick."

# Chapter Seventeen

As they traveled back to Vakkiod via path, Siobhan's head swam with information and questions. What was the endgame? She turned it over and over again in her mind, occasionally shaking it at different angles, but it still didn't add up.

Iron Dragain attacking Lirah's group hadn't made any sense to her. Granted, Siobhan hadn't a good culprit in mind, as attacking the party didn't have any rhyme or reason to it that she could see. But a guild from Orin hadn't even registered as a *possibility*.

Why would a guild from Orin even care what two guilds on different continents were planning?

She had thought that if she just knew who attacked Lirah, then all of the pieces would fall together. So why did she feel that she had simply exchanged one set of questions for another?

As soon as she had her feet back on Vakkiod soil, she went straight to her temporary house, calling, "Sylvie!"

Markl appeared in the doorway. "She's not here. She's

speaking with Lirah."

Perfect. Siobhan reversed directions and went toward Lirah's. She could hear Markl jog to catch up.

"Wait, what did you find out?"

She shot him a quick glance over her shoulder. "I want to only say it once."

She found both women sitting outside, heads close together as they conversed quietly. At her approach, they stopped and looked up.

"Siobhan, what did he say?' Lirah asked, half-dreading the answer.

"You're not going to believe this." She wasn't sure if she fully believed it, although she didn't doubt the veracity of the facts. With hands braced on both hips, she said plainly, "A guild from Coravine, Orin ordered the attack."

She was met with stunned silence.

Heaving a long sigh, she admitted, "That's how I feel about it."

"Who?" Lirah demanded, rising to her feet in a sharp movement.

"That's as much as I know."

"Why?"

"That's as much as I know," she repeated. "Sylvie, I'm waiting for you to make sense of this."

The woman gave a helpless shrug. "I've got nothing."

Siobhan grumbled, "Wrong answer. Lirah? What were you sent to do *exactly*? I can't imagine that assassins would be sent after you over a simple trade agreement."

"There's nothing simple about it," Lirah admitted. "In fact, trade negotiations are to be between Iron Dragain, Blackstone, and Silver Moon."

"My father's involved in this?" Markl demanded incredulously.

Lirah's eyes cut to him. "Oh? Then you are from *the* Hammons? Yes, he was invited to the talks some weeks ago. I understand that Guildmaster Hammon himself is coming."

"You didn't know?" Wolf asked.

"I haven't had any contact with my family in two months at least," Markl explained. He looked disturbed. "I had no idea of any of this. What are the odds that he's already arrived?"

"Quite good," Lirah assured him. "I was actually delayed in leaving."

Would that matter? Siobhan couldn't help but wonder. Silent Order lived in Sateren. They could just keep watchers on the city's walls and attack when their target was within range. It reminded her of an unwary fly entering a spider's web.

Of course, Lirah didn't know the attackers came from Sateren. Siobhan couldn't explain, either, considering the promise she had made.

Well, best not to borrow trouble. Markl's father could well have made it safely to the city without mishap. If she had only known he was mixed in with this, she could have asked Knives. Tch. Why did she always realize *after* the fact what she should have done?

"Lirah, I've a mind to move to Sateren today, if your men are able." Seeing her about to protest, she cut in firmly, "Right now, no one but enemies knows you're alive. So either Iron Dragain thinks Silver Moon has done you in somehow, or Silver Moon suspects Iron Dragain. Either way, it's not a good situation and we best not let it stew."

"Well, I agree with you, but they're not up to a three hour ride in a wagon." She bit her lip in agitation. "Although I suppose I could go alone, leave them here to recuperate and follow later."

The Ahbiren would have a fit if he heard *that* idea.

"What about a trip by path?" Grae pressed. "I finished one yesterday."

From within the depths of the house came a deep, gravelly voice, "Miss Lirah, we have the strength for that."

Lirah glanced back, visibly hesitant.

Wolf, seeing that, ruthlessly added more pressure. "The guild that attacked you was ordered *not* to kill you, to just rough you up. But the situation has changed."

"The true mastermind behind the attack is basically known, so the original plan of framing someone has failed," Lirah finished heavily, shoulders slumped as if the weight of the world rested there. "It's only a matter of time before our nameless enemy realizes this and switches to a new plan, which might not leave us with our lives. That's what you mean, isn't it?"

Siobhan could only nod grimly. "We have a small window to get under cover. Iron Dragain is our nearest refuge."

"Miss Lirah," a female voice from within the house called weakly, "we must go."

Lirah looked off blankly into the distance for some time. With one hand raised in surrender, she capitulated. "Siobhan, send word ahead. Have Iron Dragain guard us as we go into the city."

Not a bad thought, that one. "Will do. Rune, Grae, let's go back."

Wolf made a noise of protest.

"Yes, yes, you can come too." Wolf still didn't trust Rune out of his sight, eh? Or maybe it was the idea of her going into a city with known assassins lurking in the shadows that made him paranoid.

Either way, they all were a little safer in larger groups.

They made the return trip by path and were back in Sateren within minutes. This time, Siobhan tried to mentally rehearse what to say, how to approach explaining all of this to where it would make sense and not take a lot of time. She didn't pay strict attention to where they were going, trusting Rune to lead her there safely.

At least, she didn't pay attention until they ran smack into a tall, imposing gate of black iron that barred their path.

Two tall, very daunting men in black uniform stepped forward, hands on sword hilts, and demanded in near unison, "What business do you have here?"

Siobhan stepped around Rune to answer, "I am Siobhan Maley, Guildmaster of Deepwoods and spokeswoman for Lirah Darrens of Blackstone. I must speak with your guildmaster. NOW."

The guard on her left looked confused by this rattling of names, but the one on the right clearly recognized enough to understand the urgency. His eyes widened and he nodded once before spinning around sharply, calling to the guards on the other side of the gate, "Open the gate! Let them through!"

As the tall gate slowly swung open, Siobhan's eyes caught the crest wrought in the middle. She recognized the dagger with the dragon twined around it very well. Oh. Rune had taken her directly to Iron Dragain's main compound? Well, that was the best option, she supposed.

The guards let her through, one pair splitting off and escorting them across the compound. Siobhan took in the place with glances as she tried to match the quick pace the guards had set. Like every other section of this city, the compound didn't have any spare space. Buildings were crowded against each other, so tightly that a person could barely squeeze in between. Most of them were built of the same grey stone, the roofs black and sloping along the edges before rising to a sharp peak. The whole place reeked of intimidation, which she rather expected out of a Wynngaardian guild.

Also in accordance with Sateren tradition, the paths leading in and around the buildings had more curves and switchbacks than the wrinkles on an old woman's face. Siobhan's sense of direction got lost after the third turn, and she knew without a shadow of a doubt that it would take a guide to get her back to the main gate again.

Oh? This building looked different. And by different, she meant larger. Instead of a small building crowded in, this one sprawled in every direction, rising a full two stories, with a smaller version of an iron gate around it. Guards also stood here, forcing her to repeat herself nearly verbatim. This time, they didn't immediately let her through but called for someone to come.

It took a few minutes, but eventually a middle-aged

man with a dignified bearing and slight limp came down the short staircase and to the gate. Siobhan judged him to be the majordomo just from his attitude alone. Well, the prominent crest on his coat and the high quality of his clothes influenced that snap judgment too.

"I am told that a Guildmaster of Deepwoods seeks audience with Guildmaster Jarnsmor," he said in perfectly flawless Robargean.

"I do." She took a step forward. "I am Siobhan Maley of Deepwoods. I carry a message on behalf of Lirah Darrens of Blackstone."

His brows twitched together either in a gesture of disbelief or interest, she couldn't quite tell which. "Forgive me, but do you have identification on you?"

She pulled out the Deepwoods seal from a pocket and flipped the leather flap open so he could see it.

He verified it with a brief, but thorough scrutiny. "But you say Lirah Darrens? We expected her some time ago but have not seen anyone from Blackstone."

"She was ambushed before she could arrive," Siobhan informed him grimly. "Within sight of *your* city gates, no less."

He blanched at this. "You jest...no, I can see from your expression you do not. She is well?"

"I wish I could say so, but no. Most of her party is heavily injured. Sir, I must speak with your guildmaster as quickly as possible. Lives are at stake here."

"Nortin is my name, Guildmaster Maley. I will take you to him." He nodded to the guards, who quickly unlocked the gates and ushered them through.

Nortin, for a man that had an obvious bad leg, could move like lightning. Siobhan had to once again lengthen her stride in order to keep up. He pushed through the main door and inside of the building without pause, leading them from strong daylight into much dimmer lighting. Siobhan had to blink several times to adjust her vision to this cool interior.

She had the impression of smooth, polished wooden

floors and white stucco walls before Nortin took a sharp left, into a room that branched off the main hallway. Siobhan followed him in only to stop abruptly at the doorway. When Nortin said he would take her to his guildmaster, he hadn't been kidding. This had to be the man's personal study. There were floor to ceiling bookshelves dominating one wall, a massive desk that sat squarely in the middle of the room, and a small gathering of wooden stools around an oblong table that took up the other half of the room. The table had been completely overtaken in paper and maps, with a slightly older man leaning over the surface. He looked up at their entrance, dark brows drawn together in a frown of confusion.

"Nortin? Who's this?"

"Guildmaster Siobhan Maley of Deepwoods, Master Jarnsmor. She comes to speak with you as Lirah Darren's Voice."

Oh, was that the proper way to say it? Siobhan mentally noted that even as she took in Jarnsmor with frank appraisal. So this was the most powerful man of northern Wynngaard, eh? He certainly looked the part. His pepper-grey hair spoke of age, as did the harsh lines around his eyes and mouth, but there was nothing weak about the rest of him. His black eyes were sharp, shoulders broad, and his clothes did nothing to hide the powerful muscles of his arms and thighs. If someone told Siobhan that this man was capable of splitting boulders with brute strength alone, she would believe it.

"Lirah Darrens?" he exclaimed, voice booming out at an almost deafening volume. "Guildmaster Maley, have you an idea of where she is?"

"I know exactly where she is." Siobhan concealed a wince as her abused ears protested. "Sir, there is much that needs to be explained and I will happily do so, but right now I need an escort of your strongest men. Lirah's party was ambushed by assassins and they are gravely hurt. They need refuge."

"They have it," he granted immediately, without a

second's hesitation. "Nortin, arrange a guard of fifty men. Guildmaster Maley, do you judge that to be sufficient?"

She judged that to be overkill but wasn't about to say so. "Thank you, yes."

Nortin gave a short bow before disappearing from the room.

"Where are they?" Jarnsmor pressed, coming around the table to speak with her more directly. "You said ambushed? Where?"

"They are in Vakkiod, and yes, ambushed. In fact, Lirah was within sight of Sateren when they were hit."

Jarnsmor couldn't conceal a wince. "In my own front yard? By who?!"

"I swore not to say their name," she apologized, spreading her palms in a helpless gesture.

Rune, at her shoulder, cleared his throat. "Actually, ya promised not ta tell *Blackstone* who attacked them."

Oh? Come to think of it, he was right. Siobhan gave him an admiring glance. "Rune, you crafty rascal. You're quite right, I did promise them only that, didn't I? In that case...Guildmaster, it was Silent Order that did the attack. In all fairness, however, they were hired to do so and did not know the identity of their victims."

"Silent Order," he hissed between clenched teeth. "Hired or not, they should have known better. Who hired them?"

"Now that's a question I don't have a whole answer to. The only thing that my informant could tell me was that it was a guild from Coravine."

Jarnsmor blinked at her blankly. "Coravine? Coravine, *Orin?*"

"You know, that's exactly what my reaction was." Siobhan rubbed at the bridge of her nose briefly. "It still doesn't make an ounce of sense to me. I hope that once you, and the guildmaster of Silver Moon, put your heads together with Lirah, you can come up with a good explanation. I'd even take a good theory at this point."

He rubbed at his chin in deep contemplation. "Of all

the ideas I entertained, this wasn't among them. How very mysterious. But theorizing can wait, I think, until they are safely here. How many are injured?"

"Thirteen heavily injured, two lightly so," Wolf supplied behind her.

"I'll make preparations."

"Sir, I haven't found a moment yet to send word back to Blackstone reassuring Darrens that we found them," Siobhan offered.

"I'll notify him as well," Jarnsmor promised.

"Also, can you tell me if Guildmaster Hammon has arrived safely?"

"Indeed he has, two weeks ago." Jarnsmor tapped a fist against his lips. "I wonder why he wasn't attacked as well?"

Also a question she wanted an answer to. Siobhan had quite a stack of things that didn't make sense to her at the moment and she didn't like it. "I'm just as grateful he wasn't, sir, as his son is in my guild."

Jarnsmor's brows shot up. "Is he now? Then should I inform Hammon he's coming?"

"It wouldn't hurt." She'd certainly tell Markl his father was safe and sound. "But for now, I'd like to go back to Vakkiod and help Lirah get everyone ready for transport. I have a Pathfinder standing by, ready to bring people here. If you can have your escort wait for us at the path's end? We only need them for escort through the city and to here."

"Certainly. No one can attack while you're on the path, after all."

True. An open path was impenetrable to anyone outside of it. It was one of the benefits of traveling that Siobhan enjoyed. That and skipping over hundreds of spans within minutes.

"Then with your leave, we'll return shortly."

# Chapter Eighteen

It was no mean feat moving all of Lirah's party to Iron Dragain's main compound. Her people were willing, but hurting, and everyone took care to move them as painlessly as possible. Even with dedicated help, it took most of the day to make the trip and get them settled again.

At least they were in better quarters now. Jarnsmor gave them a whole wing of rooms that were right in the main building, each room a near copy of its neighbor. The rooms all had two mid-sized poster beds, a small table and chairs in the center of the room, with a window that looked out over a manicured garden. It had an airiness that the cramped storage room in Vakkiod had not, and Siobhan fancied that a person couldn't help but feel a little better staying in rooms these nice.

Because of her preoccupation with Blackstone's people, Siobhan missed it when Hammon Senior came and found his eldest son. In fact, she hadn't even known the man was in the building until she went into the common room that linked all the rooms together.

Markl, who sat facing her direction, caught her eye and waved her forward. She did so without hesitation, openly studying the man sitting on the couch next to him. Superficially, he didn't look in the least like Markl. His hair was a dark chestnut, skin pale from lack of sun, with a paunch that suggested he preferred sitting at a desk over being out and about. But then he turned to look at her, smiling in greeting, and she saw the similarity. He had the same smile and easy charm as his son.

He rose to his feet at her approach, Markl rising with him and offering the introductions, "Father, this is Siobhan Maley, Guildmaster of Deepwoods. Siobhan, my father, Nuel Hammon, Guildmaster of Silver Moon."

"Exaltations and blessings upon your house, family, and companions," Nuel Hammon greeted, extending a hand.

She blinked, not expecting this highly formal greeting, but managed to accept the hand with a firm grip and reply in kind, "Exaltations and joy to you and yours."

Judging from that slightly startled look from Hammon, he hadn't expected her to know the proper way to respond, but was pleased by it. Why he thought that, she had no idea. Anyone spending any amount of time around Markl would pick up on all the niceties eventually. She'd never met a more polite man. "Thank you. Forgive my surprise, Guildmaster Maley. I have heard of you and your reputation is excellent, but I had not thought you to be so young."

Siobhan couldn't help but laugh ruefully. "I was made guildmaster at a ridiculously early age. I am relieved to see that you arrived here without trouble, sir."

"I'm just as glad to *be* here without being attacked, although I am very sorry that Lirah Darrens' party was not as fortunate. Markl has told me what you have discovered and I have some theories regarding the matter."

She cocked her head slightly. "I would certainly like to hear them. My mind has twisted itself into knots trying to make sense of this."

He waved her to a nearby chair, silently inviting her to make herself comfortable. After the day she'd had, he didn't have to twist her arm. She promptly settled herself into a wing backed chair that faced the couch.

The common room had been designed to either conduct business meetings in or for socializing. It had a variety of chairs, couches, and settees that were arranged in small circles so that people could comfortably sit and converse. It had no windows here, as it sat in the middle of the building, but someone had installed skylights in the ceiling which cast enough natural light for the room to naturally glow. One spot of sunlight hit the chair she sat in and warmed it up quite pleasantly. She unconsciously smiled as the warmth settled along her back.

As soon as she'd settled, Hammon relaxed back into his own seat, legs comfortably crossed and hands resting on his stomach. "Markl tells me that you're aware of the purpose of Silver Moon, Blackstone and Iron Dragain all meeting?"

"To form a trade monopoly," she responded bluntly.

"Quite so." A brief smile darted over his face. "We'd hoped that by doing so we could afford to expand and raise the levels of the bridges, as I'm afraid that if we don't start fixing them *now,* they'll become nigh unusable in fifty years."

He might very well be right. It took luck, timing, and speed to cross the bridges now, and the larger caravans had to do it in stages in order to clear them before the tides rose to a dangerous level. If something wasn't done about them soon, it would be impossible to cross the bridges quickly enough, and they'd have to abandon them altogether and start shipping everything by sea. Just the idea made her wince. "So, the monopoly was in fact proposed to finance the project."

He spread his hands in a helpless shrug. "We couldn't come up with another viable option. No one guild has the means to do such a thing, and it's dangerous for just one guild to be in charge of the project to begin with. It would encourage a sense of...ownership, I'm afraid. And if they feel that they own the bridge, all sorts of trouble will eventually arise from it."

Like levies and taxes that no one would be willing to pay but would be willing to fight about. Yes, didn't that picture just give her a headache. "I see your point."

"We'd thought that with three of us, we'd have the means to fix the bridges, and no one guild would be responsible for it, so it would avoid trouble. Of course, many are going to be unhappy about our creating a monopoly on select trade goods in order to manage this... but we've only so many resources to draw upon. In order to make this happen, *something* needs to be sacrificed."

She lifted a hand and rubbed at one temple. "Someone in Coravine disagrees with you, sir."

He grimaced. "And more vehemently than I predicted, too. We knew that people would be unhappy with what we did here, at least in the beginning, but to actually send *assassins*? That was completely outside of our predictions."

"Fallen Ward is the guild over Coravine. Do you believe them to be behind this?"

"I can't imagine that an attack of this significance was planned and executed without their knowledge. Were they the ones behind it? I don't know. I wouldn't think them this foolhardy, to attack Blackstone openly like this, but then I didn't imagine that anyone would send assassins period."

Markl cleared his throat slightly. "We believe that their plan was made so that we would never know their identity. It was meant to frame either Iron Dragain or Silver Moon for the attack so that we would never suspect anyone else."

"If not for the fact that I stumbled across a man who used to work for Silent Order, and he brought me to an informant of that guild, we might not have put it all together," Siobhan added. "If you think about it, that was an amazingly fortunate stroke of luck that I was able to pull it off. In normal circumstances, I'd never have been able to manage that in a foreign city. Of course, Iron Dragain would have been able to find the same information..."

"But under the circumstances, with them being the suspects, if they'd come to us and said that it was a guild from Orin that had ordered the attack, we'd never have believed them," Markl finished grimly. "It's only because you were the one that discovered it that everyone can believe it."

"So really, their original plan had a very high success rate," she concluded, lifting her shoulders in a shrug. "We're fortunate that things happened as they did, although it sounds callous to say so."

"Indeed, but I understand what you mean. The thing that bothers me in all of this is their response to the proposed monopoly. I expected them to react, yes, because Orin has always struggled financially. Their location and lack of specialized products have cost them dearly when it comes to economic growth. But *attacking* a guild that has a direct impact on their markets is nigh akin to financial suicide. Blackstone alone has the power to shut down a third of the market in Orin. In fact, if Darrens doesn't do just that after hearing what happened to his daughter, I'll be highly surprised."

Siobhan knew with grim certainty that Darrens would likely do just that. He was a fair man in many respects, but he was a ruthless one and everyone understood that crossing him would cost you dearly. The nameless guild of Orin was a fool to attack Lirah.

"I can't imagine that they wouldn't know what the consequences would be," Markl stated slowly, perplexed. "No matter how high your rate of success is likely to be, isn't it foolhardy to not expect repercussions?"

"And that's what is bothering me," his father agreed, mouth pursed. "In their shoes, I wouldn't be trying to end the monopoly, I'd be fighting to *join* it. For them, this is a golden opportunity that comes along once in a lifetime.

Or once in every several lifetimes. They need a boost of some sort to help their economy, and this trade agreement would have been the perfect stimulus. So why try to sabotage it?"

Siobhan stared at him in stunned silence for a moment. She hadn't even considered that, but he was right. Why wouldn't Orin try to join in? As much as the agreement would have hurt them, it would have done worlds of good, too, if they'd been a part of it. "Were they panicking? Unable to think clearly?"

"Perhaps," Hammon allowed, although his tone said he didn't think that was the case. "But I'm inclined to think that there is something else, some other part of this puzzle that we are not seeing. I believe that Coravine is up to something, something that they've kept from the eyes of the world, that would influence them to attack first instead of bargaining."

"What?" Markl demanded.

"I have no idea," Hammon admitted. "But it is imperative that we find out, and soon, otherwise I think this whole situation will quickly degenerate."

That wasn't the end of the conversation, and with Lirah's people settled, her own guild came and joined them in the common room. But as much as they discussed, and offered theories, none of them felt they had really arrived at an answer. After dinner, they unanimously went to bed rather than pick up the debate again.

Siobhan's guild had been given a set of rooms that was near Blackstone's, theirs being on the opposite end of the common room. Her own room, shared with Sylvie, was a mirror image of every other room in this wing. She couldn't seem to relax in it, as nice as it was, but instead found herself tossing and turning in the bed.

Giving up, she threw back the covers and retreated to

the miniature garden that she could see from her window.

No one else was awake, and nothing stirred. She sat on the edge of the porch, in nothing but loose pants and an oversized shirt, letting her bare feet dangle in the shallow fish pond. The cool water felt good to her aching feet. She'd been on them most of the day and her body told her in detail about how it didn't appreciate that.

As tired as she was physically, her mind wouldn't let her rest and insisted on going over everything said today. She'd hoped that the stillness of this moonlit garden would soothe her and her thoughts would settle, but after sitting here for several minutes, that wish proved to be in vain.

Something didn't feel right about this.

Siobhan couldn't quite put her finger on it, but she was missing something. Something vital, at that. The reasons and theories of this afternoon made sense, certainly, but she felt that there should be something more to this. Something...with a deeper significance that would drive a guild to such desperate lengths. And it *was* desperate— picking a fight with *three* of the major guilds on two continents that could directly affect trade with all of Orin couldn't be described as anything else. In fact, Siobhan labeled it as the plan of a madman.

But what? What could possibly be so important that it would justify hiring assassins and making enemies of major guilds?

The hallway door softly opened and closed behind her, Wolf's familiar heavy tread making the floorboards vibrate slightly. With a muted grunt, he sat down with legs on either side of her, then put both arms around her waist, chin resting on top of her head.

Despite her heavy thoughts, she couldn't help but smile. He only did this when he was certain no one was watching, as if embarrassed to be caught doing anything so sentimental, but she loved it when he did. Siobhan felt the weight of her duties very strongly. She had from the very first day of being guildmaster. Sometimes, like now, the weight became almost crushing. Her decisions, good or bad, directly influenced the lives around her. A careless or poorly thought-out command could cost her a friend. Thinking like this made her job hard to bear sometimes.

But whenever she hit a low point, Wolf always seemed to appear in that moment, and he would wrap her up in his arms like this. For just a few selfish moments, she leaned against his strength and let him support her completely. Siobhan let her eyes fall closed as she entrusted her body weight to him. She took in a deep breath, letting the scent of him fill her head, mixed in with the cool night air. Then she took another, and when she opened her eyes, she felt strong enough to face the world again.

"Something's not adding up," Wolf murmured to her lowly. "It's troubling you."

"And you," she acknowledged. "If trade monopolies were really what scared them into action, then why do it this way? It doesn't make sense. I mean, even if the plan succeeded, it would only be short term. In the long run, Blackstone and Iron Dragain would have figured out the truth. When they did, Orin would be in an even worse situation, as I can't imagine that either guild wouldn't exact revenge."

He grunted agreement. "Delaying tactics, that's what this feels like to me."

She couldn't help but think the same. "But delaying for *what?*"

"Wish I knew. This I can tell you—it has to be strong enough, somehow, to turn the tides. Orin has to think it'll give 'em an upper hand so no other guild can harm 'em."

Yes, it was that unquantified potential for power that made the marrow in her bones tremble. She cuddled in a little harder and tried not to think about it.

"Siobhan, I have to ask, what do you intend to do with Rune?"

She blinked at this question, coming from nowhere. "Do with him? Am I supposed to do something with him?"

Wolf let out a gusty sigh. "You really adopted an assassin without thinking it through? He has bad habits, dangerous habits, y'know. His first instinct will be to ignore trouble as long as it won't have anything to do with him. His second instinct will be to kill anything that *does* trouble him."

"That's—" she closed her mouth on the instinctive denial and frowned when she realized he was right. In fact, that was exactly how Wolf had been at first. Oh, not with her, but he owed her a huge debt for buying him out of a terrible life. He'd felt duty-bound to protect her, at the very least. But Rune...how did Rune perceive her? "Is that why you don't trust him? You think he'll cause trouble?"

"And that," he rumbled darkly. "You don't see it, because he acts differently around you, but the *only* person that boy responds to in this guild is you. He ignores everyone else."

"Because I named him?" she hazarded.

"And you fed him. And bargained for his freedom. He has little idea how to respond to kindness, and only reacts to what we do for him out of bewildered obligation." Wolf let out another sigh, this one longer than the first. "He's the type to do things to please others without any true emotion behind it. I don't trust a man like that."

Ohhh. So he *did* have a concrete reason to distrust Rune. True, Siobhan had noticed that as well. If she suggested something, Rune did it without hesitation or complaint. Even when cutting his hair he hadn't done more than be sure she wanted it done. This willingness to blindly obey her had disturbed her, but Wolf had been the same at first, afraid of upsetting her. She'd hoped that with time and patience, Rune would work his way through it.

But if he was only responding that way in her presence and ignoring the rest of the guild...that was not a good sign. Not at all.

"Keep an eye on him," she requested slowly. "Interfere if you see his old habits kicking in."

"I will, but the question still stands: what do you intend to do with him?"

Siobhan rubbed at the bridge of her nose with one hand, feeling a headache coming on. "I wish I knew."

# Chapter Nineteen

Siobhan barely had her boots on when there came a quick rap on the door. Without waiting for a response, Conli stuck his head inside the room. "Siobhan, I need to borrow Rune."

"Good morning to you as well, Conli," she responded mock-genially. "I slept well, thank you for asking."

He shoved the door aside impatiently, toe tapping. "I don't have time for pleasantries, Siobhan. They don't have the necessary medical supplies here for me to properly treat people. I used up the last of my supply last night. I need to go shopping in the city, expeditiously, and I need a guide to do it."

"Hence why you want Rune," she finished, setting aside her teasing. "But why ask my permission? Go get him yourself."

Conli was shaking his head before she finished speaking. "That boy doesn't want to move unless he knows *you* ordered it done. I'm not about to start an argument with him about it. It's easier if you just tell him yourself."

Again. Again someone had told her that Rune only followed what she said. Siobhan's forehead crinkled into a disturbed frown. She needed to do something about this, somehow break this distance that Rune was keeping from the guild, or trouble would certainly follow. As she had no business to attend to, it would behoove her to start working on that problem today.

"Fine. I'll track down Rune. You go fetch Sylvie."

With a thankful nod, he turned and disappeared into the hallway.

Still frowning, she laced up her boots and grabbed her jacket before heading out of the bedroom. As she went, she called out in arbitrary directions, "Rune! Rune?"

Sure enough, just as she turned a corner, he appeared from seemingly thin air. He asked no questions, just looked at her steadily, as if awaiting orders.

Oh yes. This needed to be fixed.

"Conli needs to go shopping for medical supplies," she informed him. "He requests that you guide him through the city."

"Sure, sure," he responded with a lackadaisical shrug.

Taking him in from head to toe, she belatedly realized that he was dressed in the mismatched clothes that Beirly had scrounged for him. "Actually, while we're out, do you want to shop for you? Those clothes don't really fit right."

He glanced down at himself. "That's fine."

Not that she expected him to disagree about that, but... if the clothes really had bothered him, wouldn't he have already fixed the situation himself? He knew this city and where to go to shop, after all. Again, the impression that he was just doing whatever she wished. Suppressing a sigh, she waved her hand, gesturing for him to follow her.

They all met at the main entrance to Iron Dragain's compound. To Siobhan's surprise, it wasn't just Conli and Sylvie waiting on them, but Denney and Wolf as well. Well, no, she should have expected the other two to show up. If Conli went out, Denney normally went with him. Those two were nigh inseparable. And Wolf, after hearing that she and Conli would be going out alone with Rune, likely panicked at the thought and joined to keep an eye on the assassin.

Not caring about the extra additions to the party—they could all do as they wished, after all—she waved Rune to lead them. He did so without a word, taking them to the main street and immediately to the left, into a section of the city that she had never been to before.

Wolf fell into step beside her, and as he did, gave a significant look at the back of Rune's head. She nodded grim agreement, indicating that she finally understood what he had meant last night.

The party was unusually subdued as they wound their way through the morning crowd and into the market. Siobhan quickly found that the only way to press through the throng was to hide behind Wolf, as he made a marvelous trailblazer. She glanced back and found that Sylvie and Denney were using Conli to the same purpose. Part of the trouble came from the narrow, winding street they were on—with the kiosks, street stalls, and such, the path became significantly smaller. People were crushed together and walking at a shuffle, trying to force their way through.

"Rune!" she called around Wolf's arm. "Do we have to go this way?"

"Only medicine stalls are farther down this way," he explained, voice barely loud enough to carry over the din. "Gets less crowded in a bit."

So if they could survive long enough, they'd be able to escape? She clung to that thought and stayed at Wolf's back as much as possible.

Rune's words became nearly prophetic, as moments later they crossed an intersection and the traffic abruptly thinned out. She went from being nearly pressed like a grape in a wine press to having more than enough room to dance in the street if she felt like it. Heaving out a breath of relief, she came around to walk at Wolf's side.

Conli stepped around her, stretching his legs to a fast

walk. "Rune, I need a variety of herbs, ointments, and bandages. Where should I go?"

Rune pointed to a row of shops ahead and to the right of the street. "There."

With a nod of thanks, he went ahead of the group and ducked into a shop that had clearly not seen a fresh coat of paint in well over three decades. Siobhan took one look at the dark, confining interior of the place and decided she'd wait outside. Denney, Wolf and Sylvie all must have come to the same conclusion, as no one braved the doorway.

"Sylvie," Siobhan waited until the woman turned to face her, "I think while we're out, we should find Rune some better fitting clothes. He needs more than what he has on anyway."

"That's fine." Sylvie lifted her shoulder in a shrug, not troubled by the idea of more shopping. "Rune, what's your preference?"

He gave her the blankest expression Siobhan had ever seen from him. "Preference?"

"What kind of clothes do you like to wear?" Sylvie explained patiently. "Things like what Wolf wears? Or more of the traditional Wynngaardian style that we've seen here in the city? I know you are wearing these clothes because it was the only thing that Beirly could find that would mostly fit you. So what do you choose to wear?"

Rune seemed nonplussed and not sure how to answer this, which Siobhan found somewhat strange. Did he not pay attention to his wardrobe at all?

"Close-fitti'n clothes," he finally answered. "Not heavy material, but flexible."

In other words, good clothes to skulk in. She should have guessed.

Sylvie seemed to realize that was the best answer she was going to get, so smiled and pointed back the way they had come. "Then while Conli is shopping, why don't we go back to that store on the corner? I saw some things displayed outside that might work on you."

Rune looked to Siobhan for permission, which she

gave, urging him silently to go with her. Wolf, unsettled by the idea of Sylvie going off alone with Rune, took an instinctive step to follow before glancing back at Siobhan and Denney. Then he stopped dead, clearly torn between which group he should be protecting.

True, leaving Denney alone outside the shop with Siobhan was likely not a good choice. They were still in Wynngaard, after all. To make it easier on her enforcer, Siobhan stuck her head into the store and called to Conli, "We'll be at the clothing store on the corner!"

"Fine!" Conli called back from some dingy recess in the back.

He likely wouldn't miss them for a good hour anyway, not with that shopping list of supplies.

That sorted, she led the other two and caught up with Sylvie and Rune just as they entered the clothing store. In terms of lighting and such, this store was in much better condition. It contained every variety of clothing imaginable crammed inside, with shirts and pants in a wide range of sizes hung up on nails all the way to the ceiling. Dresses, skirts, and traditional women's clothing were in the back of the store, while men's clothing took up the front.

Siobhan belatedly realized that quite a bit of gear had been lost or damaged in Lirah's party during their mad escape from the assassins who'd attacked them. She'd been so focused on getting them to a safe place that she hadn't really thought about that until just now. "Denney, help me pick out some shirts and pants that might fit our Blackstone group," she requested. "I don't think they have much left after everything that happened."

"Oh!" Denney said, snapping her fingers. "That's a good thought. I'm not sure of everyone's sizes, though."

"They'll need looser clothing to cover the bandages and splints anyway," Sylvie called over her shoulder, already arm-deep in a stack of shirts. "Just guess and then go a little bigger."

"Sound advice," Siobhan approved. "Wolf, you wear a

thirty-two or so in shirts?"

"About that," he agreed.

"Isn't Luvaas about your size?"

"A mite smaller, more like Conli's size."

"Conli is a thirty," Denney offered. "Well, he's actually a twenty-nine, but he prefers a looser fit."

"Then let's get a thirty for Luvaas."

Siobhan lost track of time as they browsed and picked up shirts, sweaters, and pants, discussing and guessing what size people wore. At some point, Wolf started taking things out of her hands and carrying them to the counter, where the woman there started folding and figuring up the total so that the girls weren't forced to carry the whole lot of it around and start a clothing avalanche.

Denney paused in her browsing and looked up through the store window. "There's Conli. Uh-oh."

"Uh-oh?" Siobhan repeated, looking up to see what the trouble was.

Conli was tottering their direction with arms overflowing in packages, bundles, and bags. It seemed only a matter of seconds before something would slip and fall to the street.

"Denney, go rescue him," Siobhan urged. Her words were unnecessary, as the young woman was already moving, heading quickly out the door at a half-lope, the fastest pace she could manage through the crowd outside.

But her progress abruptly stopped when two men grabbed her by the arm, dragging her to a halt. Siobhan recognized the situation for what it was within a heartbeat. Once again, because of Denney's obviously half-Teheranian heritage, she'd been mistaken as a prostitute. Siobhan waited three seconds, just to see if Denney could reason her way out of it. But the cheap flasks in the men's hands were half-consumed and they were obviously too drunk to understand 'no.'

Growling under her breath, she looked back toward the counter. "Wolf. Denney."

Wolf pushed forward, an angry tic in his jaw. "What,

again?"

"Conli's in no position to help her, either. His hands are full." She almost said, 'go help her,' when she caught sight of Rune's face. The assassin hadn't even looked up at their exchange, but was examining the shirt Sylvie had pressed into his hands. His complete disinterest in what was happening disturbed her. Wolf hadn't exaggerated the matter—if trouble arose, and it didn't affect Rune, he truly wouldn't respond.

Making a snap decision, she ordered, "Rune. Go help Denney."

With nothing more than a glance to show that he had heard her, he passed the shirt back to Sylvie before leaving the store in a quick stride.

Wolf came in close and murmured, "Is that a good idea?"

"I've got to get him in the habit of thinking of the guild as *his* guild," she muttered back. "Otherwise trouble is going to arise. But go after him and step in if things get out of hand."

"Right." Wolf lengthened his stride and left the store in little more than a blink of an eye.

Siobhan, worried that things might go from bad to worse, followed after him but couldn't quite keep up as the crowd outside blocked her. She had to use her elbows and sheer brute force to carve a path toward Denney.

Because of that, she missed what happened when Rune first reached Denney. All she knew was that the crowd abruptly shied away from the middle of the street, scattering all directions, and left her a clear view. Wolf had Rune by the arm, his iron right hand blocking the assassin completely from what appeared to be a lethal strike toward one of the drunks. Denney was on her knees, arms over her head, although she was peeking upward. The drunks were flat on their backs nearby, hands also held protectively over their heads, their eyes squeezed tight in fear.

What by the four winds...?!

"Easy, kiō," Wolf rumbled, his stance as solid as a mountain. "Don't kill the poor blighters."

Rune's head cocked in puzzlement as he looked up at Wolf. "Isn't that what she wanted me to do?"

"No," Wolf denied patiently. "We don't kill people unless we absolutely have to. Breaking bones is one thing, ending lives another."

Rune slowly extracted his hands, which Wolf allowed without fuss. Seeing her nearby, Rune gave her that same puzzled, uncomprehending frown. "Didn't you send me out here to take care of the situation?"

Siobhan resisted the urge to go find a flat, hard surface and start banging her head against it. Taking in a deep breath, she tried to find the right words to explain. "Rune, I said *help*. I meant, go protect Denney and discourage the lack-heads from flirting with her. They're drunk and mistaken about her profession. That's not a crime worth losing their lives over."

Said drunks were nodding vigorously in avid support of this.

She could just tell by Rune's expression that he still didn't get it. Was his training really that deeply ingrained, or was she just not explaining it right? Giving up for the moment, she ducked around the men and offered a hand up to Denney.

Conli beat her there, hands frantically checking for any injuries even as he demanded, "Are you alright? I couldn't see what happened, did these men hurt you before Wolf got here?"

"I'm fine," Denney assured her uncle, then Siobhan. "Fine. Rune hit those two hard and fast, and I lost my balance too, I was so surprised. But I'm fine. Conli, your packages? Where are they?"

"I dropped them all," he admitted. Peeking over his shoulder, he said morosely, "I think some of them broke. I heard glass cracking."

Oh joy of wonders. That meant he'd have to go *back* to the store to replace things. This was turning into quite the shopping trip. Blowing out her breath, Siobhan started pointing fingers at people. "Wolf, you and Rune go finish the shopping with Sylvie. Then meet us at the herbal store. Conli, Denney, let's wrap this up and get back to Iron Dragain."

The faster they left this potential hotbed of trouble, the better.

Siobhan's punishment for adopting an assassin without thinking it through was having to *deal* with said assassin and his bad habits. After returning to Iron Dragain the day before, she'd done her best to explain the do's and don'ts when helping someone out of a sticky situation. She'd also tried to explain that she hadn't taken Rune away from Vakkiod because she'd wanted an assassin at her beck and call. Rune had assured her he understood, and that he wouldn't kill people unless necessary, but he'd still looked confused at the end of the conversation.

She could only hope that he would figure it out on his own, as she didn't know how else to explain.

A full day had passed since their disastrous shopping trip and her worries were only growing. Siobhan had mistakenly believed that if she could just find Lirah and her missing escort, then all would be well. But in truth, their rescue carried a great many troubles with it. Rune just complicated matters more.

She sat outside and looked up at the half moon overhead, her toes just grazing the tip of the pond water. It felt ice cold to her skin, but strangely pleasant, probably because she'd once again been on her feet all day.

A door opened and closed behind her. She smiled as she recognized the heavy tread and greeted without turning her head, "Evening, Wolf."

"Evening." He sank down to sit beside her, making the

wood of the porch creak under his weight. "You out here thinking again?"

"Yes." Blowing out a gusty sigh, she whined, "What do I do with Rune?"

"Ah, finally see the trouble that boy brings, eh?" Wolf responded in a distinctly unsympathetic tone.

"*You* never went around randomly trying to kill people," she responded indignantly, trying to justify herself.

"*I* was never an assassin, I was a mercenary," he refuted calmly. "There's a difference."

Yes, apparently quite a difference. She started grumbling under her breath, unable to argue the point.

"It might get worse."

She looked at him from the corner of her eye. "Why?"

"He's disappearing during the day."

"What?!"

"He did it yesterday, after he saw us back to the compound, and again this morning." Wolf rubbed a palm against his jaw, making a rasping sound against his night stubble. "I don't know if he's trying to get back into his old guild or not. It might be that he's just not comfortable here, in his old enemy's headquarters."

She let her head thunk against his shoulder. "Great. Wonderful. Now what do I do?"

"Nothing you can do. You can't control a man's heart, Siobhan."

That was less than comforting.

"But I think you're more worried about other things, and less about Rune." He cocked his head as he looked down at her. "You're wondering why Lirah's group was attacked, aren't you?"

She nodded in grim agreement. "There's too many holes in her story, too many things that don't make sense. It's like I'm staring at a puzzle with half the pieces missing."

"It's not our job to solve the puzzle," he pointed out. "Our job ended when we found Lirah. It's just because you're worried about them that we're staying on and letting Conli treat everyone."

"Well, yes, I know...."

"But?" he prompted, knowing well there was a 'but' coming.

"But it doesn't sit right with me to just let the mystery hang like this. I don't see anyone stepping forward and trying to solve it, either."

Wolf slipped an arm around her shoulder and hugged her into him. "I know you don't like things left loose like this, unexplained, but we'll be walking into trouble if you try to sort this one out."

"I think we'll be in more trouble if we *don't* figure it out. My instincts say that, anyway." Siobhan sat there, weighing out options for a long moment, but in reality she knew what they needed to do. "Erik."

Wolf jerked his head down to look at her, eyes wide in surprise. She'd only ever called his true name a handful of times in the past ten years.

She looked up at him with firm resolve. "We shouldn't sit here. Lirah might not be able to move, but we can, and we should. We need to go to Coravine and investigate, find out what they're up to. Otherwise we won't know how to prepare for the storm that's coming."

He nodded solemnly. "Eh, I agree. It's folly to sit here. But you think this small guild is strong enough to go there alone?"

"I don't know. I don't think we'll face trouble just by traveling there, though. We're not directly connected to either Iron Dragain or Silver Moon. We're small enough in number that it won't look odd for us to travel toward Orin. And if we need a cover story," she realized, bemused and amused, "We've got one on hand. Markl will be our stand-in client."

"Ah?" His head canted as he thought about it, before he shrugged ruefully. "It's not even a lie, quite. Heh. I like it. We can even stay for several days on the excuse that he's studying things. Right, well. Leave in the morning?"

Siobhan wanted to, but life wasn't quite that convenient. "We'll need to find a boat first. And make preparations. We'll be lucky to get out of here the day after tomorrow."

"Well, might not take as long, if we ask Jarnsmor for a ship," he pointed out.

True, that. Although it would still take them three or four hours by ship to cross the Dual Channel to reach Orin. Never before had Siobhan regretted the limits of Pathmaking like she did now. Why, why wouldn't it work over water? The fact that it was restrained to land—and only fertile land, to boot—drove her mad some days. "I'll ask him first thing in the morning."

"Ya won't be able ta if ya don't sleep now," Rune's voice laconically pointed out from...somewhere above them.

Siobhan jumped—now when had he gotten into the rafters again?—but Wolf nearly leaped out of his skin. He scrambled to his feet like a guilty teenager caught kissing his girlfriend, and even in this dim lighting it was easy to see the vivid blush on his cheeks.

Rune laughed outright from the safety of his hiding place, amused at Wolf's reaction. The laughter helped her pinpoint his position better. He'd found some sort of crawl space between the roof and the ceiling, apparently, as he had to be almost directly above her head.

Seeing the murderous look that Wolf aimed at the ceiling, not to mention the way his hands twitched as if hungering for a weapon, Siobhan put a constraining hand on his shoulder. "You can't kill him."

He shot her a look that said, *Want to bet?*

"It's one of those unwritten rules about being a guest," she explained mock-somberly. "You're not supposed to kill people in someone else's home."

Rune cracked up laughing again.

"Just maim him a little bit, alright?"

Wolf gave her a predatory smile. "Define 'a little.'"

The ex-assassin's nerves broke, and with a yelp, he

quickly scrambled out of the area.

She looked in the direction he'd retreated, even though she couldn't see through the wood. "Apparently he didn't realize I was kidding."

"Apparently he realized I wasn't," Wolf growled, a wicked gleam in his eyes. With a gentle pat on her head, he wished her a good night before stalking back into the building.

Siobhan watched him go and said under her breath, "Run, Rune, run."

Conli
Rorona

# Chapter Twenty

Siobhan preferred not to make major decisions that affected the whole guild without discussing it with them first. After her conversation with Wolf the night before, she felt that this was one of those times where she needed to hear everyone's opinions. So she called for a general meeting of the guild before breakfast. They retreated to the common room, the only space that could hold all of them and had enough privacy where they could talk without interruption.

Everyone found a place on either the couches or chairs. Denney chose the floor next to Conli's feet, where the dogs could curl in next to her. Rune was in the farthest chair, not directly facing the group, although the way he had his ear cocked in her direction made her think he was at least listening in.

Once they'd settled, she drew in a breath and began. "Alright. We have a decision in front of us. Our original job is complete—we found Lirah and her people, we've notified Blackstone where they are, and she's got the protection she needs to make it safely back home again. For all intents and purposes, we're done."

"I hear a 'but' in that somewhere." Grae sat forward, eyes studying her carefully. "Is there something else going on, Shi?"

She nodded somberly. "Grae, I don't feel right walking away at this point. There's too many unanswered questions. Why this elaborate setup? Why would a guild from Orin attack Blackstone? What is so important that a game should be played at high stakes, using people's lives as the chips?"

"It's bothering me, too," Sylvie admitted with a troubled sigh.

"You want us to investigate," Fei said neutrally.

"Can you think of someone better to send?" Siobhan asked him while spreading her palms. "We intimately know the ins and outs of the situation, better than anyone in Iron Dragain does. No one from Blackstone is fit to leave and look into it. We have two natives of Orin right in this room that would be able to find out more information than an outsider asking."

"Just as vital, we need to know." Hammon had open approval on his face. "If this—whatever this is—can hurt Blackstone guildsmen this far from home, what is to prevent it from happening again in Goldschmidt itself?"

That was another worry that had occurred to her last night. "Exactly."

"I personally don't like the idea of having an unknown enemy," Wolf added darkly.

"As much as I hate to agree with him," Tran grumbled, "I feel the same way."

"Any objections?"

"Have you talked about this to Jarnsmor or Lirah?" Beirly asked her. "Guildmasters are a touchy bunch. They don't like people going off and doing things without their knowing."

"I plan to ask them next," she assured him. "I just didn't want to go talk to them about it without hearing your opinions first. After all, this delays us going home by days, weeks, I have no way of knowing."

"I don't think that really bothers anyone." Beirly looked around the group.

Siobhan did the same, reading their expressions. Sylvie didn't look particularly happy to be going to Orin, but she never did. Her parents usually gave her trouble when she was within arm's reach of them. Denney, Conli, and Grae seemed ambivalent with the idea. They felt the need to go and get answers and didn't particularly mind if that delayed their departure home for a few weeks. Her enforcers were already gearing up for potential trouble, and, judging by that smile, Wolf looked forward to it.

Only Rune didn't seem to care or have an opinion. He still didn't face their direction, but only sat there because she'd called him into the room. Well, he was a problem she'd have to sort out later.

Siobhan blew out a breath that she hadn't realized she was holding. "I think we have a general consensus here. You realize we'll be walking into unknown danger?"

"I think I prefer that over keeping an eye on our backs for the next several months." Denney raised a hand. "All in favor of going to Orin?"

Every hand went up into the air, almost without any hesitation.

She felt relieved at their willingness but also strangely tense, as she realized that she had taken on another set of problems and responsibilities as her own. Walking into unknown danger hadn't been an exaggeration. But she truly felt that she didn't have any other choice. "Well then. I'll go find Jarnsmor and see if I can convince him."

Jarnsmor, as expected of a major guildmaster, could not be easily pinned down. Even with help, Siobhan spent a good hour trying to find him in this huge labyrinth of a compound. She only managed it because he always had breakfast at the same time in the same place. Once she found Nortin, he knew where to direct her. Otherwise she knew with absolute certainty that she would have spent the rest of the day searching for him in vain.

He sat in this out of the way little room that seemed to be made entirely of windows, like a greenhouse, with a single round table in the center that took up most of the space. She entered and abruptly slowed at the doorway to avoid running into anything. The windows let out over the same garden she had been in last night, only with the morning sun now pouring through, she could see much more of it. Waaahhh, what a pretty sight to stare at while eating. No wonder he had breakfast here without fail.

As soon as she stepped into the room, Jarnsmor looked up, a cup halfway to his mouth, and he dipped his head in greeting. "Guildmaster Maley. I trust your sleep last night was comfortable."

"Quite, sir. Thank you. You are a good host." Wolf had coached her to say that, just in case. It was the right thing to respond with, as Jarnsmor openly beamed at her. "I wanted to speak with you, if that's alright?"

"Of course, of course." He waved her into the chair across from his. "Sit, eat."

Siobhan felt it odd to discuss business *without* eating, so she sat without further encouragement and loaded up a small plate with different foods before pouring a hot cup of tea. "I had a thought last night," she began.

"About?"

"This whole odd situation. Markl mentioned that he found this nameless guild in Orin strange. If they knew about the monopoly you were forming here, why attack and try to destroy it? Why not join it instead?"

Jarnsmor grunted. "He's quite right."

"I thought so as well. I think that someone needs to go to Orin, investigate further, see if we can pinpoint who it was exactly that sent assassins after Blackstone and why. It's the 'why' I truly want answered. My sixth sense is telling me that there's a very deep and compelling reason for this reaction."

Holding his cup with both hands, he stared over the rim at her. "You want to go."

"Do you have a better candidate?" she replied, not trying to come off as arrogant or cocky. "One of my people is from Coravine. I have two that are from Orin altogether. I've traveled that continent many times. We are not tied down here for any reason and are free to go and investigate. More, we are fully aware of what the situation is and so know what to look for."

His open palm accepted the argument. "I have no qualms with you going. In truth, I'm in a quandary over this. You see, I have my own people that are in Coravine to keep an eye on things."

She nodded in understanding. Every major guild had at least a few spies in their neighbor's guilds. It was common business practice.

"I lost contact with them several weeks ago," Jarnsmor admitted with a troubled frown. "We've sent several messages but haven't received any reply. I'm afraid that they've been found out."

And most likely executed or imprisoned. She could see why he was worried. "You can't send any of your people in after them."

"Not without giving the game away," he agreed, mouth in a flat line. "If they are undiscovered, but unable to respond for some reason, I risk exposing them. It's a small chance that's the case, but I don't dare react hastily. But no one knows you or your connection to me. It would be safe enough to send you in, I think. But I want you to report your findings to me."

"I had every intention of doing so," she agreed, mouth quirked up mischievously. "But if you want me to go and bring news quickly, it'd help if you lent me a ship."

"Ah, *that's* what you're after." His eyes crinkled up in amusement. "Alright, I'll arrange it. Be ready to depart in the next few days."

"I will." Well, that was one problem sorted. Now to make preparations for everything else. "Can I ask when exactly you lost contact with them?"

"Some two months or so ago, we noticed that it had been a long time since we'd received any information from them." Jarnsmor picked up his glass and twirled the liquid about in an idle way. "We don't get regular updates from them, you understand, just when they have something to report. It could well be that their disappearance can be linked to the change of leadership in Fallen Ward."

Siobhan blinked. "Fallen Ward has a new guildmaster?"

"As of about six months or so ago. The old leader had quite the funeral, I understand. I can't tell you much about his successor, however. Actually, it was because I wanted information about the new guildmaster that I contacted my people. But ever since the change in leadership, we haven't heard a single peep from across the channel. I haven't the faintest idea if the new guildmaster is a man or woman. It could be some mythical creature for all I know!" he said disgruntledly.

She nodded understanding, well able to imagine how frustrating this must be. Information was vital when trying to conduct business with other guildmasters. If Darrens had been here, he'd have likely hit the table with a closed fist at this point, in sheer frustration. "I'll try and find every bit of information I can," she promised him.

"Good. Thank you."

They ate in companionable silence for a moment before Jarnsmor cleared his throat and ventured, "The young man that is in your guild. He bears a striking resemblance to an assassin that hails from this city. Bloodless, I believe his name is."

Hooo, so he'd figured it out that quickly? Or someone in his guild had recognized Rune and reported it. She looked him dead in the eye. "His name is Rune and he's a member of Deepwoods."

Jarnsmor held up a hand in a placating manner. "I'm

not trying to stir up anything. If he's with you, he's with you. I've seen the way that young man responds to you, after all. I don't expect trouble from him. But I am curious, how did you bring him over to your side? I've met a few people from Silent Order before and they are cold souls, like empty dolls. I'd never thought that they could be brought into a good guild."

Yes, she'd had a few doubts about that herself the first few days with Rune. It was her experience with Wolf that had made her try at all.

"Did you seduce him away somehow?" Jarnsmor asked, head cocked.

"No." The memory made her smile as she answered. "I scribbled on his face. Much more effective."

"Eh?" Jarnsmor blinked, uncomprehendingly, then put his breakfast aside completely. "Now, you *must* explain that."

Chuckling, she obliged and told him the story as she ate. Jarnsmor proved to be a good listener, only interrupting once to ask a question and otherwise paying strict attention to her. But then, this man ruled one of the largest guilds of the four continents. A man in his position had to be very, very good at communicating in order to stay in power.

When she'd finished, Jarnsmor laughed aloud. "Card games and doodling on people's faces...now there's a tactic I've never heard of before. I salute you, madam, as your tactics obviously worked."

"I think it was the kindness that worked." She wore a sad smile as she stared at her plate, idly moving a piece of fruit around and around. "He doesn't know how to respond to kindness, it's such a stranger to him. Being able to laugh and joke with us was just the final clincher."

"Ah, I see." His deep voice softened slightly. "But then, I suppose you have experience in dealing with dark guild members."

She looked up at him askance.

"Your enforcer Wolf has all the markings of a former

mercenary. I assumed that he was once in a dark guild as well. Am I wrong?"

This man...just how good were his eyes? "No, you're not."

"How long has he been with you?"

"Ten years."

He pursued his lips in a soundless whistle. "A long time. Do you plan to keep Rune with you that long?"

"That's entirely his decision to make. I promised to help him leave the continent in exchange for his help. What he does after we leave Island Pass is up to him."

"Hmmm." Jarnsmor let the subject rest there and instead switched topics. "The Blackstone guildmembers will be safe here while you go and investigate. I sent my own message to Darrens assuring him of such. When you do go to Orin, I request that you leave your physician Conli behind. He's been very helpful to us in caring for people."

She translated the 'request' for 'demand' without a problem. "Of course. I'd doubt I'd be able to pry him away at this point anyway."

"Good."

With Jarnsmor preparing the ship, Siobhan went to tell her people the news and get them in motion. She saw people in the halls and the gardens, all of them on their own pursuits, and told them as she passed. They all assured her they'd be ready, and she had no doubt of it.

Siobhan found Wolf and Conli, the last two, in the common room just outside of the Blackstone area. Since people were likely sleeping—the heavily injured tended to sleep more than not—Siobhan didn't hail them but simply waved to get their attention as she walked across the room. Wolf and Conli paused in their conversation and looked up, waiting for her.

"I just spoke with Jarnsmor," she said in a low tone. "He's arranging a ship for us and we leave for Orin in the next few days."

Wolf nodded in satisfaction.

Turning to Conli, she added, "He did request that you stay and tend to the Blackstone members."

"I intended to," Conli assured her.

"I thought as much."

"And Grae?"

Siobhan blinked, then slapped herself on the forehead. "Oh, right! I'd nearly forgotten how badly he gets seasick. I'll have him stay here with you."

"And Rune?" Wolf asked her, a trace of bitterness in the question.

Siobhan stared blankly at him, not understanding what he was asking.

"You intend to bring him along with us?" Wolf elaborated patiently.

She cocked her head. "Why wouldn't I? Oh, did you catch up with him last night?"

Wolf grumbled something inaudible, which she took to mean 'no.'

"Well, if he's still in one piece, then why wouldn't I bring him along? It would be awkward to leave him here in Sateren, after all."

He didn't have a response to that, just looked away, a resigned sigh escaping from his mouth.

"You don't need to worry, Wolf." Conli had an odd quirk to his mouth, as if he were biting back a smile.

"Worry?" Wolf repeated in a growl befitting his nickname.

"Siobhan isn't a love interest for Rune," he clarified. His expression warred between being sympathetic and amused. "He doesn't see her that way."

Wolf went very, very still. His eyes focused sharply as he studied Conli's expression as if trying to read the man's mind. "Oh? You seem to be quite certain of this. If that's so, then what does he see her as?"

"A mother."

Even Siobhan felt surprised at this answer. Mother? Absurd! Rune was only eight, nine years her junior. The very idea was preposterous.

Seeing the disbelieving expressions aimed his direction, Conli started defending his opinion, ticking things off on his fingers as he went. "He checks in with her before he goes anywhere. He eats when she tells him to. He comes and shares little things with her like a child showing off. Shall I continue?"

Trotted out like that, she had a hard time refuting anything. But...but still... "A *mother*?"

"Wolf, you've experienced life in a dark guild." Conli cocked his head slightly, tone a simple statement of fact. "You know better than I what life is like there. I heard you describe it as *living darkness*. Being in an environment like that would take its toll on any heart. You, at least, came from a loving home and knew light from darkness. Rune never experienced anything else. Now, suddenly, he has. All of us aside, he has a woman who shows concern for his wellbeing and smiles at his antics. Is it really so strange that he's attached himself to her the way a duckling would?"

Wolf scrubbed a hand over his face for a moment before he let out a heavy, drawn-out sigh. "Your theory makes too much sense."

"It does," Siobhan admitted. "Although the idea of it feels awkward."

"Well, he may think of you more as a big sister," Conli added thoughtfully.

That did sit better with her. Or at least, she could wrap her head around it better. Still, now that she had this knowledge, what was she supposed to do with it?

"Don't think too much on this," Conli advised them both. "In fact, act like you've always done. Just be aware that his intentions are not nefarious."

"He acts like he didn't just put a spike in the wheel," Siobhan complained to Wolf. He gave her a sour grunt in return.

"You asked," Conli pointed out mildly.

"No, I didn't!" she sputtered. "Wolf did!"

Wolf rubbed at his forehead in a pained gesture. "Believe me, I'm sorry I brought it up."

"Just keep in mind that taking him with you to Orin will be fine." Conli smiled at the two of them, lips quirked in an almost-smile. "That's all you need to remember."

Siobhan lightly slapped both of her cheeks to erase the weird expression she was surely wearing. "Thank you, Conli, for adding to the general strangeness. With that lovely idea in mind, I'm going to hunt Rune down and tell him about the trip. Wolf, get packing."

She turned on a heel without waiting for any response and tried to organize the lines of her face into a general, neutral expression. Stupid Conli and his unnecessary theories. *Don't think much on this? Act like you've always done?* Now how was she supposed to pull any of that off? One of these days, she'd find the right size cork to stick in that mouth of his. He always told her more than she wanted to know.

Muttering to herself, she went looking for an assassin.

# Chapter Twenty-One

"Shi, there's a problem."

She looked up wearily toward the doorway. Beirly had that *look* to him, the one that said he wasn't budging until she either fixed the problem or gave him a solution. He stood solidly in front of her chair, arms crossed over his chest, beard bristling like a bear contemplating a rampage.

This was the third time in the past hour that she'd picked up her book only to be forced to set it down again. Resigned, she closed it and set it aside on the table. "Alright, which one are you referring to?"

"There's more than one problem?" he asked in genuine concern.

"In this guild, when isn't there?" she countered crossly. "Just sit, and tell me what it is you want."

"You know that Rune is disappearing into the city every day?"

At least he had waited until the common room was empty before speaking to her about this. Siobhan gathered up some patience from somewhere and managed to respond steadily, "I know."

"He's likely contacting his old guild, you know that too?"

"That I highly doubt."

Beirly blinked at her. "Why?"

"That's not an answer I can give without...breaking faith with him." Not that Rune had really told her anything, per se, but she'd been able to read a great deal into the way he flinched. Also his habits of responding to danger or even just general trouble told her what his life must have been like before she'd taken him on. His life here might be difficult, bewildering, even confusing, but it was infinitely better than where he had been. She didn't believe for one second that he wished to go back to Silent Order.

Beirly sat back in his seat with a slight huff and regarded her for several seconds through narrowed eyes. "You know something."

"I know very little and have a lot of guesses."

He snorted, not believing this. "Then why is he leaving every day, only coming back at night."

"My theory? He's not comfortable in his former enemy's main headquarters."

That bushy red beard twitched. "Didn't think of that."

Siobhan rubbed at one temple with her fingertips. "Just tell me that you didn't spread this theory of Rune defecting to his old guild around?"

"Wasn't the one that thought of it," he confessed.

Glory. That meant she had at least half the guild to straighten out.

Markl came around her chair and sat on the adjoining loveseat, sinking into it without invitation. "I have the real reason for you, if you want to hear it."

They both looked at him in interest.

"Iron Dragain is hassling him," Markl informed them without prompting. "I caught them doing it this morning as he was leaving. The leaders here don't do anything more than look at him sideways, but the lower ranking members are giving him grief even though he's not doing anything to provoke them."

Siobhan winced. After all, she'd seen what Rune thought of as 'an appropriate reaction' to trouble. "And... there's no body count yet?"

"He's letting it slide."

She blinked at him. Then blinked again. No, that still didn't make sense. "What?"

"He's letting it slide," Markl repeated. "He doesn't say anything, doesn't do anything, just brushes past them and quickly disappears into the city."

"That...seems like an odd way for him to react." Beirly frowned at the floor, mulling this over. "Why put up with it?"

Like a sack of rocks, it hit Siobhan all at once. She let out a long groan and slumped forward, burying her face in her hands. "Because I told him to."

"What?" both men demanded in confusion.

Scrubbing at her face with both hands, she gave a succinct version of what had happened with Denney on their shopping trip the other day, finishing with, "We told him to not kill people when they caused trouble. I told him that I didn't bring him into the guild because of his assassination skills."

"So because he knows that you don't want him to use violence unless absolutely necessary, he doesn't do anything to them because they're not actually hurting him?" Markl finished slowly. "Siobhan, that's wrong. On many levels."

"I know," she growled. "And that's *not* what I meant when I told him that! Of course he shouldn't let people run roughshod over him. I just didn't want him killing people at random either. *Arrrghhhh.*"

"Maybe you should clarify," Beirly offered.

She shot him a look that could melt steel. "I thought I had. I spent a long time talking to him about this. Clearly, I don't know the right words to get it across. At this point, I'm open to suggestions."

Markl and Beirly looked at each other, neither one of them knowing what to say.

Siobhan flopped back into her chair. "Fine, fine, I'll figure it out. In the meantime, why don't you go back to whoever it was that told you their pet theory on Rune's disappearance and straighten them out?"

"Yes ma'am," Beirly responded humbly.

Now she had to come up with some way to explain the proper method of self-defense to an assassin.

Half the problem of speaking to Rune was *finding* Rune. He tended to disappear very early in the morning—earlier than she could manage to wake up—and come back late in the evening, after most people had gone to bed. Even then she didn't always know where he went. The bed that had been prepared for him never looked slept in.

She spent a good hour wandering around the compound, looking for him, before realizing that if he didn't want to be found, he wouldn't be. She'd have to somehow wake up early in the morning and waylay him as he went out the door.

Resigned, she turned around and headed back to her room.

As she passed the common room, however, she heard two familiar voices coming through the cracked doorway. Pausing, she cocked her ear in an effort to hear what was being said.

"—if she knew about this, she would not let it happen," Fei said steadily.

"I've caused her too much trouble already. This is nothi'n." Rune sounded dismissive, uncaring.

Hmm? What was this? She crept a little closer to the door and unabashedly eavesdropped.

"She will not think of it as such. But I'll let you handle that as you wish. The assassins that are coming for you nightly, however, must be addressed."

Assassins?! What assassins?!

"I ain't killi'n them, like she wants."

"Yes, I know. But Rune-xian, why won't you tell anyone that your old guild is out for your life? Why won't you ask for help?"

Stubborn silence.

Siobhan closed her eyes and resisted the urge to bang her head against the wall a few times. Just how much was Rune dealing with that she wasn't aware of? Assassins, for pity's sake! Was this going on *nightly*? Was he actually leaving the guild on a daily basis to draw some of the danger away from here?

"I followed you today not because I suspected you, but because I was concerned," Fei continued when Rune didn't speak. "Trouble has been haunting your footsteps and you have given no hint of it. You do not see Deepwoods as your guild, I know. Most here do not accept you yet."

"You...do?" Rune asked hesitantly.

"I see much of myself in you. You are not my enemy. It is you who refuses to be my ally."

Siobhan blinked. How in the world were Rune and Fei alike?

"I'm...like ya?" Rune parroted dubiously.

Fei chuckled, a low and rough sound. "Yes. Your curiosity of the world, the thirst you have for knowledge, the way you wish to experience life to the fullest. That, you and I have in common."

Rune didn't seem to know how to respond to this.

"Siobhan is not your only ally here," Fei assured him gently. "The others are not sure of your intentions and so do not trust you."

"I don't know why I'm here," Rune admitted with a long sigh.

"Yes, I see your confusion clearly. Siobhan brought you here for her own reasons, which she has not explained to me. But her reasons are solely hers. You must ask yourself, what do you wish?"

"It's not my choice ta make."

"Certainly, it is. If not yours, then who's could it be? You have an open path here. Carve it, direct it where you will. If you wish to stay with us, then do so."

"How?" Rune objected. "No one trusts me!"

"What reason have you given them to trust you?" Fei countered. "My young friend, in your life, you have not been shown how to make strong ties with people. But in truth, it is very simple. This is all you need to do: show them that their well-being is your priority."

Siobhan blinked. It sounded ridiculously simple, but in truth, that really was how friendships were formed and how strong relationships were maintained.

Rune seemed to feel this was too simplistic. "That's it?"

"It sounds simple, but think about what that means. You must safeguard them, be thoughtful of their needs and wants, and provide comfort in their darkest hours. Showing concern can be done with both silence and words. Have you not seen this, in how Siobhan-ajie cares for the whole guild?"

"Safeguard," Rune repeated in a quieter, more contemplative tone.

"That, I understand, is how Wolf won the trust of the guild. He proved to them that no matter what happened, he would protect them from danger. It is a small but vital step. I think you are capable of doing such. The question is, do you wish to be here?"

Silence fell.

Siobhan found herself holding her breath.

"If...if I can."

She closed her eyes in abject relief and blew out a long, silent breath.

"Then let me tell you the best way to earn their respect, yes?" There was a smile in Fei's voice. "Let us start with Grae-ren."

She listened in for a few more minutes as he gave a

precise summary of Grae's personality, and a few hints on how to interact with him, but didn't linger more than that. It was clear that Fei, at least, had figured out what it was Rune lacked and was giving him the information he needed. So, Rune hadn't tried to form any bonds with them simply because he didn't know how? That had never occurred to her. Bless Fei and his extraordinary ability to read people. He was the perfect person to guide Rune.

Just as importantly, Rune wanted to stay. That was the only information she really needed in order to know what to do next.

With a bounce in her step, she headed for her bed, content that after this Rune would sort things out on his own. Whatever assassins came after him tonight Fei would help him deal with, too, although she would need to step in at some point and do something about that situation.

She owed Fei a serious hug.

# Fei
# Man Lei

2014 Christa Triumph

# Chapter Twenty-Two

"Rune!" Siobhan ducked into the common room, half-expecting him to be there, but also aware that he might be completely tucked out of sight. Fei had assured her he hadn't gone into the city this morning, but was still on the compound. Somewhere.

She stopped a few steps inside the room, looking carefully into every corner but not seeing him. Rain and drought, but she needed to tell him about everything she'd done this morning. How was she supposed to do that when she couldn't even find him?

"Yes?"

Startled, she whirled around on her toes. Rune stood directly behind her, relaxed and calm, as if he'd been there for quite some time. Putting a hand up to keep her jumping heart in her chest, she requested in exasperation, "Can't you make noise when you walk?!"

Mouth quirked, he confided, "Actually, I can't."

"You're going to give me heart failure at this rate," she grumbled to herself. An assassin that couldn't make noise when he moved. Lovely.

"Ya wanted me?" he prompted when she didn't continue.

"Ah, yes." Reminded of her purpose, she put a hand into her coat pocket and drew out a small leather badge. "Jarnsmor informed me that he couldn't let you board any ship of his unless you were officially registered as a member of Deepwoods. So, here's your crest. I put it in a leather holder—most of us carry one that way—but you can put it anywhere or wear it any way you wish."

Rune accepted the seal she handed out to him with both hands, eyes wide with surprise. "I'm...a member of yer guild?"

"Officially, as of..." she glanced at the clock on the wall, "about two hours ago. Welcome! I'll tell everyone else about it as I see them. Now, make sure not to lose this. They're ridiculously expensive to replace."

He flipped open the top of the badge so he could look at the seal. The Deepwoods crest wasn't anything fancy. Siobhan had been stuck for a name and symbol to use for the guild when she'd created it nearly a decade ago, and so had chosen a name that she and Grae had used for their secret hideout as children. The "D" with its stem and leaf design had been done by Beirly, the only person in the guild who had any artistic talent. They could probably afford to have a better version done now, but they were so established with that name and symbol, Siobhan felt it better to leave things be.

Rune certainly didn't seem to mind that the crest had so little flair to it. He flipped it closed again and turned it over in his hand, looking at the back.

Then he froze.

When the silence stretched to an uncomfortable length, she cleared her throat and offered, "I hope you don't mind?"

"It...says..."

"Rune Maley," she confirmed.

If a feather had landed on his shoulder at that

moment, the ex-assassin would have fallen straight to the floor. He didn't even seem to breathe.

Siobhan watched his expression carefully, trying to gauge if he was upset with what she had done or not. But he seemed so stunned that he didn't know how to react at all.

"Maley," he whispered in a hoarse tone. "Isn't that... yer last name?"

"Yes, so it is," she responded carefully. "When I went to register you a member of my guild, and get your crest made, they told me you had to have a full name to do any of that. I figured, I half-named you already. I might as well finish the job."

His eyes finally rose to meet hers. In those clear blue eyes were all the wonder, joy, and life that a child would reflect after receiving a lifelong wish. She could see it all in that moment—he had never expected her to do anything like this for him.

"The Maley family is from Widstoe," she told him with a soft smile. "We're an old family, usually made up of carpenters and weavers. I'm the odd one in the bunch, with my habit of traveling. It's a good name, with a good reputation." Reaching up, she cupped the back of his head and mussed his hair in an affectionate way. "So take care of it."

"I—" he had to clear his throat and try again. "I will."

"Good."

"You want me to do what?"

Rune's impish grin widened a notch. "Learn ta skulk."

So she had heard him right. Siobhan closed the book in her hands and leaned forward in the chair. She'd squirreled herself into a corner of the common room, enjoying a moment of peace, and the last thing she'd expected was this random invitation from Rune. It was, in fact, the first thing he'd ever asked her to do and showed tremendous progress on his part. Seeing the enthusiasm in his eyes, she didn't have the heart to tell him that crawling around in spider-infested rafters was the *last* thing she wanted to do. "Well, alright, why not?"

"Excellent. This way." He grabbed her by the wrist and hauled her easily to her feet.

Somewhat bemused by this odd turn of events, she followed him down the hallway and into a narrow access that he opened to get into the roof. He had to boost her up, actually, as she didn't have the necessary upper body strength to haul herself inside.

Siobhan sat near the opening and looked around. It was dim, with barely any light to see by, which could be a mercy. Not seeing how many spiders were up here was a blessing. The dust was so strong her nose kept twitching, threatening to sneeze.

Rune boosted himself up with a simple heave before replacing the ceiling board. In a low tone, he told her, "Yer eyes will get used ta it up here, no worries."

"Right." How in the world had she gotten talked into this?

As he led the way, he explained in a whisper, "The *best* part of skulki'n is spyi'n on people. It's fun ta watch."

"Hence why you're always up here?"

He just chuckled mischievously, like a boy that had been handed an unexpected present.

"How in the world do you know where you're going?" she asked in true curiosity. She'd never thought to question that before, but now that she was up here, it was just a huge expanse of open, dark space. There wasn't anything to signify what rooms were below her, except the odd chimney here and there.

Rune tapped a finger to his temple. "Got the place memorized. Did that first day. First lesson: ya got ta know the layout of the buildi'n otherwise ya get lost quick-like."

She could certainly see why. The space up here was barely tall enough for them to walk at a stooped level.

"Second question: why aren't you hunched like an old man by now? You can't walk properly up here."

Rune shrugged, not concerned about this. He was apparently used to it after all these years.

"So where are we now?"

"Just above the common room, headi'n toward the main dini'n room." Rune paused and half turned to see her face. "I saw Wolf, Tran and Markl headi'n that direction."

"Ah, hence your desire to spy on them?"

He gave a sage nod which belied the devilry in his eyes. "Don't ya want ta know what they do when yer not watchi'n?"

"I know what they do, trust me," she responded dryly. "Because I usually have to pay for it."

Rune gave a shrug of agreement but didn't stop leading her. Then he paused and sank down onto his haunches, pointing downward. Siobhan knelt next to him and saw that there was a small knothole that allowed her to see the center of the room, or at least part of it. A table, some chairs, and a small patch of floor were visible but not much else. Siobhan opened her mouth to ask if he was sure that those three were coming here when she heard Wolf speak.

"It's *cha-po*, not *chapo*."

"It's a word from my native tongue, Wolf," Tran responded in exasperation. "I should know how to say it!"

"No, it can't be," Wolf denied. "I hear it used in Robarge all the time."

"That's 'cause people adopted it. It didn't come from there."

Rune glanced up at her and whispered in a barely audible tone, "Is that all they do? Argue?"

"That and eat," she replied sourly. "When they need to, they partner up and fight together seamlessly. But when there's no one to fight, they fight each other."

He gave her an odd look. "And ya let 'em?"

"I stop them when I see it, but they're two grown men.

I'm not going to mother them."

For some reason, Rune found that even stranger. Had in-fighting been completely outlawed in his previous guild? No, Jarnsmor had said that Silent Order had regular fights that killed off its own members. Perhaps Rune expected her to stop such nonsense and found her unwillingness to dictate Wolf and Tran's every action odd.

"I've never traveled to Teherani," Markl said in a cautious tone. "And I'm barely familiar with Tran's language. I can't begin to offer an opinion."

"But *cha-po* is something you hear in Robarge, yes?" Wolf pressed.

"Oh, constantly."

"It's *chapo*, you lughead," Tran snapped. "At least say it right!"

A chair abruptly scraped back in a screeching sound. "I am saying it right, you ham-handed fool!"

Siobhan let out a weary sigh. "I give it five seconds before the first fist flies."

Rune cocked his head. "They don't fight every time they argue."

"Trust me, that's a fight waiting to happen." Seeing that he didn't believe her, she asked, "Want to bet?"

"Terms?"

"We always wager the same thing," Siobhan explained. "It's traditional in the guild now. Whoever loses buys the other person's next meal. Or snack, if that's preferred."

Rune gave a silent 'ahh' of understanding. Then he held out a hand. "Bet taken."

She solemnly shook to seal the deal. Siobhan cocked her ear toward the hole, listening to the argument escalate.

"Is not!" Wolf thundered.

"Is too!" Tran snapped back.

"Is not!"

"Five..." she muttered under her breath.

"Markl, who's right?!"

"Four..."

"I told you, I don't know enough to be sure—"

"Three..."

"You've got brains the size of a bird's, who'd believe you!"

"Two..."

A meaty thunk sounded below, a familiar sound that she knew well. Someone's fist had rammed into someone else's face. Hopefully it wasn't Wolf's iron fist, as the last time he'd used that against a face, he'd broken the man's jaw.

Rune leaned down and put his eye directly against the knothole. "Ya even have it *timed*," he said in amazement.

"It's just experience. Live with them for another five years, and you can do the same thing." She shook her head in exasperation. "Is Markl fighting too? Can you see them?"

"Sure is."

"Poor man. I forgot to warn him. If another man is nearby when those two start fighting, he's inevitably drawn into it somehow. Keep that in mind." Rising to her feet, she asked, "Where's the quickest way down?"

"I thought ya didn't stop them."

"I said I didn't mother them. I stop them when I see them fighting. Besides, if I don't stop this quick, they're going to damage Jarnsmor's furniture, and I'd rather that not happen. He's been a perfectly good host so far."

Rune's open hand said she had a good point. He rose to his feet and gestured her to follow, leading her about ten steps away before he knelt again and opened another ceiling panel. If he hadn't led her to it, she'd have never known it was there. Lifting the board free, he eyed the distance to the ground. "How good are ya at jumping?"

"About as good as climbing."

"Ah. In that case, me first. I'll catch ya."

She blinked at him in surprise. "You and I are about the same size. You sure you can catch me?"

He gave her a long look, as if indignant she questioned such a thing.

Holding up her hands in surrender, she didn't press the point. After all, if he was sure, he was sure. If he was wrong, he'd just end up squashed under her.

Rune hopped through the hole and landed as easily as a cat, not at all bothered by the eight foot drop. With a breath for courage, she maneuvered her legs through the hole first then pushed off, dropping the rest of the way. Proving he was right, Rune caught her easily under the arms and set her to her feet without any noticeable strain on his part. Great winds, he was stronger than he looked! She'd met few men that had the strength to do what he'd just done.

Smiling, she patted him on the shoulder in silent thanks before pushing away and looking around. They were in the hallway just outside the dining room door. Oh good. She was close. Pushing through the door, she drew air into her lungs and yelled, "STOP!"

The tableau froze.

Wolf had one fist drawn back, ready to strike. Tran had a hand up to block the strike, the other around the arm Markl had around his neck. Markl was apparently trying to draw Tran away from the fight, but against the bigger man, he wasn't having much of an effect. When she stepped inside, all three of them looked at her cautiously.

"Markl," she said kindly, "I know you're not at fault in this so you're not in trouble. Be forewarned, however, that this usually happens if you are around these two. If they start arguing, just walk away. Otherwise you'll get drawn into the fight."

"Ahhh..." he slowly released Tran and stepped back. "Right."

Still with that sweet smile on her face, she turned to the other two. "Now. It's clear to me that if you have the energy to fight over how to pronounce a *word*, then you need something to do."

"How did you know what we were fighting about?" Tran questioned slowly, eyes suspicious.

She crossed her arms over her chest and gave him

a self-righteous look. "I was learning the finer art of skulking. I overheard you."

All three men gave her an incredulous look before their eyes darted to the ceiling.

Rune popped up behind her and waggled his fingers in a little wave at them.

"Ah," Wolf grunted. "I should have guessed. He's corrupting you."

"Corrupti'n's an awful word," Rune mourned with mock-innocence. "I'm teachi'n her!"

Wolf rolled his eyes.

Siobhan cleared her throat to get their attention back. "Regardless of how I learned it, the matter stands. We are not going to cause our hosts trouble, we are *not* going to destroy their furniture, and I will not stand for further fighting on these grounds. Clear? Good. Now, Wolf and Tran, you need to find something to do that doesn't involve each other's company."

With nods and sighs, they complied and filed out of the room, going in different directions once they hit the hallway. Hopefully they stayed away from each other for the rest of the day.

Siobhan had to admit that this skulking thing had advantages. "Rune, let's go back up."

He brightened perceptibly. "It's fun, ain't it?"

Yes, it surprisingly was.

# Chapter Twenty-Three

While Iron Dragain had a very nice complex, and the members here went out of their way to be hospitable, Siobhan could hardly stay on their grounds day in and day out without risking her sanity. What she had left of it, anyway. She tried to find other things to do, but packing for the trip hadn't taken more than a few minutes. After picking up and setting down the same book three times, sharpening her swords, and picking at a mid-morning snack, she finally gave up. Maybe a good stroll around the city would help.

Walking around and doing some sightseeing appealed to her, but she knew good and well that this place was a labyrinth. She in no way wanted to stay lost for the rest of the day, or worse, wander into the wrong part of town alone. No, better to have a guide.

Leaning back in her chair, she called to the ceiling, "Rune?"

No answer.

Hmm, now that was strange. Since Fei had taken Rune

under his wing, Rune had been up in the rafters nearly nonstop. Perhaps he was spying on someone else instead of her for a change? Come to think of it, she didn't know how much time he spent on any one person before moving on. He seemed to know what everyone was up to, but he couldn't possibly do that without splitting his time among them.

With a scrape of the chair, she left the table and walked out into the hallway, calling to the ceiling as she went. "Rune? Rune! How strange, where did he get off to? Sound carries up there quite well, he usually hears me. Rune!"

Two women passing by gave her strange looks. Siobhan managed an embarrassed smile and rubbed at the back of her neck. Oh, right. This would look strange to anyone else, her calling a person's name to a blank ceiling. Come to think of it, should she be advertising that Rune spent his time up above everyone's heads? Hmmm.

At that moment, Sylvie rounded the corner at a dead run, spied her, and relief washed over her face. "Siobhan! Oh thank the stars, quick, come stop them!"

"Stop who?" she demanded, reflex kicking in so that she automatically ran forward.

"Rune and a few men from Iron Dragain," Sylvie explained quickly.

"Rune? Why?"

"I don't know!" Sylvie practically wailed. "I was just walking by and saw one of Iron Dragain's men—Kark? Kirk? Something like that—take a swing at Rune. Of course, Rune dodged it, but right now he's up against three of them!"

No matter how good a fighter he was, those were steep odds. "Where?"

"Dead ahead, take two lefts, it will dump you into the right courtyard," Sylvie rapidly instructed.

Siobhan lengthened her stride, quickly leaving Sylvie behind, as the other woman wasn't a particularly fast runner. She followed the directions to the letter and skidded to a halt just inside the doorway that led out into the courtyard.

If she hadn't stopped, she'd have lost her head.

She took in the sight with open dismay and a sick sensation twisting her gut. Hadn't Sylvie said three?! She counted a good half-dozen men in there now, all trying to tear a strip off of Rune's hide. The former assassin was dodging and weaving, focusing so totally on defense that he barely got any strikes in himself. She could tell from the controlled way his fists moved that he was taking care to *not* seriously injure anyone.

Great thunder and rain, just what was she supposed to do to stop *this*? Three men might listen to her, but six guildmembers of Iron Dragain would not heed the words of a Robargean guildmaster. At the same time, she didn't want to go hunt down one of the officers of the guild, either, for fear that the situation would abruptly become worse the moment her eyes left them.

From another doorway, on the left side of the courtyard, Wolf and Fei appeared. They took in the scene with its grunts, curses, and flash of weapons with open surprise, but then a devilish smile came over Wolf's face. He said something to Fei, which made Fei shake his head in resignation, before Wolf jumped off the porch and onto the paving stones. With a whoop, he punched the nearest man, sending him flying, then dodged and weaved until he came to Rune's back.

Siobhan, all set to protest this, stopped mid-step at the look on Rune's face. He was...not just amazed that Wolf had come to fight at his side, but touched by it as well. For the first time that she had known him, he gave a genuine smile. Then with a whoop of his own, he started fighting in earnest and actually doing damage to people.

She hesitated. While fighting with the men of one's hosting guildmaster was wrong—very wrong—she instinctively felt that this was an important moment. Trust between those two was building in front of her eyes. With every punch, every opponent knocked down, they were learning how to fight with each other, how to coordinate their attacks. That experience would be invaluable in the future, she knew that for a fact.

Didn't change the fact that fighting with their hosts was wrong, though.

"Two minutes," she promised herself in an undertone. "I'll give them two more minutes. Then I step in and stop them. Somehow."

Sylvie slid to a stop beside her, took in the raging fight, and groaned. "Oh no. When did Wolf join in? And Fei?!"

"Fei?" Siobhan repeated, eyes darting about madly to spot him. Oh heavens, Sylvie was right, he had joined in at some point and she hadn't noticed. Even now he was slowly maneuvering his way to fight with Wolf and Rune. "Oh for the love of—! He's supposed to be the *sensible* one! Why did he...arghhhh."

"Well, granted, they are outnumbered otherwise," Sylvie reasoned in a remarkably cool way.

"It's Wolf out there," Siobhan protested. "No they're not!"

"Ooooh, I've never seen Rune fight before. He's quite good, isn't he? I'd say on par with either Wolf or Tran." Sylvie leaned in, watching every move with keen eyes. "If we had him fight Wolf or Tran, I wonder what would happen?"

"The furniture wouldn't survive, that's what would happen," she groaned. As it was, she wasn't sure the courtyard would survive under this madness. So far, the men had managed to trample every flower, bush, and the single bench that had been out here.

The question of how she would stop the fight resolved itself very quickly once Fei started fighting. Within minutes, the Iron Dragain members were down, most of them sporting nothing more than a broken bone or three with enough bruises to resemble a patchwork quilt. Since they were all still conscious, Siobhan took advantage of the situation and stalked into the middle of them, glaring about as she did so. Seeing the bloody lip on Rune's face, the minor cuts on his chest and arms, made her vision go red and the calm speech she'd prepared in her head disappeared in a puff of smoke. Instead her voice rose to a loud, thundering roar.

"WHAT IN THE FOUR WINDS DID YOU THINK YOU WERE DOING?!"

Every man there flinched, at the sheer volume of her voice, if nothing else. She spun on her heel with a snarl, lip curled in a menacing baring of teeth. "We are Jarnsmor's guests. We are here on Blackstone's behalf. How dare you attack one of my own?!"

One of the men—she didn't recognize him, especially since he was holding his bloody nose—spoke up in a surly manner. "He's not one of yours. He's Silent Order. We know him."

"He *was* Silent Order," she corrected sharply, the words snapping like a whip. "He's now Deepwoods."

"He's an assassin and a thief," someone else said from behind her. She whirled around to face him, feeling blood roar to her head. The man met her eyes unflinchingly. "We won't have him here."

"You won't have him here," she repeated with lethal calm. "Even though your guildmaster said differently? Oh? You didn't think Jarnsmor knew about him? But he did. We discussed it, he and I, and Rune is here because I vouched for him. He obviously didn't want trouble, he's been avoiding all contact with your guild from the first day. Wind and stars, but even when you deliberately pick on him, he doesn't retaliate! So what did you think you were doing, dragging him out here and buying a fight that he didn't want to sell?"

None of them could quite meet her eyes after that. She huffed out a disgusted breath and pointed sharply for the door. "Go. Go! Before I change my mind and finish what my men left."

With grunts of pain and mutterings, they gathered themselves up and limped away. Siobhan took in a deep breath, trying to calm herself. One breath didn't cut it, so she took in another, then another. It didn't noticeably calm her heart any, but it did give her the appearance of control at least. Turning to Rune, she asked, "How badly are you hurt?"

He didn't answer immediately, just stared at her with weighing eyes for a long moment. "Ya vouched for me?"

Patience. She took in another breath. "Rune, do you honestly think that Jarnsmor would have let you walk through his doors without someone speaking on your behalf?"

At that, he really seemed lost for words.

"Think about it later, Rune-xian," Fei advised. "Answer us first. Are you hurt badly anywhere, or is it just what we see?"

"Just what ya see," he slowly answered, eyes studying their faces in turn as if wondering what they truly thought.

Well enough. Although she'd still drag him to Conli in a moment for treatment. "And you, Wolf? Fei?"

"Fine," Wolf assured her, pleased with the fight. "Got my blood pumping."

Fei shrugged, one hand splayed that indicated he was fine, although she noticed he had a neat slice along one leg that needed tending to.

"What were you two thinking, anyway, by jumping in like that?" Although a part of her was glad they had, there *were* better ways to handle the situation. She might not have the lung power to shout down a group of fighting men but Wolf certainly did. For that matter, Fei had become an expert on breaking up brawls after years of dealing with Wolf and Tran. He could have stopped it if he wanted to.

Wolf drew himself up in a dignified manner. "Real friends don't let friends do stupid things alone."

She closed her eyes, pained. "Why does that sound ridiculously logical coming out of your mouth?"

"He needed help," Fei justified himself.

Why had she even bothered to ask? "Oh, never mind. You three go see Conli and get patched up. I need to hunt down Jarnsmor and tell him what happened." Before some garbled version reached his ears. "Sylvie, escort them there. Do not allow detours."

Sylvie gave her a half-bow of acknowledgement before grabbing Wolf by the arm and towing him along. The other two—one pleased, the other bewildered—trailed in her wake. As they went, she could hear Fei ask Rune exactly how everything had started (which was a question she wanted an answer to) but she let them go off alone. She'd get the full version later.

And to think, she had complained about being bored and restless earlier.

She found Jarnsmor in his study, and sat at the paper-buried table to report what had happened. Jarnsmor heard her out with a pained frown, and he kept pinching at the bridge of his nose as if fighting off a headache. When she finished, he let out a low breath. "Guildmaster Maley, my apologies. I had made it clear to everyone that you and your people should be treated with all due courtesy. I *thought* I had made it clear, at least."

"I know you did," she assured him, more out of sympathy than politeness. "But I also know that you always have a few members in a guild that are stubborn and rock-headed who do things their own way. Fortunately, it was all just bruises and minor cuts from this fight with no real damage. Hopefully we can avoid any conflict in the future."

A hard look came into his eyes. "I will talk with them personally."

She almost felt pity for those poor idiots in that moment. Almost. "I must ask, however, just how bad is the blood between Iron Dragain and Silent Order that they felt so compelled to fight Rune?"

"Bad," he admitted with splayed palms. "Silent Order

has existed almost as long as Iron Dragain and we've been constantly fighting each other for as long as anyone can remember. Once in a while, we work out a treaty of sorts with them so that they don't attack our people or allies, which lasts for a few years. When I first became guildmaster, there was such an agreement in place that almost lasted a full decade. But Silent Order doesn't keep the same guildmaster for long—too much infighting, belike—and our understandings with them only last until the next man takes over. Worse, every time they change guildmasters, the whole city feels the aftermath, like a tidal wave sweeping the streets. It's like the new guildmaster has to prove himself to be more ruthless than the former one. He flexes his power, demonstrating it for several months before things steady out again."

That made ice run through her veins. "Are they such a large guild, then?"

"Not as large as us," he refuted with a shake of the head. "In fact, not particularly large at all. We can't know their exact number, but I guess them to be about a hundred strong. They might grow if they can ever stop their members from killing each other off periodically. But every time an old guildmaster falls, anyone loyal to him dies too, which wipes out dozens of men at a time."

How horrifying. Siobhan felt relieved with every word that she had managed to take Rune away from that future. She really didn't want to ask this, but it begged to be known. "Please answer the next question frankly. Has Rune personally done anything to Iron Dragain?"

"That I'm aware of? No. I think my men have crossed paths with him before but we know him by his reputation and little else."

She blew out a covert breath of relief. Honestly, she hadn't known what she would do if the answer to that question had been 'yes.' "I'm glad. Hopefully our trip to Orin will let heads cool."

"You'll take him with you, then?" Jarnsmor studied her with narrowed eyes. "Doing so risks him leaving you,

you know. Once he's on a different continent, you'll have no hold over him."

Siobhan gave him an enigmatic smile. "You think so?"

His head slanted slightly in puzzlement. "Unless you know something I don't?"

Shaking her head, she declined to answer and instead stood. "Thank you for handling this. I'll get my people ready to leave tomorrow."

Jarnsmor looked like he wanted to press the matter but let it go with a wave of the hand. "As you will. I'll be curious to see if he comes back with you or not."

It was just as well that they were set to leave soon. After what happened with Rune, no one seemed able to rest easy in Iron Dragain. Without Siobhan being aware of it, some discussion had happened, and as a result everyone closed in ranks around Rune. He didn't go anywhere alone, but always had at least one other person with him. In the course of preparing for their departure tomorrow, Siobhan saw him with three different people. At one point, she even saw him sitting with Conli, getting his bandages swapped out, with both Pyper and Pete sitting on his feet.

The whole scene just warmed her heart.

People might still be debating on whether or not they fully trusted Rune, but they did feel some sort of connection to him, or they wouldn't be reacting this way. Word had spread quickly through the guild of what had happened that morning and Siobhan saw many a snide glance being aimed at her assassin. It never went further than that, however. Whether it was because of Jarnsmor's instructions or her own people's vigilance, she wasn't sure.

As long as no trouble started, she didn't care what the reason was, either.

Now, let's see, what else did she need to do? She

herself was packed, as was most of the guild, but she did want to speak with Lirah before they left. Where could she find her at this point in the day?

"Siobhan!"

She turned, halfway inside the common room, spying Sylvie and Rune coming her direction. "Yes?"

Sylvie rubbed her fingers against her thumbs in a clear gesture that asked for money. "We need to outfit Rune."

Oh. Right. The clothes they'd bought for him earlier hadn't survived the gamut of assassins. She had a feeling that Rune was rough on clothes anyway, but the nightly attacks were certainly destroying his wardrobe. "Yes, of course. I'm glad you thought of that." She took the cloth purse out of her side pouch and handed it over. "Try to only spend half of that, alright?"

Usually Sylvie would shrug assent, but this time she hesitated as she took the bag. "Umm, that might be a bit difficult. Markl gave me a shopping list for Rune as well."

"Oh?" Her eyes darted to Rune's face. Markl? And why was Rune avoiding her eyes?

Sylvie glanced at Rune as well before she dropped her voice to a confidential tone. "Siobhan. Rune can't read."

WHAT?! Her eyes nearly bugged out of her head. No, wait, calm down. She should have expected this. He was from a dark guild, after all; people were rarely educated in those circles. Wolf had been one of the few exceptions, but it was his hometown that had educated him, not the guild who'd bought him. She took in a breath to steady her voice before speaking. "So, Rune, has Markl offered to teach you?"

Rune searched her eyes, as if trying to see any pity or disgust she might feel, but he steadied out when she just looked at him levelly. "No. He demanded ta teach me."

That made her chuckle. "Now, why is it easy for me to picture him doing that? Lucky for you, then. I can't imagine a better teacher than him. What did he say you needed?"

"A primer book, a practice book, quill and ink, and

some scratch paper," Sylvie listed, ticking things off on her fingers. "Any book is pricier here than in Robarge, so it's going to be a bit steep."

Siobhan waved this off. "It's worth it. We can't have Rune wandering around the world without being able to read. It'll put him at too much of a disadvantage."

Rune made a wordless protest. "This wasn't part of the deal."

She put a hand on his shoulder and snared his eyes with hers. "You are guild, Rune. Until the day you decide to leave, you are guild, and I will treat you as such. Now, do you want to learn how to read?"

He nodded once, firmly, eyes locked with hers.

"Then learn." Giving his shoulder a final squeeze, she let go before focusing on Sylvie. "Try not to bankrupt me. We have quite a bit of traveling to do before we get home after all."

Sylvie gave a mocking bow. "I'll do my best. I need to teach him a few things too while we're out."

Both Rune and Siobhan gave her a blank look.

"Like?" Rune asked in puzzlement.

"Like how to shop and properly bargain with people," Sylvie answered promptly, giving him a pointed look. "Rune, my dear, you have *no* survival skills to speak of."

Siobhan bit her tongue and tried not to laugh at the poleaxed expression on Rune's face. So, assassination didn't count as a survival skill, eh? Well, it likely wouldn't in Sylvie's opinion.

"Have fun, then." She waved them away. Actually, she blessed Sylvie's idea in taking him out of Iron Dragain. It not only gave Rune the things he needed, but removed him from this tense atmosphere, which they all needed. She took all of one step before a thought struck. Turning about, she called to their retreating backs, "Rune?"

Rune stopped mid-step and looked back over his shoulder. "Yes?"

"Protect Sylvie." Siobhan's mouth quirked in a wry manner. "She tends to attract the wrong sort of attention from men."

Rune glanced at Sylvie, who couldn't do anything more than shrug in resigned agreement, before he assured her, "Geta."

"Good man." Siobhan waved him on again, feeling a little like a mother that had just sent two siblings out for a day of shopping. Well, in a way, that's exactly what she had done. She couldn't put Rune in any better hands, though. Sylvie could make a kor stretch until it squirmed and begged for mercy.

Now, what had she been doing before being interrupted? Oh right, talk to Lirah.

# Chapter Twenty-Four

Late that evening, after most of Iron Dragain had settled in for the night, she had everyone in Deepwoods meet again in the common room. During the whole course of the day, she'd been running from pillar to post, and because of that, she hadn't been able to meet with her people to check in.

Once again they found places either on the couches or chairs to sit, although this time Denney didn't choose the floor next to the dogs, but instead stuck close to Conli. The older man had an arm around her shoulders in silent support. Siobhan noted this position with a slight frown. Denney normally chose to be close to Conli, but for her to openly cling like this was unusual. Had something happened?

Making a note to ask later, she cleared her throat to get everyone's attention. "The ship leaves the day after tomorrow on the morning tide, so I expect people to be on board by eight sharp. We are, technically, investigating on Iron Dragain's behalf and Jarnsmor has funded us for the trip. I've got individual purses for each of you, but mind that it'll not be until we reach home that you'll get paid again, so make it last."

People nodded or said a word of agreement in response.

"Now, is everyone packed? Anything that we need to get before we go?"

No one said anything at this, just looked at each other as if to say, *You? No, I'm fine.*

"Conli?" she prompted. "How badly were they injured?"

"Scratches and bruises," Conli assured her. "Nothing that required any stitches. Assuming they keep the wounds clean, they'll heal perfectly in a week or two."

Well enough. "I'm not sure if everyone knows this or not, but Conli is staying behind to see after the Blackstone people. So Fei will be in charge of any injuries for the duration of this trip. Conli, does Fei already have the black bag?"

"I do, Siobhan-ajie," Fei assured her calmly.

"That said, I do not *want* injuries," she said this as strongly as she knew how.

"Wolf? Tran?" Grae had a smirk on his face. "I think she's talking to you."

"I wasn't in the fight this morning," Tran pointed out.

Wolf put an innocent hand to his heart. "And I didn't start it."

Grae rolled his eyes heavenward. "According to you, you *never* start it."

He looked wounded by this, as if he couldn't understand why Grae was picking on him.

Not one person in the room believed his innocence either.

Siobhan blew out a year's worth of sighs. "Moving on... no fights, people. Not if you can help it. I especially don't want injuries when we're on foreign soil far from home. Now, that out of the way, Rune? Did Sylvie outfit you?"

"And then some," he assured her, brightening

perceptibly.

"He now has three shirts, two pants, an extra pair of boots, a coat, and a new belt," Sylvie listed this off while ticking it away on her fingers. "Plus the books and papers that Markl requested I buy him. I bought a leather satchel for him to put it all in, but the strap is a bit damaged. Beirly, can you fix that for him tonight? The bag is in perfect shape except the strap."

"And you got an absolute steal on it because of that," Beirly guessed dryly.

Sylvie grinned like a cat that had just polished off a dish of forbidden cream.

"I'll take a look and fix it, one way or another," Beirly promised. "Rune, bring it to me after this."

Rune ducked his head in agreement, bewildered but pleased by this ready offer of help from Beirly.

"I think that's all we need to cover." Siobhan stood from her chair, clapping her hands in dismissal. "Go to bed, and remember, stay out of trouble before we leave."

People started moving, some heading toward their rooms, others trying to catch someone else's attention. Siobhan had her own back to the room, heading for bed, when she heard Conli call to Rune.

Eh? Conli said Rune was fine...she turned back to see what it was he wanted.

Conli had caught Rune's attention, but it was Denney that stepped forward, closing the distance between them. She had a serious set to her jaw, as did Conli. Siobhan cocked her head slightly. What was this about?

"Rune." Denney's voice shook ever so slightly but she stood steadfast in front of the assassin.

Rune went abruptly still, almost motionless, as if he didn't even breathe. He watched her cautiously, having no idea what to expect from her.

"What you did for me earlier..." Denney's lips curved in a helpless smile. "For protecting me the way you did, I cannot find the words to thank you. Because of that, I hope you will take this as my thanks." From inside her vest, she drew out a mid-sized hunting knife and presented it to him on her open palms.

Siobhan's eyes went wide. What he did for her? Protected Denney? What was this about? What had Rune done that was so weighty that Denney felt the need to give him a present in return?

The whole guild had taken notice of this interaction by now and had turned back to watch the scene play out.

Rune seemed oblivious to their attention as he reached out slowly with one hand that never quite touched the knife. "Are those...marks?"

"You weren't registered with your own hunter's marks that I could find," she explained, still holding the knife out toward him on steady hands. "So I registered a set of marks for you."

Siobhan felt her knees give way and she had to lock them to keep her feet. What Denney had done was *huge*. In all the four continents, only a handful of laws were universally obeyed, but the hunter's law was one of them. No man could claim another's prey if a hunter's marks were found there. A man was not considered to be a whole man until he had his own marks to lay claim with. Siobhan had named Rune but hadn't thought it wise to push getting him marks as well, all things considered.

Seeing that look on his face, his expression of open wonder, made her realize she was a fool for not doing so.

Rune swallowed hard before he finally raised his other hand and took the knife from Denney with both hands. In a gesture of utmost respect, he drew the knife from its sheath and looked it over carefully. Denney hadn't spared any expense—the metal shone brightly under the light, the etching near the hilt fine and detailed. Three flat lines with two circles were engraved into the dark wood of the hilt, and that, too, gleamed. A hunting knife was the traditional method of gifting a hunter's marks to a boy and Denney had chosen a very fine weapon to do it with.

He just as carefully sheathed it before saying hoarsely, "It's a good gifti'n. I thank ya for it."

Denney beamed at him. "No, Rune. Thank *you*."

Conli added in a gentle tone, "She told me what you did, and how you've stepped in several times and warned people off on her behalf. It's made you many enemies in a place where you had few allies to begin with. Because of that, I feel like we owe you something more."

"What?" Rune's head jerked back in instinctive protest. "No, sir, that's not—"

"Whatever your agreement with Siobhan," Conli cut in kindly, "you are clearly doing more than she expected. That dumbfounded expression on her face tells me that much." Conli turned and winked at her before adding, "Because of that, I give you one more gift of thanks." He snagged Rune's hand and raised it up.

Before Siobhan's—the entire guild's—astonished eyes, Conli took his bejeweled bridge ring off his own hand and slipped it onto Rune's middle finger.

"This is a bridge ring," Conli explained. "Do you know of it? No? It'll let whoever wears it travel through Island Pass without any questions asked. You can also search the records there, and request help or information from any inhabitant on that island. With this, you do not need to be bound to any place but can travel freely across the bridges as you wish to."

Rune's mouth opened and closed like a beached fish. He finally shook his head roughly. "I don't deserve this."

"Rune," Conli chided gently. "You protected someone precious to me. Multiple times. I know that you will continue to do so in the future, and that because of your actions, you will draw anger and malice to you. What kind of man would I be if I didn't help offset that by giving you a means to escape if you need it? We will, of course, protect you and safeguard you as you have us, but I do not intend to leave you trapped here unnecessarily."

"We thought the best gift we could give you was the freedom to go and make any future you wish," Denney added. "The marks and ring are for that purpose. Accept them, please."

Rune's eyes traveled from one face to another, mouth searching for words, but none were coming out. He clearly looked overwhelmed by this outpouring of gratitude and kindness and had no idea how to accept it.

Siobhan's patience snapped with an almost audible twang. "I can't take it anymore. Rune! What happened? What did you do? I've rarely seen them act like this before."

Denney turned and gave her an odd look. "He didn't tell you?"

"Tell. Me. What," Siobhan gritted out.

"The reason why he was in that fight with the Iron Dragain men this morning," Denney responded as if the answer was obvious. "The whole fight started because of me."

"*What?!*" several voices yelled at once.

Siobhan took in a deep breath. "Denney. From the beginning, please."

"Right." She half turned so she could look at the whole room. "I'd come back from the baths, heading for my room, when those idiots cornered me. They...well, it was the usual thing. They thought I was a prostitute or something and were hassling me. I wasn't sure what to do, at first. I mean, I never expected that sort of danger *here*."

Neither had Siobhan, or she would have taken precautions.

"I was a little too late in using force to get them to leave me alone, and they thought I was playing hard to get, so they cornered me. It was at that point that Rune appeared from thin air—" she glanced at Rune, head cocked in question.

"Ceili'n, actually," he corrected.

"Oh, is that where you were? I just knew you were suddenly *there*, between me and them. Rune hit them hard and fast and told me to run for it. I went straight to Conli, hoping to send help back to Rune, as I wasn't sure he could handle three men at once."

Rune snorted. Obviously, he hadn't been worried

about that.

"But by the time that I could get to him," Conli picked up the thread of the story smoothly, "Sylvie, Wolf, Fei and Siobhan were already there and Siobhan was reaming the men for daring to attack Rune. Since those three were obviously hurt, I went immediately back for my bag so I could patch them up. Besides, I was afraid of leaving Denney alone again, after what had just happened."

Denney gave Siobhan an odd look. "Didn't you tell me that he told you what happened?"

Siobhan glared at Rune. He couldn't quite meet her eyes. "I thought he had, anyway."

Rune shrugged uneasily. "She hadn't done anythi'n."

"Rune, I don't blame the victim for trouble, y'know?" Siobhan responded in exasperation. "I realize it might not seem like that, because I'm constantly yelling at Wolf and Tran when trouble breaks out, but that's because *they're* usually the ones that start things. When Sylvie or Denney are in trouble, I know good and well they didn't start it, so I'm not going to be harsh with them. You don't have to protect them from me."

Denney blinked at her, then turned to Rune with wide eyes. "You covered for me?"

Rune stared at the floor and muttered something unintelligible.

Rubbing her eyes with both hands, Siobhan blew out a long breath. "So, in other words, it's not just Rune we need to look out for, but Denney as well? Rain and drought, but this is ridiculous. I'll speak with Jarnsmor again, but for now, no one goes anywhere alone. Do you hear me? *None of you.*"

Everyone gave her nods or voiced some sort of assent.

She smiled grimly. The next fool that decided one of her own was easy prey wouldn't live long enough to regret it. But for now, she needed to say something else. Stepping forward, she ruffled the back of Rune's hair with an affectionate toss. "You did good, kid."

Rune glanced at her from the corner of his eye with

that almost-smile she was beginning to love. He openly basked in the praise.

Her eyes took in Conli and Denney as she repeated, "You did good." If she had known all that Rune was doing behind the scenes, she'd have put together a reward for him herself, but having it come unsolicited from Conli and Denney meant the world to him. Perhaps it was best that she hadn't known anything until now.

They both gave her understanding smiles.

Beirly cleared his throat and offered, "Rune, why don't me and you put those marks on your things? Now that you have 'em, let's put 'em to use."

Rune nodded his head in agreement, pleased with the suggestion.

# Chapter Twenty-Five

"There's assassins after our assassin."

Siobhan blinked and stared at Fei. She'd been in the middle of finishing preparations for tomorrow, but he apparently wanted her attention, so she dropped everything in her hands and turned toward the door. "I assume you're talking about the nightly attacks from Silent Order? The ones that you've been helping Rune deal with?"

Fei cocked his head slightly. "I was not aware that you knew of them."

"Oh, I know more than you think I do." Not much more, though. "I would have thought they'd given up, though, as they've not been the least bit successful so far."

"They are far from giving up," Fei denied with a grim shake of the head. "In fact, the numbers they send increase every night. It has now reached the point that it is...difficult for only I and Rune-xian to deal with them."

Difficult? When Fei said 'difficult,' he meant 'impossible.' She was almost afraid to ask. "How many are you expecting to show up tonight?"

He thought about that for a moment before offering, "Twenty or so?"

"Twenty?!" she spluttered. "Great wind and stars, man, how many showed up last night?"

"About a dozen."

They'd been dealing with a dozen by themselves? No wonder he'd come to fetch her first thing in the morning and report. "Fei, my dear, why are you only asking for help *now?* Even a dozen is unreasonable for just two men to deal with!"

"Well, a few from Iron Dragain stepped in and helped."

Oh sure, she knew exactly what he meant by that. In other words, a few men from Iron Dragain came and hauled unconscious and/or injured assassins away. They probably hadn't interfered in the fight itself, not when it meant protecting Rune. She let out a pained groan. "Alright. I'd thought this had stopped or resolved itself, as no one told me there was a problem. I would have stepped in before this if I'd realized how serious it had become."

She aimed a pointed glare at him. Fei didn't falter, just offered a half-bow of apology. "What do you wish to do?"

"Why don't we start with asking Jarnsmor how he wants us to handle this?"

"Can't you just kill them?" Jarnsmor requested plaintively.

Siobhan started, not at all expecting that response. For once, she hadn't found the man in his study, but just outside the main holding complex, where Iron Dragain kept all of their prisoners. The place reeked of cold, being built of granite, and looked dismal and unwelcoming. It gave Siobhan the creeps just standing outside the main door.

"You want me to order my men to kill anyone that attacks them," she repeated neutrally.

Jarnsmor's shoulders slumped slightly. "No, I suppose I can't say that. I would be violating my own laws if I did. But Guildmaster Maley, you've given me quite the predicament by bringing that young man here. He's drawing in assassins from Silent Order like flies to rotting meat. My jail is practically full already. I'm running out of places to put people!"

Ahhhh. *That* was the problem. "Can't you start judging these men and sentencing them?" she riposted. "You know them and at least some of the crimes they've committed. Surely you can let the law handle things from here."

"That takes *time*," he complained. "And what am I supposed to do with all of them while the Sateren Court judges each man?"

"Let the Sateren city jail hold them," Fei suggested. "Isn't that what they're made for?"

Jarnsmor regarded him thoughtfully. "True. They should be holding these men to begin with. I'm not sure how full they are, though. They might not be able to take them all either."

"They don't need to," Siobhan pointed out. "They just need to take whatever you don't have room for."

He snapped his fingers, expression brightening. "An excellent point. Alright, how many did you say you were expecting tonight? Twenty or so?"

"If they follow the same pattern as before," Fei responded with polite deference. "They usually increase in number by at least five more than the previous night."

"We'll plan for thirty, then, just in case." His lips pressed together in a tight, unhappy line. "You realize that I don't appreciate having assassins coming into my home on a regular basis."

Siobhan concealed a wince. "You don't like having them in your city, either. Think of this as an opportunity to rid yourself of some of them."

"Hmph." Still unhappy, he turned and stalked away,

calling out orders to people as he moved to get ready for the attack tonight.

She puffed out a breath of relief. "That went better than I'd hoped."

"Truly," Fei agreed. Lowering his voice, he asked, "Should I ask Wolf-ren and Tran-ren to help tonight? Or should we leave it up to Jarnsmor's men?"

She gave him quite the look. "Did you seriously just suggest planning an ambush without inviting our two fight-loving maniacs to join in? Wolf would pout for *weeks*."

Fei chuckled. "I'll go tell them, then."

Her nerves jangled the rest of the day, leaving her restless and moody, waiting for a fight that she wouldn't actually participate in. All four of her enforcers—Wolf especially—told her in no uncertain terms that they could handle it and didn't need help. She understood what they actually meant: the men coming were ruthless and likely more skilled than she, and no one wanted her in danger's way. Normally their protectiveness didn't bother her. If she had a choice, she'd prefer not to fight, but that didn't mean she could idly sit by while people she cared about were in serious trouble, either.

Siobhan understood that she wouldn't be able to help much even if she participated in the ambush tonight. She really, truly did. But she just couldn't stay safely away from the main building. After pacing her bedroom restlessly for several minutes, and then the common room for several minutes more, her feet automatically took her toward the main doors. The only way for people to enter was through the main gates, as Jarnsmor had tight security around his perimeter. The few holes he'd had were pointed out by previous attacks and corrected. Fei and Rune felt certain that the attack would come in through the front tonight.

She entered the main hallway cautiously, one sword held at the ready, eyes searching for any sign of life. Not a soul was nearby, but she could clearly hear the battle raging in the main foyer dead ahead. The light here was dim, barely any gleam coming through the windows, and it became progressively darker the further she went. The foyer was closed off from her view by two thick wooden doors, but even then it didn't muffle the sounds of metal clanging, men cursing, and feet stomping on the floor. Was that really only thirty or so men fighting ahead? It sounded like a hundred.

Reaching the door, Siobhan paused with her hand on the latch. Did she dare open it and peek, satisfying her curiosity? Opening the door would allow her to see them, true, but it would also allow *them* to see *her*. If discovered, she would be in a world of trouble with Wolf. And Rune. And Tran. And Fei.

Just imagining it made her wince. Perhaps this wasn't the best of ideas.

"Fei, *duck!*" Tran bellowed.

In sheer instinct she wrenched the door open and took a step through, sword up and eyes frantically searching for her people.

She found them in a split second, not ten feet away from where she stood and to the right. Fei, Tran and Rune had grouped together so that they watched each other's backs, each of them striking out hard and fast only to fall back into position. Her eyes could barely track their hands and feet, they moved so quickly. They already had several men lying comatose at their feet, silent proof of how deadly they fought.

Wolf was some three feet away from them, fighting earnestly with shield and sword, a berserker grin on his face that sent chills down her spine. Even as she watched, he used his shield like a battering ram and slammed it into his opponent's face, which no doubt broke the man's nose. It sent him flying back and landing against the floor in an inelegant sprawl.

Her eyes skipped across the rest of the room. Jarnsmor had indeed deployed some of his men to help—she recognized four of them—and it seemed they were competent fighters. In fact, the battle looked to be more or less over, as bodies littered the ground in every possible position and very few were still standing and fighting.

Grinning, she took a few quick steps forward and slammed her sword hilt into the back of one greasy head, sending the man slumping to the floor with a gasp of pain. Rune looked up, startled that his opponent had so suddenly collapsed, and found her smiling at him. "Hey!" he protested with an unhappy scowl. "Yer not supposed to come."

"Fight's over," she pointed out. "And as your guildmaster, I can be anywhere I please."

"Always stubborn like that," Tran mourned.

Another crunch of broken bones came from behind her. She half-turned to see that Wolf had finished the last Silent Order guildsman with the flat of his sword. Also with a scowl on his face, he stepped over the gasping, injured man and strode to her. "Siobhan," he growled between clenched teeth, "the fight was *not* over yet."

"Shilly-shally," she negated with a careless toss of the hand, sheathing her sword. "My, you boys were effective. I can't believe they really showed up like you predicted, Fei. I felt sure they'd learn from their mistakes."

"Matter of power, it is," Rune explained. He looked more resigned than upset over the situation. "Guildmaster can't let a man go and have him join a good guild like I did. It sets the idea in other's minds they can do the same."

Which meant that a dark guildmaster would potentially lose most of his people, as the benefits of belonging to a good guild far outweighed being in a dark guild. Besides, it was probably a matter of sheer stubbornness at this point, too. Rune was supposed to suffer a terrible fate after having failed to obey orders, not luck into a better situation.

Rune turned to Tran and thumped his heart twice with an open palm before bowing his head. Tran blinked, not at all expecting to have Rune properly thank him using Teheranian manners. Siobhan felt a little surprised to see this too, but she knew the source of the young Wyngaardian's sudden etiquette—Fei. He had indeed been paying attention to Fei's lessons on how to treat everyone in Deepwoods.

Tran, after that startled reaction, relaxed into a slight smile and gave a bow back. Then he reached out and clapped Rune on the shoulder in a comradely gesture, which made Rune smile back at him.

Turning, Rune looked to Fei next and offered, "We will drink and speak of this later."

Fei's eyes crinkled up in silent approval. He folded his arm against his ribs and extended a free hand, which Rune mirrored before accepting the hand in a firm clasp.

Only then did Rune turn to Wolf. She watched with bated breath. Her stubborn enforcer had watched Rune properly thank each man in their own ways for their help tonight. Rune was honestly trying, but would he see that for what it was and accept it?

Rune seemed to take in a breath before saying quietly, "Heill ok sael."

Wolf stared at him for a long second before lifting his right hand in acknowledgement, but he did not return the greeting, simply turned away and started to help with the cleanup.

Siobhan resisted the urge to go over and kick him. Stubborn, boneheaded, crepehanger! After everything Rune had done, he *still* couldn't trust him? She stole a peek at Rune's face, but he didn't seem disappointed or surprised at Wolf's reaction. Well, she shouldn't have been either. It was easier to get the sun to change its course than to change Wolf's opinion on something.

Sighing, she gave up on that for the moment and went to help clear bodies away.

Sylvie
Waverly

(c) 2014 Christa Triumph

# Chapter Twenty-Six

Siobhan didn't like ships for one specific reason: ceilings.

She wasn't a giant, not like some women from Teherani could be, but she did have an unusually tall stature for a woman. In fact, she could look most of her men in the eye with the exceptions of Tran and Wolf, her two giants. Most of the time her height came in handy, but whenever she boarded a ship, she had to hunch over to avoid hitting her head on the ceiling, or the top of the door jambs. It was one of those things that she remembered the first six times and forgot the seventh, so she always landed with some sort of bruise on her head.

After smacking her head on the ceiling three times, Siobhan gave up and went to the foredeck. It might be colder there with the sea breeze, but at least she wouldn't land on Orin with bumps on top of her bumps.

Tran and Wolf quickly followed her example and retreated to the forecastle, the only possible place for them to really sit without being in someone's way. She'd seen them smack their heads more times than she had, so it didn't surprise her they chose cold over pain. She put her back to the railing, sitting cross-legged on the wooden deck, and looked out over the sea. Even though they'd only been on the ship for an hour, she could barely see Wynngaard as a thin line in the distance. Her nose twitched at the strong scent of salt and tar. Still, an itchy nose was preferable to being down below.

Without a word, Tran sat on one side of her, Wolf on the other, and between the two of them they blocked the wind quite nicely. She shifted into a more comfortable position and smiled in satisfaction.

"Shi-maee."

"Hmm?" She turned to look at Tran.

"What do you expect to find? In Orin."

"I have no idea," she admitted frankly. "At this point, I'm not sure if anything could surprise me. Maybe whatever reason that drove the Coravine guild to attack Blackstone is very obvious and we'll see it once we're in the city. Or we might need to spend days looking and asking questions before we figure it out. I don't know. It's just that my gut is telling me that there's something important we haven't figured out yet."

He grunted understanding.

Silence passed comfortably between them as they sat there with their own thoughts. Siobhan let her eyes rove over the ship. It wasn't the largest merchant vessel she had ever seen, but it had a good size to it. Jarnsmor hadn't put them on a cheap, flimsy ship to say the least. At the speed they were going, she'd say they'd arrive in Orin about lunchtime. (Fortunate, that; Fei and ships didn't exactly get along where food was concerned.)

Wolf craned his head to look toward the bowsprit at the very front of the ship. "Those two look like seagulls."

Siobhan shifted about to look. Heh. He was right. Fei and Rune were balanced on the edge of the bowsprit, not seemingly disturbed by the idea that dropping into the ocean at that angle would certainly get them killed. They were animatedly talking about something, Rune's hands rising to illustrate some point he was making. The wind blew and snatched away their words before she could hear them, so she hadn't the faintest idea what subject had ensnared them so.

"I've noticed that Fei talks to Rune often," Tran noted slowly.

"They're kindred souls, those two," Siobhan said with a smile. "They both like high places. I wonder if they were birds in a previous life?"

Wolf shook his head slightly. "It's not that."

Her eyes cut to him. Oh? That sounded like a knowing tone. "What?"

"I asked Fei about it. He said that Rune reminds him of himself."

Tran blinked at him. "Eh? How?"

"That's as much as he said." Wolf gave a shrug.

Rune reminded Fei of himself? Fei had said that before, but she still didn't see the similarity. Those two were as different as day and night except their preference for high places and general sneakiness. Or at least, it looked like that to her on the surface, but in truth, there was a great deal that she didn't know about both men. Rune's past was a complete mystery to her aside from him belonging to a dark guild. He didn't trust her enough to share his secrets and she hadn't yet figured out whether she should ask or not. Sometimes old wounds bleed anew if they're prodded at.

Fei, in many aspects, was just as much a stranger. He'd been in the guild for eight years, and was one of the older members, but he'd never once told her why he was so far from home. He never had anyone contact him from Saoleord, either. He'd been eighteen when he'd come to her, which was a very tender age to be alone in a foreign country. She'd been willing to take him in just because of his youth, but he'd proven to be a good fighter when Wolf tested him, so she hadn't adopted him as a member on sympathy alone. As time passed, she had learned not to ask about his family or find out more of his story. Clearly, it was too painful to talk about. It might always be that way.

She watched the two sneaks sitting out there chatting avidly with weighing eyes. They were similar, huh. Now there was food for thought.

"You should trust Rune," Tran announced firmly.

At first Siobhan thought he said that to her, but when she looked up, she found his eyes locked with Wolf's. Oh, now this was interesting. Tran was trying to change Wolf's opinion on Rune?

Wolf's brows slammed together and a tic developed at his jaw. "I don't want to hear that from you. And since when did you come up with that, anyway?"

"You should trust him," Tran repeated stubbornly. "Did you know that he checks in on every person before he goes to bed himself? He does it again after he wakes up, too."

Siobhan sat up abruptly. "How do you know?"

"Fei told me," Tran answered her patiently. "I don't know how he knows, though. All I know is, Rune's honestly concerned about every person in the guild. That boy has been sleeping with an eye open ever since we took him on. He's dealt with threats we didn't see."

Hooo...and here she thought Wolf's senses of danger were too sharp to miss anything. She glanced at him and found him frowning.

"How far out is he patrolling?" Wolf asked slowly.

"Farther than you are. Whatever you set the limit at, he goes out further." Tran's tone remained carefully neutral as if, for once, he wasn't trying to challenge Wolf or start a fight. "I think he's afraid to lose Siobhan."

"Because we're safe to him, and he's never had that before," Siobhan translated his unspoken words with a long, exhaled breath.

Tran tapped his heart twice in quick agreement. "Wolf. That boy's no danger to us. You have to treat him as guild, or the next time we're in a fight, your eyes will be in the wrong place."

Wolf held up a hand to stay him. "I know, I know. I realized Conli was right in that. But what are we supposed to do with him?"

"We're not going to do anything with him," Siobhan interrupted. "Remember? It's his decision where to go once we are through Island Pass."

Both men gave her a dumbfounded *Is she kidding?* look.

"What?" she demanded in exasperation. "Did I miss something?"

Tran looked up at Wolf. "Usual wager?"

"I don't take sure bets," Wolf denied. "Bet with Sylvie or Markl."

"They wouldn't bet with me either," Tran complained.

"That's because it's a sure bet."

Siobhan grabbed both of Tran's cheeks with her hands. "You either cough up an explanation, or your smile is going to grow a lot bigger."

He grabbed her wrists and pushed her hands down easily, eyes twinkling in laughter. "Shi-maee, you think that boy is going anywhere? After all you've done to win him over?"

She thought about that for a second. Then thought about it again. "...What are we going to do with him?"

"You see it now, eh." Wolf shook his head. "That kid isn't going anywhere. You just got adopted by an assassin."

"It's because you fed it," Tran told her mock-seriously. "I told you not to feed everything that comes to you. They just end up staying."

"Now what was I supposed to do?" she riposted, playing along. "He was hungry. And he needed a nice place to sleep after being neglected for so long."

"Yes, but now that he knows you'll feed him, you won't be able to get rid of him."

"There's truth," Wolf muttered to himself. "So, Siobhan? What are you going to do with him?"

"I guess we keep him."

301

Wolf rolled his eyes heavenward in a clear plea for patience. "What are we supposed to do with an assassin?"

"I would suggest being nice to him, unless you want to be murdered in your sleep."

Tran laughed. "That's a start."

"Will you two be serious?"

"No," she and Tran said in unison.

He dropped his head into one hand and shook it in resignation.

"Siobhan-ajie!"

She twisted around and craned her neck to look up at Fei, who had risen up to his knees in order to call to her. "What?"

"Come up."

Huh? He sounded perfectly serious—unusual for him—and the way that his eyes never deviated from the horizon said without words that she needed to see something.

She put a hand on her sword hilts to keep them out of her way as she grabbed the edge of the railing and hauled herself upright and over, clambering up to where Rune and Fei sat. Rune gave her a hand up for the last foot, which she took, and he hauled her easily to his side. Sinking onto one knee, she looked at him briefly before turning to the direction Fei stared at.

Oh.

*Oh.*

Finally, *finally* this was starting to make sense.

In front of her incredulous eyes, stretching out over the water, was a bridge. It was like the Grey Bridges connecting through Island Pass. She could barely see details from this distance, but it was obvious that it wasn't that far along. It only went out about a span or so. Not as massive as the bridges it was obviously copied from, but sufficiently large enough for trade.

Pieces started to click into place. Siobhan felt like swearing but couldn't think of any words strong enough to fit the situation. She could barely tell what it was. In fact, if he hadn't pointed it out, she'd have never spotted it.

"That thing looks like it's only about four or five months old," Fei told her. "It's not big enough to have been there any longer than that."

"It's bei'n worked on even now," Rune added. Pointing a finger, he tried to draw her attention to the right area. "Ya see there, at the end, that trail of ropes? I see people hauli'n stones and such."

Their eyes were better than hers, then.

Wolf rose to his feet and called to them. "What is it?"

She waved for him to wait and had the boys follow her back to the forecastle to avoid shouting over the wind. Once they were there, she answered Wolf numbly, "There's a bridge being built from Orin's shores." The full situation was still sinking into her mind. "It's quite large, or at least it looks that way, although from this distance it's hard to tell."

"A bridge?" he repeated. He whipped around, one hand rising to shield his eyes from the sun. "I...can barely see it."

"If Rune hadn't pointed it out, I certainly wouldn't have." She sat there like a bump on a log, staring at the bridge. That bridge was a game changer. "Tran, call the others up here. We need to talk about this."

It took barely a minute to call them up. She sat heavily, the others following suit and finding space on the decking to sit as well. When they were settled, she looked at the curious faces surrounding her. In short, clipped tones, she explained what she'd seen.

Fei and Rune joined her, adding in a few details that she hadn't been able to make out over the distance, but which they apparently could. Just how good were their eyes, anyway? When they were done, they sat in a circle and just stared at each other, minds whirling.

It was Sylvie who broke the silence with a long sigh. "I get it now. This is a war of finances. They barely have the funds as it is to build a bridge with. But a trade monopoly between three of the most influential guilds in Robarge and Wynngaard would be economically devastating." Sylvie steepled her hands in front of her, obscuring half her face. "And with no trade specialty to offer, they have little bartering power to change the situation with."

"I'd have more sympathy for them if they weren't sending assassins after people," Siobhan growled irately.

Sylvie grimaced agreement. "Still, their initial plan is not wrong, a direct connection to Wynngaard will help them a great deal."

"I'm not sure if that is truly the case any longer, not after what they did," Markl disagreed. "Iron Dragain is *the* trading guild of Wynngaard. They unofficially set policy for all the trade on the continent. Framing them for an assassination has not endeared Orin to Iron Dragain."

Sylvie's open palm acceded the point. "It was a poor choice."

Siobhan sighed. "I wish we knew which guild it was that is actually over all of this. We know the bridge is being built from Coravine, but is that simply because it's the shortest distance to Wynngaard?"

"Even if this isn't Fallen Ward's idea, I can't imagine that they aren't a major part of the planning," Sylvie volunteered. "You don't build something near someone else's city without their approval and help. Fallen Ward is the only guild of any influence in Coravine; it must be them."

"Does it matter if it's them or not?" Denney asked, scratching at one cheek with an idle finger. "I mean, the bridge isn't really an option anymore, right?"

"Even if the bridge is no longer a usable option, I think Fallen Ward will be forced to continue down this path." Sylvie sounded unhappy with her own words. "Bridge or no, a trade monopoly will cripple them. Orin already struggles economically. They can't afford any loss in trade."

As a native of Orin, and Coravine, Sylvie would understand that better than anyone.

"So what do we do?" Rune asked.

Siobhan made a split second decision. "This doesn't change our immediate plans. We still go into Coravine and find out the guild that's behind all of this. But we gather more information about the bridge as we go. We need to know how much time it's going to take to build that thing and just where they're trying to build it *to*. We're here to get information, not make decisions that will affect the four continents." Fortunate, that. She didn't even begin to want to make *those* kinds of decisions.

"And if we can't find it out easily?" Markl asked quietly.

Siobhan met his eyes. "Two days. We've got two days. I don't think that we can afford more time than that. The rest of the world needs to know about this bridge and quickly, otherwise it's only going to become more dangerous."

# Chapter Twenty-Seven

"You...is your head there just to add to your height?"

"You chapo! Do you find breathing bothersome? *Eh?!*"

Siobhan let her head fall back and she groaned aloud. She was on top of the forecastle but could clearly hear both Wolf and Tran arguing below. Of course, both men could be thunderously loud when they were of a mind to be. From the sounds of it, they were about ten seconds from letting fists fly. She asked the sky, "Wasn't someone supposed to remind me that putting Wolf and Tran in a small area, for any length of time, is a bad idea?"

Sylvie answered the rhetorical question with a lackadaisical tone. "But they've been behaving recently."

"They've been behaving because they were both keeping an eye on Rune," Siobhan grumbled. "But now they've decided he's semi-trustworthy, so they're free to pick fights with each other again."

"Ahhh, is *that* why it's been so peaceful the last few days," Sylvie smirked.

Markl looked between both women with a confused

quirk of the brow. "I've been wondering about this for a while. If they really are that bad, why have both of them in the guild?"

"Oh, they're fine when it's serious or there's danger of some sort," Denney assured him, her fingers absently carding through Pyper's fur. Both dogs were bracketed on either side of her. "When the guild's safety is in question, they're perfectly in sync. It's just at moments like this, when there's no enemy for them to focus on, that there's trouble between them."

Siobhan, resigned to what needed to happen next, pushed herself to her feet. "Excuse me, ladies and gentlemen, I need to knock some heads together."

"Need a lift?" Fei asked mock-seriously. "I'm not sure if you're tall enough to reach their heads."

"Ha ha." She wrinkled her nose at him when he grinned impishly. "They're slouching at the moment to avoid hitting the ceiling, so I'll manage. But you know, a *true* friend would offer to intervene for me."

"No, that would make it worse," Fei disagreed. "If a man goes down, he'll just get pulled into the fight. But if *you* go, they'll break off. They'd never hurt you."

"I can't fault your logic," she agreed ruefully. With a shrug and a wave, she went down the short steps to the deck below and ducked into the tiny room that her giant enforcers were supposedly making plans in.

Tran and Wolf were practically nose to nose, hurtling insults at each other, which looked particularly ridiculous since they were hunched over to avoid the ceiling. When she darkened the doorway, they stopped mid-sentence and looked in her direction for all the world like two boys that had dragged mud all over the floor.

Clearing her throat meaningfully, she asked them with a cold smile, "Boys. Are we fighting?"

"Ah, no, Shi-maee," Tran assured her quickly.

"Really?"

"Not one bit," Wolf substantiated this, carefully hiding his iron hand behind his back.

She eyed that subtle movement and wondered just what had he been planning to do...no, she shouldn't ask. She probably wouldn't want to know. "That's good, because if memory serves, you still haven't worked off the fines for the *last* fight you two had. And we'd rather not wreck Master Jarnsmor's ship that he leant us, all things considered. Right?"

They nodded warily.

She beamed at them sunnily. "Excellent. Now, just to avoid any possible conflict, Tran, why don't you come up with me. When Wolf is done down here, you two can switch places."

Neither man could argue that they were grown adults and could govern themselves. Not after the spectacular fights they'd had in the past and the buildings that they'd destroyed. Tran meekly followed her upstairs and sat next to her as she regained her former seat on the deck.

Siobhan noticed with interest that in the few minutes she'd been gone, Sylvie had shifted positions. She had turned and was now leaning her back against Markl's arm, for all the world treating him like a piece of furniture to prop herself up with. Even more interesting was that Markl didn't seem to mind this one bit. In fact, he had a soft expression in his eyes as he looked at the woman so comfortably reclining against him.

Was something developing there? Siobhan knew that Sylvie liked Markl just because he was a gentleman and she didn't need to worry about being around him. When had that developed into...*that*?

Beirly, who sat nearby whittling something, caught her eye and gave a meaningful glance at the two. She nodded thoughtfully, making a mental note to keep an eye on the situation. It'd be interesting to see if her suspicions proved true.

Markl caught Tran's attention with a wave of the hand and ventured, "I've been meaning to ask, when did you join the guild?"

"Hmmm, I came in about six years ago," Tran

responded, rubbing at his chin thoughtfully. "Has it been that long?"

"Closer to seven," Sylvie corrected.

"Guess it would be." He shrugged, not really concerned either way. "I was working as a caravan guard, going back and forth across Robarge, when I came to Goldschmidt. It had just hit off-season, and I was looking for winter work, when I saw this beauty getting hassled in the street." He grinned at Sylvie, smile teasing.

Sylvie pulled a face. "In those days, it happened more often. That was before Wolf put his foot down and said we weren't allowed to go out alone anymore."

"Too many fights broke out because of you, that's why," Siobhan drawled.

"It's hard being this beautiful," Sylvie lamented, a hand raised to her forehead like a wilting damsel in distress.

Laughing, Tran continued the story. "I didn't know what was going on, but it was four men against her. She was holding her own, but it still made me mad to watch it. So I stepped in and helped a little."

"That means he broke two noses, three arms, and a few ribs," Sylvie translated for Markl, who was listening with wide eyes.

"When the dust settled, I offered to escort her back to her home." Tran's smile went crooked. "I'm not sure if she trusted me at first, but she went with it."

"What I didn't know was that Wolf had gotten worried about me," Sylvie picked up the thread of the story smoothly. "And he was coming my direction, looking for me. When he saw me with an unknown man, his first reaction was to think I'd gotten into trouble somehow. So he let a punch fly."

Tran rubbed at his chin in memory. "Nearly broke my jaw."

"They had quite the fight in the middle of the street before I was able to get them to stop and explain the situation." Sylvie shook her head at the memory. "Then

I felt bad, because Tran had gotten into *two* fights on my account, so I brought him back to the Hall to clean him up and give him a place to stay for the night."

"I was thankful for that, as I didn't know the city at all. Then Shi-maee," he put a hand on Siobhan's shoulder in demonstration, "got the story, liked what she heard, and offered me a place in the guild."

Markl's eyebrows rose. "And Wolf?"

"Raised the roof, he yelled so loud." There was an evil smile on Tran's face. "But she wouldn't hear it. Shi-maee likes people that can fight toe-to-toe with Wolf, which aren't many, and men that she can trust to protect her own. So to her mind, I was a perfect fit."

"Ahhh, I see." Markl ruminated on this for a moment before offering, "Is your initial meeting the reason why you two are always fighting?"

Beirly snorted. "Nothing like that. It's just having two roosters in the same hen yard is all."

Tran let out a squawk of protest, which set Siobhan and Denney to laughing.

Markl smiled too, enjoying the banter, but he wouldn't be deterred from the subject. "Siobhan, is that how you pick your people? By how capable they are at fighting?"

"Great winds, no! Think about it, did I ask you that question?"

He paused, opened his mouth, then closed it again thoughtfully.

"See? Now, I think it's important that we're all able to protect ourselves at least, and we all can in one way or another. But the reason why I have Wolf, Tran, and Fei... well, Rune too now...as enforcers is because some of us are not as good at fighting as others. Some of us need more help in that area and they take up the slack."

Markl's head cocked slightly in question. "Then what *are* you looking for, if you don't mind my asking?"

"Hmm, a few things. A good working attitude for the most part. The skills and talents needed to make a guild work. You'll notice, most of us have wildly different abilities from the others, but it's all those talents combined that give us strength." She hadn't really thought about it or tried to frame it into words before and discovered that she had to really struggle to find the right way to explain. "But it's more than just that. It's...selflessness, I guess. Kindness."

Fei nodded in support of this. "The value of a man resides in what he gives, not in what he is capable of receiving."

She gave him a frustrated look. "How is it that I can struggle to say something and every single time, you say it better than I can?"

Being a wise man, he didn't try to respond, just shrugged and looked innocent.

"Kindness...huh." Rune stirred from his perch on the railing and looked at every person with new eyes. "That's why?"

Everyone turned to look at him, wondering what he meant by that.

"What do you think, Rune?" Markl asked him gently. "Seeing this guild work together, despite how different they are, what do you think of them?"

"Didn't know what ta think." Rune caught Siobhan's eyes, his own expression pensive but also somehow lost. "Never saw the like of this before. Ya watch out for each other, and work together, and talk without words. It didn't make sense ta me. Still doesn't. But ya say it's kindness?" The way he put a twist on the word made it clear that he didn't understand at all.

Siobhan felt it strongly in that moment. She had a chance of reaching Rune's heart and changing him for the better, if only she handled this right. Praying she had the words, she got to her feet and crossed to him. He watched her carefully, like a wounded animal ready to take flight the second he sensed danger. Just as carefully, she reached out and picked up one of his hands, holding it in a loose grip. "Rune. True strength *is* kindness. Because only the truly strong can show it. Cruelty is a sign of weakness."

He swallowed hard, eyes searching hers. "B-but...."

"Think about it," she urged him softly. "You've seen Fei in action. You've sparred with him. Do you see him as being weak?"

Rune instantly shook his head, almost emphatically.

"But you know, he's one of the kindest men I've ever met. He's also one of the wisest. I've never heard him raise his voice at anyone unless they were trying to hurt one of his own. Whenever I need wise council, he's one of the men I turn to. There's not a trace of cruelty to be found in him. Forsaking kindness wouldn't make him stronger."

A war of emotions struggled across Rune's face. "Ta do the job, ya leave the heart behind."

He said it like he'd heard it a thousand times, repeated it a thousand more. Siobhan's denial was instinctive. "No. Anything that requires sacrificing your heart isn't worth it. It's evil work that destroys you. Rune, who taught you such a lie?"

"I...don't remember." He looked away from her for a moment as if searching his memory.

Had he been raised on this insanity since infancy? Oh for the love of...she took in a deep breath and exhaled it.

"The top of my old guild are strong," he whispered.

"But not stronger than the ones you've met in this guild, or in Iron Dragain," she challenged. "Your old guild even sent dozens of assassins after you and not *one* of them managed to kill you! Rune, you've been fed this line about not showing kindness, not feeling anything, but you can see with your own eyes it's not true. *It's not true*," she repeated emphatically.

"He knows," Fei assured her from behind, voice gentle.

Siobhan half-turned, looking at Fei askance.

"He knows, Siobhan-ajie," he repeated patiently, eyes crinkled in a silent smile. "Flowers do not bloom in dead trees."

Puffing out a breath, she rubbed at a temple. "You're too deep, Fei. Translate that."

"He never fully believed that he must sacrifice his

heart. He kept it safe, hidden. He must have, or he would not have been able to respond to the kindness shown him." Fei shifted to look Rune straight in the eye. "Right?"

Rune looked away, a little uneasily. "...Yer right."

Ducking her head, she tried to catch his eyes again. "Rune?"

"It's why...I was sent out alone." He kept his eyes on the decking, unable to look up at her. "I was sent out ta burn a man's house. I didn't."

*Finally* she was getting the story of how he'd ended up where he did. "Why not?" she asked, tone coaxing.

"His wife was pregnant."

Unable to stop herself, she put her free arm around his neck and drew him in for a hug. He started in surprise, body tense, but she didn't let up and whispered against his ear, "Good choice."

Rune truly didn't know how to handle this, and stayed stiff like a hardened plank of wood, obviously uneasy with the embrace. He started again when a hand settled on his back. Siobhan lifted her eyes enough to see that at some point, Wolf had come in. He met Rune's startled eyes with open approval and repeated Siobhan's words. "Good choice."

The former assassin's mouth parted as if he wanted to say something only couldn't find the words.

"It's alright," Wolf assured him, as if understanding the turmoil broiling inside of Rune. "I was saved by her too."

Rune really didn't know how to respond to that. He blew out a breath. "Yer both confusing."

For some reason, Wolf found this funny, as he chuckled lowly, like a mountain rumbling. "She is," he agreed. "But give it time."

"He included you in that," Siobhan corrected him, crossing her arms over her chest and giving him a long look.

"I'm not confusing," he denied mildly. "I like to hit things, eat good food, and flirt with pretty women.

Nothing complicated in that."

"A candle illuminates others and exterminates itself," Fei observed factually.

Wolf jerked a thumb at him. "If you want confusing, *he's* confusing."

Every person there agreed with emphatic nods, which made Fei grin mischievously. Siobhan could swear some days that he said cryptic things just to confuse and irritate people. That expression on his face right now rather proved it.

From the main deck there came a loud booming voice: "RAISE ALL SAILS! PREPARE TO LAY ANCHOR!"

"Well, I think that's our cue." Siobhan clapped her hands together. "Grab your gear, people. Let's get ready to disembark."

Beirly
Kierkegaard

Christa Triumph 2011

# Chapter Twenty-Eight

It was a well-known fact throughout the four continents that Coravine was not a particularly wealthy or prosperous place. Knowing that intellectually and seeing it with her own eyes were two very different things. Siobhan's head turned this way and that as she took in the city, her boots vibrating on the wooden gangplank leading down to a stone dock. The smell of the sea was strong here, stronger than it had been while she was crossing the Dual Channel, and her nose wrinkled in protest. It was more than the salt mixed in with the wind, but other things—decaying fish, refuse molding in piles under the docks, the smell of rot. This place made the Sateren shoreline look like a paradise in comparison.

Just as disturbing to her was the *lack* of sounds. It felt almost eerie here, the place was so empty. She counted perhaps two dozen people working and the rest were suspiciously absent. How strange. It took more people than that to handle the workload here, surely. Unless... unless all possible manpower had been diverted to help build that bridge? She couldn't see it from here. Rows of warehouses, dry docks, and small restaurants blocked her view.

"Inn first?" Beirly asked her.

"Inn first," she agreed, not wanting to lug around her bags any more than she had to. "After that, I think we can split up and meet back at the inn for dinner. Sylvie, suggestions?"

"I know a good one." With a wave of the arm, she gestured for them to follow her as she took the lead.

Rune fell into step beside Siobhan and asked in a low tone, "She knows the place well?"

"Born and raised here." Siobhan cast him a quick glance. "She's only been in Deepwoods about seven years. Before she went to Robarge, she'd lived her entire life here." Hence her amazing trade skills. It took that level of ability to survive in this city. Sylvie had learned how to negotiate a rabbit out of its fur when she was only knee-high.

Rune's head tilted back as he did some quick math. "She turned guildie same time as Tran?"

"Thereabouts. If memory serves, Sylvie came in about two months before Tran did."

"Lucky," he observed.

"Truly." If not for Sylvie, she'd never have met Tran. Despite the headaches he caused her, Siobhan didn't for one minute regret bringing him into the guild.

Sylvie led them confidently away from the docks and into a section of town that made Siobhan's hand itch for her sword. It reminded her strongly of that section in Quigg that had sheltered the street rats, the only difference being there were more signs of life here with people walking about in the open. If this represented a *good* section of the town, then she hated to think of what the *bad* section would look like.

As if sensing their unease, Sylvie called back over her shoulder, "It's rough here, but the inn's good."

Right, so this wasn't necessarily a decent part of town.

Should she be relieved or not?

Sylvie proved right—she usually was in these matters—and the inn proved better than Siobhan's paranoid fantasies. In fact, it was rather on par with their favorite inn on Island Pass. Siobhan paid for five rooms without worry, glad to have a good place to lay her head. They threw their bags into the rooms, locked them, and gathered back down at the main porch.

As soon as Markl joined them, the last to do so, she turned to him and ordered, "We need information, and you're the best at gathering that without raising too much suspicion. Take at least one person with you and just walk around town, get some intel. Beirly, I want you to take a good look at that bridge. How solid is it going to be and how long is it going to take to build?" Each man nodded understanding. "The rest of you divide yourselves up."

"And you?" Tran asked her.

Siobhan linked her arm with Sylvie's. "Let's go for a walk, shall we?"

"Oh, marvelous idea," Sylvie agreed easily. She already had a predatory eye on the street ahead of them.

"Not alone," Wolf objected.

"You're not coming with us," Siobhan said firmly.

He gave a wordless protest.

"You intimidate people just standing there and breathing," Sylvie added, backing Siobhan up. "You'll just be in the way. We'll be fine."

Siobhan gave them a little wave as she started off. "Go find something to do. Something that doesn't involve bloodshed or broken buildings."

He didn't look happy but he stayed where he was. Siobhan could hear his low voice murmuring something, and Tran's voice responding. Hopefully the two of them wouldn't go somewhere *together,* as that was a sure fire way of getting into trouble.

She and Sylvie made it all of ten steps when the brunette murmured for her ears alone, "Rune's following us, isn't he?"

319

"Fei is too."

"Did Wolf sic them on us?"

"Probably." Siobhan didn't have a problem with this, as at least those two knew how to follow people discreetly. Wolf couldn't blend in with his environment if his life depended on it.

Sylvie dismissed this with a shrug. "Are we using our usual plan?"

"Why not?"

"Excellent." Sylvie pretended to think about this for a moment. "I want a new winter cloak. You?"

"Boots would be good. Something knee-high to block this icy wind."

"I haven't seen any good clothing shops yet...." Sylvie raised a hand to shade her eyes and peer further down the street. They'd finally walked far enough along to get to a nicer, more business-oriented side of town, so they actually had choices in front of them. "But I think I see one. That green sign down there, isn't that a boot carved into it?"

"It certainly looks like one." Siobhan had a hard time seeing it clearly with the sun glaring off of it.

They struck off for the store, for all the world appearing to be two women on a shopping expedition. Sylvie's eyes proved right, and the store had a great quantity of leather boots, work rough and fine in every possible size. The store seemed fit to burst, in fact, with the quantity of them. Siobhan quickly discovered that quantity did not equal *quality,* as the first two boots she picked up were obviously second hand and ill-used. Hmm. It would take some digging to find anything decent.

As she shopped, Sylvie leaned against the counter where a middle aged woman was waiting. "I'm looking for a good cloak," she said with a warm smile. "Is there any store here you'd recommend?"

"Oh, certainly," the woman responded, voice slightly nasally. She leaned over the counter, which creaked under her ponderous weight. "There's a shop two down from here on your left side, but don't go into it. The man's a shyster. Go further down, past the old tavern, and there's another store on your right with bright purple trim around the door. *That's* the best place to shop."

Siobhan glanced at her over one shoulder doubtfully. Considering the state of the woman's wares, she had to question her taste in quality.

Sylvie pretended not to notice. "My friend here is looking for knee-high boots, something that will keep her legs warm while she's traveling. Do you have anything like that?"

"Oh, a few," she said. "Most of my women's shoes are only ankle high, though. Dearie, what size are you? Twenty-two, twenty-three?"

"Twenty-five, actually," Siobhan admitted.

"Oh my! I won't have anything that large."

Yes, so she could see. Siobhan just sighed in resignation. "It's fine. Do you have anything like it in men's shoes?"

"Oh." The woman stood from her stool to see over the counter. "Ohhh, you've got men's shoes on, I see. Hard to find your size, eh? Well, you're so tall, it's no wonder. Here, see this back corner near me? That's the right area to look."

"Thank you." Siobhan turned sideways and eased around one stack of shoes, carefully stepping to avoid creating a shoe avalanche.

Sylvie recaptured the woman's attention. "When we came in, we saw a bridge being constructed on the shoreline. Where's it going to? I mean, I don't think there's any land out in the channel until you reach Wynngaard."

"There isn't." The woman leaned in a little closer. "They told everyone in the city to keep this hushed for as long as we can, although why they thought that would work, I don't know. The thing sticks out over the water like a sore thumb. Eventually enough sailors will spread the word. But they're building a bridge to Wynngaard, like the

Grey Bridges."

Sylvie gave a shocked expression that would have made any credible actor envious. "Oh my! Are you serious?"

"Yes, yes. I don't remember where it's supposed to connect..." the woman trailed off, staring up at the ceiling as if she was trying to recall. "Somewhere on the continent, anyway."

"But that's a long ways!" Sylvie protested, more genuine this time.

"Oh, I know it. It's supposed to take another forty years, they said. Long past when I'm dead and buried, leastways. But can you imagine what it will do for this city? Why, trade will shoot right up!"

"Who's behind the building of it? It'll take a pretty penny to build something that size."

"That's the thing." The woman leaned forward even more, her voice lowering to a conspiratory tone. "No one knows."

Siobhan snapped around to stare at her incredulously. "What?"

"No one knows," the woman repeated with a furtive look toward the door. "We all suspected Fallen Ward, but they're denying it, and it's true—we never see their members working on the bridge. It's always workers and masons from other cities that come and do the construction."

She shared a speaking look with Sylvie. This just got stranger and stranger. Even the people of this city didn't know?

After a little more digging, Siobhan found a good pair of boots that only had light wear to them, and she bought them for a reasonable price thanks to Sylvie's bartering. They exited the shop and went ten steps down the street before daring to speak to each other.

"It's *not* Fallen Ward?" Siobhan said in confusion. "How can that be possible?"

"It can't be," Sylvie denied. "No way. Can you imagine

a guild coming into Goldschmidt and building something that large without Blackstone somehow being involved? No, they're working with someone behind the scenes. This attitude of 'not involved' is camouflage. Why they're bothering to act innocent, I don't know."

Siobhan rubbed a temple, feeling the pangs of a headache coming on. "I'm getting more confused, not less. And we're here so I can be less confused!"

"I hear you. Cloak?"

"Why are ya shoppi'n anyway?" A familiar male voice asked from above their heads.

Both women stopped and craned their necks around to look up. Rune squatted casually on the edge of a nearby roof, looking as comfortable up there as a cat in a sunny perch.

Sylvie didn't even look surprised to find him up there when she explained, "Buying something is the easiest way to loosen a shop owner's tongue. Thereby, shopping is the most effective method of gathering information."

Rune gave her a look that said he didn't buy that for one second. "Ya like ta shop."

"You bet." Sylvie winked at him, lips curled in a smirk. "You don't have to lurk on the rooftops, you know. You can join us."

He held up a hand in refusal. One shopping trip with Sylvie was enough for him, eh? "Ya keep goi'n."

"Suit yourself." With a shrug, Sylvie kept walking, Siobhan keeping pace with her.

"At the rate we're going, we might need to buy a whole wardrobe before we find all the information we need," Siobhan muttered.

"You think Iron Dragain will reimburse us?" Sylvie batted innocent eyes. "After all, it's a business expense."

"I highly doubt it, but can you pitch the idea to Jarnsmor when we get back? The expression on his face is bound to be priceless."

"I bet you I can," Sylvie challenged with a gleam in her eye.

"Usual bet?"

"Usual bet."

"You're on."

# Chapter Twenty-Nine

Siobhan's joke about buying a whole wardrobe turned out to be more accurate than she'd predicted. Between the two of them, they managed to buy a cloak, coat, shirt, boots, and two pairs of pants in their search. In spite of their intense pursuit and Sylvie's silver tongue, they didn't get much more information.

As night threatened to fall, the whole guild met back up at their inn's tavern room and sat down at a round table for dinner. The lighting in here wasn't the best, so the room with its low ceiling seemed casted in warm lantern light and cool shadows. After spending the majority of the day in harsh sunlight, Siobhan was thankful for the cool darkness.

She did feel somewhat sorry for Tran and Wolf, though, as they kept knocking their foreheads against the rafters.

A thick beef casserole of some sort was dished out onto plates with warm biscuits and set on the table. Silence descended as everyone focused on the food, and it wasn't until the second serving was half-consumed that Siobhan felt it safe to ask questions. "So...how did it go today?"

Everyone just grimaced at her or gave a glum shrug.

"Well, now, that's informative," she said sarcastically, pushing her plate away from her. "Come on, people, tell me what you *do* know."

Beirly, being a brave sort, started after clearing his throat. "Bridge is solid. Good construction, good design. When I went to get a closer look, the foreman there tried to hire me on the spot. Said he was short on workers. From what I see, they're taking any man who can lift a stone, no matter where he comes from. Bridge isn't as big as the ones near Island Pass, about half the width, but that's wide enough for caravans and the like."

"Did he mention how long it will take to build?"

"He said it's due to be finished in 37 years."

A more accurate timeline had been gained, then. "Did he mention where exactly it was supposed to end up?"

"They're going straight across, so just northeast of Quigg."

Sylvie let out a low whistle. "If they do that, I can imagine that Quigg will rapidly expand that direction."

"Either that or another city will start up nearby," Markl agreed. "We talked to a great many people and no one knew who was behind it. Now, according to the masons' guild here in the city—they're apparently over the design and construction of the bridge—they've gotten approval from Fallen Ward to construct it. But they were adamant that it wasn't them who funded the project."

Siobhan's brows arched. He'd learned something that she hadn't. "So who did?"

"Client privileged information," he said sourly, with a tone that indicated he'd heard nothing but that phrase all day.

"That's a fancy way of saying, 'I won't tell you.'" Beiryl shook his head. "We heard that a lot today."

"Whoever did this is very good at covering their tracks." Markl braced his forearms against the table and leaned across the surface wearily. "In fact, the way the information has been so thoroughly squashed makes me believe it really *is* Fallen Ward. Only the main guild of a city could exert this kind of influence over everyone."

Truly. A city guildmaster was like a minor deity to its city. No one would dare to disobey for fear of the consequences, which could range from anything between a fine to being stripped of all possessions and thrown out. "Speaking of, anyone gain any information about the new guildmaster?"

"Not a thing," Markl sighed. "People would tell us about the funeral of the old guildmaster—apparently it was quite a grand affair and the whole city got drunk for three days—but no one seems to know about the new one. Ever since the guild's changed hands, the security around their main compound has tightened to the point that very few can enter or leave."

Hence why Jarnsmor hadn't been able to get any messages from his people. If they truly were still alive, and in there, they were probably unable to leave long enough to send any message out. She nodded understanding. "Sylvie and I didn't do much better. Anyone else find out anything? Anything at all?"

People shrugged or grimaced but no one spoke.

"Alright, that begs the question," Siobhan raised an illustrative finger, "will we gain more answers if we stay longer?"

Most of the table shook their heads no.

"I think between all of us, we covered most of the city today." Denney grimaced and stretched. "Or at least, my feet say we did. Siobhan, honestly, I don't know who else to *ask*. The few people that are in this city that know all the answers aren't going to tell the likes of us. So unless you want to start a war right here in the city—"

Tran, Wolf, and Rune all perked up and eyed their guildmaster hopefully.

"—and force information out of people, then I don't know what else we can try," Denney finished with a sour look at the men.

"I *highly* doubt that we're allowed to start a war here," Siobhan responded dryly, giving the men quelling looks. It didn't have quite the effect she was going for, as they seemed more crestfallen and disappointed than afraid of her future wrath. "In that case, I think we should leave in the morning. Beirly, find the ship's master and relay a message to him that we'd like to go back to Sateren in the morning."

Beirly gave her a casual salute of acknowledgement.

Pushing back from the table with a scrape, she stretched her arms above her head with a yawn. "See you in the morning."

"Siobhan."

"Uhhhh." She batted the hand away and attempted to roll over. This effort was thwarted by the wall that she smacked her forehead into. The beds in the inn were clean, but one could not describe them as *wide*.

A hand grabbed her by the shoulder and insistently shook her awake. "Siobhan!"

She cracked open one eye and aimed a murderous glare over her shoulder. Markl was leaning over her with a lantern in one hand, illuminating a worried expression on his face. Judging from the narrow window behind him, it was still in the middle of the night.

Uh-oh. Her brain woke up enough to point out to her that the only time anyone woke her up like this, something had happened. It usually involved property damages, too. "Who's injured?" she slurred out, dragging her hair out of her face as she sat up.

"Wolf and Tran, although it doesn't look too serious," he answered promptly.

"Where?"

"Tavern across the street."

She stopped with her legs half off the bed and gave him a long look. In a painfully level tone, she said, "Wolf and Tran went to a tavern. Together."

"Umm...yes?"

"And no one stopped them?"

"Were we supposed to?"

She dropped her head into one hand and just groaned, long and loud. "How much damage did they do?"

Markl hesitated, searching her face and judging what words to say. When she just stared back at him steadily, he gave up and with a shrug told her bluntly, "I'm honestly surprised the building is still standing."

Lovely. Shooing him out with one hand, she threw on the first clothes she found, dragged her hair back in a rough ponytail, and stuffed her feet into her new boots. Snagging her purse—and praying it had enough money to fix this situation—she stomped out of the room, down the short stairs, and into the cold night air. Rubbing her arms briskly, she got all of two steps when Fei appeared at her elbow like magic. He had a medical satchel in his hands, the sort that Conli issued to take care of minor medical emergencies.

Without a word to him, she crossed the street in quick strides to the tavern and shoved what was left of the door aside. The way it creaked and hung, the whole thing would likely need to be replaced.

Once she got a look at the room, she realized in dismay that the door was in *good* shape compared to everything else.

There was not one chair still intact. They were all broken, scattered over the floor like so much kindling. Only a handful of tables were still erect, two of which Wolf and Tran sat on. The bar behind them had mostly withstood the fight, but it had long scores in the wood, like a dragon had gnawed on it. People were laying injured, comatose, or just passed out drunk in every possible angle and position. She had to maneuver her way around the bodies, sometimes stepping over people, to get to her own.

Wolf and Tran looked up, spotted her approach, and gave her neutral expressions. That look alone told her that this fight was, indeed, their fault. For some strange reason, both of them were half-naked, only their trousers still on, and Tran was even missing a boot. She'd never seen a bar fight that had escalated to the point that it had *stripped* people before. Stopping in front of them, she planted her feet, crossed her arms over her chest, and gave them The Look.

"Boys. Why were you fighting?"

"I have a headache," Wolf volunteered easily.

Tran half raised a hand. "I have a stomach ache."

Patience. She had to exercise patience. "And how does that tie into getting into a bar fight?"

"Well," Wolf explained innocently, "destroying things makes us feel better, so...."

Behind her, Fei choked on a laugh. Without looking, Siobhan threw an elbow into his ribs, which he mostly dodged, the rat. "Be serious."

The two men exchanged glances, heaved identical shrugs, and came clean.

"Actually," Tran admitted, "the real reason isn't much better. See, we were arguing over who has the most scars—"

"Never did agree on that," Wolf muttered to himself, as if only just realizing this.

"—and for some reason, the tables around us got really into it," Tran continued with a cough and exasperated glance at Wolf. "One side said it was me, the other table said it was Wolf. So they got up and started wrestling our clothes off."

Ahhh, *that* was why they were half-naked.

"And then one man said, 'Let me help even it out!' and he came at us with two kitchen knives," Wolf held up his hands a good foot apart, "about yay big. Almost short swords, they were so long."

"If they'd had a hilt, I'd have thought they were," Tran agreed. "Anyway, he comes straight at Wolf. Without that metal hand of his, he'd have *lost* a hand."

"Then the rest of the crowd thinks he's got a point, or something, 'cause *they* pull out swords too and go at us." Wolf shrugged, a grin on his face in memory, because in truth, he didn't care what the reason was as long as he got to be a little rowdy. One quelling look from Siobhan and his smile instantly dropped from his face. "Anyway. We were defending ourselves," he ended with righteous indignation that almost sounded genuine.

The master of the tavern came from a back room with a broom in his hands. He'd apparently overheard most of their exchange, as he came up to them with a deferential bow and offered, "It truly wasn't them that started this, Miss...?"

"Siobhan Maley," she introduced herself with strained politeness, offering a hand. "I'm their guildmaster."

"Oh, pleasure, certainly, a pleasure," he bobbed his head nervously and grasped her hand in a quick, flimsy way before letting go. "Guildmaster, don't be too harsh on them. As I said, they didn't start it. And they did their best to end it quick, to not let things get out of hand. But well, most of the men here are from other places and far from home, so they tend to drink too much and things like this..." he trailed off as he looked around him in dismay, "well, this isn't the first time it's happened."

The poor man. If this was a regular occurrence, how by the four winds was he staying in business? "Regardless, my men were in the fight and caused damage. I'll compensate you as much as I can."

He gave a duck of the head, rubbing at his neck sheepishly. "Obliged, much obliged, I'm sure. But I won't take more than two golds. I know these men's taskmaster, I'll get the rest from him."

Well that wasn't half-bad, compared to the other spectacular fights these two idiots had gotten involved in. Siobhan, with a secret sigh of relief, handed the golds over. Then she turned back to her enforcers with a quirked brow. "Since you two aren't screaming with pain or bleeding anywhere, I assume you got through it relatively safe?"

"A few bruises," Wolf admitted.

"I think I did get cut on my back," Tran twisted about as if to see, which of course he couldn't. "But I'm not sure how bad it is."

Fei came around the table, opened up the small black satchel, and set about tending to Tran.

Siobhan just sighed, eyes closed for a moment, offering a silent prayer of thanks to any god listening. Then she called out, "Rune?"

From somewhere above her head, the assassin responded, "Yes?"

She'd just *known* he was around somewhere. "You didn't get involved in this too, did you?"

There was a suspicious moment of silence. "I might've knocked a few heads together."

Of course he'd joined in. She pointed an accusing finger at Wolf. "You're setting a bad example for the children."

"He had bad habits *before* he met me," Wolf protested, not at all upset with the accusation.

"I don't want those bad habits to continue. Having *two* of you is bad enough. I do not want THREE." That said, she craned her head around, trying to spot Rune. In vain. How a man could possibly hide up in those airy log rafters, she had no idea, but he'd managed it somehow. "You didn't get hurt, did you?"

"Naw, I'm fine," he assured her, voice amused.

Under her breath, she muttered, "Thank the winds for that. Alright, now that the fun is over, I expect everyone to go to bed and *stay* there until dawn. At least. Am I clear?"

A chorus of obedient "Yes, ma'am" came to her. Satisfied, she turned on her heel and went back to the inn, shivering. As she went, she grumbled to herself, "Seriously. What part of 'we do not want to start a war here' did they not understand?"

Ugh. Men.

✦ ✦ ✦

After the late night misadventures, Siobhan found it hard to get up the next morning. Since the ship was at their beck and call, she took advantage of it a little and didn't try to rush getting ready. In fact, she went down to breakfast a good hour later than she normally did, only to find that most of the guild had also risen late.

Waving good morning to people, she sat and filled up a plate but didn't try to really talk until she had consumed about half of it. At that point, she realized that the table had two notable absentees. "Where's Sylvie and Rune?"

"They were gone when I came down," Markl responded, a slightly unhappy set to his mouth. "The innkeeper said they left early this morning together."

*Yes, and you're jealous of that, aren't you?* Siobhan carefully bit the inside of her lip to keep herself from smiling. Markl wouldn't take any sign of amusement well. "I see. Is everyone packed and ready to board the ship?"

"We can't leave until those two show up," Tran pointed out, calmly eating.

"I'm aware. I'm also aware that out of this entire group, it's the *men* that are always ready to leave last." She cast the repeat offenders pointed looks, although none of them looked particularly abashed at her silent scolding. "So be ready to leave the minute they're back."

Getting grunts and waves of acknowledgement, she felt satisfied she'd gotten the point across and resumed eating.

As it turned out, everyone was downstairs with their bags packed, just chatting, when the errant duo finally returned. Sylvie looked particularly put-out with the world, a scowl twisting her mouth. Siobhan didn't have to ask to know where the other woman had been. Sylvie must have been visiting her parents while she was in town.

They'd been through here several times over the years, and it was always the same whenever Sylvie went home.

333

Her parents were dead set on living in Coravine, heaven only knew why, but they couldn't really make much of a living here. In fact, all seven of their children had left the city—some of them had left the continent altogether—and made homes elsewhere because of Coravine's poor economy. Sylvie tried to convince her parents on every trip to move, to go to one of the places where their children lived, but they wouldn't hear of it. Instead, they wanted Sylvie to live *here* and take care of them in their older years.

Siobhan gave her points for trying, but her parents would have to be in a far more desperate situation before they'd finally give up and leave the city. Until then, anything Sylvie said was just a waste of breath.

More curious to her was, why had Rune gone with her? Simply because he was worried about Sylvie being out and about on her own? "Where have you two been?" she asked them.

"Morning market, and a few other places," Sylvie responded. "Is that my bag? Thanks."

"Morning market?" Markl repeated in confusion.

Rune came to stand in front of Siobhan and handed her a small bundle wrapped in a grey handkerchief. Bemused, she took it and hefted it in her hands. Strange, it felt warm and was that...did she smell apple? "What's this?"

"I lost the bet, remember?" Rune reminded her. "Sylvie says ya like these."

Bet? Oh, right! When they were in the rafters together. They'd bet on whether or not Wolf and Tran would fight. Having a good idea of what he'd bought her, she nonetheless unwrapped it and found two small fried apple pies, still steaming and fresh. "She's right. I do. Thank you, Rune."

He gave her a boyish grin.

Siobhan grinned back, wrapping them up again. "I'll eat these on the ship. Alright, people, let's go back to Wynngaard."

# Chapter Thirty

During the course of her term as guildmaster, Siobhan had reported to various other guildmasters about the status of things. However, she had never reported to *three* guildmasters of major city guilds all at once before. Well, alright, Lirah was standing in for her father, but it was the principle of the thing.

As soon as they'd landed, Siobhan went straight to Jarnsmor's study to report their findings. She hadn't expected Hammon and Lirah to already be there, all of them seated around the table, but was half glad that they were present. It saved her from hunting them down later and repeating herself.

"Guildmaster Maley," Jarnsmor greeted with open relief. "You came back quite quickly! Please, sit, sit."

She took a seat next to him with subtle pleasure. Sitting on something that didn't sway back and forth was a blessing.

"You were able to gather information expediently," Hammon noted, eyes sharp on her. "Or you weren't able to find out anything at all. Which is it?"

Siobhan grimaced. "A little of both. Good news is, we've found the reason why they're so adamantly against the trade agreement between you. It is, in fact, blatantly obvious if you get close enough to Coravine. They're building a bridge."

"A *bridge?*" Hammon repeated in shock, eyes wide in his face.

"It's quite sizeable." Siobhan's hands rose in illustration as she tried to describe it. "Not as wide as the Grey Bridges, I'd say it's about half the width, but that's more than large enough for trade caravans and such to go across. According to rumor, it'll connect directly over to Wynngaardian soil, just northeast of Quigg."

Jarnsmor turned in his seat to look at the map hanging on the wall nearby. "There's no cities or villages in that area."

"Yet," Lirah corrected, mouth a flat line. "You know as well as I that if you build a bridge that connects there, then a city will develop around it by default. Trade always has such an effect on places."

"She's right," Hammon agreed. "No, the lack of city or such doesn't matter in the long run. I think whoever is building that bridge knows it, too, which is why they chose to build a bridge the shortest distance possible."

Siobhan couldn't help but agree with all of this. It was very similar to Sylvie's conclusions. "They haven't been working on it long, about four or five months. They're years from completing it."

"Of course they would be." Jarnsmor sat back in his chair, making the leather sigh. "That's no easy feat, building a bridge that far. But how in the world are they financing this? We're going to just build on top of an existing bridge and it's taking three guilds to finance that!"

"They must have been planning this for years, working up to it," Hammon hypothesized. "I can't imagine how they're doing this otherwise."

Lirah put her head in both hands and spoke to the

table's surface. "At least I now understand why I was attacked. Years of planning would be destroyed instantly when a trade monopoly was formed."

"Sending assassins after you was a delaying tactic and nothing more," Siobhan agreed, although she winced at the harshness of her own words. "Although, really, it still doesn't make sense to me that they chose to attack instead of join in. If they had, then they might well have been able to convince you to help them build the bridge."

"Not necessarily," Hammon disagreed, his expression smooth and unreadable. "Our agreement was based upon the market trends and economics of the world as they stand. Making trade easier with Orin would not be to our benefit."

Which someone in Orin had obviously realized, hence the lack of effort to join the monopoly. Siobhan let out a resigned sigh. If people had been thinking less about lining their pockets and more about the good of the world as a whole, they wouldn't be in such a mess right now. "Bad news is, I couldn't get any information about the new guildmaster of Fallen Ward. Even the people in the city don't know anything. Ever since the death of the old guildmaster, the main compound has been completely sealed tight. It's hard for anyone to even approach the gates."

"Hence why I can't get in contact with my people," Jarnsmor sighed. He rapped his fingers against the tabletop. "But you didn't hear anything? Not even rumors?"

"Not a thing. It's very strange."

"Yes, so it is," Nuel Hammon agreed slowly.

Siobhan was left with the obvious question. "So what now?"

"We ignore it." Jarnsmor's mouth twitched in a brief, dry smile. "Oh, we'll keep an eye on them and make sure that we're prepared for more assassins, if they choose to send them after us. But really, with the monopoly now formed, there's not much they can do. We know the bridge is there—it loses its threat because it's incomplete. The money that they've managed to save can't possibly be enough to complete the project."

She searched his face, looking for some insecurity or worry, but he seemed entirely confident of his own opinion. "You think ignoring them will work?"

"Yes."

"We've little other choice," Hammon added, tone reassuring. "We *must* focus on the renovations of the Grey Bridges. If we lose them, then it's not just the economy of Orin that will take a plunge, but all four continents."

Well, he had a good point, but....

"Speaking of," Jarnsmor caught her eye, "Miss Darrens and I have been discussing logistics. We have a team of architects that will be traveling to Island Pass in the next few days in order to study the bridges and make plans. Might we employ you as escorts for them?"

Siobhan blinked at this unexpected offer. "Well, I certainly don't mind." She glanced at Lirah, not quite sure if she should accept or not.

"I assured him you can go," Lirah responded as if she had asked the question aloud. "After all, my people aren't going to be in any shape to move for weeks yet and there's still the finer details of our agreement that need to be settled on. There's no reason for you to sit here waiting about on my behalf."

"I've assured her that when it's time for her to return home, I'll send an escort with her," Jarnsmor added.

Oh. Well, in that case.... "Certainly, we'll act as escorts for your people. Would you wish for us to stay with them and bring them back after they're done with their work?"

He shook his head. "No need. They'll stay on and oversee the masons. The architects are only the first wave, you see."

"I'm gathering masons and building supplies along with Blackstone that will join the architects in a month or so," Hammon explained. "So once you take the architects to the Pass, there's no reason to remain."

So they could all go home shortly, in other words. She was relieved to hear it. "In that case, we'd be more than willing to take on the job."

"Excellent. Your whole guild will do so, I assume?"

She understood what he meant and gave him a smug smile. If he'd placed a bet that Rune would desert her, he'd lost it. "*All* of my people are accounted for."

"I see." The other two were confused but neither Siobhan nor Jarnsmor felt it necessary to explain it to them. He continued with an inviting smile, "It will be some days before we're ready, so take this time to relax and rest."

Siobhan gave him a strained smile in return. Several days? They'd be here for several days with nothing to do? Could she keep her rowdy boys in check that long?

No.

She was doomed.

Rune
Maley

# Chapter Thirty-One

After spending the majority of the day in meetings, Siobhan had to have a hot bath and a massage from Denney to get all the kinks out of her back. Even then, she found it hard to sleep and ended up outside on the back porch overlooking the garden. She sat down in what was fast becoming her favorite spot, letting her feet hang over the side and in the cool pond water. Ahhh, paradise. The night air was a bit too chilly to sit out here long, but her cloak dispelled most of the cold, and sitting here cleared her head.

From behind her, the door opened and quietly shut. She half-turned, and wasn't really surprised to see Wolf coming toward her. In the few days they'd been here, they'd both developed the habit of sitting for a while, looking over the garden, before going to bed.

He sat next to her with a muted grunt, also letting his feet dangle in the pond. For several moments they sat in companionable silence before he asked in a quiet rumble, "Did you spend all day up in meetings?"

"Well, the majority of it," she admitted. "I'd much rather have joined Rune back in the rafters."

"You'd rather have crawled around in dusty, spider-infested rafters than sit through meetings," Wolf repeated in bemusement.

She shrugged, grin stretching over her face. "It was surprisingly fun."

Wolf eyed her sideways. "Rune mentioned in passing that you gave him your last name?"

"I rather felt I should. I mean, he needed a full name just to be registered a guildmember, and to be able to book passage on the ship. I'd started the job, after all, so I might as well finish it." She cocked her head at him. "Why are you looking at me like that?"

He shook his head in wry amusement. "Siobhan. Giving your name to him like that is an astonishing gesture of trust and affection. Didn't you learn ten years ago? Trusting someone like that is powerful."

She opened her mouth to retort, thought about that first moment when Rune had realized she'd given him a family name, and the joy on his face, and couldn't find a way to argue. Intellectually, she'd known that naming people in Wynngaardian culture was huge, but she hadn't really *understood* it until she'd seen that expression of Rune's. Even after that, though, she hadn't thought of it as a gesture of trust. But in Wynngaard, where a name meant everything to a man's reputation, it would be a colossal offering on her part.

"Didn't you realize how important it was to me, ten years ago?" Wolf asked her softly. "Despite all my bad history, you trusted me completely. That trust was healing to me. It's your absolute trust in Rune that's healing him."

"I didn't think of it as a gesture of trust," she responded, feeling her way through the words as she said them. "He reminds me so strongly of you, what you were like the first year in Deepwoods. You were so cautious, so bewildered by kindness. The first time that you asked if I wanted to go somewhere with you, I wanted to just hug you because I knew you'd finally opened up to me a little. And when Rune asked to teach me how to skulk, I felt the same then, too."

"That's trust, Siobhan," he assured her patiently. "At that point, I trusted you enough to ask. *He* trusts you enough to ask."

She sat there and thought about it, but the whole situation still didn't make sense to her. "Giving him the Maley name really means that much? I mean, it took a solid three months of working on you to get you to that point!"

"Yes, Siobhan," Wolf said patiently, "it really means that much."

"But that doesn't explain why he's bonded with everyone else too," she objected.

"I think it's helped that the whole guild is working with you as well. When I came in, Grae thought you were insane to take me on and only Beirly was open to the idea. This time, it's not just you trying to win him over."

Also a very good point. "Still, that's a load off my mind."

"He's not completely won yet." Wolf shrugged slightly. "That's just going to take more time. But he at least trusts that *you* trust him, and that makes all the difference."

Her mouth curled up in a satisfied smile and she leaned her head against his shoulder. Hearing all of that did her heart good and she just let his words sink in so that she could bask in them for a while.

After a long moment of silence, he asked, "You have plans for tomorrow?"

"I was going to check in with Jarnsmor, see if I could get a more accurate head count of who we're escorting, start making plans of our own. Other than that, nothing. You?"

"Beirly hit upon the idea of teaching me how to build a handcart. He said if all we need the cart for is pulling supplies along the path from one city to the next, then we don't need to bring Kit every time. We'll do a trial version up here, sell it, then make a better one when we're home again."

Not a bad thought, that. Without the additional weight of Kit, the load that Grae had to carry would be drastically reduced. "You think you can pull a cart that has the whole guild on top?"

"If it's designed right, two strong men can manage it." Wolf shrugged. "Besides, it won't be the whole guild. Tran and I will probably be pulling, and Grae walks in front. At that slow pace of his, I think we'd be fine."

Those two put together could move small mountain ranges. She didn't doubt that if they put their minds to it, they'd manage. "Keep me updated on that. I'd like to know if it worked."

"We'll likely have to load everyone into the cart to test it, so I think I can safely promise you that." He grinned at her, a brief flash of white in the darkness.

Struck by the image of Wolf with a tool in his hand, she couldn't help but ask, "Do you even know how to build something?"

"Not a bit. But Beirly informed me he gave me a natural hammer," Wolf held up his iron right hand in demonstration, "and it's about time I learned how to use it."

She snorted. "He *does* rather have a point."

"I certainly couldn't think of a way to argue with him."

"Well," she shrugged, "I think that as long as you don't manage to accidentally cut off your other hand, you'll be fine."

Siobhan awoke slowly, not quite sure why she felt the need to awaken. Something seemed out of place, or more like, she sensed something that she shouldn't have. Puzzled, she raised her head from its pillow and looked around the room. Her roommate was still dead asleep in the other bed, only her dark hair visible. Soft moonlight and shadows flickered through the window, indicating the sun wasn't anywhere close to rising. It felt like the wee hours of the morning.

Her ears perked at a foreign sound. Aside from her and Sylvie's breathing, another sound rose and fell. Cautiously, she shifted to look over the edge of the bed and at the floor.

There, curled up on his side, lay Rune. He was fully dressed, sans boots, eyes closed as if fast asleep. Now when did he get there? For that matter, *why* was he asleep there? She knew for a fact that he had a perfectly good bed to sleep in, not two doors down.

An old memory flashed through her mind. Wolf used to do something like this, the first year he'd been in the guild. He'd never entered her room, but he'd propped himself against her doorway many a time, dozing. It had taken her years to finally get him to confess why he'd done so. Wolf admitted that on the nights he had the darkest dreams, it comforted him to know that she was there. Just being able to hear her breathe, peacefully sleeping, gave him a sense of well-being.

She stared at Rune's sleeping face for a long moment. Was it the same? Had Rune felt compelled to sleep near her for a similar reason? Or was there something else going on that she didn't know about?

Siobhan still found it strange that Rune had attached himself to her so quickly and with such devotion. Conli hadn't thought it so. Neither had Wolf. Rune had tested her several times, done things to irritate her or make her uncomfortable, but she'd never rejected him because of it. Conli said that once Rune felt sure of her, he hadn't needed anything else.

The proof of that could be seen right in front of her eyes.

Had she adopted an assassin, or had he adopted her? It was hard to tell.

Either way, it wasn't something she wanted to stay up

all night debating with herself. She grasped the extra quilt laying at the foot of the bed and leaned up on her knees long enough to shake it out and lay it carefully over Rune's sleeping form.

Of course, he awoke the second that the blanket touched him. He didn't start awake, just opened one eye and looked up at her.

"Everything alright?" she asked him softly, barely more than a whisper.

"There's no danger," he whispered back.

*That didn't quite answer my question.* Shaking her head slightly, she decided not to push it any further. "You're not cold down there?"

He dragged the quilt up around his shoulders a little more. "I'm fine."

Shrugging, she let him be. He was the one that would wake up with a crick in his neck, not her. Instead she rolled back into her bed and let her eyes fall closed. If he wanted to sleep down there, she'd let him.

"Siobhan."

Her eyes flew open. He'd never called her by her name before. "Yes?" she responded carefully.

"Did ya really take in Wolf knowi'n he was from a dark guild?"

"I did," she admitted. Now, where had he heard about that?

"Ya trust him in spite of that."

"I trust him because of it."

Rune twisted about to look up at her. "What?"

"I trust him because of it," she repeated. "Because I know that he hated living in that darkness. He'll do everything he can to avoid it. He'll never let us fall into it, either."

His brows furrowed together as he turned that over in his mind. "Did ya...did ya take me on thinki'n I'd be like him?"

"No." She had to be careful how she answered this. "At first, I honestly only wanted you to help me. I was desperate for help. But I hoped you'd be like him. I see the same potential in you as I did in him."

A strangely content expression settled over his face. He almost looked like he was smiling, although the faint light of the room made it hard to be sure. With a nod, he rolled back over to his side and curled up again, as if going back to sleep.

Siobhan rolled onto her back and let out a low breath. Phew, why did she feel as if she'd just passed some sort of test? That conversation had been vitally important. How, she still wasn't quite sure. Perhaps Rune wanted to know if he really could become like Wolf, an accepted member of a good guild? Come to think of it, she hadn't yet made it clear to him that he was welcome to stay in Deepwoods if he wanted to. She'd discussed it with every other member of the guild, but never when he was within earshot. Did he even know that he could stay if he wanted to?

She rolled over and stole a peek over the side of the bed. This time he truly did seem sound asleep, as his breathing had deepened to an almost snore. Considering how little rest he normally got at night, she was loath to wake him up. Besides, there should be a certain timing in telling him such an important thing. Some wee hour of the morning while he was asleep on her bedroom floor didn't seem like the right moment. She'd have to either find the right moment or create it later.

Sighing, she flopped onto her back with a slight squeak of springs.

Now how in the world was she supposed to go back to sleep?

Siobhan studied the list in her hands as she walked back toward the main building of Iron Dragain. Nortin had thoughtfully written one out for her, as well as the predicted schedule of when they were expected to be ready to leave, all in neat penmanship. It looked like they'd be ready to go by the end of next week, which was faster than she'd anticipated. Siobhan silently sent a prayer of thanks to the gods. She didn't know how much longer she could keep Wolf and Tran out of trouble in this city. They tended to stay near the compound in case trouble arose. Which led to a different sort of trouble occurring on a regular basis. She'd argue against it, but their concerns weren't exactly groundless. They weren't sure of Fallen Ward's tactics. Would they attack again? Do something else entirely? So far no one had been able to predict what that guild would do.

She shook the worries away and focused on the list again. For now, she needed to find Grae. Now that they had a list of people and equipment, they could estimate how much weight it would be and he could start building a path to Quigg. Siobhan really, truly wanted to get those architects to Island Pass before winter really hit Wynngaard. They were a good month and a half away from season's change, but it was already getting colder by the day and she wanted to be safely home before she got buried under twenty feet of snow.

As they'd learned from previous experience, a path buried in snow did not work well.

Another body slammed suddenly into hers and she stumbled back a step with a grunt of surprise.

Two strong hands caught her arms and steadied her. "Sorry, Siobhan, sorry!" Conli apologized, but he was already pushing past her and running before the words could fully leave his mouth.

She blinked, startled, but instinct had her turning and chasing after him. Conli rarely looked rattled, but when he did, it was usually because someone was seriously hurt. "What happened?" she asked, lengthening her stride into a jog.

"Pyper came to me with a message," he said, not slowing his pace. The dog, hearing her name, barked once, tail wagging, but she kept running too. "Wolf and Tran are hurt."

"WHAT?" Siobhan demanded in open dismay. "Weren't they with Beirly building something?"

"A cart, yes, near the docks. Someone over there lent them the tools. Denney's message wasn't long on explanations. She just said grab a bag and a lot of bandages."

Well that didn't sound good.

Siobhan followed close on his heels, weaving through the narrow, maze-like streets of Sateren. Pyper ran ahead with great confidence, as if absolutely sure of where to go, but if not for her, Siobhan and Conli would have gotten quickly lost.

Eventually they exited the city through the Sea Gate, letting them out near the docks. The smell of the sea hit her strong here, mixed in with fish, tar, and some other unidentified scents. Pyper went around the corner, passing a dry dock with a half-finished ship on it, and through a doorway that led into what appeared to be a warehouse. Siobhan blinked as she went from sunlight to the dimmer interior of the building, letting her eyes adjust. She barely processed the worktables on both sides of the room, and the tools and wood shavings lying about before her eyes fell on the bloody scene in front of her.

What looked like a half-finished wooden box lay on one side, part of it smashed in. Next to it was a stack of cut lumber, which Wolf was using as a seat. Wolf had a nasty cut at his temple, multiple lacerations and bruises along his arms, and it looked like a large splinter was sticking out of his thigh. Tran lay on the ground near the other side of the half-finished cart, and his condition wasn't much better. His nose looked broken, eyes already swelling under the pressure, and the way that he had two hands protectively over his stomach spoke of an injury her eyes couldn't see.

Conli hesitated at the door, torn between whom to go to first. "Who's bleeding?" he finally blurted out.

"Tran first," Wolf rasped out past a bloody and split

lip. "I think I might have broken a rib."

Swearing, Conli dove for the other man.

Siobhan lifted her eyes to the ceiling and took in a deep breath. She let it out again slowly. Another breath in. Another breath out. "Beirly."

Her handyman had been kneeling next to Wolf, as if preparing to pull that huge splinter out, but as she called his name, he looked up grimly. "Siobhan."

"What. Happened," she gritted out between clenched teeth.

"They got into a fight."

"Obviously." She pinned him in place with her eyes, making him flinch at the obvious anger she was exuding. "Over what?"

"Um...who could work the fastest?"

"Why, *why* did you have them work on it *together*?"

"I thought that if they had a task to work on, they wouldn't get into pointless fights!" he protested in his own defense.

She honestly didn't know who to kill first at that moment. Beirly, for his good but misplaced intentions, or the other two for their rash stupidity.

Breathe, she ordered herself sternly. Breathe. They're some of the best friends you have. You can't give into temptation and strangle them. "Conli. How bad is Tran's condition?"

"Thank the gods he's so sturdy," Conli responded without taking his eyes away from his patient. "I don't think it's broken, just badly bruised. If we wrap it and he takes it easy, he'll be fully healed in a month."

"Wolf?" she asked steadily.

"Looks worse than it is," Wolf assured her. "Head wounds are always messy."

"Good." Another breath in. "Let me make this clear to the two of you, as apparently you didn't understand it before. If I find you fighting each other *one more time*, I will *finish* what you start and you won't be walking home. As it stands, you're on half pay until the end of next month."

Neither man dared to utter a peep of protest about that.

"Beirly." She waited for him to look up at her. "Your next task is to build a cage large enough to put them into it. If I see them even arguing, one or the other will go into that cage, even if I have to stuff them into it personally. You got me?"

He nodded vigorously.

Spinning on one heel, she whirled sharply about and stomped out of the warehouse. "Rune!"

Like magic, he appeared at her side, landing from... somewhere. Where had he been perched this time, anyway? She hadn't even sensed his presence. It was his habit of always spying on people that led her to believe he was nearby.

"Yes?" he asked, lengthening his stride to keep up with her.

"Lead me back to Iron Dragain, I have no idea how to get there," she ordered sharply.

"Yes ma'am." He eyed her sideways as he led her back through the Sea Gate and into the city. "Yer...scary when mad."

She gave him a cutting glare. "Then why aren't those two louts intimidated?"

"Don't know," he admitted frankly. "*I* am, and I ain't the one in trouble."

Siobhan snorted. Maybe after so many years of being exposed to her glare, it had lost its impact on those two?

"If they fight again, ya can always tell 'em I'll assassinate the next person that starts it," Rune offered helpfully.

Siobhan lifted her lip in a snarl. "Don't tempt me."

# Chapter Thirty-Two

In an effort to move things along and get home quicker, Siobhan ordered every able-bodied man—this excluded Tran, whose ribs were too sore and tender still—to help Grae build a path to Quigg. Since they had an accurate head count, and knew how much weight to calculate for, Grae could start building the path that very moment. She expected him to build a sunflower pattern, as that would be more than sufficient not just for their own group, but any future groups of people and equipment Jarnsmor sent down. Grae surprised her by announcing that morning over breakfast that he instead felt it prudent to build an evergreen pathway, something capable of handling over one hundred people.

Siobhan had outright winced. The evergreen pattern took a *lot* of stones and it would not be an easy matter to collect enough for a path back to Quigg. Grae calculated that he would need 5,670 stones in order to build the path.

Everyone groaned— well, everyone except Rune, who hadn't yet had the dubious pleasure of assisting Grae in pathmaking. He followed along with a curious look on his face as they all trooped out of the city and toward the coastline. Grae had scouted out a good location for a path the day before while waiting for exact numbers to come through, so he led them straight to a spot that was up above the tide line but close enough to the sea to gather water as needed.

Grae cleared his throat as his stone gatherers looked to him for guidance. "Alright, everyone, I mostly need stones that are about the size of a kor. However, if you find a flat one about the size of your clenched fist, let me know. I need those for centerpieces. Understood? Good, go."

Rune followed Siobhan as she headed for the beach, the most reliable and rich hunting ground for stones. In an undertone, he asked her, "What am I looki'n for?"

"I'll show you," she assured him, spitting hair out of her mouth. Lovely, the wind was picking up over the ocean. Perhaps she should have worn a hood today. "You have much experience with paths, Rune?"

He shook his head. "Just when we used 'em to get from Vakkoid to Sateren."

"Really?" she gave him an odd look. Pathmakers were unusual in the world, but not *that* rare. Most people had traveled by path at least once. "That was the only time?"

"Never left the city," he explained simply.

"Is that right. Then I better tell you the basics." They hunkered down in the wet sand, combing through it for stones. As she worked, she explained how pathmaking worked and the rules he needed to follow while on an open path. He listened with the same sort of rapt attention that Markl had when he first asked Grae how it worked.

When she finished, Rune sat back on his haunches and mulled all of that information over for a moment. "So if a path is made, anybody can use it?"

"Not quite," she corrected. "Any *Pathmaker* can use it, yes. You have to have the talent, not just the know-how, to use a path. Grae is actually being quite kind in building as large of a path as he is. He doesn't need to, y'know. A smaller pattern would work just fine for the group we're taking down to Quigg. But he's making one that a future Pathmaker can use to bring down supplies with so they won't have to make another path."

"Oh." Rune cocked his head slightly. "So there's different levels?"

"Quite a few. Grae has told me about eight of them. We tend to only use about three, though, as we're always going about in groups."

Rune twisted slightly to look over his shoulder. Grae stood some distance off, sorting through the stones people brought him. He'd brought a tarp to kneel on so that he wouldn't get his knees wet and dirty while working. Rune watched him for a long moment before asking slowly, "How good is he? At pathmaki'n."

"He's a genius. Literally." Siobhan smiled when Rune's head whipped back around, his eyes wide with surprise. "You wouldn't think that by looking at him, would you? He's such a quiet, humble man. But he invented a pattern eight years ago that took pathmaking to a whole new level. It used to be that caravans could never go by path as they were simply too large. None of the known patterns could carry that amount of weight. But Grae invented the coral pattern, which changed all of that. It's because of his pattern that we can take caravans on as escorts." And made a ridiculous amount of money doing it, too.

Rune's brows furrowed a bit in a puzzled frown. "If he's that good, then why...?"

"Why be in a small guild like Deepwoods?" she finished the question wryly. "Many people have asked him that. But Grae isn't the type that does well in large groups of people. He's far more comfortable in a smaller guild, where he only has to interact with a certain number of guildmates on a day-to-day basis."

He didn't ask another question, but his expression said he somewhat understood that.

They shifted through the sand for a few moments in silence. Siobhan had quite the pile at her feet. She'd need to bring these to Grae in a minute, before the weight became too much to carry. Stones added up quick.

Rune dug out a larger stone and held it up next to his clenched fist.

"Oh, that looks good," Siobhan noted in approval. "Take that to Grae, see if he likes it."

With a nod, he rose to his feet.

"And take these with you," she tacked on quickly, handing him the cloth bag of her own stones.

He gave her quite the look for that, but scooped up the bag without comment and strode off.

As soon as he left, Markl shifted from where he had been gathering nearby and came to kneel next to her. "Siobhan, I have to ask—how serious are you in keeping that boy?"

Her eyebrows rose in question. "Quite serious. Why?"

Markl let out a breath of relief. "I was hoping you'd say that. You're aware that I've been teaching him to read?"

She'd seen their daily lessons often, so nodded confirmation. "Yes, how's that going?"

"He's an amazingly quick study," Markl told her with a twinkle of pride in his eyes. "He memorized the Wynngaardian alphabet so quickly my head spun. Right now he's learning short words."

Her eyes nearly crossed. "In *six days?*"

"His intellectual capacity is incredible. Every time I sit down to teach him, I'm astounded all over again by how fast he learns. Given some time, and dedication, he could become a scholar."

A former assassin becoming a scholar. Her mind couldn't quite wrap its way around that. "Did you tell him that?"

"Well, I've complimented him, but I didn't want to say anything until I was sure of what you intended." He leaned in a little more, tone lowering to a more confidential level. "You will tell him soon that you want him to stay? I don't think he really feels like he can."

"I've been trying to find the right moment," she

answered, shrugging. "Maybe while we're building the path I can find a way to bring it up. You feel like he would, if he felt welcome?"

"No, Siobhan, I think he would run screaming in horror at the opportunity," Markl retorted dryly.

Alright, fine, that might have been a stupid question. Especially after finding Rune sleeping on her floor the other night. "I'll ask him," she promised. What was taking Rune so long to come back, anyway? She looked up to find that Grae had taken him to the first stepping stone being built. Both men were kneeling on the ground with stones in their hands. Under her incredulous stare, Rune placed a stone on the ground under Grae's direction, and then another.

"Markl." She couldn't tear her eyes away. "Are you seeing what I'm seeing?"

Markl peered in Grae's direction, hand lifted to block out the morning sun. "Is Grae teaching Rune how to build a path?"

"It looks that way to you too?"

He lowered his hand and looked at her questioningly. "Is that unusual?"

"Unusual? No. It's downright *strange*. I've *never* seen Grae teach anyone pathmaking before. He's never even offered." What on earth was going on?

"Siobhan..." Markl said slowly, hesitantly, "how do people know if someone has the talent for pathmaking?"

"Grae was tested for it at an early age. We all were as children."

"But would someone test street rats or children in dark guilds?"

She opened her mouth only to slowly close it again. "No, probably not."

"So is it possible for Rune to have pathmaking talent? Undiscovered talent?"

She'd have laughed and said no, of course not, just moments earlier. But she couldn't dismiss it now. Grae would not be sitting there, so patiently teaching Rune, unless he saw something that made him think Rune had the right talent. "If he does, then he has a lot of studying to do in the future. But then, from what you said, he's got the mind to learn with."

"He does." Markl rose to his feet and offered her a hand up. "I think we need to double check this."

She accepted the hand without hesitation and rose, her knees protesting a little from all of the kneeling. Siobhan went directly to Grae and Rune, standing on the other side of the stepping stone they were building. This close, she realized that Grae was not giving precise instructions. In fact, as she watched, Rune placed three stones without any direction from the man at his side, and to her eyes, it looked perfect. Heavens, she might not be an expert, but even to her it seemed obvious what was going on. In a deliberately casual way, she asked, "Oh? Rune, you helping him actually make the path?"

Rune shot her the brightest smile she'd ever seen from him. "Surely am."

*Wind and stars, look at that smile. It's the same expression Grae wears when he's building a path.* She glanced at Grae and found him watching her with quiet intensity. "You seem to be picking this up quickly."

Grae was the one that answered. "He doesn't quite understand the weight of the stones yet, and how that affects the pattern, but he's got good instincts. He's built most of this stepping stone himself."

Siobhan scanned the half-finished pattern in front of her with disbelieving eyes. *Rune* had done this? Not Grae? It looked so pristine and precise, she'd never have believed a complete amateur did this if Grae hadn't said otherwise.

"All I did was follow that un," Rune jerked his chin to indicate the other stepping stone nearby that Grae had built.

Grae didn't take his eyes from hers, his expression validating her suspicions. "It takes talent to do that, Rune. Very few can simply look at a stepping stone and duplicate it like you have done."

*Rune is a Pathmaker. A novice Pathmaker.* By the four winds, she could not have been more surprised if a star fell out of the sky and landed on her head. Her desire to keep Rune in the guild tripled in that moment. One way or another, he was staying in Deepwoods. Even if she had to twist his arm and bribe him, she'd keep him. Somehow, she kept her voice at a normal tone. "Rune, why don't you stay here with Grae and help him build the path? Since you're one of the few that can."

Oh, he liked that idea. His smile came back full force. "Sure, sure."

She forced herself to smile back even as her mind whirled. "Markl and I will go back to gathering, then."

Grabbing Markl by the arm, she hauled him away.

"Why didn't you tell him?" Markl hissed at her, stumbling along at her side.

"I can't, not right now," she whispered back quickly. "Markl, *think*. You know how rare it is for Pathmakers to be born. Sateren doesn't have *one*, even though they're a major trade city. Jarnsmor is even now hiring one from Quigg so that he can move supplies back and forth after Grae leaves. If he found out that Rune was a Pathmaker, do you know what he'd do?"

"Keep him," Markl groaned in realization.

"Rune cannot stay in that city. He especially can't stay in Iron Dragain. Pathmaker or not, they'll never accept him, not with his history. I have to take him out of here before anyone knows about his talent. It'd be even better still to tell him after he's through Island Pass," she realized this as an afterthought. "Once he's in Robarge, Darrens will never let another guild get their hands on him. He'll protect Rune."

Markl stole a glance back. "Does Grae realize all this?"

"He must, otherwise he would have said something to Rune by now." She'd have a good talk with him later, though, to make sure he understood just what was at stake. She tightened her grip on his arm, voice intense. "Do not breathe a word of this. Understand me?"

He held up a placating hand. "I won't."

"We have to bide our time, or we lose Rune entirely."

# Chapter Thirty-Three

By some minor miracle, they managed to keep Wolf and Tran from starting any fights for the next week. Tran's bruised ribs and limited movements might have had something to do with that. Regardless, the first wave of architects and bridge engineers were assembled, supplies packed and loaded, and Grae's new path toward Quigg finished.

They assembled in front of the main gate of Iron Dragain in the cool chill of the morning. Siobhan had her own people in their cart, along with what supplies they would need for the full trip home. Since they now had ready paths that took them all the way to Goldschmidt, Siobhan didn't expect it to take more than three days to get back to their guildhall. At some point during those three days, she had to find a moment to talk to Rune about staying in the guild. She still hadn't found a moment to do that yet. Every time she'd tried, she'd either been surrounded by other people, or had been interrupted. It was more than frustrating.

Rune was fascinated by the whole idea of riding a path he had helped to build. Beirly had him sit on the top bench with him so he could have a bird's-eye view once they got on the path. Siobhan felt that the safest place to put him anyway—he was less likely to fall out that way.

The total group came out to five architects, two master masons, and one of Iron Dragain's jarls, whom Siobhan had met briefly the day before. Romohr was his name, a stocky fellow that was leaning more toward fat than muscle. His hair was pitch black—a rarity in this culture—and thick bones prominent in his face so that he looked like he could crush a rock with his head. He was apparently one of Jarnsmor's right-hand men, one that he trusted completely. Siobhan didn't find it surprising that Jarnsmor would send someone to watch over this highly important project and report directly back to him.

Romohr had a silent air about him, making him hard to approach, but the same could not be said of the head architect, Ardin. If someone asked her to describe what a model father should look like, she would have pointed to Ardin without hesitation. He had that comfortable, worn-in look with the spectacles perched on his nose, shaggy haircut, and loose clothes. From every pocket—and his outfit sported several—things bulged. She found it a wonder he didn't clink as he walked. But the thing she liked best about him was his ready smile, which he always seemed to have when he saw her.

"Guildmaster Maley!" he greeted with a wave, quickening his pace to catch up to her.

Siobhan stepped away from the Deepwoods cart in order to face him. "Master Ardin. Are we ready?"

"Well, we are, or at least I hope we are." His smile faltered and stumbled, to be replaced by a worried frown. "I just received word this morning that part of the Grey Bridge has crumbled."

For a split second his words didn't make any sense at all. When they did, her eyes shot wide and she demanded in a screeching voice, "WHAT?!"

Ardin winced at the piercing volume. "I'm not sure how extensive the damage is. The report just said a good stretch of the bridge near Quigg had fallen into the ocean."

While she realized that the bridges were several hundred years old, having been built during the time of governments and kings, they were also rock solid and had been a dependable way to travel ever since their construction. The idea that even they might fall apart was akin to telling her that the moons had fallen out of the sky.

"How is this possible?" she spluttered, feeling as if someone had jerked a rug out from underneath her. "I just traveled over those bridges not a few weeks past! They were as solid as Wolf's head!"

"Hey!" Wolf protested from behind her.

"They might have appeared to be on the surface, only to hide some internal failure on a deeper level," Ardin responded, brows furrowed as he thought. "We won't know until we get down there and see the situation with our own eyes. But this is partially what we feared. The bridges are old, Guildmaster, extremely so. They've been battered by nature, storms, time, and millions of feet pounding on them. I'm astonished they've held up for as long as they did! Especially since they've only seen sporadic maintenance."

Well, he had a point, but still.... Siobhan shook the thought off. Talking about it here wouldn't do any of them good. "Knowing that the bridge has damage, do you need any other equipment or supplies to bring with you?"

"Most likely, but I won't know what until I see what the damage *is*," he responded with a helpless splay of the hands.

"Then let's go." Hopping lightly up onto the cart, Siobhan made herself visible to the whole group. "Attention, everyone!" she waited until all eyes were on her before continuing, "I've just been told that the Grey Bridge near Quigg has been damaged. We need to get there quickly and fix the situation before it gets any worse. Everyone load up, we're heading directly to the Quigg path."

People lost no time in obeying her direction. Within minutes they were out of the gate, traveling through Sateren's streets and heading toward the path that Grae had made near the coastline. Even though Siobhan had helped him build part of this, she still sat on the cart and admired the path as Grae explained the rules for the rest of the party. He'd built an evergreen pattern, something that was capable of carrying an excess of one hundred people. Not that he'd needed such a large path this time, but the other Pathmaker from Quigg had requested they do so, in anticipation of needing it in the future. In the morning sun, the stones glinted in the ground like an ancient mosaic, and it was quite pretty to look at.

With the directions and warnings given, Grae ducked down to the sea long enough to fill his flask full of water, then he darted back and activated the path. They traveled uneventfully straight to Quigg, arriving just northeast of the city.

Since Ardin was the one with the report, and knew where to go, she encouraged him to lead the way. They skirted around Quigg's outer wall—traveling through the city would have taken more time—and went directly to the bridge.

Turned out, even a blind man would have been able to find the problem.

Siobhan stumbled to a stop on the shoreline, regarding the bridge with open dismay. 'A good stretch' were poor words to describe the condition of the bridge and the extent of the damage. Several hundred feet were simply gone, fallen away into the ocean, leaving a gaping hole in the bridge. One cart could still pass on the far right side, but certainly not more, and the once eight-cart width had been reduced to rubble. Even from here she could see giant cracks in the support pillars and the stonework. "That...does not look good."

"Understatement," Denney groaned beside her. "What *happened?* It was fine when we crossed it!"

"We'll find out," Ardin promised, jaw set in a determined line. "Guildmaster Maley, until we get a chance to thoroughly inspect that bridge, I don't suggest that anyone cross it. Especially not any distance, which you'll have to do to reach Island Pass. I know that you only intended to drop us off here and then go home, but can you stay for a few days?"

"We'll need her to anyway," Romohr rumbled. Siobhan turned to look at him, as he had been walking behind her. He met her eyes levelly. "We will need your Pathmaker. Damage like this can't wait to be repaired. We'll need supplies and masons sent down immediately from Sateren."

He was right, of course. At the very least, they would need Grae's help to send a message speedily to report the situation. "Yes, of course. Grae!" Her Pathmaker perked up in response to the call. "You be ready to go back to Sateren whenever they need you."

Grae gave her a casual salute. "Right-o."

Even though this wasn't, technically, her party, she felt responsible since she was the escort. To Ardin, she said, "We'll move the carts closer to the bridge so you can have easy access to any supplies you need. Then we'll be on standby to help however we can until you're ready to send a message back."

Ardin gave her a relieved smile. "Thank you, Guildmaster. Men! Let's get to work!"

As they went off, Siobhan turned and hailed Sylvie. "Find an inn that has enough space for us, somewhere that's nearby. See if you can get enough food for everyone so that they can work and eat without worrying about going into the city."

"Sure thing."

"Tran, go with her." With that dispatched, Siobhan focused on moving the entire crew closer to the bridge.

By the time that they had moved the carts to the very edge of the bridge and gotten a workstation set up, the architects had crawled over every part of it. One of them even jumped into the sea and did an underwater examination. An hour slowly passed as they studied the situation. Siobhan went from alert and anxious for an answer to dozing in the sun, comfortably propped in the back of the cart.

"Guildmaster Maley!" Ardin waved an arm above his head, trying to get her attention.

Whoops! Naptime must be over. She waved back so he knew he had succeeded, but didn't try to yell over that kind of distance, just hopped out of the cart and crossed to him. Markl, who had been sitting next to her, followed along to also hear the answer. "How is it? How bad is the damage?"

"Bad, but it's also strange." He glanced back at the bridge over his shoulder, eyebrows furrowing. "Guildmaster, I don't believe this was natural."

She went very still as his words penetrated. "Not natural? Someone did this deliberately?"

"I think so." His face fell into grim lines. "Oh, they took the trouble to make it look like it was just the ground giving way under the supports, so the bridge would collapse on its own, but it's not like that. I'd bet my eye teeth someone set a submersible charge and blew apart the pillars. The way the damage looks isn't natural."

Her blood went cold. Who in their right mind would purposefully try to destroy the bridge? The entire economy of the four continents depended on the Grey Bridges. Destroying them would cause such upheaval that most of the poorer classes would starve before the bridges could be fixed!

As her head was spinning, Markl demanded, "How much time is it going to take to fix this?"

"I don't know," Ardin admitted frankly. "We're still assessing how much damage the bridge took. Explosions on a structure like this will cause fissures throughout the whole frame. I wouldn't suggest putting any weight on it right now, not more than we need to, until I can figure out how dangerous it is. But, Guildmaster, this was a deliberate attack, and I don't think that whoever started this is finished."

Siobhan was very afraid that he was right. Making a snap decision, she promised him firmly, "We'll guard you. I'll send a report back to Iron Dragain and Blackstone telling them what's really happened. You write one as well, give them details so they know what help to send." Turning, she ordered, "Markl, get my enforcers over here. We're setting up round the clock protection as of *now*."

He nodded somberly before spinning on one heel and racing off, calling for people as he went.

Thoughts racing, she tried to consider all angles and prepare for the worst. "Ardin, I don't know anyone in Quigg, and honestly, I don't know who to trust from this city to call for help. For all we know, they're in league with whoever destroyed the bridge."

"But *why*?" he demanded, throwing up both of his hands in pure confusion. "The bridges are Quigg's lifeline when it comes to trade! Destroying one doesn't make any sense."

"This isn't the work of a rational mind," she corrected. "It would take a madman to do this. Regardless, I don't know who to trust from this city. I'm calling for reinforcements from Blackstone. We'll guard and protect you until they get here. That might take about a week, all things considered."

Ardin gave her a relieved smile. "Yes, Guildmaster, I understand. Thank you."

"Go write," she ordered before heading to the cart. She needed to put together messages, and quickly. Fortunately, she had Grae's paths set up going to Iron Dragain, so it would be quick getting word back to Jarnsmor. She wished it would be as easy going toward Blackstone. Someone would have to spend two days crossing the Grey Bridges before they could even get to Robarge. Two and a half days there, plus the preparations necessary to form up a guard of men and bring them all back here. She'd be lucky if it only took a week to manage that.

The logistics she would worry about later. Right now, she had around the clock protection to arrange.

# Chapter Thirty-Four

The challenge of setting up watch was figuring how to divide the fighting strength evenly. After all, some of the guild were like minor deities when they fought, and others were barely capable of protecting themselves. She didn't want to put all of the true fighting strength on one watch, only to leave a different watch weakened.

Even more fun, she had eleven people to sort out in four different watches, which didn't divide evenly. Siobhan finally gave up and went to Romohr, asking if he would be willing to stand watch with her people. He readily accepted, which surprised her, but as he pointed out, the bridges were also his responsibility. And he didn't have anything constructive to do except oversee things anyway.

She finally settled on Beirly, Conli, and Denney on the first watch, Fei, Grae and Markl on the second, Wolf, Romohr and Sylvie on the third watch with herself, Rune and Tran on the last watch.

With that settled, they went their own directions, some of them going for an early dinner before taking the watch, some of them taking the chance to explore the city a little more. Siobhan retired early in the inn that Sylvie had found, only to rise in the pre-dawn hours and quietly dress to face the day. She snuck downstairs, not wanting to wake anyone, and found that Rune and Tran were already at the door waiting on her.

Without a word, Tran handed her a steaming meat bun. How he'd managed to lay hands on it at this obscene hour of the morning, she had no idea, but she consumed it gratefully.

They walked in the cold night air, huddling in their cloaks and rubbing their hands together as they traveled down silent streets toward the bridge. Even Rune, who seemed impervious to cold, shivered a little and grumbled under his breath.

Rune kept up with her as they walked, eyes searching every shadow they passed in sheer habit. She supposed paranoia was an occupational hazard for assassins.

"Siobhan."

"Hmm?"

"This whole thing," he waved a hand to indicate the bridge now visible in front of them, "don't make sense ta me. Why destroy the bridge?"

"Trade logistics," she responded promptly. It didn't surprise her that he didn't understand the motivations behind what was going on. He'd never needed to know or think about things like this before after all. But she, as a businesswoman that catered professional escorting, had to understand it just to survive. "Look, the only way to get from Teherani to Wynngaard is by either using the bridge or going by ship, right?"

"Right."

"So what happens if the bridge is out of commission? What if you *have* to send things by ship instead?"

His brow furrowed a bit. "Ain't it more expensive?"

"It certainly is. Now, if shipping charges go up, prices go up. It's inevitable. If prices go up, it has a ripple effect on the market that will shake the economy. But it's not just one country's trade with another that's affected. It's all four because we all use the bridges to get things to and from Wynngaard. By destroying the bridge, they've managed to cause serious damage to every major trader." It might outright destroy the smaller traders, the ones that survived from caravan to caravan.

"Fallen Ward must be behind this," Tran said quietly, expression hard.

She nodded unhappily. It was a conclusion that she had reached hours ago. "They sent assassins to Lirah to disrupt the trade agreement, but even Wolf said that was nothing more than a delaying tactic. When it didn't delay them more than a couple weeks, they hatched another plan instead: destroy one of the bridges and disrupt all trade entirely. It'll take months, if not a year, to repair the damage done. They've bought themselves some time to work on their own bridge."

"And when it's fixed?" Rune's eyes darted between them. "Then what do ya think they'll do?"

"Destroy another part of it," Tran answered grimly. "I think this will be a never-ending game we'll play."

Siobhan was afraid he was right. "I said as much in my letters to Blackstone and Iron Dragain. I hope they're planning on dispatching guards at every entrance to the bridge, to protect them, because we can't afford to go through this again. Honestly, we're lucky that this is fall, and not in the height of trade season. I can't imagine how much the economy would suffer if it was."

Tran grunted agreement.

They stepped onto the bridge at that point. Siobhan looked around carefully but didn't see any signs that there had been visitors. The bell that they had set up near the entrance was untouched. It was there to sound an alarm, to call for help when needed, but she hoped she wouldn't need to ring it. In this inky black night, the place looked dangerously shadowed.

Wolf saw their approach and waved his metal hand in greeting, the moonlight glinting off of it. "End of watch?"

"Yes," she confirmed, walking toward him. "Where's everyone else?"

"We discovered we can't see under the bridge from here," Wolf explained, heaving himself off the railing, where he had been casually sitting. "So Sylvie took up the other side, and Romohr went underneath to keep watch there."

That sounded feasible, although she didn't like the idea of one man down there by himself, out of sight of his companions. "Are you sure he's fine?"

"He found a place where he can keep watch on the whole area, and Sylvie—" Wolf pointed to where she sat on the opposite side of the bridge "—can see him."

Oh. Well, alright, she felt better about that. "I suppose we should take up the same positions. Alright, who wants to be where?"

Tran raised a hand. "I'll go down. I think Rune will have a fit if he's underneath something for long." He flashed a teasing, wicked grin at the assassin.

Rune glared back. "Ha, ha. Fine, I'll stay up here and keep an eye on *him*, assumi'n I can see him in the dark."

"I'll blend in quite well down there," Tran agreed, still chuckling at his own joke.

"I think we're sorted, then." Siobhan waved a hand at Wolf. "Go, go to bed."

"You don't have to tell me twice." Rubbing his hands together, Wolf called to his fellow watchmen and led them off, back toward the inn.

Her group went to their designated areas. Siobhan chose not to emulate Wolf and sit on the bridge's railing, as the stone was ice-cold and froze her behind when she tried it. Instead, she paced back and forth, eyes scanning the area.

Standing watch gave one time to think. Sometimes too much time. As she walked back and forth, the cold sea wind kept her mind clear and racing with thoughts. When Markl had come to her all those weeks ago, looking for a guild to stay with, she'd never imagined that it would turn out like this. Never mind having to go on an emergency rescue trip across the world, but she hadn't expected to adopt an assassin either. She'd grown rather attached to both of them, but the truth of the matter was, she didn't have any real hold over either man. One of them was perfectly frank that he didn't know how long he would stay and he had every right to leave whenever he wanted. The fact that Markl let her order him about was astonishing, really, because any other man with his background and position certainly wouldn't put up with it.

Siobhan harbored the suspicion that Sylvie liked him, perhaps more than she showed. For her sake, she hoped that Markl would eventually decide to stay. But she also realized that Markl could go anywhere and be anything he wanted. He had proven to be a very capable and intelligent man, after all. Why he chose to focus on studying the world instead of running a business, or creating a guild, was somewhat confusing to her.

On the other hand, she had Rune to think about. Also a skilled man, he didn't have any of the connections or backing that Markl had but he did have every bit the freedom. Their deal ended as soon as she could get him to Island Pass. What he would do then, she had no idea. Siobhan thought he'd rather grown fond of her, and liked being in their guild, but that didn't guarantee that he would stay. She needed to tell him soon, too, that he was a Pathmaker. She wanted him to take Grae as a master, but wasn't sure how to broach the idea. How could she approach him and extend the offer without pressuring him into accepting?

"Rune," she said under her breath, testing out the words, "I realize our original deal was that I would bring you to Island Pass and then you would be free to go wherever you want to, but you have to realize that finding another guild that will accept you is going to be beyond difficult...no, wait, that won't work." Frowning, she chewed on her bottom lip and thought about it some more. "Mmm, how about: Rune, I know I said that you can go your own way when we hit Island Pass, but I hope you'll reconsider. We've all become rather fond of you and wouldn't mind if you stayed. Oh. Oh, I like that one better. It doesn't pressure him. Although should I also say—"

"SIOBHAN!" Rune thundered in warning, his voice echoing.

She spun about in alarm, boots grinding against the stone, eyes searching madly for the danger he had seen.

They melted from the darkness, their silhouettes barely visible in the moonlight as they crossed the bridge.

Siobhan stared at the three men slowly approaching her, all of them with swords in their hands at an en guard position, their faces masked by dark hats and night shadow. She drew both of her swords in a hiss of steel against steel, eyes darting from one to the other in an attempt to keep them all in her view. A warm presence abruptly appeared at her back with nothing but the faintest hint of sound, a whisper of displaced air. She started in alarm and half-turned to glance over her shoulder.

"Hey, Siobhan," Rune greeted calmly. "I think six men is too much ta ask for a girl ta take on alone."

Rune? Oh thank heavens. "You're quite right," she agreed with false neutrality. It felt like her heart was trying to beat its way out of her chest. "Six?"

"Ya didn't see the other three sneaking up on ya," he explained.

Rain and drought, had there really been three trying to ambush her from behind?! How had they even gotten there? Did they climb up the sides somehow? "Rune, my darling?"

"Yes?" he responded with amusement in his voice.

"Guard my back, won't you?"

"My pleasure," he assured her, and this time there was a feral quality in his tone.

They had no more time for words. In the next instant, the three in front of her sprang forward, swords raised.

Siobhan raised her own, swords crossed, before

she exploded forward, swinging both swords wide to force them to either retreat or block her. The swords clashed and reverberated in her hands as they struck the opponents' weapons. She didn't stay still but instantly moved again, sliding the blades up and toward the men. They had to throw their arms up a little, ducking their heads, to avoid being beheaded. She spun low, knees bent, and slashed out again, one sword coming up and over her head, the other coming forward in a deadly arc.

The one coming directly at her swung at her feet and she nimbly jumped over the blade before landing on her back leg and lashing out with the front one, catching him squarely in the chest and sending him flying backward. She spared no attention to how he landed, but instead caught the blade of the right man with her own sword and spun again, robbing it of its force and sending him half-stumbling toward his own ally.

Another blade whistled at her in the darkness, only the moonlight glinting off of it making it visible enough for her to dodge. She had to kick herself up in a half-horizontal flip to avoid it completely, which unfortunately put her back within range of all three of them again. As she landed, she used the proximity to her advantage and put her back to one man, raising her arm up enough to slam her elbow into his nose sharply three times. He grunted at each impact, blood spraying, and stumbled back. Not giving him an opportunity to regain his balance, she kicked his legs out from under him as she turned again, facing the other two. He landed with a sickening thud, as if his head had cracked against the hard stone.

Taking a page from their book, she aimed next for their legs, swords held parallel to each other. But they had also learned from her and kicked themselves up and over in a sideways flip that neatly avoided the danger.

Worried, perhaps, that she had better fighting technique than they did, the last two standing retreated a few steps and gave themselves some breathing room. Siobhan rotated both swords in her hands with an easy turn of the wrist, deliberately egging them on.

Not taking the bait, eh? Her breath came loud in her ears, sweat starting to dew her temples, but she wasn't tired. She felt warm and ready to fight. They didn't seem to have quite her stamina, as their breath came loud and fast, expelled in white puffs of smoke in this cold night air.

She had no desire to stay out here all night fighting. Fine, if they wouldn't come, she'd go to them. With three quick steps, she closed the distance and lashed out again.

This time they tried to flank her, each coming around to a different side, lashing out at the same time. She spun like a dancer, both swords whistling up and around, blocking the attack and taking her out of the center of danger.

Siobhan raised one blade high, going for an overhead attack, and when the other man raised his sword high to block it, she kicked him square in the chest. His breath exploded from his lungs in a gasp and he stumbled back, clutching at himself as he struggled to get air.

The last man standing lost his head at seeing his friends defeated and he rushed her with a growl of frustration. His strikes became sloppy, predictable, and she smacked him hard in the ribs with one sword as she fended him off with the other. He doubled over in pure reflex, gasping in pain, and as he did she rammed an elbow against the back of his neck. With nothing more than a groan, he slid to the ground face-first with a soft thud.

Siobhan took in a breath and looked around, but none of them were moving. She whipped around to look for Rune only to find him in the center of equally still opponents. He looked unfazed by their brief skirmish, and he had a thoughtful hand against his chin and an admiring look in his eye.

"Injuries?" she demanded of him, not sure if the darkness was hiding something.

Rune waved this away with a negligent flick of the fingers. "Fine. But ya know, Siobhan, ya led me ta believe yer not that good a fighter."

She raised an eyebrow at him as she slid both swords home. "I'm not."

He snorted. "Who ya compari'n yerself to? Wolf-dog? Tran? 'Cause those two are monsters. Not many can face them. But I watched ya just now, and ya fought like a goddess of war. Sent chills up my spine, it did."

"Rune," she said patiently, "you finished off three opponents while I was still downing my second one, and you want to say I'm a good fighter?"

"I'm a monster too, ya know," he responded with a wicked grin.

He rather had a point there. Well, perhaps she had understated her fighting abilities a little. Just a little. But she could argue the point later, right now there were more important things. "Did they attack below too? How's Tran?"

"Fine," he assured her. "Tran saw 'em comi'n."

"Go check on him," she ordered. "I'm ringing the bell."

# Chapter Thirty-Five

Even though they were more vigilant after that pre-dawn attack, nothing happened that day or the next night. Siobhan wasn't sure if this was a good sign or not. Now that the enemy knew they were prepared to fend them off, would they change tactics again? Or would they stick to this idea and simply send in more manpower?

The men they did capture weren't at all helpful. They were from a dark guild of Quigg, something similar to Silent Order in Sateren, and the information they possessed was little indeed. They were hired by a foreign guild to stop anyone working on the bridge. That was all they knew and all they cared to know. Questioning them further proved to not only be futile, but frustrating.

In the end, they turned the whole lot of them over to the enforcing guild of Quigg—who was delighted to have known criminals in their custody—and returned to guarding the bridge.

Grae went back with Romohr to deliver reports and letters on a daily basis, coming back with teams of masons, stones, and mortar so that repairs could be started. Beirly explained to her that they had a very limited time to work on the bridge and get anything constructive done. The weather had to be warm enough for the mortar to set, and they were quickly losing the year's heat. When winter set in, they would be forced to stop and wait for spring.

Perhaps because they were racing against time, both Jarnsmor and Darrens promised to send guards for the bridges by the end of the week. All Deepwoods had to do was keep the place safe for another four days.

Siobhan prayed they'd be able to manage that.

This silence and lack of enemy movement made her nervous. It had been proven to her several times over that if one plan failed, they wouldn't give up, but simply switch to something else. She also realized that so far, they had never been able to predict what their enemy would do next. This uncertainty of what to expect made her stomach tie itself into knots. How could she possibly prepare for the unknown?

Siobhan retired that night uneasy, and even though her bed was inviting and warm, she kept tossing and turning on it. Four days. They had to hold out for four days and then it would be someone else's problem to worry over. For what had started as a quick rescue mission, she certainly had become involved in a lot of the world's problems.

Growling, she flopped over onto her other side with a squeak of bedsprings, punching her pillow a little to fluff it up, trying to get her nerves to settle. Sleep. She needed to sleep. She was on third watch this time and it would mean getting up in five hours. Siobhan was not the type to function well on only a few hours of sleep, so it was vital to get whatever rest she could.

Her eyes slowly closed. Deep breaths. Conli had taught her how to relax each main muscle, breathing deeply as she did so, in order to fall asleep. Feet first. Calves. Thighs. Back. Good, she could feel herself relaxing.

The sound of a bell being frantically rung reverberated

through the still night air, loud enough that she could clearly hear it through the shuttered window. *DONG DONG DONG.*

Her eyes flew wide and she threw back the covers, hastily throwing on clothes while trying to jam her feet into her boots at the same time. She didn't even bother to belt on her swords, just grabbed them, flinging the door open and racing down the stairs. Three rings meant someone was on the bridge, an enemy, and she needed to get there *now.*

Everyone stumbled out of their rooms at nearly the same time, but she wasted no breath calling for a head count, just kept going. The cold air slapped her in the face as she made it through the front door, making her gasp for breath, but that didn't make her falter either. She lengthened her stride, running at full speed. Even still, Tran and Rune quickly outstripped her, Fei following close on their heels. How in the four winds could they be so *fast*? She wasn't that slow!

It was just as well that they were that fast.

Her heart stumbled over a beat when she finally came into full view of the bridge. This wasn't the half a dozen attackers of two nights ago, but what looked to be a full guild of fighters. Every person on the bridge was engaged with at least two opponents, fighting hard and desperately, but there were still some enemies left over with...were those barrels? Small kegs? In this hazy moonlight, it made it hard to see details.

Markl, who was panting along behind her, managed to gasp out, "Those are...black powder barrels, aren't they?"

Her blood ran cold when she realized he was right. Great wind and stars! Were they planning on finishing the job and blowing up the rest of the bridge?!

Making a snap decision, she barked out orders. "Denney, set the dogs on them, harry them so they can't light those fuses. Sylvie, call for more help, we're going to need it. Conli, Markl, help me push those barrels off into the ocean. If they're wet, they can't be used."

She heard and registered the chorus of assents, but did not focus on them, just sprinted the last distance and engaged the nearest men. Like their compatriots two nights ago, these men wore dark clothing and black cloth wound about their faces. She could only see the whites of their eyes as they looked up, seeing her approach.

They'd been laying out fuses, rags rolled up with oil and black powder, preparing to blow the kegs. She quickly hacked through three of them and kicked them aside, taking precautions against them being used, before charging forward.

It quickly became a melee of confusion. These men weren't better swordsmen than the last ones she'd faced, but they had numbers on their side. Siobhan quickly found herself fighting back-to-back with Markl, her swords a blur in her hands as she fought desperately to not only protect herself, but him. All around her were the sounds of Pyper and Pete barking and snarling, the clang of metal clashing against metal, and the grunts of pain when a weapon struck flesh. The sounds didn't tell her if they were winning this fight or not, but it was distracting to her, as she couldn't decipher who was hit, friend or foe.

Her opponents were less focused on her and more focused on quickly getting the job done and leaving the bridge as fast as they could. It made them sloppy, distracted, and Siobhan found an opening to down two of them. As they fell, a gap opened up, letting her access two of the kegs. "Markl?"

"Go!" he encouraged her, the weapon in his hand rotating as he simultaneously blocked one strike and slashed at another.

She had no time to question if he were truly alright against three opponents. Siobhan trusted his judgment and darted forward, kicking the kegs out of their place and quickly rolling them toward the uneven edge of the bridge before forcing them to fall into the water. They fell, one after another, with satisfying *splashing* sounds, the cold sea water spraying upward and onto her in the process.

Shivering, she wiped the drops from her face as she turned back and raced to Markl.

Three barrels had not significantly helped. Markl had defeated one man while she had her back turned, and as she watched, he slashed at another, sending the man to the ground with a gasp of pain. Her eyes scanned the area, head jerking as she looked this way and that, trying to take it all in. It was complete madness, no matter where she looked. Almost everyone was fighting, black-clothed figures lying still on the bridge. To her dismay, she saw Tran leaning against the railing behind Fei, one arm clamped around his ribs. Oh no, had he reinjured himself? Conli had been very clear that he shouldn't be fighting for another three weeks yet.

Where was Sylvie with those reinforcements?!

But worse than all of that, she could see several barrels farther along the bridge, on the other side of the destroyed section, and they were perfectly fine. None of her people were anywhere near them, either. How had they managed to get all the way over there, past the people on watch, she had no idea. But it was a problem she would have to deal with, as she was the only one free to do something about it.

Swearing, Siobhan ran toward the next group of barrels, skirting as close to the edge of the bridge as she dared to avoid getting tangled into any of the fights. She reached the trio of barrels stacked against each other and without ceremony kicked it into the water.

Good. Next.

She could hear footsteps thundering behind her and found that Markl was struggling to catch up with her. He was shouting something, but she couldn't quite decipher the words, and only his tone got through. He was worried, frantic about something, and pointing ahead of her.

What? Siobhan turned her head, looking up, trying to see what it was that had panicked him so.

In front of her, several feet ahead, was a small light on the ground that traveled forward quickly. For the second time that night, alarm shot through her and cold dread seized her heart as she realized what it was. The enemy, in desperation, did the one thing she didn't want them to do. They had lit one of the fuses and were even now trying to disengage with her guild, desperate to get off the bridge before it blew.

Siobhan swore viciously and stretched out her legs, trying to run faster toward the kegs waiting nearby. At this point, she couldn't make it off the bridge in time before those things exploded. Her only hope was to get to the barrels and dump them into the water first.

"Siobhan, NO!" Markl screamed behind her.

She didn't glance back, didn't do anything but strive with every muscle in her body to beat that fuse. "GET OFF THE BRIDGE!" she screamed as she ran, not sure if the rest of the guild realized what was happening during the heat of the moment. "GET OFF, GET OFF, GET OFF!"

In that moment, she reached the kegs.

And so had the fuse.

Something hard slammed into her, forcing her swords to drop from her hands. Siobhan barely had time to grunt at the impact as she sailed through the air before her body hit the hard, icy water of the sea.

Heat exploded through the air, brushing past her face briefly before her head went under the water.

The world went black.

"CONLI! GET HERE NOW! SHE'S NOT BREATHING!"

The words faded, and darkness descended again. Vaguely she was aware of being cold, cold enough to shiver and shake, with wet clothes clinging to her. A sense of wrongness stirred in her mind but she found it impossible to react to it.

"Markl?!"

A sloshing noise, and water sprayed over her face, followed by a male grunt of effort.

Markl...this was important. Markl was in trouble. Markl had fallen with her.

It faded from her, sealed again with darkness before she could act or react.

"—on her back, seal your mouth over hers and blow hard."

Her back touched cold stone, hard and unforgiving. Something warm touched her mouth and air was forced into her. She twitched ever so slightly under the force of it. The air came again, stronger, and this time her lungs filled with it. In instinct, she weakly pushed away and tried to roll to her side as the sea water in her lungs rushed forward. Gasping, wheezing for breath, she coughed and spluttered, grimacing as the harsh salt in the water scraped at her throat. It felt like a sea monster had crawled into her mouth and died, very messily.

"Breathe, Siobhan," Wolf sounded frantic, panicked, as he rubbed a hand over her back in soothing circles. "Breathe. Throw all that water up and breathe."

She did her best to comply, drawing air frantically into deprived lungs. Stars swam in her vision for a few moments as she battled for proper breath. As soon as she felt she could manage it, she grabbed his arm and demanded hoarsely, "Markl?"

"He's fine, he's fine," Wolf assured her. He wrapped an arm around her waist and hauled her up so that she could lean against him. "We pulled him out after you, and look, see? He's breathing."

She managed to get her eyes focused on where he pointed. Markl was being supported by Conli and Sylvie as he also coughed up seawater and struggled to breathe. He lifted his head and saw her, and relief flashed over his face. She waved at him, and he choked on a laugh as he waved back.

Relieved, she sank back against Wolf and let him support her completely. "Tell me we're all accounted for."

"We're all here," he answered, shrugging out of his coat and draping it around her. "It was only you and Markl that we almost lost."

Good? She was sort of glad to hear that, anyway. "The men that attacked?"

"We defeated some, but they ran before the bridge exploded."

Of course they had. "More mercenaries from a dark guild, huh."

"Probably," he agreed.

"The bridge?" she looked up to see the situation with her own eyes. She and Markl had been dragged onto the banks near the bridge. The gap that had been there previously was larger now, longer than it had been, but she was beyond relieved to see that most of the bridge was still intact. At least this way, they wouldn't be set back and forced to rebuild a full section of the bridge. Her insane bid to try to protect it had partially succeeded, then. "Who pulled us out?"

Fei and Beirly, both sopping wet, raised their hands. Oh, of course. She should have figured that. They were the strongest swimmers in the guild, after all. "Thank you," she said to them sincerely, or tried to through her chattering teeth.

Wolf put both arms underneath her and rose to his feet. "We can talk about it later, after you are warm and dry."

Wonderful plan.

# Chapter Thirty-Six

After hearing what had happened, Jarnsmor and Darrens wasted no time in sending guards. Jarnsmor's men, having a ready path to travel, arrived first, with the Blackstone men due in two days later. Siobhan and Markl spent the next day in bed, as neither of them had escaped the explosion completely unscathed. Markl's quick reflexes had saved them from being burned, but chunks of stone had still impacted the water hard enough to hit them as well, leaving behind bruises and one fractured wrist. Markl was good-natured about his injury, claiming it was a privilege to be wounded in defense of a pretty woman. Siobhan, feeling equal parts guilty and thankful, determined that she'd find the perfect moment in the future to pay him back the debt.

A soft knock came at the door before Wolf put his head into the room. "You awake?"

She had spent most of the morning sleeping, still recovering from her near-death experience of the night before. She waved him inside. "How is everything?"

"It's fine," he assured her as he fully entered, taking the small wooden chair next to her bed and moving it around to where he could face her comfortably and talk. "Iron Dragain's guildsmen are arranged all around the bridge and I coached them what to look out for. Ardin said that while the explosion did do significant damage to that portion of the bridge, it didn't shake the overall frame of it, so he thinks small parties can cross without danger."

She breathed out a sigh of relief. "So we can pass over it and go home."

Wolf nodded confirmation. "And trade won't stop completely, it'll just be bogged up a bit as people try to enter and exit Quigg. They'll manage a way around that until the repairs are complete."

"They'd have to think of some sort of system anyway," she mused aloud, sitting up more comfortably in bed. "After all, the bridges are going to be under renovations for years to come. We're all going to have to manage travel on it despite that."

He shrugged, hand splayed in silent agreement. "And you? How are you feeling?"

"Sore, a little tired still," she admitted frankly. "But I'm also ready to be home, I think. How is Markl?"

"I'm not...actually sure," Wolf said with an odd smile on his face.

She turned his words over, but if there was a deeper meaning behind them, she didn't get it. "And why wouldn't you be?" she asked slowly, studying his expression.

"Well, Conli said that aside from being tired, and that fractured wrist, Markl was in good condition. And yet I haven't seen the man peek a toe out from underneath his covers yet." There was a light of devilry sparkling in Wolf's eyes. "Sylvie's been perched on the edge of his bed all this while."

"Sylvie's playing nursemaid," Siobhan said in enlightenment. "Ahhh. Well, if I were Markl, I wouldn't be moving either."

"He's a smart man," Wolf agreed mock-somberly. "If I were him, I'd do the same."

She couldn't help but chuckle softly, a hand lifted over her mouth to try to stifle the sound less it be heard in Markl's room next door. "Wolf, tell me," she leaned forward to ask him in a confidential tone, "how serious is it between those two? Do you know?"

He splayed his hands out in an uncertain shrug. "I don't think even they know, yet. Sylvie's attracted to him simply because he's a kind man, and she's met few of those in her life. Markl's attracted because he's not blind nor an idiot. You'd have to be both to not want Sylvie."

"You never were," she pointed out archly. "Nor Tran. Or Fei."

"That's because she's our guild-sister, and we've always seen her that way. I think we all recognized from our first meeting that what Sylvie needed was a pack of protective brothers, not more lecherous men. Markl is seeing her as a woman, one who's been protected for many years, and that's a different thing entirely from the Sylvie of seven years ago."

Truly. Sylvie had been very nervous, wary even, of being too close to men when she'd first joined the guild. A woman of her beauty had to be, in order to avoid dangerous situations. She had relaxed considerably after being so fiercely protected in Deepwoods.

Wolf watched her for a long moment before stating, "You're hoping that Markl's attachment to Sylvie will make him stay in Deepwoods."

"I am," she admitted frankly. "The longer I'm around Markl, the more I hope for that. Where would I have been, if not for him?"

He shook his head grimly. "I don't even want to imagine that."

"But it's not even his actions last night that make me think so. Think how many times Markl's knowledge, his empathy with people, his quiet charm, has opened doors for us where there were no doors to open? He's become an amazing asset to the guild, one that I didn't realize was missing. More, I think he's becoming at home with us. No offense to his father, or the family that raised him, but I don't think he ever felt he really belonged with them. If he had, he'd have accepted his position as heir instead of running away from it."

"I can't argue that." Wolf leaned back in the chair, making the wood creak dangerously under his weight. "Well, I have no doubt you'll sweet talk him into staying eventually. If you can do it with a former dark guild mercenary, then anything is possible."

Siobhan snorted. "You weren't a hard sale at all. You were so deprived of kindness and acceptance that all I had to do was feed you and give you a smile and you were ready to stay."

He opened his mouth, paused, then snorted. "Was I really that pitiful?" he muttered to himself, eyes on the ceiling as if pondering this.

"Yes," she answered wryly. "You were. Fortunately, you grew out of that. But onto other matters: so, Iron Dragain's men are here. Guards are set up. Markl and I are healthy enough to travel. Any sign of my swords?"

Wolf shook his head. "Lost to the bottom of the sea, most likely."

Rain and drought, she'd been afraid of that. She'd have to commission a new pair once she got back to Goldschmidt. In the meantime, she'd have to rely on her long daggers and make do. Great wind and stars, but she hated walking around half-armed!

Heaving a gusty sigh, she set the worry aside, to when she would actually need to do something about it. "I feel terrible about leaving at the moment, like I'm leaving a job half done."

"Well, it *is* half done, but there's nothing we can do about that." He gave an easy shrug. "We don't have the skills, time, or money to finish this task. We're through with what we were asked to do."

"Yes," she nodded, but still felt unsatisfied even

though he was right. "It's just...something tells me that this situation is far from resolved. We don't even know who's really behind all these attacks. We suspect Fallen Ward, but really, do they have the resources to reach this far and do as much damage as what's been done?"

"I wouldn't have thought so." Wolf rubbed at his chin thoughtfully. "But there's much about all of this that's in want of an explanation."

Siobhan couldn't have agreed more. "I don't think we're done with this, Wolf. I think we're going to be pulled back into this mess somehow."

He grimaced. "I'm afraid you're right. But let's not focus on future trouble, eh? Not until we need to."

"You're right." Pushing back the covers, she swung her feet out of the bed. "Spread the word to get ready. We're going home."

# Epilogue

Island Pass, at last. Siobhan felt that the journey here had taken at least three times longer than it really needed to. And yet, she couldn't help but wish it had taken even longer still, for just one reason.

Rune.

In the past hectic days and crazy nights of fending off saboteurs, she hadn't had a chance to really talk to Rune about his future. Now that they had arrived on the island, the moment was upon them, and if she didn't say something right now then she might lose all of her chances with him. And yet it didn't feel right to start such a heavy, important conversation right here in the middle of the road, either.

Taking a deep breath, she looked at the sky. They had perhaps an hour left of daylight. So she could talk to him about it over dinner. Right, that was a good plan. No, wait, no it wasn't! That was assuming he would stay with them for dinner, and stay at the same inn, and he might think that he should go his own way now that they were on the island. She really couldn't wait.

Whether or not this was the appropriate place to speak to him, she had to say something *now*.

They were all riding on the cart, piled up on top of each other, with Rune on the opposite side of where Siobhan sat. She tucked her knees up against her chest and spun about in a tight turn so that she could hop off the side.

"Siobhan?" Wolf asked in bewilderment, lifting up to watch her land. "What are you doing...? Hey!"

She ignored him and quickly walked around and to the other side, grabbing Rune's wrist and tugging at him insistently. "Rune, get down. I need to talk to you."

Rune's eyes narrowed, questioning, but he slowly complied and got down.

Beirly called back from the driver's seat, "What, *now*?"

"Stop the cart, Beirly!" she ordered firmly.

He muttered something about 'crazy woman' and 'no patience sometimes' but he pulled the cart more off to the side of the bridge before stopping it completely. Most of the guild studied her in blatant confusion, except Markl and Grae, who knew good and well what she would say next.

"Grae, you too," she ordered, although her eyes never left Rune. "I know that I said you could go wherever you wanted when we reached this point, but there's two things I need to tell you first."

Rune swallowed hard. "I'm listeni'n."

"First thing." She paused, searching for the right words and fumbling. "You remember when you helped Grae build the path to Quigg? You remember what he said?"

Rune's eyes darted to Grae and back again. "He said I was good at it."

"He said it took *talent* to do what you did," she corrected. "Rune. You are a Pathmaker."

His jaw dropped so hard it was a wonder it didn't crack the stones under their feet. "C-can't be!" he protested, his denial instinctive and disbelieving.

"You are." Grae came to stand at Siobhan's side, voice not just persuasive but intense. "You are. I saw the potential in you when you started picking out the right stones for the stepping stone. But only a Pathmaker could have understood the pattern like you did and laid it out so perfectly. You have enormous talent, Rune. It surprised us as well to see it."

His eyes went blind, staring off into the north as if he simply couldn't believe what he was being told.

"Sorry for not telling you before," Siobhan apologized in all sincerity. "I felt like I couldn't, not until we got you out of Wynngaard. If Jarnsmor had learned what you are, you'd never have been allowed to leave Sateren. He would have kept a stranglehold on you and I think you deserve the right to decide where to go. If you want to go back, I'll help you do so, but it should be your choice."

"Your future is limitless once you're trained. Markl said you're a quick study, and I saw that when you built the path with me earlier, so I don't think it'll take you long to learn what you need to," Grae assured him. "I'll teach you myself. Or, if you want to go somewhere else, I'll introduce you to another Pathmaker to be your master. I know all of them."

Considering there was only about two dozen known Pathmakers in the world, that wasn't much of a feat.

Rune searched Grae's face for a long moment. "Ya...yer willi'n ta teach me."

"Of course!" Grae seemed surprised that Rune even questioned this. "You're a good student and an easy man to work with. I'd think it'd be quite fun to teach you."

Siobhan had to bite back a smile. She knew good and well why Rune had that poleaxed expression on his face right then. She'd told him Grae's reputation, so he knew that a master, a genius in his field, had just offered to be Rune's master. Only a fool would pass up that invitation.

"But that mean's I'd..." he trailed off uncertainly, looking at Siobhan.

Why was he hesitating? Oh. Oh, right, in order for him to be Grae's student, he'd have to stay in Deepwoods and she hadn't made it clear yet that he was welcome to stay.

Deep breath in. Right, here goes. "I know that our original deal was that you could do whatever you wanted once we reached Island Pass. And you've done a marvelous job holding up your end of the deal. I mean, you helped me even when I didn't know the right questions to ask! And you took us to Sateren and made sure we were safe there the entire time—Tran told me about your night patrols, thank you for that, I never said that before—but you helped us even when we weren't in Sateren, which wasn't part of the deal at all—"

"Siobhan," Wolf said patiently, laying a restraining hand on her shoulder.

"Wait, I'm not finished, I have to say this right," she responded in irritation, shaking off his hand. "I didn't get a chance to say anything to him before, so don't interrupt me! Rune, what I'm trying to say is that I've come to really like you and respect your skills. The way that you've watched out for my well-being has meant the world to me. And I don't think it's wrong for me to say that the rest of the guild feels the same way—"

"Siobhan," Conli interrupted.

"Will you both be quiet?" she demanded, exasperated. "I've completely lost my thought now! Where was I?"

"That's a good thing," Denney assured her dryly. "Because you're babbling. You have a bad habit of doing that when you're nervous." Squeezing around, she put a hand on Rune's shoulder, who was watching the whole group with wide, bewildered eyes. "Rune, what's she trying to say, and is too nervous to, is that she wants you to stay in the guild."

Siobhan blinked at her. "Right. Didn't I already say that?"

"No," several voices chorused, all of them amused.

"Oh. Rain and drought, I meant to say that first thing." She reviewed the speech she had mentally prepared but

396

couldn't remember the right order to say anything, so gave up on it with a shrug. "Rune, I want you to stay. I don't want you to feel pressured into staying, mind. If you feel like going off and exploring the world for a while and thinking about joining us, you're welcome to do so. After all, I don't think you've seen anything outside of Sateren, much less outside of Wynngaard."

Rune's expression turned into one of lopsided bemusement as he regarded her. "When we made our deal, ya said I could go wherever I wish when we came ta this point."

Had she really worded it that way? "Well, yes, that's right."

His smile became mischievous. "Then I'll go with all of ya."

A worry that had been eating at her dropped away and she openly beamed at him. Unable to resist, she threw her arms around his neck and hugged him tight before bouncing back. "Good! That's settled then. Will you take Grae as your master, too? Should I find you someone else?"

Rune shook his head with a shy smile. "I'll take him as my master."

Grae openly beamed.

She blew out a long breath. "Good. I'm glad that's all sorted. Let's go to the inn. We'll have a grand feast to welcome you officially to the guild!"

Rune blinked at her and pointed to their spectators. "Wait! Don't they get a say in this? A chance ta agree or not?"

"Any objections are overruled," she informed him cheerfully. "It's one of the perks of being guildmaster. They can't nay-say me about who joins."

"Otherwise Tran would never have made it in," Wolf muttered under his breath.

"Otherwise *you* would never have made it in," Grae drawled with a pointed look. "I didn't like you at first either."

Wolf opened his mouth to protest that, thought about it, then looked at Siobhan in a considering way. "Maybe it's better she has the final say."

Siobhan patted him on the arm, gave him a winsome smile, and started off for the inn with a bounce in her stride. "This way, everyone!"

# Author

Over thirty years ago, in the hills of Tennessee, a nice, unsuspecting young couple had their first child. Their home has since then been slowly turned into a library as their daughter consistently brought books home over the years.

No one was surprised when she grew up, went to college, and got her Bachelor's in English. Despite the fact that she has a degree, and looks like a mature young woman, she's never grown out of her love for dragons, fairies and other fantastical creatures. With school done, she's ready to start her career, hopefully by blending two of her loves: books and fantasy.

Her website can be found here: http://www.honorraconteur.com or if you wish to speak directly with the author, visit her forum at: http://z13.invisionfree.com/adventmage/

# Don't Miss These Other Fantastic Adventures!

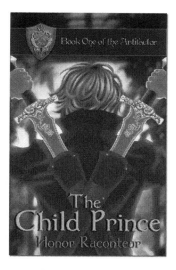

Kingslayer
Honor Raconteur
978-0-9891485-6-6
$9.99

The Child Prince
Book One of the
Artifactor
978-0-9910395-2-4
$14.99

Raconteur House
*Characters to Aspire to*
www.raconteurhouse.com

Available on Amazon, Barnes and Noble, and Smashwords.

Made in the USA
San Bernardino, CA
02 September 2016